D1002617

MARION ZIMMER BRADLEY'S SWORD AND SORCERESS XXII

Edited by Elisabeth Waters

Copyright © 2007 by The Marion Zimmer Bradley Literary Works Trust

All Rights Reserved.

Cover Painting:

"Joan of Arc" by Harold Hume Piffard (1867-1938).

Cover Design Copyright © 2007 by Vera Nazarian

ISBN-13: 978-1-934169-90-2
ISBN-10: 1-934169-90-0

First Edition
Trade Paperback Edition

November 15, 2007

A Publication of
Norilana Books
P. O. Box 2188
Winnetka, CA 91396
www.norilana.com

Printed in the United States of America

ACKNOWLEDGMENTS

Introduction © 2007 by Elisabeth Waters
"Edra's Arrow" © 2007 by Esther M. Friesner
"A Nose for Trouble" © 2007 by Patricia B. Cirone
"Night Watches" © 2007 by Catherine Soto
"Vanishing Village" © 2007 by Margaret L. Carter
"Pearl of Fire" © 2007 by Deborah J. Ross
"The Ironwood Box" © 2007 by Kimberly L. Maughan
"Bearing Shadows" © 2007 by Dave Smeds
"Black Ghost, Red Ghost" © 2007 by Jonathan Moeller
"The Decisive Princess" © 2007 by Catherine Mintz
"Child of the Father" © 2007 by Alanna Morland
"Child of Ice, Child of Flame" © 2007 by Marian Allen
"Skin and Bones" © 2007 by Heather Rose Jones
"Crosswort Puzzle" © 2007 by Michael Spence & Elisabeth Waters
"Fairy Debt" © 2007 by T. Borregaard
"Tontine" © 2007 by Robert E. Vardeman
"The Menagerie" © 2007 by Sarah Dozier

Marion Zimmer Bradley's
Sword and Sorceress XXII

Norilana Books
Fantasy

www.norilana.com

Marion Zimmer Bradley's

Sword

and

Sorceress

XXII

Edited by

Elisabeth Waters

CONTENTS

INTRODUCTION

by Elisabeth Waters

I had forgotten how much fun it was to edit *Sword & Sorceress*. Of course, the last time I did it, I was doing three volumes at once while coping with Marion Zimmer Bradley's death, and nothing in my life was much fun at that point.

It was great to see how many of "MZB's writers" submitted stories to this anthology. I wish I could have bought stories from all of them, but by now there are over 300 of them, and we're trying to maintain Marion's goal of discovering new writers as well as publishing stories by established ones. Trying to maintain a balance between old and new writers and between swords and sorcery makes selecting a final line-up a real challenge. In the end, what I looked for most was originality. I still had to send back some stories I would have loved to keep, so I'm really hoping we'll be doing another volume next year.

Marion started training me to edit these with *Sword & Sorceress IV*, and I've worked on just about every one since. I miss her advice and support, but I spent two decades in her company, so her voice still lingers in my head. I hope she would be proud of this book. I know she would be glad that her legacy still continues.

EDRA'S ARROW

by Esther M. Friesner

Esther M. Friesner is a Nebula Award winner, as well as being the author of 31 novels, over 150 short stories, and assorted poetry and plays. I remember attending a performance of one of her plays, a spoof of the medieval morality plays, at a Worldcon. The author sitting next to me, who had an extensive medieval background, laughed so hard that she actually fell out of her chair into the aisle. Esther has also edited seven anthologies—including the infamous *Chicks In Chainmail* series—and her articles on writing have appeared in *Writer's Market* (one of MZB's all-time favorite—and most recommended—magazines).

Her most recent novels are *Temping Fate* (how come my temp jobs were never that interesting?) and *Nobody's Princess*, which is being published as I write this. The sequel, *Nobody's Prize*, is due in Spring 2008.

By the time she was reading for *Sword And Sorceress III* in 1985, Marion was rejecting stories where people told the protagonist that she couldn't do something because she was a woman; Marion said it should be assumed—at least for the purpose of the anthology—that a woman could do anything. But, regardless of your abilities, should you do something against the customs of your society? And what are the consequences of doing or not doing it?

The hunting was poor and had been poor for months. Edra stood alone in the great pine forest, sifting the scents of fallen needles, withered mushrooms fallen to spores and dust, and the heady smoke from the distant cookfires. *Cookfires with nothing to cook,* she thought bitterly. *Not unless you count the few fish we've been able to catch from the lake, but they're pitiful things, more bones than flesh, scarcely enough to keep all of us this side of starvation. Fish and roots and acorn mush can't sustain so many. We need meat, real meat. And where's it to come from? Two days on the trails and nothing. There isn't even the scent of a deer here any longer, or the dream of one. Goddess, what's happened to this land, these woods? The season of blue cold will be here soon. We can't stay, but we haven't the supplies we need for the trek to the lowlands. What's going to become of us?*

She knelt on the path that once had boasted the marks of so many cloven hooves that the rawest hunter-in-training could follow the herds' passage and find a respectable target. Now the earth showed a layer of undisturbed pine needles, wind-blown dust, and one or two piles of scat so old that a breath would turn them to powder. *Where are the beasts?* Edra wondered. *It's not time for the migration. The great river's still too wild for them or us to cross, so they shouldn't have any usable route to their wintering lands. Even if the river had subsided earlier, we would have heard the animals, seen them as they traveled down to the plains. There was no warning. Stranger than that, there was no hint of their departure. They were simply...gone.*

Edra hunkered down, staring at the abandoned game track as if she were a fire priestess, seeking answers in flame, ember and ash. Her little silver-tipped bow rested across her updrawn knees, the string wound tightly around her right fist. If a miracle happened and the gods saw fit to let a fat buck leap out of the earth right in front of her, Edra would have her bow strung and an arrow nocked and flying true before the creature could take two steps. She was proud of her skill as archer and huntress, but all the skill in the world couldn't turn a straw target into a suitable quarry. Her people couldn't live on the ghosts of deer.

The longer Edra stared at the barren trail, the more her head echoed with the words of her sister, Jir, who'd entered training with the old fire priestess just before the last season of blue cold: *You're too stubborn, Edra. You think that no one can command you, but I know otherwise. Making you obey is easy. All I need to do is order you to do the opposite of whatever I want. No one wanted you to become a hunter. The fire goddess herself gave the first bow to her son Skel. When he died, she howled her grief so loudly that it shattered his bones into the hundred sacred arrows, the inheritance of his sons. His* sons, *sister! Using the bow and arrow for sport is one thing, but we women should know better than to use them for bloodshed.*

It's not forbidden, Edra countered.

It ought to be. Jir wore her primmest expression. *The gods trust us to know right from wrong and watch to see if we take the path that pleases them. They give us the privilege of choice. We should be grateful for that, not arrogant. A woman who uses a man's weapons in the hunt tempts their anger and their punishment.*

And again Edra heard her own merry voice reply: *Your words would carry more righteousness, sister, if your chin wasn't shining with the grease from one of my kills!*

Oh, how Jir had blushed! How fiercely she'd scrubbed at her chin, glowering at Edra while the other women joined in the huntress' laughter! But the men stayed silent, their eyes hard and hot in the firelight, their stares hostile and piercing.

You think you're funny, Jir spat. *You think you've climbed so high that nothing can touch you. But mark me, sister, even mountains crumble. The gods have eternity to teach you better manners.*

I'm not laughing at the gods, Edra said lightly.

At me, then? Jir's face looked like a storm cloud. She began to mutter strange words under her breath, the seeds of a fire priestess's curse. She hadn't voiced more than a dozen of the ancient syllables before a gnarled brown hand fell from the shadows behind the firelight, closing like a hawk's talons around her wrist. Jir cried out in pain.

A curse on your own blood? The old fire priestess, Mirani, glared at her pupil. The crone's eyes were red and yellow, like the heart of the flame she served. *And for what great offense? Wounding your petty pride? Is this how you use the lore I teach you? May the goddess take my bones, I chose poorly when I chose you to succeed me. Praise be, while I live, it's not too late to unchoose.*

Jir yowled, filling the night with her pleas for forgiveness, her promises to be worthy of Mirani's teachings.

She even flung herself face down on the campground earth, sobbing and apologizing to Edra for the ill she'd almost done her own sister. Mirani and the rest of the people seemed satisfied with the girl's contrition, but Edra caught a glimpse of her sister's face when Jir lifted her head at last. There were no damp smears of earth on her cheeks, no sign she'd shed a single tear. There was nothing but resentment smoldering in her eyes.

Edra snapped her thoughts out of the past, jerking her awareness sharply back into the present. What good did it do her to dwell on Jir's old anger? The memory held no clues to where all the game had gone, and the image of her sister's surly stare would fill no bellies. The huntress rested her fingertips on the ground, seeking the heartbeat of the earth, the breath of the forest. She sensed nothing but solitude, emptiness. It was as if the blue cold season had come early, casting the net of its ruthless ice storms over the land, freezing everything to the marrow, even sound. She couldn't even hear the creaking of tree limbs or the whir of insect wings.

This is wrong, she thought. *It's late in the year, but still, there's always at least one unlucky bug left behind to pipe a final note. And the birds, gone too? But the blackwings winter over comfortably, picking at carrion, and the red-crests always manage to find some way to feed themselves until spring!* She stood up, her wiry young body tense in the silence under the trees. *Was it like this on all the other days I returned to our camp empty-handed? I should have listened more carefully, but I was too busy filling my ears with curses over my bad luck on the trail. And I'm not the only one who's found nothing to hunt in this forest. The men have shared my ill fortune. The elders can't blame me alone for failing to bring back meat. All of us hunters must share the burden of our people's hunger.*

A dark thought stole into her mind: *They haven't blamed me alone...yet. That doesn't mean they'll never hold me responsible for what's happening. Empty bellies breed short tempers. Everyone feels helpless. Laying blame for what's happening won't fix the trouble, but it will give our elders the illusion that they're doing* something. *And Jir will be there, ready and eager to support the first person who'll suggest that the gods have taken away the game because of me. She'll remind the people how badly and how often I've* offended *the gods. Before anyone can stop her, she'll start chanting the tale of Skel's sacred arrows and his sons', sons', sons' sole right to be hunters. She'll chant, and the people will listen, and then...*

Edra lifted her bow, holding it sideways at arm's length so that it became the line of an imaginary horizon of gently rolling, golden hills. She let her eyes rest fondly on the perfect curve of the tawny wood, the glimmer of the silver tips with their artfully formed lion's heads. It was a gift from the dead, a sacred trust received from her mother's hands on the day she'd stolen one of the boys' bows and killed a buck whose antlers spread wider than she was tall.

This was your father's bow, Mother told her. It was the first and last time she spoke of him to Edra. *This is your inheritance, all that he left in my care, when he died. He said, "Edra will want this. So young, yet still her eyes gauge distance like a hunter's. Her tiny hand grasps mine with the grip of a born archer. My blood is hers, and I hear it calling out for its birthright. I won't live to answer that call, but she must. When the time is right, give her this bow. May she use it to bring home all that she desires.*

She closed both fists around the unstrung bow, holding it so tightly that its golden line trembled against the dark green of the pine boughs, the silver of the ancient tree trunks...*and the people will listen to Jir as she chants the tale of Skel's hundred sacred arrows, and the curse of hunger I've brought down upon us by using this bow to follow Skel's way, even though they claim it's an unfit path for a woman.* She could feel the whorls of wood even through the hardened skin of her palms. The voice of the bow, she called it, though she'd never mentioned such an outrageous thing to anyone else. Who would ever understand? *They'll listen to Jir, and they'll try to lift the hunger-curse by taking you from me.* Edra lowered the bow. Her jaw was set, grim. *They'll* try. *I wonder, will Jir feel any sorrow when I die, fighting to hold onto what's mine?*

Edra began to run. Her feet made no sound, though they pounded hard against the earth. She chose the trail back to her people's campsite, hating herself for returning empty-handed. Her belly knotted at the thought of what sort of a reception she'd have. *Better to face it now,* she thought. *Best to deal with it and be done, one way or the other.*

It didn't take her long to return. She'd traveled the hunting paths so many times that she could find her way at top speed in the dark. The location of every rock, every downed tree, every abandoned burrow was as well known to her as the faces of her tribemates. She burst into the clearing where they'd camped since midsummer. Wood smoke hung heavy on the air, weaving through the scent of soup that held more dried-up roots than good, nourishing meat. Edra saw the faces of hunger, the old and the young, the pinched cheeks and hopeless eyes. *The other hunters have had as little success as I,* she thought. *Why will no one claim the gods are angry with them?*

She stalked through the camp with her head high, her father's bow clenched in one hand. She did her best to keep from looking too many of her tribefolk in the eyes. At the center of the camp, Mirani stood beside the chieftain, both of them already wrapped in the fur robes that would see them through the blue cold season. Rumor claimed that Mirani and the chieftain had been lovers in their youth, that sometimes they still shared warmth. True or not, it didn't matter. The fire priestess's authority and power didn't depend on the chieftain's favor. Both were hers, both absolute and, in time, both would be Jir's inheritance as her disciple.

As my father's bow is mine, Edra thought. *Does Jir even think about how she'd feel, what she'd do if someone declared that the fire goddess is like the other gods and will listen only to men? Ah, see there! It looks like she's trying to get the feel of her fire priestess power already.* She saw her sister standing just behind Mirani. *Look at her! She's smiling. She knows I've failed. My cursed luck feeds her better than any meat. She fattens on it! Oh, Jir, we were true sisters, once! When did you become a stranger to me?*

She bit her lip against the pain of memories. *Did the coldness steal between us little by little, or did it happen suddenly, so suddenly that I dismissed it, refusing to believe such a thing* could *happen? You spoke harshly to me at old Iri's burial, but all of us were raw with grief then. He was our shaman, the one who opened the path between us and the gods. Was that when it began?*

"Edra?" The chieftain's voice tugged her back into the present. "Welcome." He stretched out his arms to her. "What luck?"

Edra did not attempt to look away. Even if she had nothing to bring to the cookfires, she refused to act as though her empty-handed return was shameful. *No one can fault me for failing to bring down a quarry that isn't there.*

"The same luck every man here's had these past months," she replied boldly. "The deer are gone. The smaller beasts have vanished, too. I heard no sounds of life in the woods. It's not natural."

"*You're* not natural! If the life's left the forest, it's because even the dumb beasts fear dwelling near a monster, cursed by the gods." The voice was a man's. One of the younger hunters stepped forward. His name was Tokal, Iri's lastborn son. Edra remembered how she'd brought down three big bucks for the shaman's grave feast, the last substantial kills she'd made with her father's bow. The moon had been dark on the night Iri went into the earth by torchlight. Before she showed her full silver mask again, the game had vanished.

"You didn't think I was such a monster when you tried to make me share your furs, Tokal," Edra replied evenly. "You didn't hesitate to ask a monster's help when you begged me to speak for you to the people, when you dreamed of taking your father's place as our shaman."

"Lies!" Tokal's voice shook almost as much as the finger he pointed at the huntress. "I respect our ways. I know enough to keep my feet on the true paths. When my father's spirit finally chooses to speak, *he* will name our next shaman. How could a creature like *you* be of any help there?"

"You have a short memory, Tokal," Edra said, trying not to smile at his childish outburst. "When I first refused your wooing, you sweetened your pleas with promises. You said, 'The naming of a new shaman requires only two voices: One to receive the vision, one to witness it. Be that second voice for me, Edra, and I will share my power with you for as long as we live!'"

In spite of her best efforts, Edra's lips parted in a wide grin. "Then you tried to share your...*power* with me again. But I said no to all that you offered."

"You said *nothing!*" Tokal's hands became fists. "Your mouth is full of venom, the truth dies on your tongue. As if I would ever filthy my furs with *you.*" His rage was real, but from somewhere in the crowd came the sound of laughter.

Bad move, Tokal, Edra thought. *Our people may be hungry, but their memories are still keen and they know the truth. Many here remember how you trailed after me for weeks, like a starving dog. Many know how badly you wanted to assume your father's place and power, and how badly you failed.*

"Silence!" Jir broke from Mirani's shadow. She stamped her foot, and the strands of glinting metal beads wound around her ankles clashed loudly. Such ornaments were few and precious, drawn from the rocks by an old magic that had died with Iri. Wearing them was an honor reserved alone for those who served the gods. "Tokal speaks with more wisdom than the rest of you will ever know. You think the gods are as short-lived and shallow-minded as you? They're deathless, not witless, and it takes wit to hear their words and read the signs they set before our eyes. Tokal has heard and seen clearly." She turned toward the young hunter and smiled.

I know that look. To be an accomplished huntress meant more than being able to hit the mark. The difference between success and failure on the trail also lay in being able to read the subtlest signs. Anyone could follow a track of hoof prints in soft earth, but when the game chose a path over raw rock, only the true hunters could still find and follow it. *Is that the answer, my sister? You want Tokal, I see it. But is that why you've gone against me?*

"What about you, Jir?" Mirani fixed her student with a piercing look. "How clear is your vision? I can guess what it's revealed to you: That your sister must lay down her bow and sit at the fireside with the other women." She spoke coldly, scorn clinging to every word. "What will satisfy your small heart? For our tribe to lose the most skilled hunter we've ever had?"

In spite of the fire priestess' authority and support, murmurs of dissent came from the crowd:

"Skilled? Tell that to my children's empty bellies!"

"You worry too much about that monstrous girl and too little about the rest of us, Mirani!"

"Maybe if we fed our fires with her bow and arrows, the gods would be pleased and feed *us* again!"

This last idea was greeted with many strident cries of agreement. A trio of Tokal's fellow huntsmen exchanged conspiratorial looks and silently began to move towards Edra. She didn't wait to second-guess their intentions or try to stand against them. If anyone in the tribe had objected—even if they feared to do more than speak out against the men's obvious purpose—she would have held her ground. If the chieftain had spoken up, ordering them to keep their places, she might have lingered, but when he said nothing, his silence became a nod of approval. He'd let them wrest her father's bow away, crush it to a heap of splinters, yet keep his own hands clean.

She sprang away before the men had taken three steps. She was a puff of dust in the firelight, a breeze flying far from the campsite, a ripple of shadows swallowed by the forest. Angry shouts faded in the distance behind her. She didn't bother to glance back to see if anyone was trying to run her down in the oncoming dark. She heard no footfalls, no branches snapping, no harsh breathing as the men tried to match her speed. That was how she understood her flight was unchallenged, that her people no longer cared enough about her fate to bother going after her.

In a small clearing a fair distance away from the campsite, she sat down on a fallen tree trunk and pondered her situation. *If I go back, they'll break my arrows and my bow. They might as well break me. If I don't return, I'll have to make my own way on the land. I could live well enough without any of them, but as things are, with the woods deserted...*She rested her head in her hands wearily as the night settled over her. With the chill of darkness came the whispers of doubt.

Maybe...maybe I'm wrong. Maybe the gods are against me for taking the path I've chosen. Have I sacrificed my people for the sake of my own desires? If that's so— She picked up her father's bow and looked at it sadly *—if that's so, it's time I made a different sacrifice.*

Tears trickled down her cheeks as she unstrung the great weapon and held it at arm's length in both hands. Head bowed, knuckles white, she began to bend the silver-tipped wood in a way it could not bear for long. Her own sob stifled the bow's first faint groan of protest.

Edra...Edra...

The words caressed her mind, not her ears, a whisper that came from nowhere, everywhere at once. She jerked her head up and darted glances into the surrounding woodland. She had the bow restrung as swift as thought, and an arrow nocked to the string. "Who's there?"

Child, don't you know me? Am I such a dreadful memory? Or have you changed so much since I've been gone? This isn't the girl I knew, the bold one, the fox-eyed little hunter who filled my old belly with meat and my old eyes with joy.

Edra stood up, a wisp of apprehension shuddering over her bones as she recognized the voice. "Iri..." She breathed the dead shaman's name and the forest answered with an old man's laughter.

Something moved through the moonlight against the background of trees. Edra followed it, or tried to do so. Though she had trained her eyes to see almost as well by night as by day, what she tracked now was no fixed shape, but an *absence*, seen and not-seen at once. *Like morning mist when the sun's heat touches it,* she thought, and suddenly she felt deathly cold.

Don't be afraid, Edra. The voice came again, stronger. *You did me no wrong in life. I mean you no harm.*

"I'm not afraid." The tip of her arrowhead swept slowly across the line of trees.

Oho! Then why were you poised to cast away your other self? Great sacrifices come only from great fear. But you are as wrong to fear the gods as you are to fear me.

"I fear neither you nor the gods, Iri," Edra said, her words soft-spoken but steady. "If I fear anything, it's for our people."

Do you love them so much, Edra? The spirit's voice painted an image in Edra's mind of Iri's living face, the old shaman's bright eyes wide with mock disbelief. *And how much do you think they love you? How much would* they *sacrifice for* your *sake?*

"I don't want them to sacrifice anything for me. If I was ready to give up my bow, it was of my own free will for them."

For them? Iri's voice was amused, skeptical. *All of them, Edra?*

She paused a moment, then shook her head. "No. Not for all of them. For the children. None of them blame me for the famine, yet they suffer for it. If breaking my bow will break their hunger, I'll do it in a heartbeat."

Good, good. The best sacrifices, the true ones, the only ones that please the gods are those that come from whole and willing hearts.

"The gods—" Edra snorted. "Our people say that the land is barren because of me, that soon even the fish will be gone, that the lakes and streams will go the way of the forest. They whisper that the gods have turned away from us because I am a woman and a hunter."

The dead man chortled. *You've hunted for more seasons than I can recall, and our people have eaten your kills greedily enough. Can any of our tribe explain why it took our gods so long to get angry about it?*

Edra's expression hardened. "You're turning this into a joke."

More laughter sounded through her mind. *You will have to forgive me, child. Death has been cruel to my body but kind to my sense of humor. It's hard to take the world seriously when one dwells beyond its reach. But in honesty, why* would *the gods wait so many seasons to show their displeasure?*

"That was your doing, your prayers keeping the gods' anger at bay."

Was it? The dead shaman sounded surprised. *I never suspected one person's prayer was better than another's. Die and learn.*

"Stop toying with me. While you lived, you spoke to the gods for us—all the gods except the fire goddess. Our next shaman would have done the same, but you didn't name him before you died. Nor after. Your son Tokal still waits for word that he's the chosen one."

Does he? It isn't wise to keep someone waiting, god or mortal. Dead needles rattled on the pine branches. *And if the gods are angry because I've named no one among you to serve them after me...*Iri's voice trailed off.

The young woman tensed. "Is—is that why you've come to me now?"

Ah! Now *I've frightened you!*

"I told you, I'm not afrai—"

Now, now, no lies. My eyes may be dust, but I can still see clearly. You are *afraid, Edra. You dread hearing that I've returned to name Tokal our shaman.*

"N-no." Her hold on bow and arrow didn't slacken, though her voice faltered just a bit. "If that were so, I'd accept it. One shaman names the next. It's always been that way."

And since when are you *so ready to accept the way things have "always" been?* Iri's spirit chuckled.

Edra took a deep breath. "All right then: If you're here to name Tokal as your heir, why come to *me*? What good is a vision that doesn't appear to the one who must heed it?"

What good indeed? The dead man's voice turned sad. *What good are any visions while our people live under the wings of a curse? It flew here on the breath of rash words, and you were only moments from making the same mistake, throwing the gods' gift back in their faces.*

Edra's hands began to tingle. She looked at her father's bow and gasped as the arrow she held ready flared with a cold green flame but did not burn away. "The gods' gift," she whispered.

That? A frigid wind knifed past Edra's face, capturing the arrow, green flame and all, in a thin shroud of ice. *The gods' true gifts to you are greater than mere* things*, no matter how deeply touched by magic. What use is the bow without the arm to draw it? What use is hope without valor, or knowledge without the courage to embrace it?*

"And what use are riddles while our people starve?" Edra told the air. "Tell me *how* to use whatever gifts the gods have given me. Show me *how* to break the curse."

The frosty wind swirled around the young huntress, sending twinkling stars of ice dancing along her bow. The frozen dart vanished. A second arrow made of ice and starlight floated in the air before Edra's eyes. Her free hand moved as if through the depths of the sea to close around it. The shimmering faded, leaving a pale core of bone in the huntress' grasp.

Skel's arrow, Edra, the dead shaman said. *The sacred dart made from the bones of a dead hero. You clasp a legend in your hand, and only a strong hand can master it. You will only have to tell it what you seek and it will find your quarry. You will not need to aim for it to fly unerringly to the target. It will not fail to kill.*

Edra laughed nervously. "It hunts, it finds, it aims, it strikes true...This arrow needs nothing from me!"

The arrow needs the bow, the bow needs the hunter. Without your hand to draw back the bowstring, Skel's arrow is no more than a sliver of ancient bone. But what does the hunter need?

"Not more riddles, I'll tell you that much." For the first time in too long, Edra found hope enough to smile. "Lead me, Iri. Lend me wisdom. Show me the first step on the trail I must follow."

The wind rose, and the trees swayed. The branches overhanging the path leading back to her people's campsite parted at the touch of invisible hands, making her path clear. Edra's mouth went dry.

What does the hunter need? Iri's voice repeated, fading on the wind. *Only the heart to do what must be done.*

⋅⋅⋅⋅⋅

The people knew she had returned to them from an encounter with something more than human. She saw it in their faces the moment she stepped back into the circle of firelight, her bow in hand, the white fletching of Skel's arrow pricking her fingertips. Young mothers held their children close, pinch-cheeked toddlers and infants too hungry to cry. Strong-limbed men stepped aside to let her pass. The few elders, frail-boned, with skin as thin and fragile as dead leaves, murmured among themselves and made trembling hand-signs to ward off calamity.

No one else spoke a word—not even the chieftain—until Mirani ventured forward and knelt at Edra's feet.

"Mirani?" Edra scarcely recognized her own voice, echoing strangely in her ears. "What are you doing?"

The fire priestess lifted her face. "You can't see yourself, Edra. You don't see what we do, or you would understand. Fires dance around you, bright and cold, soft as the down on a hatchling red-crest. And then, you bring us this." Her slender hands hovered reverently above the waiting arrow. "Something found you in the forest."

Edra nodded. She told her people all that had happened since she'd fled them: Iri's spirit, his gift, her mission. As she spoke, she saw how her every word conjured fresh fear into her people's faces. No one could escape the news she brought: The curse would be lifted, but at a life's cost. A sacrifice must come.

When she was done, the chieftain spoke: "A sacrifice...A sacrifice by one of Skel's own arrows. May the gods hear me, even though I am no shaman. May the gods receive my thanks for giving our people a fresh chance, even though one of us must—must—" He took a deep breath and let it out slowly as his eyes passed from one frightened, firelit face to the next. "Let it be done."

Edra raised her bow. She felt the barbed tip of Skel's arrow vibrating, pulling at the bow, at her arms, at her entire body. It was seeking its quarry, choosing its rightful target. Her mouth filled with sour liquid as the arrow forced her to follow its slow, agonizing track from one person to the next. Every face held endlessly repeated cries of *No, please, no, please, no,* except for the young mothers. They hunched their shoulders, trying to hide their children's bodies with their own, while their eyes cried out *Take my life, Edra! Take my life and spare his, spare hers, take mine!*

And then the pull of the arrow stopped.

"Jir?" Horrified, Edra met her sister's eyes. It was astounding: There was no fear in them. The fire priestess' apprentice looked as though the arrow's choice were welcome. Certainly she did not look surprised.

"Well hunted, sister," Jir said calmly. "Why do you hesitate? Give the gods what they demand. Give our people back

the deer. Give old Iri's spirit a second chance to name his heir—
a willing one, this time—after I am gone."

Edra felt cold sweat mist her brow as the dead shaman's
words came back: *What good is a vision that doesn't appear to
the one who must heed it?* "Iri came to you, Jir? Goddess,
when?"

Her sister closed her eyes as though savoring a pleasant
dream. "Two days after his burial. Tokal was...with me. At first
he thought his father's spirit had come to bring him the news he
was so hungry to hear." She cast a fond glance at the shaman's
lastborn son. He looked half mad with grief. "Tokal, my love,
don't weep," Jir said tenderly. "I've made my own doom. I
brought the curse of hunger on our people the moment that I told
your father's spirit I would never be our shaman. How could I?
It's one thing to serve the fire goddess, as women have always
done, but for a woman to be brazen enough to speak to the gods?
Our people would never stand for it. I was sure they'd destroy
me first. Bad enough we already had one woman who'd gone
against the 'natural' way of things." She gave Edra a rueful
smile. "I refused to believe that Iri's spirit brought me the true
desires of the gods. I turned my back on them, and so they
turned their backs on us."

"It isn't fair!" Tokal cried out. "Everyone knows that
only the fire goddess can be served by women. That's how it's
always been! Jir shouldn't be punished for doing what we all
know is right." He scowled ferociously at Edra. "If your arrow
kills her, you'd better have a second one waiting to kill me."

Edra saw Tokal's hand close around the hilt of his long
knife. He took a step toward her, but before he could take
another, Jir flew to his side and held his hands immobile.

"No, beloved," she said quietly. "You mustn't interfere.
I've brought enough misfortune to our people, enough
humiliation to you." She looked at her sister. "After I refused the
gods' call, I saw a way for me to wield a shaman's power
without risk. If Tokal could be named his father's successor, he
would pretend to walk the path between our people and the gods,
but I would be the one to tread it for him. I sent him to woo you
because we needed you to lie for us. Too many eyes saw how

things were—are—between Tokal and me. Too many wouldn't believe it if I swore that Iri chose him."

Jir turned wistful eyes to her people. "I clung to the old ways out of cowardice, not virtue. I have refused the gods' command, endangered us all, tried to manipulate my own sister and treated her harshly when she wouldn't bend to my plans. I wanted power without risk, and now I find that I've risked and lost everything." She kissed Tokal long and sweetly, then opened her arms to Edra and the silver-tipped bow.

"I love you, my sister. Forgive me. Let the arrow fly."

Edra drew back the bowstring. Skel's arrow whined in her ear, eager for release. She looked down the pale shaft to her sister's face. The lifeless woods surrounded her with their silence. All she had to do was set the arrow free and the curse would be lifted, the gods' anger sated, the deer would return, the hunger would be over.

Set the arrow free, Edra, Iri's voice whispered from the snowy fletching. *Set Skel's arrow free.*

Into my sister's heart? Her hands tightened in the bow. *No. Things change, even the ways of gods and heroes. It's not Skel's arrow now. The gods' gift, yes, but in* my *hands. My father's bow, Skel's arrow, but my choice to rule how they'll be used.* Mine.

The silver-tipped bow cut the night air like an eagle's wing as Edra swept her aim skyward to the stars. Her shout was so loud that afterwards there were many to swear that the moon itself shook at the sound like a pebble-rippled pool. She released the bowstring, and the arrow soared into the heavens, a streak of white so blinding that the people shaded their eyes against brilliance almost too dazzling to bear. As they watched, transfixed, the arrow made from a hero's shattered bones shattered again into countless shards of light. They dropped swiftly, and the hunters cried out in happy astonishment as a fat, spirited stag sprang out of the earth wherever a gleaming fragment fell. The deer snorted and plunged into the trees, the hunters scrambling for their spears and bows and arrows as they raced off in pursuit.

Her bow in hand, Edra took her weeping sister into her arms. And from the forest came the sound of drowsy birds, of little bright-eyed creatures, of the great herds' return, and of a spirit's slowly fading laughter.

A NOSE FOR TROUBLE

by *Patricia B. Cirone*

Patricia B. Cirone has been writing for a number of years, and has sold more than a dozen short stories, some of which were published by Marion Zimmer Bradley. One of her greatest joys is that she got to meet Marion several times and talk to her about writing, life, and writing some more. In her day job as a librarian, she spends more time talking about books than reading or writing them, but she is currently working on a novel which she hopes to finish before the characters in it get so frustrated they stop talking to her. She lives in New England with her husband, two cats, and a fencing foil that is a lot easier to maneuver in stories than in real life.

Marina paused, stilling even her breathing, in order to listen. Yes, those were footsteps approaching, and rapidly. Not the soft furtive scrape of soles worn to nothingness, but the sure, swift tread of boots. Marina looked around frantically. Nothing except the trash underfoot offered any kind of cover in the dark winding alley. Its high walls did not have windows to press up against; glass was too expensive for residents of the warrens, and no one was fool enough to open a square covered only by shutters onto the smells and type of foot traffic that dominated an alley. The few doorways that opened onto its darkness were flush with the walls and soundly locked.

Only the narrow jut of wall where two buildings didn't meet flush with each other offered any type of protection. It was that or stand stock still and let the stranger run smack into her when he came around the curve. Marina ducked sideways and pressed herself against the scant inches of cover, pressing even the back of her head as hard as she could against the dank bricks. Her hand flicked down and took a hard grip on her skirt, gathering it back against the wall so that even the faint breath of air that stole down the alley wouldn't cause it to flutter, and betray her presence.

And then he was upon her...and passing, never looking back. Marina held her breath, not believing her luck. It was a Makepeace man, all right, and not even an alley beater, with a night stick and whistle, but an officer, with shiny buttons and one of those new-fangled guns flopping at his belt. It looked kinda funny, so short compared to a good long sword, but Marina felt no inclination to laugh. It was probably his being an officer that had saved her; he wasn't out looking for folks out after curfew, but had more important business. Why he was walking down an alley instead of striding down a street was a mystery, but one Marina had no intention of lingering to find out.

She waited, still holding her breath, until he was around the next curve in the alley and then slipped away from the wall and scurried forward again. The sudden sound of a scuffle and a sharp cry from behind her froze her in her tracks for a moment, and then she began to run. Softly, on quiet, slipper-shod feet. She didn't know what was going on tonight, but she wanted to be far away from it.

She knew she shouldn't have stayed so late at her mam's, but it had felt so good to be home—with the familiar smell of onions and warm fire, instead of incense and cold, heatless lamps—that she had lingered. Her mam had fussed over her, giving her an extra half-bowl of stew, even though she was eating well now, and even her older sister had stopped fussing over her children long enough to sit and listen while Marina had told her all about the medium's house, making it sound better than it really was. Now she was paying for her folly.

The curfew bells had rung a good fifteen minutes ago and she was still far from Madame's house. If she was caught out, she'd not only lose her job, but the fines might well be too high for her family to pay. Well, she'd just have to make sure she wasn't caught. It hadn't been that long since she had run the streets with all the other grubby urchins of the poor quarter, dodging patrols; she just had to pay attention to what she was doing and not clump along with her head in the clouds.

The rest of her run passed without incident. Soon the heavy, cloying smell of fish and dying seaweed filled the air. She skirted the pools of light from the few oil lamps that swung high above the quay, darted towards the middle-class quarter that bordered the busy docks, and ducked down the alley that led to the back of her employer's house. This alley was much wider and cleaner than the ones in the warrens. Soon she was slipping into the back door of Madame Fertaglio's, and into the equally cloying smells of incense and candles that masked the scent of fish that wafted from the docks. She lit a lamp with the aid of the embers from the banked kitchen fire and turned to lift the heavy night bar across the door.

She was back safe. Her half-day was over, her month's pay was safely in her mam's hands, and the next month, she wouldn't linger so long she was out after curfew!

The next day her mistress was even more demanding than usual. Nothing Marina did was right, from the way she cooked the morning egg to the precise height at which she trimmed the candles.

"You don't understand!" cried Madame Fertaglio dramatically. "The atmosphere, it is all in the atmosphere. It *must* be just right, or the spirits won't come!"

Atmosphere, my eye, thought Marina. It was all in the drugs with which "Madame" laced her incense. Why else did Marina hear tinny, far off voices and catch glimpses of shadows out of the corner of her eyes whenever Madame did readings in the incense-filled room at the front of the house? And did she think Marina didn't know why Madame had shooed Marina away and opened the back door herself, when that sailor had knocked a few weeks ago? Madame, who never lifted a finger to do anything for herself? She had bought something she didn't want Marina to know about. It had to be either drugs or bought spells, as Madame was no spell-caster herself, and she suspected Madame was too cheap to pay for magic.

But it certainly wasn't for her to complain or be pointing out her understanding to her mistress. Madame had made clear she didn't like questions, and if Marina wanted to keep this job it would pay her to keep her thoughts and observations to herself. Growing up in the warrens you learned not to see what you weren't supposed to see, even when it was right in front of your nose.

So Marina never even raised her eyes when Madame continued to complain about the lunch, and the way Marina's skirt made too much noise when she walked about doing the chores, and the why those gulls had to shriek so, and wasn't there something Marina could do about it.

The latter had Marina biting her lip, thinking of more than gulls' voices she'd like to silence.

It was with relief that she gathered up the basket and headed for the market to buy what was needed for dinner and the evening guests. As she moved from stall to stall, she kept her ears open for the gossip. Madame always wanted to know what was being talked about—some of it had a way of showing up in her readings.

Today the voices were hushed and excited...

Did you hear about the Peacemaker...head bashed in...Peacemaker! killed! not far from here!...they say his head was mashed something awful...brought the sniffers in...say they're looking for a girl...something to do with the sea...a girl! how'd a girl kill a Peacemaker like that?...no, sniffers say to look for a girl, and you know they're never wrong...they're going to be bringing the sniffers to the docks, I hear, on account of the girl having something to do with the sea...how can a girl have something to do with the sea? Can't be no sailor and haven't seen no foreign girls coming on a ship—would have heard about that...death of a Peacemaker...won't be any rest in the city, till they've caught someone for it, right or wrong!

Madame would certainly be interested in this! A death, and a violent one, and some foreign girl! A medium could hardly ask for something better to bring people flocking to her readings! All would be wondering if Madame would hear anything from the spirit world, and Madame would make certain that she dropped mysterious hints that would keep people coming back.

Marina went back to the stall that sold nuts. She would have to bake plenty of the little nut delicacies Madame liked to have on hand for her guests. It was as she was leaving the nut stall that she glanced up and saw the official, blue-bordered notice of the Peacemaker's murder pinned on the market notice board. It had a sketch of the man. Something about him looked familiar, and Marina pushed her way closer to look.

She gasped, as she realized it was the man from last night, the one who had hurried past her in the alleyway.

Marina felt a cold chill move down the back of her neck and settle like lead over her heart. *She* had been there last night. And now that she worked for Madame, she lived near the docks. And her name—her mam had told her that her name meant a pretty place where ships went, because her father had been a sailor. *That* had something to do with the sea. The sniffers were after *her!*

Marina rushed home from the market as if the sniffers were right on her tail. She dropped her basket on the table, and hunched over it, panting. Gradually she realized no one had actually chased her, and she still had the chores to do, but her hands shook as she made the little nut delicacies for the evening reading. Her thoughts scurried like mice, over and around and through her head.

I didn't have anything to do *with him getting killed.... I didn't even know he* had *been killed.... That scuffle. That must have been when it happened. There had been a cry, too....*

But why were the sniffers describing her? She *hadn't had anything to do with it; she'd just been there. Out. After curfew. Too close to something bad....*

Surely she was safe, here, in Madame's house. Could the sniffers find her here, behind a locked door? They say they used magic, that's how they knew stuff. They looked at a body, or went round some place where a crime had taken place, and they just sniffed out knowledge, the way a hound sniffed out scents. She should never have stayed too late at Mam's...now look what had happened...but surely she could explain she had had nothing to do with his death—she hadn't even seen who had done it!

ঙ৫জ৯৮

Aian Donal came to the end of the report he had been reading and ran his fingers through his hair in frustration. He looked across at the specialist who'd wrote it, one of those the commoners called "sniffers," and asked: "So, none of you have *any* clue on who actually murdered young Jokcelyn?"

Petrie shook his head. "The 'no see' spell they used was thorough—no thought, no sight, no sound, not even an odor from the actual moment. It's as if it never happened. Except for the fact we have a body, that is. I'd like to know *what* spell they used to wipe all traces from the scene—I've never run up across anything like it before and we can't work up a counter if we don't know the original spell.

"All we sensed is the girl. *Her* presence comes across so strong, she had to be involved—either part of murder—though if she was, it seems strange they wouldn't have protected her by the 'no see'—or else she witnessed it. Either way, she's the only lead we have."

"And you've traced her to Madame Fertaglio's house?"

"Yes. Should we pull Madame Fertaglio in for questioning?"

"No. At least, not yet. Madame is a pompous windbag, who is also a tad shady, but by no stretch of the imagination could she be called 'a girl.' No, it wasn't she in the warrens when Jokcelyn was killed. Someone else. Someone who fled to her, or went to her for a private reading, or has some other connection with that house. I'll see what I can do to ferret out what connection this might have with the Madame.

"You and your men go canvass the dock area. See if you can find any trace of the girl there. Or rumors of a new spell-caster, or anything of a nature that would cast some light on this 'no see' spell you can't break."

"Right," Petrie said with a sigh. "Though you know, if someone on the wrong side of the law has the ability to spell something like this, they're not going to be broadcasting it."

"You never know," replied Aian. "Sometimes we get a break. Asha knows we need one on this. I've got the Lord

Commissioner screaming about how I could have 'let' one of my officers get killed, and young Jokcelyn's noble relatives demanding information, and nothing to tell either. Other than he wound up dead, with his head bashed in, in a quarter of the warrens he shouldn't have been in, while not another living soul was present within one hundred yards—according to *you* folks."

"I never said there wasn't anyone else present—just that they left no trace."

"I know, I know," Aian sighed. "But that doesn't help me any. He was *supposed* to be watching Kiasie, that foreigner that we were warned might be smuggling black magic. Or possibly smuggling something else. Or maybe just 'trouble.' I don't know if Jokcelyn was murdered because he saw Kiasie doing something suspicious, or because he was wandering around the warrens looking for some prostitute to bed, in which case his death could be from a simple mugging!"

"No simple mugger has a 'no see' like that one."

"I know, I know. I'm just saying we don't have anything definitive to tell anyone at this point. Either the Lord Commissioner *or* Jokcelyn's relatives. At least nothing I'd care to share. Go find me something."

"We'll try," Petrie said while smothering a yawn. He got up and shuffled wearily out the door. Aian ran his fingers through his disordered hair once again, as if he could pull clues from its strands.

ଔଔଔଔ

Marina's fingers trembled slightly as she lit the candles for the evening; she still felt chilled to the bone, as if it were mid-winter instead of late spring. Madame bustled about, her mood of earlier forgotten.

"Here, add one drop of this to each of the incense holders," Madame said, handing Marina a small vial containing a clear liquid. "Just *one* drop, mind you. This costs as much as two client fees!" She hurried away, humming.

Marina went over to one of the incense holders and carefully lifted the stopper on the vial. She almost dropped it, the smell that wafted up was so powerful. Madame wanted *this* added to the incense? It wasn't a pleasant scent, but maybe, like a powerful perfume, it would smell better when diluted. Or maybe it was one of the drugs Marina suspected Madame used, to play with the senses of her guests. Carefully Marina dropped one drop onto the cake of incense, re-stoppered the vial, and moved to the next holder.

As she was adding the drop to the third incense holder, her hand shook just enough that part of the drop fell onto her finger. She rubbed it off onto the cake of incense, not liking the oily feel of the liquid on her skin, and not wanting to wipe it off on her clothes. Bad enough she had to smell it now, she didn't want it lingering on her all night.

She finished adding the liquid to the incense and went out to the kitchen to check on the nut delicacies she was baking. Madame liked them to be still warm from the oven when the guests arrived. Her finger itched where the oily liquid from the vial had landed, so she scrubbed it hard, both to relieve the itch and also to get the scent out. She wished she knew what the stuff was, but she didn't dare ask Madame if it was dangerous to get it on your skin; Madame would be more concerned with the loss of a quarter of a drop of her precious liquid than anything Marina might suffer from getting it on herself.

The itch went away, and if it was replaced by a dull tingling, Marina didn't notice as she rushed through the rest of the preparations for the evening. Madame may be in a good mood now, but that didn't mean she was any less demanding.

The nut delicacies were safely removed from the oven, the candles were burning at an even rate and the incense was spreading a pleasant (thank heavens!) scent throughout the room when Marina began answering the door to let in the guests. Each discreetly handed Marina their fee, which Marina just as discreetly locked away in the small drawer in the chest placed by the entrance. Madame was too "spiritual" to handle money—at least within sight of the customers.

Mr. Terweg, a regular, a small, birdlike man with watery brown eyes, was the first to arrive. He was followed shortly by Mrs. Hasse and Lady Lorent, both of whom had attended several times since Marina had been employed by Madame. The next man was a foreigner, with strange yellow hair and eyes that were such a light hazel they seemed almost as yellow as his hair. By that time, Madame had entered the room and was greeting her guests effusively. She swept past Marina to welcome the next, a tall, somewhat florid man, whom she greeted as Lord Tiebold, fussing over him as if he were the King himself. Another stranger, at least to Marina, arrived, followed by Miss Sebrings, who came to Madame's readings almost as often as Mr. Terweg.

Marina made sure all those who wanted something to drink were served, and then began ushering them into chairs around the table. Her work for the evening was almost done. Once everyone was seated, all she had to do was sit quietly in a corner and make sure none of the candles burned out, none of the incense holders smoked too much, or no other minor disaster occurred.

She noticed the dark-haired man who had arrived just before Miss Sebrings kept glancing her way, and wondered if he were one of those men who thought servant girls were fair game for their amorous intentions. Well, she'd rather be stared at by him than that yellow-haired stranger. Something about him gave her the chills as much as the thought of sniffers being on her trail.

The thought of the sniffers made her remember the events of the night before, so much so she didn't notice the humming with which Madame always started her readings. Voices droned behind her, asking Madame and her "spirit" questions, which Madame answered in that strange voice she always used during the readings. More of Madame's "atmosphere."

What would she do if the sniffers came looking for her at Madame's? It wasn't as if she could run very far. They'd find her in the warrens as easily as here. She shivered and glanced over at the candles, to make sure all were still burning evenly, and bit back an exasperated hiss.

One of the guests had left his seat at the table. That wasn't allowed. She was amazed Madame hadn't already called her over to "make the guest comfortable," by sitting him back down.

As she stood to lead the guest back to the table, his face grew brighter. And the chill that still numbed her fingers spread throughout her body.

It was the Peacemaker. The one who had been killed. Standing there, staring at her.

"What are you doing here? Go away!" Marina cried, oblivious to the guests starting to turn and look at her.

"I need your help," the man whispered. He turned, slowly, and pointed to his head. With a shudder, Marina saw the bloody, misshapen pulp that used to be the back of his head. "I was murdered," the man continued.

"I know," moaned Marina. "Just go away! I don't want to see that. I don't want to see *you!*"

"Marina!" Madame cried sharply, her soothing "reading" voice absent. "Who are you talking to?"

"Nobody," Marina said, thinking if she got rid of...him...fast enough, no one would connect her with the girl the sniffers were looking for. But how could she get rid of him? Why was he here?

Her thoughts felt sluggish and slow, as if energy was draining out of her. Just standing was an effort, trying to move towards the apparition felt as though she was dragging her feet through thick, oozing mud.

"What are you doing!" exclaimed Madame Fertaglio. "Sit back down and behave yourself. You're interrupting the reading! All the spirits have fled!

"Help, these days," she murmured in a lower exasperated tone, becoming aware of the guests staring back and forth between her and the girl. "It's so impossible to find good help these days!"

"No, he hasn't fled," said Marina. "I wish he would!"

Someone at the table snorted.

"You have to listen to me!" cried the murdered Peacemaker.

A chorus of gasps from the table let Marina know the guests had heard him as clearly as she had. That, and the sudden, overwhelming of energy being sucked right out of her, made her realize what was happening. She was being used as a medium.

Not a fake one, like Madame Fertaglio, but a *real* one. That was the ghost of the Peacemaker, and he was speaking through her.

She staggered, both from exhaustion and fear. The dark-haired man at the table leapt up and rushed over to her.

"You need to sit down," he said, pushing her back onto her stool. "You're using up energy too fast. You're not used to this, are you?"

"I've never...this can't be happening! I don't even believe in spirits!"

"Will someone *please* tell me what is going on?" Madame Fertaglio demanded in a loud voice. She, apparently, was one of the few in the room who had not heard the murdered Peacemaker speak.

"Just relax," the dark-haired man said. "Just let it happen, and it will be easier on you. I've worked with lots of sniffer...er, specialists, and it's the same with them."

"How can I relax, when that...that bloody apparition is standing right there!" Marina demanded, beginning to feel hysterical.

"You *have* to," the man said sharply, and Marina felt her spine stiffen.

"*Please* listen to me," the murdered Peacemaker said, in a softer tone, and the gasps at the table turned into soft murmurs of excitement from the guests.

"Go ahead," said the dark-haired man, standing behind Marina, and holding her steady on the stool.

"Trying to report, sir," the ghost said, wanly.

"I know," Aian Donal replied sadly.

"Kiasie—he's right over there."

"I know," replied Aian.

With a sharp noise of disgust, the yellow-haired stranger who had made Marina uneasy shoved back his chair and got to his feet. "I don't know what you're playing at, but I refuse to be a part of this!" He stormed out of the room.

"Stop him!" gasped the ghost.

"Don't worry, he won't get very far," Aian reassured him. "Just tell me what you know, before this young girl collapses from exhaustion."

Marina stirred beneath his hands. "I'm fine," she said defiantly. She was starting to get the hang of this...she thought. The man behind her had been right about relaxing, and not fighting the drain of energy. She had more control over it, this way, instead of feeling like a fish on the mudflats, thrashing and gasping for air. But she hadn't liked his reference to the sniffers....

"Kiasie isn't smuggling black magic spells," the murdered Peacemaker gasped, rushing his words. "He's a spell-caster—a black one—and he's working with Lord Tiebold, there, who is paying him for a whole series of spells to try and overthrow the King!"

"I say!" sputtered Lord Tiebold. "What nonsense is this!?" But Marina noticed he had turned a sickly, pale gray, with spots of red burning in his cheeks.

"Sit back down," commanded Aian.

"They met here to exchange the payment," Jokcelyn's ghost went on. "You'll find an envelope from Lord Tiebold in the drawer in the lobby here, hidden under the payment for this reading. Kiasie was going to lift it when he was leaving, so no one would see it exchange hands. I overheard Kiasie's underling making the arrangement with Lord Tiebold's seneschal. But I must have given myself away, because Kiasie's underling followed me and murdered me."

"All right, you've done well," said Aian. "It's time for you to head for the follow-grounds, before you get stuck here, in this state. We'll find the proof for this, now that we know what to look for."

"He stole my gun," said the ghost, fingering the pale, transparent holster at his hip. "And took it back to Kiasie, who has it in his cabin on his ship. He's studying it to see if he can work a black spell on it, and use it for one of the spells Lord Tiebold's commissioned."

"We'll find it. Now you need to go," said Aian Donal.

"But..." protested the ghost of Jokcelyn.

But Marina, who had been studying the cord of energy leaving from her, as well as paying attention to the conversation, quietly but firmly pinched it off.

The young Peacemaker looked surprised for a moment, then relieved, as he faded away to nothingness.

"Good girl," said Aian.

"I'm *not* a girl," Marina said sharply.

"Ahh, you'll make a feisty sniffer," Aian said approvingly.

"I'm no sniffer!"

"Ah, sorry. *Specialist*. None of you lot like to be called sniffers."

"I'll agree I might be a medium. But I'm not, and never will be a sniffer!"

"Well, that's for the future to see, but you've got the talent. *And* the nose for trouble."

"That's the part I don't understand. If I can do something like...like *this*, how come it's never happened to me before?"

"Well, most of you...*specialists*...have to start with a bit of a spell—lucky, or you'd be walking about hearing voices and seeing things from the otherside all the time. Drive you crazy. Does, to some of those who can do it without touching a spell. Did you buy any love potion or some such recently?"

"Of *course* not!" Marina replied huffily. "What would I want with one of those!"

"Well, you must have touched or swallowed something that was magicked within the last few hours," Aian said.

That drop of liquid that spilled, Marina thought, and looked down at her hand. Then she closed her other hand over it, as if the drop could still be seen, and glanced over at Madame, who was sitting at her own table, looking like a stuffed trout. Well, she'd just keep quiet about Madame's little vial. She didn't want to be a sniffer, which meant she needed to keep this job. At least for now....

"I must have touched something down at the market, when I was buying the food for tonight," Marina said. Out of the corner of her eye, she saw Madame Fertaglio relax a bit. Though she still didn't look very...happy.

"Shouldn't you be chasing after that Kiasie man?" Marina asked, changing the subject.

"No. I told the men I brought with me *and* the ones I ran into who were following Kiasie to detain him if he left here before I did. I expect we'll find him, and Lord Tiebold's little envelope full of money, safely in custody. We'll pick up Jokcelyn's gun from his cabin and have the sniffers go over it for spells and anything else they can find, and we should have a nice tight case against Kiasie."

"I never paid him any money!" Lord Tiebold protested. "You've made all this up, you and your...your sniffer, there!"

"I'm sure we'll get all this straightened out to everyone's satisfaction," Aian said cheerfully, in a tone that did not seem to cheer Lord Tiebold up at all.

He moved over to collect the older man and escort him towards the door. The remaining guests began to ease back from the edges of their chairs. Miss Sebrings fluttered over to Marina.

"Are you going to be doing the readings, now?" she asked, in a whispery, excited tone.

"That will be up to Madame Fertaglio," Marina said politely. "I'm just her apprentice," elevating herself about three rungs from general dogsbody and maid of all work.

Madame Fertaglio reared up from her chair like a whale breaching the water. "Yes, you're coming along quite nicely, dear, but I think we'll have to spend a bit more time with practice before you do another session. Very...chaotic. Not very professional, at all, you know. But you're coming along."

"Thank you, Madame," Marina replied, already planning a few other changes in her terms of employment.

NIGHT WATCHES

by Catherine Soto

Catherine Soto's work first appeared in *Sword & Sorceress XXI* with a story in which Lin Mei and her brother acquired a pair of kittens while traveling with a caravan. Now they're in winter quarters and have more problems than just hired assassins—and I still think there's something strange about those cats....

Catherine says that she wants to write a novel about these characters. One way to produce a novel is to keep writing short stories about the same characters. It worked for Mercedes Lackey.

The courtyard was empty, bathed in moonlight, and serene in the stillness. Even so, there was an air of menace about it. Lin Mei shivered in her quilted jacket. She rested her hand on the hilt of her sword, drawing some comfort from it. The companion dagger rested in the sash next to it. They were smaller twins to her brother's sword and dagger, and their blades gave the two of them unparalleled fighting power. But something in the night made her uneasy nevertheless.

"Another bad dream?" her brother asked behind her. Biao Mei also wore a quilted jacket and his sword and dagger. Tragedy had taught them harsh lessons; neither went out unarmed.

She nodded. "The same one. It's the third time in three nights."

"The snake again?"

"It does not seem to be malevolent," she said. "But it is dangerous." She heard him sigh. Although he had fifteen to her seventeen years, he had taken over the role of her protector, which she did not mind, since he was stocky and strong, although she was stronger and tougher than her willowy form suggested. Still, she often had to do the thinking for both of them, and then convince him that the result was his idea.

"Not malevolent, but dangerous," he mused. "At least it's not both. Thank Heaven for small graces," he said ironically.

Annoyed, she made a sudden decision. "Let's see to the cats," she said. "I want to be certain they are safe." Without waiting for agreement she went down the stairs of the veranda and started across the courtyard to the stables...and stopped after only a few steps, the hair on the back of her neck rising. Biao Mei froze beside her, his hand on the hilt of his sword. So he felt it too....

"Back to the veranda," he whispered. Silently they retraced their steps to the barracks for the compound's guards, which was their home—and occupation—for the winter. With their backs to the door, and a roof over them, they could observe any potential attack.

"Left," she whispered. He nodded. So, it was not only in her mind....

Unmoving, save for their eyes, they both carefully examined the courtyard, then checked the roofs of the adjoining buildings. Lin Mei spoke first.

"Footprints in the sand," she whispered.

Her brother nodded. They moved down the veranda toward the small sand garden at one end of the courtyard. They slowed as they neared the sand, making some distance between them as they did so, enough to allow a free swing of their swords but not so much as to allow either to be cut off from the other.

The prints were clear, if few. Three human footprints, leading from the paved area of the courtyard to the water-worn river stone at the other end. Biao Mei pointed at the door just before them, which opened on the storage area where goods unloaded from caravans were kept. It was always kept locked. Now it was slightly ajar.

"Should we call the alarm?" Lin Mei asked softly. Biao Mei shook his head.

"Let's first see if there is reason to," he said. There was a soft click as he loosened his sword in its scabbard.

The door opened silently on well-oiled hinges as he pushed. The interior was dark, illuminated only by moonlight coming in through narrow windows near the ceiling. He led the way, eyes scanning the darkness.

A dark mass fell from the ceiling above him. His body dropped into a quick roll forward, sending him and his attacker to the floor in a tangle. Lin Mei drew her sword, but hesitated until she could differentiate between her brother and his attacker.

That moment saved her life, as she became aware that someone had come behind her. She dropped automatically to one knee, stabbed backward over her head, and was rewarded with a pained grunt. Not waiting to see what or whom she had struck, she jerked her sword free and rolled forward into the darkness.

She came up against her brother and his attacker, still locked in combat. A felt boot knocked against her head. It was Biao Mei's. The split toed boots of thick cloth must therefore belong to his opponent. There was no room for the sword, so she drew her dagger and stabbed as hard as she could at the man's calf.

Her brother took advantage of the distraction to draw his dagger and strike. A ghastly death hiss, followed by a rattling cough, told her that his blow had been fatal. Their lives had encompassed enough death that she knew the sounds. She came to her feet and swung her sword in an arc through the darkness to ensure that the area about her was clear of any danger.

"I think we can give the alarm now," her brother said.

છ૱ળૹ

"Anshazhe," Shin Hu, the caravan master, said, using the toe of his boot to prod the body of the man Biao Mei had killed. The first rays of the sun were starting to filter in through the windows. The dead man was clothed all in black. His mask had been ripped off to reveal a nondescript face. His sword had been kicked to one side.

"I think I hit another," Lin Mei said, indicating a splash of blood on the floor near the door.

Shin Hu nodded, eyeing the blood.

"How is it that you were up?" he asked.

"I had a bad dream," Lin Mei replied. "I went outside for some air. Biao Mei followed, and we saw the opened door."

Shin Hu eyed her closely.

"We met these scum on the road here," he noted. "Now they appear here in Kendar." He looked down at the dead man. "Anshazhe," he said, "are hired assassins, deadly fighters. You are fortunate to encounter two and survive."

"What were they doing here? " Biao Mei asked.

"That is a very good question," Shin Hu said. "They are not normally thieves. Murder for hire is their trade."

"They were not alone," Hua Chan said, coming in. "The tracks in the sand were not theirs." He motioned with his lance and they all followed him outside. The morning light illuminated the sand garden. He pointed with his lance at the prints. "Those tracks were made by bare feet. The Anshazhe wear cloth boots."

"Another mystery," Shin Hu said.

⋯⋯⋯⋯

Two hours later, with breakfast and a pot of tea in their bellies, Lin Mei and Biao Mei were in the stables. "They seem well," Biao Mei said, eyeing the kittens in the basket in an unused stall.

Lin Mei squatted, a finger poking softly at two of the kittens. The other three were cute, striped like little tigers, but the two she was interested in were cream colored with dark faces, paws, ears, and tails. Despite the differences, all were suckled by the mother cat lying on the blanket that lined the basket. She had adopted the two orphans that Lin Mei and Biao Mei had found in an abandoned temple in the mountains above Kendar when Shin Hu's caravan spent a night there. Lin Mei had named the male Shadow and the female Twilight.

Hua Chan came in, his lance in hand. "Shin Hu wants to see you. The Magistrate's men are here and you two are to make a statement." They followed the lancer to the main hall.

Wang Liu, the merchant who had taken the caravan into his household for the rainy season, was there also.

The Magistrate's men were two clerks and two armsmen. Statements were taken, a few perfunctory questions were asked, and the official party departed, taking the dead man with them.

"Is that all?" Lin Mei asked. Wang Liu looked at her for a moment.

"I don't think so," he replied. "Sin Wai Tsu, who is the District Governor, is no fool. If questions were scant it is because knowledge is not. At least, not in his quarters." He stopped to take a sip of tea. "But I would know more. Why were Anshazhe in my storeroom?"

"Your clerks report nothing missing," Shin Hu said.

"There is also the matter of the footprints on the sand, which do not match the boots worn by the Anshazhe," Hua Chan noted. He lounged by the door, his lance still in his hand.

"Truth," Wang Liu said. "The women's quarters were locked, and the prints were made by bare feet. Women in this compound do not go barefoot."

"Mysteries," Shin Hu noted. "I dislike mysteries. We will have a full guard at night until this matter is resolved." Wang Liu nodded, and the meeting broke up.

Lin Mei and her brother decided to get something to eat. They went to the kitchen, where they got steaming bowls of rice and noodles, and went to sit on the barracks' veranda to eat.

"May I join you?" a voice asked. They looked up to see a woman, dressed in a divided skirt and quilted leather jacket.

"You are—?" Lin Mei asked, her hand motioning to a spot next to them.

"Ro Min," the woman replied, sinking gracefully to a seated position. "Of the household."

Lin Mei nodded. She had seen her and another woman around the compound; they were bodyguards attached to the women's quarters.

"Much excitement last night, we hear."

"Anshazhe, hired killers," Biao Mei said. "Two of them, and one got away."

"And mysterious footprints not left by either," Ro Min noted. "I examined them earlier. They don't match anyone here. Too slender."

Lin Mei nodded. Ro Min was seeking information, trading what she knew for whatever Lin Mei and her brother might know. She noted that Ro Min, despite being a bit more muscular than most women, was nonetheless attractive, and that Biao Mei was warming to her. She suppressed a smile. She would work it to her advantage.

"Has any knowledge been gained of the Anshazhe Biao Mei killed?" she asked.

Ro Min shook her head slowly. "Anshazhe do not work this far from the capital. There are quarrels here, sometimes fatal, but people do their own killing." She nodded at Biao Mei. "They are dangerous. Good work killing one."

Biao Mei actually blushed. "What would bring them this far west?" she asked.

Ro Min shrugged. "Money, power, political intrigue. All the same thing, actually. Kendar has grown in this generation. It is no longer the frontier border town it used to be. The Khans have unified the mountain kingdoms to the South, and peace has brought more trade. There is now more to fight over."

"We met some in the hills above the town," Biao Mei said, "when we took shelter from a storm in an abandoned temple."

"There has been much talk of that," Ro Min noted. "A desperate battle against high odds—the market has been filled with gossip about it."

"Any real news?" Lin Mei asked dryly.

Ro Min smiled and shook her head. "In the marketplace? No. But gossip can hold truth. People say that the District Governor is leaving early next Season."

Lin Mei finished the last of her noodles with a loud slurp. "Has the gossip linked that to the sudden presence of Anshazhe?" she asked.

"Of course," Ro Min said. "In many ways. But no real news." The midday gong rang in the distance.

"Time to train," Lin Mei said, stacking her bowls. Ro Min rose in one graceful motion.

"It was good talking with you," she said, before moving off to the women's quarters. Lin Mei watched her, puzzled. She could not shake the feeling there had been more than was apparent in the meeting.

"Interesting," Biao Mei said. She looked at him.

"A romantic interest?" she asked grinning.

"Of course not," he stammered. "But she obviously knows a lot of what is going on."

"Maybe you can nurture your friendship, and you can learn from each other," she said.

"Perhaps," he grunted.

She hid her smile. He would have thought in that direction anyway, and now he would look for any probing on Ro Min's part.

They returned their bowls to the kitchen and went to the training rooms for the afternoon's session.

Lin Mei lunged with a padded practice lance and fell to the floor with a whump! Hua Chan had whirled away from the thrust and then back to trip her with his own lance. She felt the padded tip of his lance at her throat, holding her down. After a moment he backed off, letting her rise.

"Another bad night?" he asked.

She nodded.

"Bad dreams will kill you," he added, with a slight note of exasperation in his voice. "Rest and get some water to drink. We will start again in a short while."

Nearby Biao Mei sweated through his own routine, the heavy wooden practice sword straining his muscles. With a sigh of relief he set it down and joined her.

They went out to the well in the courtyard. The household was bustling, and they had to wait in line. Biao Mei nodded to the far end of the courtyard where Ro Min and another woman were training with their bows. As they watched Ro Min loosed an arrow that flew unwaveringly into a bundle of reeds that had been set up as a target.

"Good shooting," he observed.

Lin Mei nodded. She watched as Ro Min nocked another arrow. The release was smooth and quick and the second arrow landed beside the first. Lin Mei looked around, observing the household traffic, which was centered around the well and the cooking fire, with only a few servants sitting in the shaded verandas. She motioned toward the sand garden.

"People seem to avoid that," she said.

Biao Mei looked over and nodded. "They do," he agreed.

"That's odd." The sand was carefully raked, the plants were carefully arranged and well tended, and the rocks were tastefully chosen and set in the sand just so. It compared well with other gardens they had seen in their travels. Still, there was something menacing about it, even in the light of day.

"A pretty garden, eh?" a servant girl behind them said. "Wang Liu's young wife had it made earlier this year. She directed the making of it, in every detail. It is like the gardens in her home province."

"She is not from here?" Biao Mei asked.

The girl shook her head. "He brought her here two seasons ago. She was a lady-in-waiting in his older brother's household in Chang'An."

"So she is from the Capital?" Lin Mei asked.

The girl nodded. "A minor family. Noble, but not too wealthy. And she is the youngest daughter. This is a good match for her."

"And her guards?"

"Also from Chang'An," the girl replied.

Lin Mei and her brother looked at each other.

"Interesting," Lin Mei said later, as they walked back to the training rooms.

"So Wang Liu has ties to the Capital," her brother said. "Would that account for the presence of Anshazhe?"

Lin Mei thought for a moment, then shook her head. "The youngest daughter of minor nobility with little wealth? I doubt it. Still, it is something to keep in mind."

The rest of the afternoon passed in hard effort, and Lin Mei was glad when it ended. She made her way to the women's quarters to use the baths there. The servants had buckets of heated water ready and she gratefully took one and began to rub off the grime and sweat of the day.

"Train hard, fight easy," a voice said behind her. She turned to look. It was Ro Min, with her companion. "This is Kin Shin," she said. "May we join you?"

Lin Mei shrugged, and moved aside to make space in the small tiled room. She watched as the two women washed with quick economical movements. Afterwards they went to soak in the large heated tubs in the next room.

"Lance work," Ro Min said, pointing to the bruises on Lin Mei's body. "Hua Chan is a hard taskmaster."

"He is," she agreed. "I was watching you practice with the bow earlier. Good shooting."

"Thank you," Ro Min acknowledged. "It is just as hard to learn as the lance, although less painful."

"We heard of the fight in the storerooms last night," Kin Shin broke in. "Good work."

"Good thing I was awake," Lin Mei said. "A bad dream made it difficult to sleep."

"A bad dream?"

Lin Mei nodded. "The same as the past few nights, a large snake, dangerous, looking for something."

Ro Min and Kin Shin looked at each other. "It is unusual for the same bad dream to come more than once," Kin Shin said.

"This one does," Lin Mei said.

"Drink a small cup of white tea this evening, before bedtime," Kin Shin suggested.

Lin Mei thanked her for the suggestion and the talk drifted to memories of Chang'An, the capital.

That evening Lin Mei and Biao Mei were informed they would have the last watch, just before dawn. She recalled Kin Shin's suggestion and went to the kitchen to get a cup of white tea. While sipping it just outside the door she gazed over at the sand garden, noting the way people seemed to avoid it.

"Looking at the garden?" one of the cooks asked.

She nodded.

"Pretty garden," the cook said, "but people don't seem to like it. Bad feng shui, I say. Wang Liu's wife used a book instead of consulting a local expert. She even had that big rock brought in from the river because she liked it. You can do that in the center of the empire, but not here near the mountains. No, not here." He moved off back into the kitchen, leaving her to finish her tea and wonder about his words.

After the day's exertions Lin Mei had no trouble falling asleep. She woke just in time for their watch. They relieved the guards who had the prior watch and took a walk about the compound, partly to check the grounds and partly to come to full alertness. All seemed in order and they ended their round at the door to the storerooms where they had battled the Anshazhe the night before.

"Think they'll return?" Biao Mei asked.

"Maybe," she replied, "but I doubt if they will so soon after last night. Still, let's stay alert." She looked down at the sand garden.

They had just started another round of the compound when Lin Mei stopped in her tracks, slightly dizzy.

"Are you well?" Biao Mei asked, stepping close. After a moment the dizziness passed, leaving a feeling of fear and nausea in its place. That, and an image of danger.

"The cats!" she said suddenly. Without another word she raced across the courtyard, Biao Mei following in surprised exasperation.

She entered the stables, hand on her sword hilt, and ran down the center to the stall where the cat's basket was. At first all seemed well, but as she came closer she noticed that there was an air of agitation, with the kittens squirming about their mother. She, for her part, had her head raised. And Twilight and Shadow were sitting up, staring into the darkness. Lin Mei looked around into the shadowed interior, and froze in horror.

It was a woman. Or rather, it appeared to be a woman. She stood in the shadows, covered only by long, thick, black hair that reached down past her waist. Tall, slender, and perfectly formed, she swayed in the moonlight coming through the windows near the roof. Her eyes were cold, filled with hard calculation. Part of her mind told Lin Mei that this was easily the most beautiful woman she had seen in her short, though eventful, life. A bigger part of her mind noted that she had never before been confronted by anyone, or anything, so dangerous.

"Who are you?" Lin Mei breathed.

"Lumas," the stranger replied, her voice cold as ice.

"Lumas," Lin Mei repeated. "Why are you here?"

"You brought me here," the stranger hissed in an angry reply.

"We brought you here?" Lin Mei asked. "How?"

Before she could reply the mysterious being looked to the end of the room, her face scowling. In an instant she was gone, apparently vanishing into the dark shadows without taking a step, leaving Lin Mei with a wildly beating heart.

"What was that?" Biao Mei asked, shaking. Instead of replying Lin Mei looked down the room to where Lumas had fled. She doubted that the mysterious and dangerous being had run from something. So she had run *to* something. But what? Suddenly a certainty crystallized in her mind.

"The garden!" she yelled. Without another word she ran down the center of the stables toward the door, Biao Mei in pursuit. The door was still open and they raced through it to the space outside.

And confronted three figures in the courtyard, all dressed in black, masked, with swords out and ready. Anshazhe. Biao Mei stepped out in front of his sister, sword in ready position. Lin Mei stepped to the side, grabbed her sword hilt firmly, and proceeded to strike it loudly against the wall of the stables, all the while shouting "Intruders! Intruders!"

Within moments doors and windows were opening and people were shouting all over the compound. One of the Anshazhe motioned to his companions and they started to run. Two arrows sped through the night, striking with unerring accuracy. Two of the Anshazhe went down. The third almost made it to the nearby wall where a knotted rope waited when a dark streak brought him down. He fell, thrashing on the flagstones with Hua Chan's lance embedded in his back.

Suddenly the night was quiet, everyone staring in shock at what had happened. Shin Hu's voice broke the stillness. "Torches," he yelled. "Lanterns!"

In moments the courtyard looked like New Year, with lighted lamps and torches appearing out of nowhere. Shin Hu sent men to search the place while he took Lin Mei and her brother to the side and bade them stay still and speak to no one until he had a chance to question them.

Lin Mei said quietly as they waited, "Let's not mention the woman we saw until I have a chance to learn more."

ℭℜℬℭℬ

The sun was rising over the wall when Shin Hu returned. His men had reported that they had found no other Anshazhe. Armed messengers had gone to the magistrate's office and the head of the city's night watch, and Wang Liu had been awakened.

It was midmorning when the household of Wang Liu returned to some semblance of normalcy. The magistrate's men had come and gone, taking their reports and the bodies with them. Shin Hu had closely questioned Lin Mei and her brother. They simply said they had been checking the stables and encountered the Anshazhe on the way out. Ro Min and Kin Shin were the heroines of the day, with Hua Chan sharing credit.

"That's four dead in the last two days," Shin Hu commented. "Add in the ones we killed back at the temple in the hills and this has been a bad month for the Anshazhe. And we still don't know why they are here." He looked down at Lin Mei and Biao Mei, who were sitting on a bench inside the stables where he had taken them. "Any ideas?" They shook their heads mutely. "Well," he went on, "you two seem to have a nose for this sort of vermin hunt. If you find out anything that is useful, you will let me know, correct?" They nodded. "Good. Go and get some rest."

"Breakfast," Lin Mei said quietly as they walked across the courtyard to the kitchen, "and I want to talk to that cook."

Two bowls of rice and noodles later, along with tea, life looked better. They stacked their bowls to be washed, and went in search of the cook Lin Mei had spoken to the day before. They found him chopping some radishes for that evening's dinner. He looked up as they approached, almost as if he had been expecting them.

"So," he greeted, "more excitement and battles." Lin Mei smiled in greeting and looked around to ensure they were alone.

"What is wrong about that garden?" she asked. "It's not just the self-taught feng shui."

He finished chopping the last radish and looked up at them. "The lumas do not like to be disturbed."

"Lumas?" they both replied in unison. He smiled wryly at them.

"So you've met her?"

They nodded slowly.

"Ah," he went on. "When I was younger..." He was lost in reverie for a moment, then shook his head to come back to the present. "The lumas are serpent demons that live in stones. The people of the mountains claim they come from a union between a stone serpent demoness and the Monkey King." He looked at them to see if they were still following him.

"When Wang Liu's wife built her garden she brought a stone from the river. The lumas you met lives in that stone, and she is unhappy. She haunts the compound now, mourning the loss of her home."

"If the stone is returned to the riverbed, will she be appeased?" That was Biao Mei. The old cook shrugged.

"Perhaps," he said. "The stone demons are fickle, and their behavior is not easily predicted. You can try."

"How is it that you know of these things?" Lin Mei asked. The old cook smiled sadly.

"I was not always a cook," he said. "When I was younger I was trained to be a priest. I learned the rituals of propitiation. I learned to intercede between men and the elemental powers. Then one day, when I was performing a ritual to appease a serpent demoness whose home had been disturbed by careless men mining for gold, I let my weaker male nature get the better of me. For my sin I was banished from the monastery." He looked at Biao Mei. "She was beautiful, wasn't she?" Biao Mei blushed red.

"Can you still perform these rituals?" Lin Mei asked.

"Yes, but I cannot guarantee that they will work."

"What about the Anshazhe?" she asked.

The old cook looked at her for a long moment. "Perhaps your new friends, the ladies of the deadly bows, can help with that."

"Perhaps," Lin Mei said. "Thank you for your words." They turned to go.

"Wait," the cook said. They stopped. "Wang Liu already knows," he said.

"Knows what?" Biao Mei asked. But the man returned to his radishes. After a moment they left.

"Wang Liu and the magistrate both," Lin Mei said quietly once they were outside. "That would explain the rather brief inquiries of the last few days." Biao Mei nodded.

"Do we go and tell Shin Hu?" he asked.

"Tell him what?" Lin Mei asked in return. "So far we have tales of a 'stone demoness' and cryptic references from an old cook. Let's talk with our 'new friends' and see what light they may choose to shine on this."

They were allowed entry to the main house with an ease that made Lin Mei uneasy. It was as if they were anticipated. Ro Min met them in a side room, with tea and sweet rice buns on the low table. They sat opposite her as she poured tea with a grace and composure that seemed out of place in this provincial outpost. She set the full teacups before Lin Mei and her brother and sipped quietly from her own cup, then sat back and waited. And it hit Lin Mei with a jolt.

"You're not ordinary guards," she said. "And Wang Liu's wife is not the youngest daughter of a minor noble family." Ro Min smiled faintly.

"Imperial Guards," she said softly. "Charged with protecting the women's quarters."

Kin Shin walked in and took the other chair. They sat quietly, watching Lin Mei and her brother. They were unarmed, but Lin Mei recalled a moment two years before in the Southern jungles when they had come upon a tiger feeding on a deer. Their calm neutral eyes reminded her of the cat's gaze, and a chill ran down her spine.

"And who is Wang Liu's wife?" Biao Mei asked. Kin Shin took a cup and poured tea into it, taking a sip before setting it down and looking at him.

"The King of the Western Turks asked for the hand of the Emperor's oldest daughter," she began. "She is his favorite, and she pleaded not to be sent to live among the Western barbarians. But to refuse such a request would be a grave diplomatic insult. Fortunately the Emperor had another daughter, born of a concubine, who was almost identical in looks to the oldest daughter. She was sent off to the Western lands, where she resides in splendor, and is the mother of the Khan's sons. The Emperor's daughter was sent here for a few years, as the wife of the merchant, Wang Liu. We were sent with her."

"She accepted a life out here as the wife of an old merchant?" Biao Mei asked in disbelief.

"A marriage in name only," Ro Min replied. "At his age it does not matter to him. His sons from his prior marriage have been given positions in the Imperial Government, and he has an Imperial license to conduct trade for the Emperor here. He will die a very wealthy man. She will return home, and in the meantime he has a beautiful and refined wife and is the envy of his peers."

"What about the Anshazhe?" Lin Mei asked, already knowing the answer. Ro Min shrugged.

"We have sent a message back to Chang'An," she said casually. "Inquiries will be made."

Lin Mei looked at her knowingly. The secret had somehow been leaked, or was suspected, and blood would be spilled. She hoped it wouldn't be theirs.

"That explains why Wang Liu was so indulgent regarding the sand garden," Biao Mei said.

Ro Min and Kin Shin just smiled. Lin Mei and her brother looked at each other for a moment and reached a decision.

"That leaves the matter of the demoness," he said. The two imperial guards looked at him. Quickly Lin Mei recounted what the old cook had told them.

"He gave no guarantees," Kin Shin pointed out.

"We can try," Lin Mei replied.

ଔଔଔଔ

They assembled in the courtyard in the last hour of the third watch. Shin Hu had posted guards to ensure that the ritual was not disrupted, and the household was inside. Wang Liu and his wife watched from their rooms. All was ready except for the old cook.

"Where is he?" grumbled Shin Hu. He looked around, and stopped in his tracks. Approaching them was an aged priest, regal in his robes and staff. It took a moment to recognize the man they knew as the old cook.

"Your Reverence," Shin Hu said, without any irony or amusement in his voice, so drastic was the change in the old man. The priest nodded, looked around.

Confidently he stepped to the table that had been set up as an altar in the area before the sand garden. On it were sweet rice buns, a jar of wine, and some honey sweetened barley cakes. He lit the incense burner. As the fragrant smoke began to rise he began to chant. The words went on, incomprehensible, in the ancient tongue of the mountain tribes. It seemed to all present that the smoke was swirling in patterns that represented images.

Then she was there, standing beside the stone, still covered only in her thick, long, dark hair, perfectly beautiful and seductive as only a demon could be. There were indrawn gasps of breath as they all took in the vision. She gazed at them, her eyes as cold as a snake's, but with a wild, untamed spirit. Suddenly Lin Mei understood all the stories she had heard about the wild tribes of the mountains, and she believed the tale of their ancestry.

"Lumas," the priest chanted, "accept our deepest and most sincere regret at the disturbance to your home. Accept our offerings in the spirit we offer them, and we pray you to forgive us our transgressions."

She stepped forward, eyed him with a mixture of amusement and frank female appraisal.

"I have heard of you," she said. Her voice was as rich and sweet as honey, deep and husky, and no longer angry.

The old priest took a deep, ragged breath.

"A time of youthful indiscretions," he said. "Please forgive me."

She smiled at him, mirthful and sly at the same time.

"My sister says there is nothing to forgive. She sends her regards." She looked down at the table, stepped forward and took up a barley cake. She bit into it delicately, almost sensuously. "It's been too long since I had one," she said. Her hand waved over the table, and the offerings vanished. "I'll enjoy them later," she said. Then she was gone into the shadows.

For a while there was silence. "Is she gone?" Lin Mei asked quietly at last. The priest shook his head.

"No," he told her. "But she accepts her new home. I will leave periodic offerings, so that she will continue to accept it. She will no longer trouble the harmony of this household." He covered the incense burner, snuffing out the smoke.

As they started to disperse Lin Mei looked over at the stables and saw Shadow and Twilight watching from the doorway. "You have a unique bond with your two companions," the priest told her, following her gaze. "It will be interesting to see how it develops."

"It will be," Lin Mei said. She smiled at him, and his wise old eyes smiled back at her.

VANISHING VILLAGE

by Margaret L. Carter

Reading *Dracula* at the age of twelve ignited Margaret L. Carter's interest in a wide range of horror, fantasy, and science fiction. Vampires have always remained close to her heart (figuratively rather than literally, I hope); her first book, *Curse Of The Undead*, was an anthology of vampire fiction. Her short fiction has appeared in *Sword & Sorceress V* and *XX* as well as many other markets. Her first mass market novel, a vampire romance entitled *Embracing Darkness*, was published in March 2005 by Silhouette Intimate Moments. With her husband, retired Navy Captain Leslie Roy Carter, she has co-authored two fantasy novels, *Wild Sorceress* and *Besieged Adept*, with a sequel in progress. For more information, visit Carter's Crypt: www.margaretlcarter.com.

This story, however, has nothing to do with vampires; instead it has one of the most unusual magicians I've ever encountered.

A shadow-shrouded, foreboding stand of ancient trees blocked the road where the village of Meadowmill ought to be. The village that, according to the inhabitants of the last town up the road, had disappeared eight years before.

"I don't believe in vanishing villages," Liriel said to her partner Bertrice, mounted on the horse beside her own.

"You and me both," said Bertrice, a slim, blond woman with hair cropped to just below her ears. Like Liriel, she wore plain leather armor instead of the flowing robes most people expected of mages. That costume might look impressive but wasn't very practical for riding through the countryside. "And I don't like that emanation of vague menace."

The raven perched on Liriel's saddle horn squawked in agreement. "As far as I'm concerned, it's downright offensive," Liriel said. "As if any halfway competent sorcerer couldn't scent the odor of magic in that overblown effect." She ran her fingers through her sweat-dampened shock of short, brown hair. "Notice anything odd about that patch of woods?"

"You mean, besides being older and denser than the rest of the forest we just rode through?" Bertrice waved at the sparsely scattered, second-growth trees on either side of the rutted lane. She shaded her eyes against the noonday glare. "It looks too regular, like the same six trees duplicated over and over."

"Which also screams 'magic' to me. Good observation. You'd make a fine illusionist."

Her friend laughed. "No, I'll leave that devious magic to you. Give me a nice, straightforward fireball or lightning bolt."

"Let's find out what Brom thinks of it." Sorcerous illusions fooled only human sight, not a bird's or animal's. "Fly ahead and tell us what you see," she told her familiar. Closing her eyes, she invoked the link between her mind and the raven's.

With a caw of acknowledgment, Brom launched himself into the air and flew straight ahead into the trees. But, as Liriel saw through his eyes, the dark, glowering trees weren't there. As she'd expected, the road continued unbroken except for the sunlight-dappled woods they'd traveled through all morning. She silently directed the bird to continue following the track. The trees thinned out until the road wound through a stretch of grassy meadow into a cluster of thatch-roofed houses. Brom flapped higher above the village and spotted the stream with the mill that gave the hamlet its name. She mentally called him to return to her.

"Just as we thought," she said after the bird alighted in front of her on the saddle. "The town's still there, behind that stage set of menacing forest."

Bertrice nudged her horse into a trot up to the edge of the supposed forest. "I've never seen an illusion of that size before.

No offense meant to your talent, but could you do that?"

"Maybe for a few minutes." Liriel walked her own horse to the verge of the sorcerous mirage. "Whoever made this can maintain it permanently, judging from the disappearing village rumors. Amazing."

"I guess that's where we have to look for Lord Malkus."

Liriel sighed. "He should've listened to the locals and stuck to the main road. What possessed him to try a so-called shortcut, anyway?"

"I'd have expected him to take the long way home, if anything. If I had the Duke for a father, that's what I'd do."

With a rueful laugh, Liriel agreed.

She'd hoped finding the Duke's younger son, a month overdue for his expected return home from a routine diplomatic journey, would prove equally routine. With luck, it would have involved nothing more complicated than ambush by a band of outlaws or, best case, a side trip to dally with a compliant tavern maid. She pronounced a single word in the arcane tongue of spell-casters. Like the mouth of a tunnel, a gap appeared among the trees. Through it, she sighted the clear path Brom's reconnaissance had shown her. "We'd better leave the horses here."

She and Bertrice tethered their mounts under genuine trees surrounded by a patch of fresh grass. Liriel then cast invisibility on herself and her companion. The raven flew ahead of them, alighting on a tree limb every few minutes for the women to catch up.

As they drew near the village, they noticed shallow holes, each a couple of feet across, dug in the sward at irregular intervals. "What do you make of that?" Bertrice whispered.

"Can't imagine," said Liriel in the same low tone. Digging for water? With a stream running almost through the middle of town, the people would hardly need a well on the outskirts, not to mention that none of the holes delved deep enough for that purpose.

The houses they passed looked deserted. As they approached the village common, she heard a murmur of voices and realized most of the inhabitants must have gathered there. At the same time, she noticed an odd sensation. It took her a minute to identify it. The air had cooled. Instead of a midsummer day's sticky heat, Meadowmill enjoyed the mild climate of late spring. Even the scent of the air had changed to a floral aroma. "I think he's transmuted the weather," she murmured.

"Is that possible?" Bertrice's low-voiced question echoed her own amazement.

"I wouldn't have thought so, except in short bursts."

As soon as they reached the edge of the gathered crowd, she glimpsed Lord Malkus, unmistakable with his imposing height and golden hair. Standing with a group of people clustered near a long table, he didn't look like a captive. No shackles, no armsmen training weapons on him. Why had he lingered here? The next moment, though, her attention was diverted by a man trundling a wheelbarrow to the center of the square. He tipped the barrow to dump a load of dirt onto a blanket spread on the ground, already partly covered by several heaps of earth and uprooted turf.

Meanwhile, a woman upended a basket of leafy branches on the table.

A portly, gray-haired man dressed a bit more finely than most of the villagers held up a hand. "Enough. Stand back, everyone."

They obeyed, opening a circle around leaf-littered table and the blanket with its mounds of dirt. The people waited in expectant silence. What in the name of all gods was going on? Seconds later, she found out. A silvery glow shimmered over the cloth. When it faded, stacks of vegetables, fruits, and loaves of bread had replaced the soil and grass. The branches had changed to lengths of cloth.

Liriel heard a gasp escape from Bertrice. "Did I just see what I thought?"

"Yes, unless I've gone mad, too," Liriel whispered back. Renewed murmurs from the crowd, as people lifted the food onto the table and started handing it out, covered the slight noise of their conversation. "Somebody transmuted all that stuff at once."

"Which one did it? I don't sense magic emanating from any of them."

"Neither do I." Grasping Bertrice's hand to keep from

getting separated, she led her partner around back of a nearby cottage. "We need to talk with Lord Malkus." She took a scrap of paper from her belt pouch and focused on it. In a situation like this, using magic to imprint words on the parchment was more convenient than pen and ink. The brief message read, "My lord: Your father sent us in search of you. Please meet us beside the mill stream as soon as you can. Liriel." When she folded the note and placed it in Brom's beak, it became visible.

The two women made their way to the other side of the village, where the mill stood. "Now we wait," Liriel said. "The people looked busy enough that Brom should be able to pass the note to Lord Malkus soon, and he can probably slip away while they're distributing the goods."

"Unless he's under a spell that limits his freedom."

"He didn't look entranced."

They didn't have long to wait, resting under a clump of willows, before the Duke's son came strolling along the stream bank. Liriel gestured to remove the invisibility spell. The young lord nodded to the two mages, who bowed in return. "A pleasure to see you," he said. "For all the good it'll do. You're most likely trapped here along with us."

The word "us" reminded Liriel of the two men who'd traveled with Lord Malkus. "Your squires are well, too?"

"They're fine. We all are. Nobody has offered us any violence. They just won't let us leave."

"How did you end up here?" Bertrice cast a nervous glance toward the village.

"Don't worry, they won't bother to follow me. After all, I can't go far. Simple enough, we were hunting a stag. It ran into that patch of dark woods you must have come through. We chased after, and here we are." He added with a grim chuckle, "The villagers were grateful enough for the venison."

"So why can't you leave?" Liriel asked, although she'd guessed the reason.

"Some kind of magical barrier. Whenever we get to the edge of that fake forest, we find ourselves heading back toward town. Blasted illusions." He snorted in disgust.

Liriel didn't take offense, having long since learned how most warriors viewed magic. Except when it became useful to them, of course, as the sorcery she practiced was to the Duke. She supposed she should be grateful that he'd kept them on as hirelings after the end of the border wars, when so many combatants, both armsmen and mages, had been cast adrift without employment. Still, both she and Bertrice were counting the days until they'd fulfilled their contract and saved enough to open a shop to sell potion ingredients and other arcane necessities. The suppliers of such items made better livings than most freelance sorcerers. Bertrice even had a prospective husband lined up, a fellow mage they'd become friendly with during the war. As for Liriel, she was holding out for a steadier sort, maybe a plain-spoken, earthbound merchant to manage their shop's accounts. She looked forward to settling into that peaceful life, with no more traveling hither and yon at the whim of an overlord. Well, that would come later. For now, she had to get Lord Malkus and themselves out of this trap.

"That performance on the common," she said. "It's happened before?"

"It's the routine here. Twice a week they pile up barrows full of dirt, rocks, and leaves to be turned into food and other goods. Folks bring requests for little things they need, and usually they get them. Not much meat, though. I've seen fish appear in the stream a couple of times, and once a flock of quail landed in the village square. Lured in, I guess. I didn't see them get changed from anything else."

"But who's doing all this?"

"I've never seen the wizard," Lord Malkus said. "Apparently nobody has since all this started, except his family. He's supposed to be the son of the miller, or the man who used to be miller when they had grain to grind—or needed to. People say the mage has been providing for them like this for almost eight years."

"That's when the spell cut the village off from the outside world?"

Lord Malkus shrugged. "So they say. Turned it into a pocket paradise, with perfect weather all year round. Even the rain cooperates. Falls only at night. They let the fields go fallow a long time ago, what with the mysterious wonder-worker filling all their needs."

"Why won't he show himself, I wonder?" Liriel said.

Bertrice nodded. "You'd think he'd want to enjoy his neighbors' gratitude."

That question, Liriel figured, could wait for an answer until they met the reclusive mage. "Well, our next step is obviously to call on the ex-miller."

"They don't live in the mill cottage anymore," Lord Malkus said. "The town council gave them a bigger house on the edge of the square."

"Then lead the way if you will, my lord. We'll be right behind you." Liriel once more veiled herself and Bertrice in the glamour of invisibility. She'd take no chances with such a powerful master of both illusion and transmutation. Gods only knew what other gifts he might have. He might cast fire and lightning that would render Bertrice's strongest spells as feeble as a child's tantrum by comparison. Any sorcerer who combined that degree of power with secretiveness had to be dangerous.

On the common, people continued to pass out baskets of food and bolts of cloth. She noticed some laying broken tools and worn shoes on the table, to be repaired by a burst of scintillating light. Good; with luck the sorcerer would be too preoccupied with his wonder-working to notice their approach. With such an opponent, surprise gave them their best hope of success. They followed Lord Malkus to one of the few dwellings built of wood and stone rather than wattle-and-daub. It had two full stories, another sign of prosperity by village standards. Why didn't the mage relocate to a great city, Liriel wondered, where his gifts could bring him and his family vast wealth?

The Duke's son hung back, obviously unwilling to get caught in the middle of a magical duel. Still invisible, she tried the front door and found it bolted from within. When she knocked, a male voice called, "Who's there?"

"Visitors. We'd like to talk to the wizard."

"I don't know you. Where did you come from?"

"Inhospitable, aren't they?" she murmured. With a muttered spell, she unlocked the bolt.

The moment the door swung open, a wordless scream of outrage sounded from above. "So much for surprise," she said. At the same instant, the invisibility spell dissolved.

Two men in the group on the village common spun around and ran toward the house. "Call the watch!" one of them shouted. A teenage boy hurried in the other direction, presumably to do just that. Both men brandished daggers.

Lord Malkus drew his sword to meet their charge. Several more people broke away from the crowd to join the melee. Malkus's two squires, whom Liriel had met before but didn't know well, also rushed over. They were brothers, both coppery-haired and freckled, one burly, one wiry.

The Duke's son and his squires held the first attackers at bay with their short swords, but others dodged around them, trying to seize the two mages. Bertrice chanted a spell, and a glowing sphere materialized around her and Liriel. The first man to make a grab for them stumbled back with a cry of pain, burned by a miniature spark of lightning.

"Inside!" Liriel pulled Bertrice over the threshold and slammed the door behind them. Bertrice's energy globe vanished. Liriel's stomach churned at the thought of how quickly the mysterious wizard negated their defenses.

A thin, balding man who stood beside the hearth in the combination parlor and dining room growled at them, "Who are you? Why are you barging into my home?" He picked up a piece of firewood and swung it like a club.

When he stomped toward her, Bertrice waved her hand to whip him with a gust of wind that knocked the wood out of his grip. A second later, a fiery dart shot from her fingers to ignite the logs stacked in the fireplace. "We want to see the wizard."

A stout woman with her gray hair in a long braid hurried out of the adjacent room, drying her hands on her apron. "You can't. Please go away and leave us alone, whoever you are."

Bertrice raised her right hand, aglow with leashed energy. "Wrong answer."

"Those spells were just warning shots," Liriel said. "We don't want to hurt anybody. We only want to meet this powerful mage we've heard about. Obviously, it's not either one of you."

The man's bushy eyebrows drew together in a frown. "What gives you the right to charge in here and threaten us?"

"What gives you the right to hold Lord Malkus and his

men prisoner in your town?"

"They might've told outsiders about us," the woman said, close to tears. "We can't let that happen. Now get out. Our son has never harmed anyone, but if he decided to attack, you wouldn't stand a chance against him."

"Can he stun both of us before Bertrice gets off another bolt?" Not that Bertrice would willingly hurt a couple of unarmed old folks if given any choice, but they didn't know that.

The man's shoulders sagged. "All right. You can see him. It won't make any difference, because he won't let you leave town, either."

Maybe not, Liriel thought, but if he proved as dangerous as she feared, Bertrice might manage to strike him down while she distracted him—provided they struck quickly enough. Having the parents as hostages might help. "You." She gestured to the mother. "You're coming with my partner. Bertrice, hang onto her arm, and if her son makes a wrong move, you know what to do."

Bertrice gripped the woman's elbow, putting on her most threatening glower.

"Miller," Liriel continued, "what's your name?"

"Tyras."

"Very well, Tyras, I'm Liriel, and this is my partner, Bertrice. You introduce me to your son, and your wife comes along with Bertrice."

With the miller in the lead, they trooped through the kitchen and up a narrow flight of stairs. She noticed the old man sweating, and the woman's arm visibly trembled in Bertrice's grasp. A sour taste filled Liriel's mouth. What had her vow to the Duke's service made of her, a hired bully?

When Tyras opened the door of the chamber at the end of the upstairs corridor, she first noticed the shutters covering the single window. She blinked until her eyes adjusted to the lamplight. The room smelled clean but stale. "Why don't you open those shutters and let in sunlight and fresh air?"

"He wants it this way," said the miller's wife.

Now Liriel focused on the boy in the far corner of the room. Judging from the couple's age and their son's phenomenal powers, she'd expected a man in the prime of life. Instead, she found a slender youth no more than eighteen years old.

Dressed only in a pair of loose trousers, he sat cross-legged on the polished wood floor. His chestnut hair, loose to his shoulders, partly hid his face. He rocked forward and back like a hermit at prayer. He clasped a pale green object in one hand. A wand?

Bertrice flung another miniature flame dart. It stung the boy's fingers and forced him to drop the thing.

A cry ripped from his throat. Rocking faster, he cradled his hand against his chest.

"How dare you?" his mother burst out.

Liriel got a good look at what he'd dropped. A piece of chalk. Half embarrassed, she said, "We've seen what he's capable of. You can't blame us for being cautious."

The woman only glowered.

An elaborate mural decorated the wall in front of the boy. Otherwise, the spacious room was almost bare, with a bed and a chest the only furniture aside from a few cushions scattered over the floor. Beside the bed, a single shelf held a rainbow assortment of chalk sticks.

Tyras cleared his throat and took a step toward his son. "Robur, these visitors would like to meet you."

The boy didn't glance up. He began chanting in a monotone, "Go away, go away, go away."

"He won't talk to you," Robur's mother said. "He hardly even speaks directly to us most of the time."

Liriel swallowed the lump of pity congealing in her throat. "Has he always been this way?"

The woman nodded.

"And the magic?" Bertrice said.

Tyras edged closer to his wife and slipped an arm around her waist. "He started changing things when he was only four years old. We had no other wizard in town to advise us, not that Robur could have benefited from a teacher anyway. So we didn't know how unusual his talent might be."

"Very unusual," Liriel said. Now she realized the nature of the drawing on the wall. A map of the village, apparently with every house and tree shown. He must use the picture as a medium for his spells. Stunned at the elaborate detail of the mural, she strode over to examine it. "Beautiful work."

Although he still didn't look at her, the volume of Robur's chanting rose. "Go away, go away, go away." He rocked faster.

"You're upsetting him," his mother said.

Hearing the strain in her voice, Liriel backed away from the mural and instead walked over to the shelf full of chalk. Someone had arranged the pieces in order of color, shading tint by tint from deep blue at one end to reds and browns at the other. White, gray, and black lay in a separate row with similar gradations. She sensed an aura of magic shimmering around the drawing sticks. Fascinated, she reached out with one fingertip.

A keening howl burst from Robur. She leaped back. Bertrice, equally startled, raised a hand, poised to cast another spell.

"Don't touch that!" Tyras ordered. "He can't stand to have anybody touch his things."

The old woman scurried to her son's side. "It's all right, dear. They're leaving now." She glared at the two mages. "Aren't you?"

"You've done enough harm already." The miller's voice sounded sharp with anger now, rather than fear. "Leave him in peace."

"All right." Liriel struggled to keep her own voice from shaking. "We'll talk downstairs."

As soon as they all left the chamber and shut the door, the boy's screaming stopped. "He's your only child?" she asked on the way down to the sitting room.

"Born after many years of barrenness," the woman said with a jerky nod. "But don't you go feeling sorry for us. He has a great gift."

After they'd taken seats on a pair of benches flanking the hearth, the miller and his wife on one, the two mages on the other, Liriel said, "He does indeed. Spell-crafted food that actually nourishes. Cloth that doesn't turn into dead leaves at the next sunrise. Permanent transmutation of weather. I've never seen anything remotely like it."

"But what's the reason for that barrier around the village?" Bertrice asked.

"He's never liked people around him, except us," Tyras said. "And he won't even let us touch him. For him, it's bad enough to have the rest of the village, people he's known all his life, nearby. He hated it when strangers came into town."

"So he shut the town off from the world? When he was no more than ten years old?"

The woman nodded. "Nine. We tried to explain to him that the village couldn't survive without some outside trade. Though he doesn't talk much, he understands enough, as long as it's about things, not people. So he started working his spells to create everything we needed."

Liriel still had trouble wrapping her mind around the marvel of it. "In the outside world, you could be fabulously wealthy."

With a scowl, the miller said, "We don't need wealth. And our son would be miserable."

His wife wrung her hands. "That's why we can't let you or the others leave."

"You can't seriously expect to keep this place a secret forever," Bertrice said. "Surely Lord Malkus and his men weren't the first to stumble on it. What happened to the others?"

Tyras said with a dry laugh, "Not as many as you're probably thinking. Only three in all these years. Two runaway apprentices and, later, a young pregnant woman fleeing from a husband who beat her. Once they found out what kind of life we have here, they were glad to stay."

"The dark forest illusion scares everybody away, I suppose," Bertrice said.

"Well, this is all fascinating from a professional viewpoint," Liriel interrupted, "but Lord Malkus and his squires do want to leave, not to mention the two of us."

The miller's fists clenched at his side. "If you try, you'll be sorry, wizards or not."

She stood up. "Listen to me. Your son has great power, but he's untrained. Bertrice and I could probably take him down. And even if he managed to kill us, other people would get hurt. Including Robur himself. Furthermore, when we didn't make it home, other, stronger sorcerers would come looking for revenge." She wasn't bluffing, for if she and her partner died,

Brom would fly to one of their colleagues with the full story of their deaths lodged in his memory, ready for any mage of sufficient skill to extract.

Tyras sprang to his feet, too. "You expect us to do nothing while you bring outsiders here to ruin our lives?"

Tears glinted in his wife's eyes. "You probably think of us as ignorant country folk, but I know enough about the world to know what would happen to Robur out there. Some nobleman would put him in a cage and force him to cast monstrous spells against enemies from the next kingdom over, or they'd make him conjure that wealth you mentioned. They'd try, anyway. He'd shrivel up and die before things got that far." She wiped her eyes with the back of her hand.

With her arms folded, Liriel glared across the room at the old couple and tried to tell herself their fears had no basis in reality. She couldn't sustain that lie. How would the Duke use a mage of Robur's power? A childhood tale hammered in her brain—a maiden locked in a tower and forced, on pain of death, to spin straw into gold. She glanced at Bertrice. "Let's have a talk with Lord Malkus."

Out front, the Duke's son and the two squires stood guard at the door, while a semicircle of village men with drawn daggers hovered an arm's length away. Liriel said, "All of you might as well stand down. We've talked to Tyras and his wife, and nobody's going to get hurt." She explained the situation to Malkus. "My lord, I'm inclined to leave these folks in peace. We should go home and keep their secret."

He stroked his chin. "My father would want to hear of this miracle worker."

"You know what would happen to the boy if your father learned of his existence." She met the young lord's eyes with open defiance. How far would she go to keep him from betraying this village? She prayed she wouldn't have to make that choice.

"The mother was right," Bertrice put in. "We saw how nearly helpless he is, aside from his magic. He wouldn't survive a week as the Duke's captive. Lord Malkus, you'd be destroying these people for nothing."

He stared into the distance for a minute, then snapped,

"Very well. You're the experts in sorcery, not I. I've seen their contented way of life. Who am I to ruin it?" He said to the squires, "Well, lads, Mage Liriel and Mage Bertrice have come to rescue us. Ready to go home?"

The youths exchanged glances.

"You're not tempted to stay?" Liriel asked. "None of you?"

Lord Malkus shook his head. "Fine for a holiday, but I have responsibilities." He smiled grimly. "After all, my older brother might get gored by a wild boar or some such, and my father would need an heir."

One of the squires said, "It's a nice town, but a little too quiet for me."

The other one nodded. "Same here."

"I'll take a vow not to reveal the existence of this place," their lord said. "You must do the same."

When they hesitated, Liriel said, "Unless you want your memories magically erased."

Alarm leaped in their eyes, the fighter's aversion to magic again. "No, ma'am, that won't be necessary. We'll make the same pledge."

"You know what we can do to you if you break it," Bertrice said. Liriel knew the menace in her voice was exaggerated, but the men didn't.

"Go to the inn and pack our gear," Lord Malkus ordered. When they'd marched off, he said, "How do you suggest I explain a month's delay in getting home?"

"Forest outlaws?" Bertrice said. "They were holding you for ransom, but their message to the Duke must have gone astray. We rescued you."

Liriel smiled at the idea. "They had a low-level wizard in their band. He cast a forgetting spell on you, so you have only the vaguest memories of your time as captives, not enough to make it worthwhile trying to hunt them down."

Lord Malkus nodded in agreement. "Well plotted. That tale will save the three of us from having to concoct a detailed story and worry about sticking to it."

While he followed after his men to supervise their preparations for the journey, Liriel and Bertrice went back inside to talk with the miller and his wife. After assuring them their secret would be safe, Liriel said, "You should consider something, though. You won't live forever."

"We've thought of that," Tyras said. "I have a niece whose company Robur tolerates. She'll care for him when we're gone."

"And when he dies? Have you thought of that?"

The miller's eyes narrowed. "What do you mean?"

"If he's robust in body, decades could pass before that day comes. This village might raise a whole generation with no idea how to feed and clothe themselves. Your paradise can't last forever. Think about what your neighbors will do when it falls apart."

A few minutes later, Lord Malkus and his squires, mounted on their horses, met the two mages at the edge of town. Liriel cast a spell to rip a hole through the illusion just long enough for the five of them to penetrate it. After untethering her horse and Bertrice's, then leading them outside the perimeter of the young mage's territory, she canceled her own magic. When she turned on the road to look back, the menacing forest had reappeared.

While the three men trotted ahead, she murmured to Bertrice, "We could have stayed in that little paradise. Sent his lordship and the other two home without us. Made an excuse about magical research, catching up with them later, some such lie."

"Were you tempted?" Bertrice whispered back.

"Maybe for about ten seconds. Think of what we could teach that boy—and learn from him." The thought still dazzled her. She forcibly shook it off. "I was right the first time, it's a trap." True, her pledge to the Duke also trapped her in a way, but temporarily, not for life like these people's self-chosen captivity. With patience, she'd win her freedom. True independence, not an illusion.

She and Bertrice mounted up and started for home.

PEARL OF FIRE

by Deborah J. Ross

Deborah J. Ross began her writing career as Deborah Wheeler, so her previous stories in the *Sword & Sorceress* series are under that name, as are her Darkover short stories. Her story "Imperatrix" in the first *Sword & Sorceress* was her first professional sale, making her one of "MZB's writers." As Deborah Wheeler she also sold two science-fiction novels: *Jaydium* and *Northlight*, as well as dozens of short stories— Marion alone bought a couple dozen of them. Deborah was the person Marion chose to continue the Darkover series; she's done three novels so far, and the fourth, *The Alton Gift*—not to be confused with my short story "The Alton Gift" in *The Keeper's Price*—should be out by the time this anthology is published.

Deborah lives in the redwood forests near Santa Cruz with her husband, writer Dave Trowbridge, two cats, and a dog. In between writing, she has worked as a medical assistant to a cardiologist, lived in France—which she describes as an "alien encounter"—and revived an elementary school library. She has been active in the women's martial arts network and has spent over 25 years studying *kung fu san soo*.

She says that the idea for this story came to her in a dream. I'll bet a lot of us wish that our dreams could lend themselves to such stories.

I traveled by river barge as far as I could, as the forested hills I had known all my life fell away into rocky pastures and then fields of barley and millet. When my path led me south, I joined one trader's caravan and then another. A decrepit camel brought me across the broken, withered lands, and at last I reached

Ixtalpi, refuge of thieves and outlaws and all manner of desperate souls, huddled in the shadow of the black, volcanic Viridian Mountains.

● ● ● ● ●

I never expected to become the guardian of the Pearl. It had always passed from father to son, a closely-guarded family secret. True, I wondered why, with so few men to defend Sharaya, we had never fallen, why the dregs of the Duke's armies never harried us, why we had always been able to fend off Eaglehurst, with whom we had long maintained blood-feud.

The Pearl had been intended for my brother. Devron was fourteen, just beginning to grow broad in the shoulders, when Great-grandfather fell ill. No one knew exactly how many winters the old man had survived, but this one would be his last. He called us to him one blustery morning, when the clouds were more black than gray, and sleet rattled against every loose-paned window.

As usual, Devron could not be found. He was probably hiding in the stables. My mother and father and uncles stood around Great-grandfather's bed, the headboard carved with the scene of a hunt, the stag at bay, yet fighting on, the dogs lying dead at its feet. The rows of candles from the night before had almost burned out. I remember watching one and then another gutter into curls of smoke, still tinged with the honey scent of beeswax. I was, I suppose, a little afraid of Great-grandfather, who was wrinkled and gruff and had never so much as patted me on the head in all my ten years.

I could hear Great-grandfather's rattling breaths in between the gusts of wind outside. As the soft golden light of the candles died away, his skin turned whiter. I had the fanciful thought that when the last one had burned itself out, his life would end.

A feeling welled up in my child's breast, of loss and tenderness and a great yearning to speak before it was too late. I had been standing beside my mother, the way I did when I was little and hid myself in her full skirts. Something drew me forward. Only two candles remained, and one flickered, leaping and struggling as if the storm outside had penetrated the room.

Great-grandfather had closed his eyes, but now the lids jerked open. His eyes were full of lightning and clouds and things I could not name. His lips—so withered, so dry!—moved. I thought I heard him speak a name, but whether it was Devron's or my father's or that of someone dead long before I was born, I could not tell.

The next to the last candle went out. The stone walls shivered and grew still, expectant. My father and uncles waited, motionless, hardly breathing. I felt the pressure of my mother's fingers on my shoulder.

Again the old man struggled to speak. Tears sprang to the corners of his eyes. A pain shot through the center of my own chest.

Great-grandfather lifted one hand, one poor bony hand that quivered like a twig in a gale. The skin was all dried out and mottled with huge liver-colored spots.

No one moved.

Suddenly I could bear it no longer, that he should be calling out, reaching out, and no one would answer him. No one held him in loving arms. He had never been kind to me, but he was hurt and lost and alone.

I broke away from my mother's grasp and rushed to him. What did I know? I took his hand between both of my own.

"Great-grandpapa!" I cried out in my child's voice. "I am here!"

At first, he did not seem to know me, but when I pressed my lips against his shriveled cheek, he roused. "Is it you? Is it time at last?"

"Yes, it's me."

"Rayzel, no!" My mother's voice seemed to come from far away.

Before anyone could stop him, Great-grandfather shifted on the bed, raising up enough to slip a long silvery chain over his head. I had seen the chain before, glinting through the opened neckline of his shirt, and assumed it was some sort of priest's medallion, such as those old people wore for protection against joint-bane and fever. What dangled from it, however, was no slip of metal, but a glowing marble set in a cage of silver wire. I caught a flash of bronze in its depths, red like fire.

Then, with a grip so fast and hard it left me breathless, Great-grandfather pulled me close and looped the chain around my neck. Heat flared though the layers of my dress and shawl, as if the pendant, whatever it was, had been plucked from a fire.

One of the men—my second oldest uncle, I thought—shouted something, but I could not understand. All I could hear, above the pounding of my heart, was the whispered sigh that came from Great-grandfather.

"It is done, then."

The last candle went out.

Devron burst through the door and everyone started shouting at once, except for my mother, who was screaming, and me. I felt numb and on fire and shaken to my bones, unable to grasp what had just happened.

"It's his!" my father yelled, meaning Devron.   "Give it—"

"You fool! It's *been* given! To her!"

"But he didn't mean—he thought she was the boy—"

"Oh, that I should live to this day!" my mother wailed. "My own daughter!"

"Then take it back!"

"How can we? Until she dies...."

"Doom! Doom has come upon us all!"

"Oh, my poor sweet child!"

I slumped to the floor. I could not understand anything beyond Great-grandfather being dead. Of that, I was certain. His life had gone out of him, and I had held his hand, and surely that was not a bad thing. Why did the room seem filled with curling bronze-red smoke? Why did my chest burn as if someone had placed a live ember there? Why was my mother weeping as if I had been the one who died?

At first, I was overcome by a great weariness. My mother brought me milk and bread, and tucked me into bed. I slept for three days, and when I awoke, I felt strong and clear and hungry. My father looked grim as he told me that from this day forward, I must be like a son to him. I must ride a warhorse instead of my gentle pony, and fight with a sword, and study the plans of ancient battles, and learn how to command men. I was young enough to consider it a great adventure.

The days and weeks and years went by in a blur. I grew tall, and strong from the strenuous exercise. How had all of this happened? Why was I set apart? Why did animals, even the house cat, shy away from my touch? Few of the horses would carry me, sweating and white-eyed, for more than a few minutes. Why did my brother suddenly cease his old taunting, bullying ways?

Why was I never cut or bruised, even when my knife slipped at table or the blade of my sparring partner slashed through my guard?

Why must I always wear the Pearl, but never openly, tucked safely between my new breasts?

Sometimes, when the moon was rising, swelling towards fullness, and I stood in the darkening practice field, weary and aching, searching for the strength to lift my wooden sword one more time, I caught a glimpse of the faces of my uncles. I did not know how to read what I saw there. Pity and sorrow, I thought, and grudging respect....

They left it to my mother to explain. On one of those nights, after practice, she came down from the house. My oldest uncle, who had taken charge of my sword training, gestured a halt, and my brother and the other men retreated gratefully into the twilight.

My mother beckoned for me to come with her. We sat on the fallen log beside the horse trough, talking quietly about daily events. The house cat had returned from her rambles, and we would have kittens soon. The cook had burned the bread. The goose girl was to marry a farm hand.

The men finished tending the horses, and for a long time, silence hung over us, except for the animals tearing at the hay and the distant sound of chickens clucking, the clink of pans in the kitchen. I had been sweating hard, and now shivered in the cooling night. An owl swooped soundlessly from the top of the barn across the shadowed fields.

My mother lifted her face to the moon. It turned her into a stranger, a woman of silver.

"You want answers, Rayzel? You must see them for yourself, what the Pearl of Fire has made of you."

She led me to the trough. The water was very still. I could see the moon reflected there, glorious and shining and pure. I stepped closer, into the place my mother indicated. The cold bright light touched me, too.

"Look."

I bent over, expecting to see my own face, streaked with dust and sweat, a smear of dried mud over one cheek bone, my hair disheveled and tied back with a bit of string.

My breath froze in my throat. I shied away, for an instant unable to absorb what I saw in the water's smooth surface. An illusion born of moonlight? A fragment of a forgotten nightmare?

My mother's strong hands held me fast. Where could I run to, anyway? Slowly, slowly, I looked again.

A dragon glowered back at me, every curved metal scale and jagged spinal ridge, each fang like a curving dagger, limned in sharpest clarity. Bronze tinted the moon-silver reflection. Molten crimson lurked behind the opaque eyes.

"What magic is this?" I breathed.

Why did I feel no fear, only a sense of fatality, of resignation?

"You see?" My mother's voice belonged to someone else, harsh as a crow's. "You see what cannot be undone? Why you cannot be harmed by sword or lance or dagger?"

The Pearl had done this to me...but what could be done, could also be undone. I fumbled for the chain around my neck. It stuck to my skin as if it had melded to my body. I could not budge it. My mother stilled my hand with a touch. She shook her head. "Are you so ready to die, my daughter?"

"No, to live!"

"The Pearl of Fire passes only from the hands of one who has surrendered any hope of living." Her voice trembled with inexpressible sadness. I had never before felt so loved, or so alone.

"Who would you pass it on to? Who else will use its power to defend us? Your father, with his bad heart? His brothers, who think of nothing but their own pride? Devron? He is my son and I love him, but I know what he is."

A coward and a bully.

I left the chain around my neck. I bent to my lessons, pushing myself ever harder, hastening the day when I would stand between my family and the dangerous world. Every year, since Great-grandfather's death, the Eaglehurst raiders had grown bolder. Soon, I would go up against them, I with my hide of dragon's bronze, I who could not be harmed.

ೞೞೞೞೞ

Just past my fourteenth birthday, I went on my first foray against our old enemy. Eaglehurst had been raiding the long green valleys, burning villages and looting. We lay in wait for them, my youngest uncle in command, for my father had been laid up with chest pains. Under the stark midday sun, we hid behind the ramshackle communal barn, so that the smell of hay and barley overlaid that of fear.

The village was laid out in a series of open yards bounded by thatch-roofed cottages, storage sheds, livestock pens. Chickens scratched in the dust, and a few sheep, too stupid to run for safety, bleated as they stood in the opened gates. Not a child ventured forth to greet us.

I held my breath and caught the jangled rhythm of hoofbeats, the clang of bridle rings, men shouting.

"Wait until they pass," my uncle said, holding up his hand.

The rangy, leather-mouthed dun mare, one of the few horses who tolerated me, pranced beneath me.

My uncle pointed at me. "Go."

My sword slipped free. I clapped my heels to my horse's sides. With my uncle and his men at my heels, I burst from cover.

The dun mare leaped forward like a loosed arrow, racing toward the Eaglehurst men. They had slowed, searching for resistance. There were so many—twice our own numbers. Some carried lighted torches; a few of them, crossbows. The sun glinted off their swords, their eagle-headed helmets of leather and steel. Their captain was shouting orders, pointing at which cottages were to be burned first.

I bore down on the nearest raider. He wheeled his horse, but too slowly. I could not see his face. His own sword came up. The momentum of my charge drove my sword deep into his body beneath the arch of his ribs. The impact shivered through my whole body, almost jerking my sword out of my hands. My mare kept going and it was all I could do to hold on to it as we swept past.

My vision clouded, crimson. The taste of fire and red sulfur and blood filled my mouth. Men and horses swept past me, stumbling, bleeding. Wildfires raged behind my eyes. My skin, where the Pearl lay cradled between my breasts, burned with exquisite desire. I gulped deep breaths of air and spewed forth a charnel wind.

The hunger of the Pearl raged through me. My sword smoked with blood and more blood.

I hardly noticed when a terrible stillness fell on the common. A few riderless horses skittered away from the fallen bodies. My uncle directed his men to put out the single fire. Two of our own men were down, one unmoving, the other struggling to his feet, clutching a slashed thigh.

The dun mare came to a halt, trembling, her hide hot and wet. The fire died within me. The sky shifted from red to shivering gray. I swayed in my saddle. My sword fell from my limp hand. I felt utterly empty, used-up, bereft.

Dimly I felt my uncle's hands catch me as I toppled. Later, one of the men told me that he had carried me home in his arms.

࿔ஐ

Some years later, we enjoyed a glorious golden summer. I had been leading our men along the borders for enough seasons now that Eaglehurst had pulled back, licking its wounds. For once, the Duke was at peace with his neighbors; no mercenaries or refugees wandered our mountains. I rode watch with my uncles, but with much less urgency than before.

I also rode alone. The forest that bordered our lands and Eaglehurst, once too dangerous for even armed travelers, had now become a series of abandoned sunlit glades. The last of the spring wildflowers still lingered in the moist pockets beneath the largest trees. The very air smelled of growing things, of rich earth, of the dust that gently settled along shafts of brightness.

I swung down, loosened the girths, and tied my horse by a halter so that she could browse. The air was still and warm, the only sounds the faint whisper of a breeze and a far-off bird. Leaving my sword tied to my saddle, I dug into my saddlebags, beneath the packet of food, the whetstone and cloth for cleaning steel. My fingers brushed finely woven wool. I pulled it free, took one last look around, and skinned out of my men's tunic and breeches. The boots I could do nothing about, as my feet were too tender to run barefoot.

The dress fell around me in lamb-soft folds, emerald trimmed with lace-flower and daisies. I'd found it in a cedar chest last winter. It was probably my grandmother's, and a bit too short. I spun in circles, relishing the feel of the skirts as they swirled outward. I pulled my hair free, combed it with my fingers. For an hour, a blessed hour, I might pretend the Pearl was a love token given to me by a gray-eyed stranger. I might be just an ordinary girl.

The hour passed too quickly, leaving me wanting more. I folded the dress, tied back my hair, tightened the girths, and went home. But I came back as the wildflowers were drying and bees buzzed around the burgeoning queen's-lace and painterbrush. I came, and danced, and wept when it was time to go.

All too soon the summer neared its end, and the faint scent of must and honey hung in the air. The leaves had turned that intense, almost fiery green, when he first came.

I was dancing and singing, some mindless tune I learned from the horse boys. My feet were bare now, having toughened over the months. Although I heard nothing, I knew I was not alone. With a sense that was half-human, half-dragon, I *felt* his presence. A man, yes, I knew that, and young as I was young. Unsure and cocksure and enthralled as if by magic, drawn to my voice, yearning for something magical, beyond the ordinary. Even before I saw him, I loved him.

He stepped from the shadows. My eyes noted his ordinary hunter's clothing, vest and shirt and pants in shades of green and brown, wide leather belt around slim hips, russet hair tumbling over muscled shoulders. My heart saw only the light in those gray eyes, the catch of wonder in his breath, the way he looked at me as if I were the most wonderful, most tender thing he had ever seen.

I paused in my dance, and the green skirts fell still around me. We stood in a pool of slanting light. We talked. We danced to the music that rose, wordless, in my throat. When he reached to take my hand, a shadow passed over me. I drew back and he, taking it for maidenly modesty, plucked a strawflower, kissed it, and then held it out to me.

It was impossible, our love. Perhaps I was intoxicated. Certainly, I was heedless. I kept on, as the leaves turned orange and then crimson and then brown. He laid his cloak on the crisp leaves and we lay on it, murmuring secrets to one another.

In my madness, I kept meeting him, even when the forest was no longer safe. The Eaglehurst raiders had struck again. He never failed me, my sweet, gray-eyed lover. The hidden part of my heart, the part I thought dead forever when I accepted the Pearl, the part that was mine alone, came alive in his presence.

Of course, I did not tell him who I was. Nor did I ask. He was a younger son from one of the bordering families, it did not matter from which side.

ങ೧೩ೞ೦ಬ

As winter lowered over the forested hills, Eaglehurst pressed us hard, seeking revenge for their past defeats. One gray afternoon, we met them at the river where the slate-dark water frothed and pitched between steep, rocky banks. Here we held fast, skirmishing back and forth. As usual, I placed myself in front. I urged my horse half-way across the river, blocking the narrow ford. The air reeked of wet rocks, horse sweat, and blood.

The Eaglehurst charged at me, shouting their battle-cries. Their helmets gave them the aspect of raptors, not human men. They came at me in twos and threes, trying to slash through my guard. I had no need of defense. My body reeled under the force of their blows, but I felt nothing. Wherever I struck, they fell.

The clang of steel against steel, or perhaps against bronze, filled my head. The Pearl roused at the sound of their death screams, the blood, the terror. I felt its exultation shivering through me, consuming me.

I swung my sword again. Again. Again. Sliced air, leather, flesh, all the same. The rushing water ran red around my horse's legs.

At last, a horn sounded from the Eaglehurst side. *Fall back. Retreat. Save yourselves while you can.*

They scrambled back across the muddied banks. Their captain shouted something about not leaving any of their fellows behind. Bare-headed, he plunged into the river, on foot now, struggling to reach one who had fallen to my sword. I caught a glimpse of a gray beard, white-rimmed eyes, and then I was moving again, screaming curses, sword high. They turned and fled.

I pulled my mare to a halt. She fought me, half crazed with fight and rushing water and the dragon-stench rising from my skin. I could not let her win or she would never carry me again, and few horses could tolerate the Pearl. She dipped her head in surrender and picked her way through foam and rock.

The rider, whose body they had tried to retrieve, lay pinned by the water against the rocks. As I rode by, the current tumbled him over, so that he shifted on to his back. His helmet came free.

Russet hair, tangled like rust-stained riverweed. Eyes gray as a storm, staring and empty. One hand, palm up as if grasping the water that slipped through those strong, graceful fingers.

I should have known. I should have known.

And if I had, would I have chosen differently? Would I have denied us those brief hours for the pain of what came afterward?

The mare heaved herself up the slope, happy to be out of the surging water. I hunched over, trying to breathe. My lungs had turned to bronze.

"My lady?" someone said. "Are you well?"

"Of course, she is well." My brother's voice. "She can't be hurt, can she?"

No, not hurt. Not ever.

"Take up their fallen," someone said with my voice, harsh as a bell and distant. "Do not leave them for the river, or to be eaten by scavengers. Send a messenger under truce to Eaglehurst. Offer to return them, so that they may bury their own."

"In exchange for what?" one of the men asked.

I touched the mare with my heels and she moved off. Blood still gleamed on my sword. When I arrived home, I cleaned it, as always. I rubbed down my own horse, as always. A servant took away my muddy, blood-stained clothing. As always.

I lay in my bed, eyes staring and empty.

In exchange for what?

I moved through the days, eating and dressing and talking, each in its proper time. I beat back the Eaglehurst time and again, across the river and farther each time, until I stood in the smoking ruins of their great manor house. Their scattered remnants harried us like rats. They learned to fear the red-bronze fire of my sword.

Then my father died.

CBCREOBO

He had diminished, not just from the seizure of his heart, but in some essential part, as if his very soul had shriveled. Had he wasted away in useless hope, waiting for his grandfather to fail and pass the Pearl on to him, only to see the treasure go to his own daughter? Or was this simply how all men looked when the vital spark had fled? I had seen carnage, most of it at my own hands, and yet I had never peered into the faces of the dead as I did my father's. For the first time, I was not afraid to see death. I saw it as a release, as a benediction.

My own life stretched before me, seasons of killing and more killing, and soul-devouring loneliness. There would never be another lover for me. I would not dare.

"The Pearl of Fire passes only from the hands of one who has surrendered any hope of living," my mother had said.

The Pearl had taught me patience, so I waited. I waited to see my father buried. I waited until my mother had set aside the black veil of mourning. I waited until my brother had taken up rulership of Sharaya, now Greater Sharaya. I waited until we were alone, not in the great hall adorned with plunder from Eaglehurst and other conquests, but a moment of quiet in the stables, after riding the borders as his bodyguard.

"I will leave you now," I said.

It took him a moment to realize I meant more than returning to the manor house. "I don't understand. You can't leave. The Pearl cannot leave Sharaya."

Cannot? I looked at him slantwise, raising one eyebrow. The Pearl had also taught me silence. Then I shrugged. I had never found any difficulty in crossing the borders. He spoke from his own fears. He could lose half of what I had brought to him, and still have more than any one man needed.

I resolved, as well, that no more men would bleed away their lives for greed. Not my brother's, not mine. Not the Pearl's.

I turned and walked away, out of the stables redolent with sweet hay and the warmth of horses, into the pooling dusk.

"Where will you go? What will you do?" he shouted after me. *Without us,* he meant. *Without family or home or name?*

ᚳᚱᚷᚱᚦᚩᚱᚹ

I traveled by river barge as far as I could, as the forested hills I had known all my life fell away, and, at last, I reached Ixtalpi, refuge of desperate souls....

Once I had left the mountains, I attracted considerably less notice. Here, in the wide lands of the world, a woman with a sword, even one traveling alone, was not so unusual. Several times, fellow travelers approached me with offers of employment or simple companionship. I turned them all away.

I took a room at an insignificant inn and went walking. Beyond the city walls, the slopes of the volcanic peaks rose gently at first, then stark and steep and black. Red light flickered near the blunted peaks. Several times, the ground rumbled and shook, a vast and rancorous underground beast. Ash blackened the sky and turned the sunset a lurid crimson.

In a strange, fey mood, I took my supper in the common room of the inn. The air was close and smoky. Greasy soot coated the rough wooden walls. I found a place at the end of the long trestle table. A scrawny lad brought me a bowl of some kind of stew and a mug of ale. The ale was warm but surprisingly good, and the stew too spicy for my taste, most likely to encourage customers to order more ale and to disguise the odd flavors of the meat. I ate the stew, called for more ale, and sipped it slowly. The blend of astringent and mellow flavors slid down my throat like a memory of summer.

The ale softened my mood enough so that when my neighbors at the table struck up a conversation, I did not turn away. Across from me sat a grizzled, balding drover. The man and woman on either side of the table wore leather vests, faded and rubbed shiny along the seams, decorated with strings of shell, horn-bead and bone. They looked young and hungry, with hawk-keen eyes and skins tinged with copper. Neither bore any visible weapon, not like the knife prominently strapped to the drover's thigh, but I had no doubt they were armed. Mercenaries, perhaps. I did not recognize their accents, but the drover made a joke about their being from Raë on the Western Sea, and not to be trusted.

Soon a game of dice and castles was proposed and accepted. Having no better way to pass the evening, I ordered more ale and joined in.

Six of us made up the opening game, with the addition of two locals. The locals dropped out after the first hour and left the inn, supporting one another in their vacillating homeward path. The game went on, the stakes gradually rising. Winnings passed back and forth across the table. Ale flowed. A sense of well-being settled over me. I derived as much enjoyment from losing as from winning.

After losing three rounds in a row, the drover pushed himself away from the table. That left the two Raë and myself. The woman, Juthe, pulled out and stood, looking over her man's shoulder, one hand resting there with deceptive ease. I saw the edge of desperation, ale-tempered, in their eyes, the quick glances, the readiness to raise the stakes once again. They were gambling with assets they could not afford to lose. I thought to let them win, but the cards would not oblige me.

The man, Culliy, and I faced each other over the table. The pile of bets went back and forth, growing larger in leaps, never settling long with either of us. Having already lost my sword, I added a small knife from my boot, on to the pile.

The cards went against me. I grinned as he raked in the pile and started to leave.

"Wait," Juthe said, quick as a serpent. "Stay."

"I have nothing more to wager," I pointed out.

She jerked her chin toward my chest. The bones dangling from her vest clinked softly. "That?"

In the heat of the close dark room and the excitement of the game, I had loosened the ties of my shirt. The chain that carried the Pearl gleamed dully, crossing my sweat-bright skin and disappearing over my heart. I sat back, drew out the Pearl. It glowed like banked embers.

Culliy let out a long whistle. Juthe licked her lips.

The ale spoke to me, *Why not?*

Something stirred behind my mind, restive. If I would never use it again, why not let it pass to those who might derive some advantage from it?

Why not let the Pearl itself decide?

I slipped the chain over my head, and, to my astonishment, it came away easily. I dropped it in the center of the table, half-expecting the wood to burst into flames. It landed with a thump and a clatter of metallic links. The skin over my breastbone, where the Pearl had lain so many years, felt tender, new. My ribs ached. I drew a breath, deeper and freer than I could remember.

Culliy pushed forward the entire pile of winnings. We drew cards, one and then another, building our hands. I did not look at mine, for what did it matter? The ale and the wild mood owned me. Culliy glanced down at his cards. I saw the little signs, the tightening at the corners of his eyes, the faint pressure of Juthe's hand on his shoulder, the slightly slower movement as he sat back, his movements too controlled for true ease.

There was nothing more to bet. One hand would take all.

Culliy's face stayed stony as he laid out his cards. A good hand, but not unbeatable. I let my gaze rest on the painted designs. Then, without looking at my own cards, I slapped them down on the pile of discards.

With a shrug and a grin, I pushed myself to my feet. "That's a night, then. Good fortune to you both."

I did not look back until I had reached the far end of the common room, the narrow stairs leading to the sleeping chambers. Culliy had lifted the chain, about to drop it around Juthe's neck. The Pearl flashed iridescent, reflected in her eyes. Until that moment, I had not been certain that it would let me go.

I slept that night like one dead. If I dreamed, I had no memory when I woke. The room had only a straw pallet on a wooden frame and a table with pitcher and bowl for washing, pegs on the wall for cloak, a single rickety chair. Nothing like a mirror. If I looked in one by moonlight, what would I see? If I shattered the mirror and drew one of the pieces of glass across my skin, would I bleed? I could not remember the color of my own blood, or the taste of my tears.

ℭ𝔔ℌ𝔒ℵ

I left Ixtalpi the next morning. The innkeeper, having watched last night's game from the bar, gave me a free bowl of gruel for breakfast. It was last night's stew, watered down and simmered into mush, but it filled my belly. I had no idea where I would go or how I would earn my bread. I could not go home, that much was sure. I had some skill with a sword, but only for attack, not defense. In all likelihood, I would not survive the first skirmish. I found, to my surprise, that I disliked the notion.

Heading downslope, out of the shadowed Viridian Mountains, I paused at a crossroads. East or west? I had never traveled in either direction. It came to me that for the first time in my life, I had no ties to any land or lord, nothing to keep me from going wherever my two strong legs took me. I took the less traveled road, and then, whenever it branched, the way that seemed wilder.

The road narrowed to a trail wide enough for a single line of baggage animals. Here and there, a pile of droppings, still moist underneath, gave evidence of recent travelers. I was no tracker, but I thought there might be three or four small horses, one of them unshod, as many more men on foot, and a narrow-wheeled cart. In my mind, I spun out a story about the party, who they were, where they were going, and the songs they would sing to one another around the evening's fire.

The trail wound upward through scrub forest, skirted running streams, and dipped into sunlit glades. A pleasant passage, I thought as I stretched out under a tree in one of these meadows for a midday nap. As I allowed myself to be lulled by the hum of insects, I thought of my gray-eyed lover, remembering now not the anguish of loss but the golden afternoons we had spent together, the joy and comfort we had of each other. In my dreams, I wandered through the great house of Sharaya, but the halls and corridors lay dark and empty. The windows were open and dead leaves skirled across the floor in the chill breeze.

I jerked awake, sweating, to glimpse the last crescent of brilliance as the sun sank below the western hills. Shadows had already begun their slow reach, dimming the meadow. The open space no longer felt safe. I found the trail and hurried along it.

The trail climbed higher, and the feeling of unease lessened. I began to look for a place to spend the night, some sturdy branch, overhang, or shallow cave. The moon rose, full and bright enough to cast shadows. I went on with the vague thought that my fellow travelers must surely have made camp by now, and might allow me to join them.

Even as I was trying to convince myself of the folly of continuing on, the risk of a fall, broken bones or worse, I heard voices ahead. I could not see any lights at first, for the trail followed the twisting contour of the hillside. The voices sounded distant, oddly distorted, and they did not seem friendly. I hurried as fast as I dared, stumbling here and there over unexpected stones.

The raised voices escalated into screaming, fell away into a moment of silence, and then wild, anguished keening.

I rounded the bend and saw the campsite, limned in orange firelight. The cart stood in a little flat place just off the trail, cradled between two arms of rock. For an instant, the place looked deserted. Nothing moved. Then my fighter's vision picked out the pattern of fallen bodies from the scattered rubble. I had seen enough dead men to know them now.

The sobbing came from the far side of the camp, beside the picket line. The ponies shifted, white-eyed at the reek of blood. A woman knelt there, cradling a man's body. Rocking, weeping. Juthe, it had to be her, even with her voice distorted, stretched to the breaking point around her horror and pain.

Fools, to take on so many. Unless...unless the Pearl itself had urged her to it.

Unless the Pearl wanted fresh blood. I had thought to pass on a gift. Instead, I had burdened them with a curse.

Soft as shadow, I moved through the camp. I need not have taken any pains to be cautious, for she had no awareness of me, or of anything but the body in her arms. I knelt an armslength away, empty of words.

Her shirt was torn, ripped by a dozen blades in a dozen killing strokes. Through the rended fabric, her skin shone, untouched. The Pearl rested between her breasts, glowering, sated.

She turned to me, her eyes all tears. Had I wept like that? I supposed I had. Tears had not brought my lover back, either. The thought came to me that she might do herself harm, that she had neither kin nor oath to bind her to life. I reached out my hands. She let me take him and lay him out.

I folded Culliy's hands across his chest and smoothed his eyes closed. His body was still warm, his muscles pliable. He would stiffen in an attitude of grace.

As for Juthe, she would have nothing of comfort. Her grief burrowed inward like a canker worm. In time, she would grow numb, inured, even as I had. In time. But not yet.

She stumbled through a chant in a language I could not understand, Raëth most likely. At first, I thought it was a prayer for the dead, a requiem. But there was no sorrow in it, only a wild, consuming rage.

Her eyes changed as she reached for a knife fallen on the ground. She lifted it, pressed the flat to her forehead, then to her lips. Smoothly, she placed the point over her belly, both hands holding the hilt. She thrust again and again, grunting with the effort. The tip would not pierce her skin. Her knuckles turned white. Sweat slicked her skin.

Juthe tossed away the knife and glared at me. "Can kill—cannot die." She clawed at the Pearl where it hung between her breasts. "Curse, is this thing! You...you knew?"

I looked away.

Then she was on me, her hands on my shoulders, shaking me. Her shirt was slick with the blood of the men she'd slaughtered; the smell sickened me.

"Must die!" she shrieked. "Die in honor! Tell me how!"

A light burned in her eyes, fire and blood and madness, reflections of the inferno within the Pearl.

"Give it back to me," I said.

She whipped the chain over her neck and shoved it at me. The Pearl swung back and forth. "Take! Evil bargain!"

My fingers closed around the Pearl, stilling its motion, imprisoning it. The bronze-red globe flared, implacable. I shivered at the prospect of what I must do, endure. It would never tire, the dragon within me, never cease to thirst. I could never use it, that much was certain. It would taint every purpose.

I could not use it...but I could keep it from using anyone else.

Juthe reeled away from me. I thought she fled into the night, for I heard no sound from her as I went about the camp, straightening the fallen bodies, seeing to the weapons and the animals. I ate the burned food, banked the fire, and wrapped myself in a borrowed blanket.

The next morning, I found a spade in the cart. A little ways from the camp, I found a grassy slope, not too steep, and dug a shallow pit. I would rather have made separate graves, but I had not the strength. As it was, by the time I had dragged the first two to their resting place, I was sweating hard.

Wordless, Juthe picked up the feet of the next corpse, and together we carried him to the common grave. We worked without stopping until the camp was cleared and the earth smoothed over. Juthe returned my sword, but I buried it with the dead.

I found a small barrel of ale in the cart and we sipped it together, sitting with our legs sprawled in the dust and our backs against one of the cart wheels.

"Give you back evil thing," she said. "Now, tell me how to die!"

"You—" I stopped myself, thinking hard. "You must wait a year and a day for the spell to wear off. Then..." I shrugged, praying that I had given her grief enough time to subside.

After a time, when she made no move to get up, I asked, "What will you do now? Will you find employ with some company of mercenaries?"

She shook her head. "Culliy say quit, keep safe."

Yes, and when the money ran out, they gambled, then turned raider. How could I condemn her, I who had slain so many?

If we were together, I might be able to keep an eye on her, prevent her from getting into a situation that might test her year-and-a-day immortality. "Can you manage that cart?"

"Farm daughter." Her gaze flickered to where the Pearl lay, hidden beneath my shirt. "That?"

Who will keep us safe from that?

I saw what a few hours of exposure to the Pearl had done to her. What decades had done to my Great-Grandfather. What the desire for it had done to my father, my brother.

I will keep us safe, I thought. I must and would...because only I could.

The bronze dragon could never be beaten, never smashed, never destroyed. The mailed fist and the prideful spirit would yield at last to the lust for carnage, the seductive lure of invulnerability.

But the Pearl had no power over the open heart of a child rushing to comfort a loveless, dying old man, nor the tender heart of a young girl dancing in a sunlit glade.

Only a bruised and broken heart, a heart once filled with anguish and now turning toward hope, could tame the Pearl of Fire, could transform it into something else. What that might be, I could not imagine, only sense the possibility.

I lifted my face to the day, and felt the breeze cool against the wetness on my cheeks, now certain of my course.

My heart would guide me.

THE IRONWOOD BOX

by Kimberly L. Maughan

Kimberly L. Maughan was born in Arizona, but has also lived in Texas, Illinois, Indiana, and South Carolina. Fantasy stories have been a constant throughout her wanderings—she's one of the writers who started dictating stories before she could hold a pencil. She says she is currently writing, working as a bookseller, and earning her Masters degree in Library and Information Science—"regrettably, not always in that order."

This is her first published short story. Many people think that they're nobody special, that they have no talents or gifts, but that doesn't mean it's true.

She'd been dreaming of the box for nearly a week now, waking each night to itching palms and a restlessness that would not subside until she'd risen from her bed, padded through the darkness to the loft where Lily slept, and cooled her hands on the fine, ironwood grain of the box. It had been a week of dreams, she knew, because every night she passed the tiny window in the loft, open to the soft spring air, and watched as the moon grew from sliver to quarter. What she did not know, and could not understand, was why she was dreaming of the box at all.

It was a simple thing, a small thing, beautifully crafted and heavy, though it was no larger than the length and width of her hand, but she'd known about it for years and never once dreamt of it. Perhaps she wasn't the only one dreaming of it now? Perhaps Lily, and Rose too, found themselves waking in the middle of the night to seek it out, to reassure themselves of its substance, its safety.

Perhaps. But she rather doubted her sisters thought of little else in their waking hours, as she did.

Something sharp pricked her finger, and Pansy blinked to discover herself standing in the garden, sunlight warm on her skin, the scent of earth and lemony daffodil in her nose, and a knife in one hand. The other, she saw, pinched a twig between thumb and bleeding finger. "Oh," she said, dropping the twig and struggling to clear away the shadows of moonlight and dreams. "What...?"

"You've cut yourself." Lily spoke up beside her, reaching for the injured hand.

"Careless," Rose teased, appearing over Lily's shoulder to pluck the knife from Pansy's loosening grasp. "That's not like you."

It wasn't. They were all careful, of course, but Pansy especially so. She had no gift, as her sisters did, to protect herself.

"What happened?" Lily asked.

"I—I don't know." The truth slipped out before she could stop it, and Pansy flinched. Now they would ask questions, and how was she to explain where her thoughts had been just now?

But neither sister asked anything. Lily sighed and Rose tucked the knife into her sash, and together they ushered Pansy into the cottage. In silence, Lily salved and bandaged the cut, and only then, still holding Pansy's hand between her own, did she speak. "You're dreaming of it, aren't you? The box?"

What? The box? The question was so unexpected, Pansy could only sit, startled and speechless for a moment. "I—" she began. "Well...."

"What box?" Rose asked. "The *ironwood* box?"

"Yes," Lily replied, voice very soft. "But quietly, if you please. Remember where we are."

Rose nodded, dark brows drawn as she dropped soundlessly into the chair beside Pansy. "All right," she said. "But what's this about the box?"

"Pansy has been dreaming of it." Lily's eyes flicked to Pansy's. "At least, I believe she has." One arched, red eyebrow asked the question.

"Yes," Pansy replied slowly. "Have you known all along? Have you been dreaming too?" Oh, she hoped so....

But Lily was already shaking her head. "No. Not I. I merely woke two nights ago to find you in the loft, holding the box. I certainly thought I'd dreamed it, at first, but you woke me the next night as well. And you've been so distracted."

Rose snorted. "So you have, little one. Coming home from market with the eggs still unsold. Pouring salt in your tea. All this down to dreams?"

A faint smile curved the corners of Lily's mouth. "I imagine they're rather persistent dreams." The smile faded a little, but Lily's eyes grew brighter. "And I believe they are very important dreams."

Important? Dreams about the box? They were certainly peculiar, but important?

Rose asked the question for her. "What are you thinking, Lily?"

Lily's eyes grew brighter still, shining honey-gold in the sunlight streaming through the door. "I believe that Pansy's dreams are what we've been waiting for." One slender hand left Pansy's to find Rose's where it curled on the table. "I believe Pansy's dreams are telling us it is time to go home."

Lily's grip on her hand was so tight it hurt, but Pansy hardly noticed. The pain in her chest, sharp and hard, rose above all else. Go home? No. No, they couldn't. *She* couldn't. Her lungs hitched, fought for breath. Gasping, she yanked her hand from Lily's hold and staggered to her feet. Two pairs of identical honey-gold eyes turned to her, and at the sight of the joy rising in them, Pansy's chest pinched tighter.

"I can't," she said, the words barely a whisper through her struggling lungs. "I can't," she said again and, turning, fled the cottage.

⊰⊱⊱⊰

It was with a burning chest and aching legs that she finally stopped running, some long time later. The forest around her was unfamiliar, but at the moment she could only be glad for it: if she didn't know where she was, her sisters wouldn't know either. Panting, she sank against a tree and slid to the ground.

Above her the wind rustled through the canopy, stirring the sweet-musty air beneath, and Pansy gulped, trying to match her breaths to its slow, easy rhythm. Morning sunlight danced to the wind, as well, glowing through the leaves in ever-shifting green prisms. Pansy closed her eyes, lifted her face to it, and sighed through the rasp of her lungs.

She'd grown so used to the forest that it was strange to think she hadn't always lived inside it. A smile teased her mouth. How she'd hated it when they'd first come! The trees pressed too close, shutting out the sky, and the air was so wet it dampened her clothes even as she slept. Not that she'd slept much, at first, not with all the strange chitterings and snufflings of the forest animals, the birds singing their peculiar songs at the oddest times of day.

The forest was nothing like home, nothing like Suralis. The villagers, half a morning's walk nearer the borderlands, couldn't even pronounce *Suralis* correctly, instead flattening the vowels and hissing the sibilants. How she'd grieved in their little cottage, how they'd all grieved, losing country and home and parents and names within days of one another.

And she thought Lily and Rose still grieved, even after five years, but while she would always remember Suralis fondly, Pansy had found a place to belong in the vast tangle of the forest. Certainly, she thought, bunching her skirt in her fingers, she belonged here, silent and separate in this humble skin, this flower name, far better than she ever did as Persal, the Right Hand, third and youngest queen of Suralis, giftless and unremarkable.

For as long as memory, the queens of Suralis had been gifted, given a talent by the land itself that they might better serve their kingdom. Lily, born Linea, eldest daughter of Marit, heir to the High Queen, found her strength in words. Calm, assured, she spoke poetry as easily as council, and as Marit, herself a prophetess, had announced at Linea's birth, *all who hear must listen.*

And Rose, born Rosild, second eldest daughter of Marit, heir to the Left Hand, found her gift in warcraft. Merry and graceful, her hands shaped strategy, her body dancing death to her enemies. *All who defy must fail* had been Marit's prophecy for her second daughter.

But Persal had been born giftless, and Marit had no prophecy for her youngest daughter. *You are the best of us*, she'd say, or *How can Suralis be whole without you?* But for all her mother's kind words, Persal knew perfectly well, even as a girl, how disappointed and worried the Suralis court had been. High Queen Irin had been the first to act on her conviction that Persal must not be queen, but she was hardly alone in that belief.

Pansy's eyes pinched tighter, shadows of that long, desperate flight into hiding and safety playing on her eyelids. All this time they'd hardly dared step from the cottage, only briefly venturing to the village, exchanging the merest of greetings with their distant neighbors, speaking of Suralis only rarely and in the faintest of whispers. And now to return home? Her sisters believed the time had come, and perhaps they might go: they were true queens and Suralis needed them. But Persal was Pansy now and safer that way. As Persal, she'd been the cause of one coup. She'd not return and be the reason for another.

"So here you are." Pansy's eyes flew open to find Rose standing across the clearing, hands hooked into the bright red of her sash. "I almost didn't see you, curled up so tight. And in that gown," dark brows jumped, "you look very little like my sister and very much like an exceedingly cross rock."

Only with great effort did Pansy manage not to smile. Instead, she hunkered down tighter against the tree. "Then please," she said, "pretend you haven't seen me and go away."

Rose gave a long-suffering sigh and sauntered closer. "Won't do you any good. Your trail ends here, and so even if I couldn't see you, I'd still know you were here somewhere. And I'd look. And I'd wait. Until I did see you."

Pansy uncoiled a little. "I left a trail?"

"A trail?" Rose laughed. "Yes. You did. Plain enough for even one of the villagers to follow, little one." Dropping into a crouch, she unfolded one of Pansy's arms from around her knees and skimmed warm fingers over a criss-cross of scratches. "And it looks as though the forest left a trail on you, as well."

Pansy hadn't even noticed, but now that she knew they were there, the scratches started to sting a little.

"You need mending," Rose said. "Come along home and we'll salve them."

Salving sounded good, but.... "I don't want to go back to the cottage yet."

No surprise flickered in her sister's gaze. Encouraged, Pansy pressed further. "And I can't go back to Suralis." Rose still didn't appear surprised, but a faint frown now creased her brow. Pansy reached to smooth it, whispering, "You know I can't. I'm useless." This time Rose did look startled, but Pansy dropped her hand to her sister's mouth before she could speak. "I was young when we left, but I wasn't *that* young. I remember everything. I remember how we escaped the palace and how we made it safely to the borderlands, where Irin couldn't find us anymore, and it was you and it was Lily. Lily speaking people into leaving us alone and you fighting to win us free. But it wasn't me. I did nothing—"

Rose shook her head, pulled Pansy's hand away to say, "You were a child. Only twelve years old, little one. Of course you did nothing."

"No," Pansy protested, eyes stinging. "No. I did nothing because I can *only* do nothing. I'm giftless." Lowering her voice still further, she continued, "And 'tis because I'm giftless that mother and father and Aunt Vela and all the others died. If it hadn't been for me—"

Rose's hand sealed Pansy's mouth now, brown eyes fierce. "Stop. Stop saying such horrible things. They're not true. Not one of them is true." The hand lifted but Rose's gaze warned her to stay silent. "You weren't so very young, no, but you were young enough not to remember everything.

"Aunt Irin's ambitions didn't begin with you, little one. To hear Mother and Aunt Vela tell it, they began long ago, when Irin was no older than you are now. The natural order of Suralis, of the world itself, has never been enough for her. Knowing she must die someday, she planned to live on in her daughters—for she believed, fiercely and for years, that she would mother the next queens. Instead, she had only Alba, poor weak, rock-dull Alba, and when I was born, Irin knew it was Mother who would bear the three daughters, the three queens, and not herself.

"For a time, she convinced herself that her own daughter could take your place. We waited ten years for you, after all, and as Head Queen, Irin might have been able to persuade the court into believing Suralis had chosen two sisters and a cousin as queens, instead of the three sisters it had always provided before. But when Mother discovered she was expecting you, Irin was forced to acknowledge what I believe she knew all along: her only means of creating a legacy was by destroying us. Your being giftless was merely convenient for her plans, but she would have killed mother and father and Aunt Vela, and tried to kill us, even if you were the soul of Suralis, itself.

"So, no," Rose's hands squeezed Pansy's shoulders, "you weren't the cause of any of it. Irin had been planning her coup for years, and those courtiers who followed her did so not because you were giftless, but for her promises of power and wealth."

For a long moment, nothing but birdsong sounded in the clearing, and Pansy closed her eyes against her sister's sharp gaze, trying to think, to understand all Rose had said. Could she believe it? Rose did, that was clear, and Pansy certainly *wanted* to believe she was not at fault, but the sick guilt and fear had been with her so long she couldn't quite bring herself to accept that they were...wrong. That she had no reason to feel them. Surely, she thought, surely her lack of gift was still dangerous, even if it had not caused the deaths of so many she loved.

Swallowing to ease her dry throat, she opened her eyes and said, "But I'm still giftless, Rose, and what need has Suralis for a giftless queen?"

"If Suralis had no need for you, Persal ne-Marit, why did it provide you as our third queen?" Lily's voice pierced the quiet of the clearing, and Pansy turned to see her eldest sister where Rose had stood earlier, so still even her white blouse and red hair seemed a part of the forest beyond. There was no telling how long she'd been there, but judging by the burnt cinnamon of her eyes and the taut line of her mouth, Lily had heard more than enough.

"For centuries," Lily went on, her voice a crackling, vivid heat, "Suralis has provided each generation with three sisters. Never more, never less. Only three sisters who would someday become queens like the sisters before them. This has always been true, for Suralis requires three sisters to maintain its balance, to rule and preserve a prosperous land. I do not know why you have no gift, Persal, but you *are* as Suralis requires you to be. Rose and I cannot rule alone. You are our third. And just as Suralis struggles now beneath Irin, so it will suffer without you."

She paced closer and the sorcery shimmering in her voice softened. "We have hidden here for five years, as Mother said we must, but she also promised that one day we would go home. And that I would know when that day came. Your dreams, Persal, of the ironwood box—" Lily hesitated, then finished slowly, "After all this time, I cannot believe it coincidence."

She didn't explain, but she hardly needed to. The box, crafted from ironwood grown only in the western desertlands of Suralis, was the only thing their mother had insisted they take with them. No one knew precisely what was inside, but the box had been created after one of Marit's visions had warned her of Irin's treachery, and it had been sealed and strengthened by Vela, whose gift gave her power over trees and herbs. In every aspect, the box was tied to Suralis. And now Pansy was dreaming of it.

"Irin will know the instant we set foot on Suralis land," Rose warned. "We won't even reach the palace before her soldiers find us."

"Yes," Lily agreed. "And since she can see anything she wishes within the Suralis borders with her gift, she may choose to stay in the palace to watch. But I believe she wants the box, even without knowing what it holds. And for that, she will come herself. And when she comes, perhaps we can fight her. Perhaps Suralis will even assist us." Lily's eyes met Pansy's. "But only if you come with us, Persal. Suralis requires three. Without you, we cannot win."

There was no other answer to give, really, but that didn't make the words easy to say. Licking dry lips, she met Rose's eyes and then Lily's—both the same shade as their mother's, as her own eyes—and said, "I will come."

ෞ෦ඏ෨෦ඏ෦ண

Her hands were itching again, faint, feathery tickles teasing her palms, sweeping the tops of her knuckles. Rubbing them did no good—the sensation pricked beneath her skin—but at least this itch was tolerable. In the three days since they'd passed from the forest, over the border, and into the grasslands, Pansy had become acquainted with almost every sort of itch imaginable: the soft tingle of her fingertips; the hot, achy rawness at the heart of her palm and between her fingers; the persistent, maddening bug-bite itch on the back of her hand; the flaming lick of stings along her fingers, beneath her nails, across her palm.

That last was the worst, painful as real fire, impossible to ignore, and soothed only by the touch of cool ironwood. But since they'd crossed into Suralis, Lily and Rose both had forbidden her access to the box. Her dreams had intensified then, and several times her sisters had woken to discover Pansy hunched in the darkness, box hugged to her breast, fingers toying with the small gold latch. She mustn't open it, her sisters said, not while they still needed to lure Irin to them, and Pansy knew they were right. But only Lily and her gifted voice could convince her to release it.

It didn't make sense. Now that they'd returned to Suralis, the dreams should have stopped. Instead, she found herself thinking about the box even during the day, imagining it in her mind, smooth as satin, light catching the fine grain in gleams of cinnamon and amber, copper, russet, and gold. And the itching in her hands? It didn't distract her from her fears and worries, only intensified them. As though they weren't already worsened by the sight of the land around them.

On the surface, Suralis appeared much the same as it always had: a great spread of grasslands rolling into foothills to the south, drying to scrubby desert in the west, the horizon ragged with a slate smudge of mountains. At this time of year, Suralis was always green and vivid with wildflowers, the sun just beginning to bake an edge of silver into the grasses. Even after five years, Pansy remembered that. But the Suralis she saw around her now was nothing but brown. Brown and dry, rustling and rattling eerily in the occasional breath of wind. The air wasn't hot, but the land was the worn and weary husk of late summer. Lily had been right: Suralis was struggling.

"Ho!" Rose's shout drew her from her thoughts. "Riders to the south." Pansy's eyes darted along Rose's gaze and saw, far but not far enough, a faint cloud of dirt and dust rising into the air. Irin's soldiers, at last. And, they could only hope, Irin herself.

"Any strategy, Rosild?" Lily asked, voice brisk beneath its calm.

Rose snorted and dropped her pack to the ground. "Here is as good a place as any. No ground has the advantage, and while they've horses, we've our gifts." And catching Pansy's eyes, "And the box."

Lily nodded and dropped her pack, too, although more carefully. As she rummaged in its depths, Pansy shrugged out of her own pack and smoothed itchy fingers against her fluttering stomach.

"Here," Lily said, holding out the ironwood box. "You take charge of this. I trust you won't open it?" Pansy mumbled an assurance and reached for the box. The itching eased as her fingers touched it.

Moments later, they were ready: Pansy beside the packs, Lily some feet to her left, and Rose an equal distance to her right, curved sword in hand. The cloud of dust drew nearer. And then the soldiers, themselves, were visible. And then, at last, they arrived, hooves thundering against the ground, dust stinging Pansy's eyes as they galloped to encircle them.

Lily raised her voice, gift edging her words with command, but Pansy couldn't hear them over the clash and ring of steel on steel. All was confusion, grit and the spark of sunlight on swords, Lily shouting now, the smell of horse and Pansy's hands trembling against the box. And then, suddenly, all was still. The dust settled, and Pansy found herself in a ring of soldiers, Rose almost beside her now, three swords leveled at her chest. But Rose didn't even seem to notice the threat, lip curled and fierce eyes fixed instead somewhere to her left. Following her gaze, Pansy gasped to see Lily held tight by two more soldiers, her mouth gagged against her gift and a knife to her throat.

"Good day to you, my nieces," lilted a voice from behind them. Pansy spun to see Irin dismounting from her horse. At least, she assumed the woman was Irin. Five years had not been kind to her: wrinkles etched her eyes and scored her cheeks, and though she was just as tall as she'd ever been, she was grass-thin now, dark eyes and pale hair muted to an even brownish tone. Beside her, another woman lurched shakily from her mount—a yet thinner, more muted version of Irin. Alba, Pansy realized, less struck by the change in her cousin than she'd been by that in her aunt. Alba had always been rather small and colorless.

"Do you like my welcome?" Irin asked, shuffling closer. "Oh, don't answer. Just a moment." She reached up to pluck a wad of something from both ears. "I couldn't hear you before. Precautions, you see." She gestured at the soldiers surrounding them. "They still can't hear, although I suppose I could tell them it's safe now. Linea is well in hand, after all. Such an unfortunate gift she has. So powerful. But I've had five years to decide how to protect myself from it."

Rose growled and a cold smile folded deeper wrinkles around the queen's eyes. "And how to defeat you, Rosild. Unbeatable, if you fight. But I daresay you won't, not with Linea at the point of my knife." And then Irin's eyes met Pansy's. "But you, little Persal," she sighed. "How relieved I was not to have to concern myself with you. Giftless and harmless. I can only thank you, my dear." Pansy flinched, hands tightening on the box, and Irin's eyes darted to the small movement.

"You brought it," she chortled. "How relieved I am. Your mother used to tease me so about that box. How she and Vela plotted and planned before you were even born, Persal, always talking about that box, but never saying what was inside. I watched them almost ceaselessly, hoping they might slip and say *something*, but they never did. And now here it is. Waiting for us to open it. Oblige me, if you would?"

The box shuddered in her shaky hands, and Pansy gulped. The denial stuck in her throat, but Irin must have seen it anyway, for she took another step closer and said, "Open the box, Persal."

Pansy's eyes darted around the circle of soldiers, looking for someone, anyone, who might help. But not one appeared to even see her.

All pretense of warmth fled Irin's voice now. "Open the box, Persal. Or I shall kill your sisters." Pansy almost laughed. As though any of them would be allowed to live? She looked to her sisters, but she knew already what they were thinking: the box must not be opened. But to be responsible for their deaths? To refuse to open the box and watch them die? She pinched her eyes closed and wondered if she could bear it. The box seemed to hum in sympathy.

And then it purred. And then it buzzed. And her fingers began to burn.

"I'll open it," she heard herself say, hearing next the mumbled and shouted protests of her sisters and Irin's dry, satisfied cackle. But her eyes were on the box, on her fingers plucking at the fragile gold filigree of the latch. It gave readily beneath her touch, but her hand, her whole body, felt the press of air like lead. Slowly, struggling, she lifted the lid of the box and looked down into...nothing. The box was empty.

Irin grunted. "Just a trick, as I thought. To keep me worrying and wondering all these years. Marit and Vela—"

A scream echoed around the circle, so loud Pansy saw some of the soldiers wince even with their stoppered ears. But it wasn't until the box toppled from her fingertips and Pansy found herself dragging a deep, endless breath into her lungs that she realized the scream came from her.

And then nothing made sense anymore.

Distantly, she heard Irin yelling about a trap and then the ring of steel and then Lily's blessed voice, free and commanding once more. And beyond all of it, the scream, penetrating, chilling, and echoing from her own throat again and again. But she wasn't in pain. She didn't know what she was, Pansy or Persal, peasant or queen. Everything was light and heat, shading through her skin until she shone like glass, stirring her around, pulling her apart, picking threads of the world and weaving all back in place again.

An eternal moment later, it all stopped, and Pansy was standing in the grasslands, her sisters at her side, soldiers a bristling ring of blades around Irin and Alba. There was a hot weight glowing in her stomach and her hands, whole and work-worn, felt bathed in warm, flickering flame.

"Are you all right?" both her sisters seemed to ask at once, and Pansy merely nodded. She was all right. But something was...wrong.

The heat in her stomach tugged downward, and Pansy followed its pull until she crouched in the dry, brown grass. And then her hands met earth. Heat and light washed over her again, and this time she could see a pattern in it, a purpose. But the pattern was unbalanced, uneven, and it was the merest of efforts to make it right.

Heat and light swirled away, leaving only the weight in her stomach and the unseen flicker of flames on her hands, palms soothed by the cool earth beneath them. Grass crackled in her ears, slithered along her forearms as though urging her to stand, and only belatedly did she realize no wind existed to move it. But her eyes had already opened, already widened to see the grass beneath her shading into green.

With a dizzy lurch, she rose and turned, watching as the patch of vivid grass at her feet widened, spread, lapped outward in uneven, crackling waves. Farther and away it rolled, splashing green-silver and wildflowers across the plains, frothing the distant foothills with a profusion of new-leaf trees, even washing bright the far-off line of tawny desert and blue mountain.

Murmurs and gasps blended in the susurrus and when at last the land grew quiet, grass rustling now only beneath the light fingers of a breeze, Pansy found the soldiers standing well back, awed and watchful, swords scattered like straw around them. Irin and Alba stood alone, unprotected, Alba wide-eyed and anxious, Irin gaping and furious.

"B-but you're giftless," Irin protested.

Pansy stepped forward. "Yes," she agreed, feeling only a faint sting at the admission. Perhaps she'd somehow balanced herself as well as Suralis. "And maybe I still am giftless. But I believe Suralis has chosen me over you, anyway."

And Pansy cupped her aunt's cheek, fell into heat and light once more, and shifted the balance. It was harder this time, the pattern more complicated, and she had to remove whole pieces of it to gain even a semblance of evenness. But eventually the balance was gained, and she withdrew to see a new Irin, wrinkles smoothed, hair pale as Pansy's again, her eyes dark and soft, childlike and sweet.

"Good day," Irin lilted. "Have we met?"

Rose snorted and muttered something about improvements, but Pansy merely nodded and turned to Alba.

The girl was shaking, dusty eyes glassy with tears. "It doesn't hurt, does it?" she asked, ducking her chin at her mother.

"No," Pansy said. That odd sense in her stomach seemed to indicate there wasn't much wrong with Alba, anyway, but Pansy touched her cheek and slid into the balancing. When she opened her eyes, Alba was the same pale, simple girl-woman Pansy remembered, only more at peace than she suspected Alba had been for years.

"Thank you," Alba said, and then Pansy was alone with her sisters.

Rose's smile trembled a little at the edges. "I believe this is yours," she said, lifting the ironwood box.

Pansy eyed it a long moment. Then, her fingers sliding over the cool wood, said, "I don't know if it'll last...but I seem to balance things. Make them as they should be."

"Whole," Lily said, and laughed. "Just as Mother always used to say of you, *how can Suralis be whole without you?*" Lily laughed again, this time joined by Rose.

"She knew!" Rose cried. "I can't believe it. Mother knew all along."

"Oh, it'll last, Pansy," Lily smiled. "Your gift was in the ironwood box. That's what Aunt Vela and Mother captured inside it, safe and unknown until this moment."

A low rumble of chatter rose among the soldiers, and the three turned to see Irin cheerfully introducing herself to her former guardsmen. Rose laughed, then Lily, and finally Pansy, weighted warmth rising in her chest as their laughter joined to ripple outward over the sea of grass, over the hills, over Suralis...home.

BEARING SHADOWS

by Dave Smeds

Sword and sorcery works by Dave Smeds include his novels *The Sorcery Within* and *The Schemes Of Dragons*, and shorter pieces in such anthologies as *Enchanted Forests* and *Return To Avalon*, as well as seven previous volumes of *Sword & Sorceress*. He writes in many genres, from science fiction to contemporary fantasy to horror to superhero and others, and has been a Nebula Award finalist. He lives in the Napa/Sonoma wine country of California with his wife and son. In addition to being an author, he has been a farmer, graphic artist, and karate instructor.

He says that the inspiration for this story came to him as he was thinking of the determination of a writer he knows to have a baby, which turned out to be very challenging for her and her husband. I hope, however, that they had fewer problems than the characters in this story did.

W hen the child quickened inside her, Aerise made a pilgrimage all the way to the cairn of the First Woman, high on the bluff west of the village, and left a serving of wine from the sacred cask as a token of esteem.

The pregnancy advanced smoothly. No swollen feet. Only a little clenching in her lower back. Aerise took it as an omen. Unlike her first two offspring, this child would enjoy a full life. Week by week, the ripening grasses obscured the small graves Aerise's husband had dug on the far side of their garden. The dark sense of loss grew fainter in her memory.

Her mother was constantly at her side, patting her near-to-bursting belly, helping to chew deerhide to soften the new carrying sling Aerise had fashioned, and offering suggestions on the decoration of the child-braid Aerise would soon have the right to wear. Something with wild boar tooth, perhaps, to fend off the god of Death.

"Perhaps," Aerise replied, knowing she would in fact use mussel shell, because she loved the river.

On the day things changed, the two of them were on the verge of that river, sitting on a log. Out in the fields, a bored mule pulled a cart down a row. Villagers' harvest knives flashed, cutting stems. Bunches of grapes vaulted through the air, to land on the ever-mounting load. Aerise's husband Duran toiled in one of the crews, adding his clear voice to the vintners' chant. Aerise and her dam, shaded by a huge old oak, fulfilled their part of the great communal enterprise by honing the edges of blades the pickers had dulled over the course of the morning.

All was in its place. Soon it would be her child's place. Nine Vineyards had endured in its little valley for three centuries. The plague years had not emptied its fields. The invasion of the Horsemen had not swept it away. Aerise pictured a time three hundred years hence when her descendants would lovingly regard full vats of grapes ready for the crush, and would take their offerings to the shrines on the bluff to commemorate the lives of all the forebears who had cared for this land.

"You are not too hot?" her mother asked, startling her from her reverie.

Such a question. This deep into pregnancy, Aerise's flesh all but simmered. But the oak's leaves hung thickly overhead and a breeze was ruffling her hair, its cool breath promising fog in the night.

"I am fine."

But her mother's brow remained furrowed. "I will soak a cloth for your head," she persisted.

"There is no need," Aerise told her, but her mother was already up, unwinding her sash. The older woman slipped between the curtain of acacia fronds and disappeared over the lip of the riverbank. A few moments later Aerise heard water sloshing, followed by the splatter of drops on cobblestones as her mother wrung out the excess. Despite her protest, Aerise found herself anticipating the cool kiss of the cloth. She set aside the harvesting knife and whetstone, relaxed, and shut her eyes.

"Ahhh-oh!"

Aerise flinched. Her mother stood rigid a few steps away, the wet sash fallen onto the litter of acorns and oak twigs. She looked as aghast as if she had returned to find Aerise strung up and gutted.

"What is it?" Aerise tried to rise, but her balance eluded her. She reached out for assistance, but her mother whirled about and sped toward the workers in the field.

Plopping back down on the log, Aerise finally looked down. And discovered for herself that when the First Woman had granted her wish that her womb be filled, the great ancestress had not been showing favor.

ೞೞೞೞ

That night, the great lodge of the village was so full the odor of humanity nearly overrode the reek of fermented grapes emanating from the vats along the walls. Everyone had crowded in: The wisemen and the women's council. Laborers from Creekside and Twin Rock, newly come for the harvest. Her siblings. Her mother. Her husband.

She studied the onlookers. There was her friend Dala, who had come of age with her, been married the same month, both to younger sons of the former headman. Dala averted her gaze.

Others glared at her. She saw disbelief. She saw shock. In the dimness, what had been so difficult to accept was now impossible to ignore. Radiance poured from her abdomen, barely diminished by the presence of her maternity cloak, a brightness to rival the glow of the oil lamps on the walls. The light of her child, showing itself to be the get of a shadow man.

Irony, that the adults of the Cursed Folk could walk the land so invisibly, and yet their unborn announced themselves so plainly. It was the sorcery coming into their bodies that did it, so the bards maintained. When it manifested, the babes-in-womb were unable to contain the gleam of their own power.

The headman took his place in front of the sacred cask,

and raised his hands to silence the murmuring. "Aerise, Daughter of Makk," the elder rumbled, any pity he may have had erased by his need to be a leader, to declare what must be declared. "Your crime is apparent to all with eyes to see. You will bear the penalty. You will leave us forever. Your name will not be uttered again within this valley."

The headman turned and showed his back to her. The other wise men, and then the council of women—ultimately, anyone of status within the community—did the same.

Aerise's mother and sisters huddled toward the rear. Her mother sobbed, lifted her grooming knife, and cut off the braid that denoted Aerise. She flung it onto the wine-soaked planks at Aerise's feet.

Finally, of all the adults, only her husband still faced her.

"How could you?" Duran murmured.

She knew when it had to have happened. That night in winter, when the person she thought was Duran, returning early from the sweat hut, slipped beneath the blankets without lighting the lamp. His body had been unusually warm, but this she took to be a byproduct of the steam.

"I was deceived," she murmured. "I thought it was you."

Duran's eyelids squeezed down tight. He nodded, chin trembling, and choked back a sob. But then he, too, turned away.

This was the worst. If her spouse had refused to believe her innocence, she could have hated him a little. The pain of losing him might then have pierced her less deeply. But to have him believe her and reject her anyway? That was as bitter as acorn meal before it has been leached.

No matter whether she had been raped or tricked, she was befouled. Now no person of Nine Vineyards would let her live among them.

A five-year-old boy—her own nephew, son of her eldest brother Nal—reached into one of the many buckets of stems and spoiled raisins that waited at the feet of the crowd and flung a handful at her. A second child did the same. Within moments, Aerise was being pelted.

She crouched, shielding her face. When she made no effort to move toward the door, some exchanged the raisins for clods of dirt. If she did not leave, eventually the barrage would consist of stones. At which point, the adults would join in the flinging.

Weeping, she fled the building.

She staggered as she crossed the threshold, but a sharp impact on her buttocks straightened her up. She sprinted down the wagon way, past the cottages and lodges, out into the lanes of the vineyards. The rain of debris tapered off as parents called back their offspring. A few cruel whelps dogged her all the way into the woods.

Tripping and stumbling over roots the moon's weak light failed to reveal, she forged on until she could no longer hear the shouted threats. Only then, panting, her abdomen leaden and cramping, did she stop.

The trees loomed dark and close, hiding any sign that people lived nearby. This was the edge of her world, known to her only from forays to gather acorns or mushrooms. She had gone farther—to grind flour with the village women at the mill at Creekside, or to help her brothers and father sell wine at the fair at Traders Hollow—but never before had she been beyond the periphery of Nine Vineyards without at least one companion.

Her feet bled from the twigs she had landed on during her flight. Her throat ached from the crying, and from the dryness her panting had caused. But all her discomforts paled beside the shock of her exile.

She slapped her protruding belly. It made the babe kick, causing her to groan as her bladder received the impact, but she did it again. If the action forced her into labor, she welcomed it. Not that emptying her womb would change her fate. She was the cask that had produced vinegar, and would never be used for wine again.

She was not sure how long she raged, but by the time she was at last spent, fog had flowed in from the coast.

She had no shawl. Nor did she have a knife to cut fronds to build a shelter. She had nothing, in fact, but her cloak and the thin shift beneath it. She wormed into a thick patch of bracken she hoped would fend off a little of the mist. It was the only trace of comfort she found that night.

At last the sky lightened in the east. Aerise lay still, hoarding the warmth of the crushed bracken beneath her. For once, the baby was quiet. She had no desire to feel it squirm, knowing what it was.

She heard furtive footfalls along her trail and rolled up, reaching out in hope of finding a stout limb or a large stone to wield. Her hands were still empty when the intruder stepped into the strengthening light and she recognized her youngest sister.

Zana was carrying a bulging satchel. She set it down on the loam and rushed to Aerise's side—

—And then stopped, not touching her. She eyed the glow of Aerise's belly. Carefully she approached again and laid a hand tentatively against Aerise's cheek.

Aerise kissed her sibling's hand. "Show me what you brought."

Zana produced four loaves of bread, two rounds of cheese, and both a skin and a hornflask of wine. Aerise's stomach rumbled at the sight of the food, but in the long run she knew she would be happiest to have the vessels, because after the wine was consumed, they could be refilled with water.

Zana jiggled the satchel. "There is a knife and a tinder box and a comb. I am sorry it is so little." They both knew there could be no more than one exchange. If Aerise lingered near the village, she would be hunted down.

"It could be worse. Winter could already be here." Aerise tore off a piece of a loaf and began wolfing it down. She made no attempt at finesse; with the awakening of the child's magic had come a fierce hunger.

Zana reached into the satchel and drew out one more item, a small, lidded urn. Butter. Aerise gratefully spread a thick smear on her bread, not attempting to ration it. It would only grow rancid if she hoarded it.

As Zana perceived just how much sustenance she required, new tears welled up to replace those she had already wiped away.

"Will it be enough to reach the enclave?" Zana asked.

"The enclave?"

"The Cursed Folk encampment. I am told it is all the way up near the headwaters this year."

"I would not know," Aerise said, stiffening.

Zana put her fingertips to her mouth, color filling her

cheeks. "I did not mean—"

"Yes, you did." Aerise fought back new tears. "You believed I had made an arrangement. That I chose to be a broodwhore."

Zana looked away. She occupied her hands by helping restore the loaves to the satchel. The twitter of awakening sparrows in the branches grew loud.

"Promise me you will go there anyway," Zana said.

"I have no wish to see the one who did this to me, or his people."

Zana hiccupped. "You *must*. I want you to live, Aerise. I want you to live."

"I make no promises."

Zana knew that tone well. She fell silent.

"Go," Aerise said. "You've already risked too much to stay this long." If her absence from the village were discovered, she would be beaten severely.

Zana fled. All too soon, Aerise was again alone in the woods.

Over the next few days, as she slipped farther into the wild lands, Aerise tried to tell herself that she had meant what she implied to Zana—that she would rather die than seek out the Cursed Folk. Then, as the bread and cheese disappeared and real hunger set in, after the snuffling of a bear in the darkest part of the second night made her wet the seat of her shift in fright, after ants attacked the satchel and cheated her of the crumbs of her rations, she acknowledged that all along she had been following the course of the river toward its source, the place Zana had spoken of.

The susurrus of the stream filtered through the underbrush. Here it was a creek rather than a river, often flowing over stones and fallen logs, no longer the quiet waterway that flowed past her home. She made her way down into the gentle ravine and followed the animal trail that ran beside the stream.

Bruises aching, she clambered slowly over boulders and padded listlessly around tangles of vegetation. In early afternoon she stopped at a cave to rest, only to fall asleep on its soft sand bottom. The nap cost her too much of her remaining daylight and she was forced to spend the night there.

The next day, as she plodded up steepening slopes and the creek dwindled to a brook, she searched for some sign of the Cursed Folk. Even they could not inhabit an area without leaving evidence of their activities. But she saw only deer tracks, spent feathers, fox scat, the cast-off husks of caddis flies.

Finally her way was blocked by a short cliff. A spring welled up at its base, supplying the stream with much of its volume. Whatever sources of water lay above barely generated a dribble down the terraces of the cliff. These were the headwaters.

Zana had been wrong. The Cursed Folk were not here.

Hunger gnawed at her so desperately it made her sway. The needs of the child were overriding the disinterest in food that usually came with the second or third day of fasting. She limped back downstream. Earlier in the day she had spotted a nettleberry bush on a high bank. She clawed her way up to it and gathered what the plant had to offer. She could see that foraging bears had stripped away the bulk of the crop, but she managed to harvest two handfuls.

She had to peel open the hairy rinds. The itchy filaments lodged in her thumbs. Despite the fruit's ripeness the squirts of pulp on her tongue were so bitter they puckered her mouth. She had only ever enjoyed nettleberry as an ingredient of jam. The tiny repast only served to intensify the hollowness in her midsection. She turned over a rock and found a fat grub and wolfed it down. That only made her feel as if something were writhing at the bottom of her gullet.

Her shift caught on a broken branch on her way down the embankment, ripping the fabric so that her bare belly showed through the opening, right where she would see it every time she looked down. The sight drained away what little of her dignity she had preserved until then.

Going downhill taxed her nearly as much as climbing, because pregnancy stole her sense of where her weight was balanced. She barely kept on long enough to reach a place where the ravine flattened and permitted the stream to spread itself out and grow still. Sunlight puddled across the surface as she waded along the pool's edge to a flat boulder. Tadpoles urgently hid themselves in the clouds of silt her feet disturbed.

Aerise lowered herself to her resting spot with effort. She sighed, too spent even to dip her fingers to try to rinse the sticky nettleberry juice from her hands. She did manage to slip the satchel from her shoulder.

Her womb contracted. She knew the sensation, having been through the process of birth twice already. She tried to calm her breathing. One twinge might signify little. She estimated she was not due for another fortnight, but she could not be sure given the stresses she had been put through, or given the half-breed nature of the child. By dawn she might be lying here, spent from labor, the birthing blood attracting wolves she could not defend herself from.

The baby stirred. A sharp kick made her gasp. Looking at her belly in anger, she was startled to see that the glow was no longer steady. The light was pulsing. At its brightest, it matched the level she had become accustomed to over the past few days. At its dimmest, she could not make it out in the daylight.

Then it faded altogether.

Fingers trembling, she pulled the torn edges of the hole in her shift wider apart. The taut skin of her abdomen was its normal hue. The baby's urgent shifting had eased. She could tell it was still wakeful, but its movements were now gentle—a subtle tickling.

She could not help but think of her firstborn, how he would fuss in her arms, only to be soothed and fall asleep when Duran picked him up and nestled him.

Aerise checked right and left. Then down. The sheen on the surface of the pool included a manlike outline.

Her heart began drumming. A shadow man was lying submerged in the water, apparently devoid of the need to breathe. So insubstantial was he that the current did not alter his position. Even minnows and tadpoles passed through him. He might have placed himself there—no, *must* have placed himself there—even before she had arrived.

Awkwardly she tottered to her feet—pretending to be even clumsier than she actually was, to conceal the moment when her hand slipped into the satchel and found the knife Zana had brought, which she hid behind her back as she rose.

He rose up as well. His form began to lose its

ghostliness.

She knew it was the man who had raped her. Tall, fair-skinned, sparsely bearded, he looked enough like Duran she no longer blamed herself for being fooled in the unlit bedchamber that night. He would also have used sorcery to cloud her mind, of course.

He was naked. Aerise had not expected that, though she had been told that Cursed Folk could not bring their clothing with them when they slipped back and forth between planes of existence. Seeing him displayed in such a way made the mash of nettleberry in her stomach want to come back up.

Rivulets trickled down the muscled flesh of his body. The river sloshed and gurgled around his thighs. Suddenly he was very much a part of the world. Aerise did not waste a moment—she vaulted forward, thrusting the knife as her brother had taught her, low from her waist level, toward his gut. She committed to the leap, not caring how she landed as long as the knife reached him.

At the last instant he faded to mist. She plunged right through him, flopping into the water, which was just deep enough beyond him to receive her. She bounced off the stream bottom, bobbed back to the surface, and stumbled inelegantly to her feet, calf-deep in the midst of the pool.

She whirled about. The man was on the granite slab she had vacated. He solidified once more, taking two further steps back as he did so. He wiped the front of his torso. Blood seeped one drop at a time from a pinprick cut below his breastbone.

If she had been a moment faster, the blade would have penetrated him while he was corporeal. She had the satisfaction of seeing him realize how close he had come to being killed. She had the misery of knowing she had failed.

He was too far off now to surprise him again, in part a byproduct of how recklessly she had flung herself at him. But the knife was still in her hand, and there was one thing left she could do. She raised the weapon up, tip pointed straight at her womb.

The shadow man grew very still. She adjusted her slippery palm on the hilt, wrapping her other hand around the first, breathing so fast she was almost panting. His brow furrowed. In the alders, a squirrel peered at them, tail twitching. A frog sprang from the leaf litter into the creek. In the distance, a hawk uttered a territorial screech.

He did not rush at her, trying to overpower her. He did not plead. He simply waited.

Her grip loosened. The knife fell, splashed, and sank out of sight.

She dropped to her knees in the silt and pebbles. Water rode over her folded legs. She pulled at her hair until the pain in her scalp provoked the tears she needed. She was otherwise already drained of tears.

She could imagine all too well what she looked like at that moment—wet, bedraggled, nettleberry juice staining her chin. Wretched.

"Why?" she wailed. "Why did you do this to me? Why thrust your seed into me and not a broodwhore? Did it please you to deceive me?"

His expression contorted with such anguish her eyes widened. She stopped yanking her hair.

"It pleased me not." His accent and phrasing were archaic. "I did as I must. I did it for her." He pointed to her belly.

The glow reappeared.

She put her hand on the bulge. "Her? You can tell it's a girl?"

"Yes. And healthy she is. As I had hoped." A smile blossomed for an instant, quelled again as he continued to study her.

"The price you paid was high. I am in your debt." He reached out to her. "Will you come with me?"

He said it as if she had a choice. She did not accept his help in rising, but she nodded, and when he led the way, she followed.

ଔଔଔଔ

The enclave lay far into the forest. It was well clear of the headwaters, the man explained, so that if raiders were sent to burn them out, they would not be found where rumor indicated. His folk avoided the river unless their sentry enchantments revealed the approach of a visitor they wished to contact. Sometimes this was a woman seeking to become a broodwhore. Usually it was a trader, come to parley for goods such as only the Cursed Folk made.

They stopped when they came to a fine old blood cedar. The man reached into a niche at the tree's base and pulled out a maternity gown. It was woolen—the fabric a product of spindle and loom. He held it out to her.

Because it came from him, she nearly refused it, but the prospect of being able to cover herself better overcame her distaste. Much to her relief, while she put the article over her torn shift, he donned an ensemble of deerskin and otter pelt, finally concealing his bare skin.

The rest of the journey required three long hours of hiking, their pace hindered by her exhaustion. Finally Aerise noticed the signs of habitation she had looked for earlier—a reduced quantity of deadfall branches due to the gathering of firewood, a hint of woodsmoke on the breeze, and then actual footprints on the trail.

Near dusk they reached the edge of a large meadow. Where the trees resumed on the other side she spotted a series of tents as well as an arbor roofed with cattail and fern thatch. She saw no more than thirty Cursed Folk, half of whom were children.

The meadow was soft even this late in the season, making her work to take each additional step. Aerise sighed and rubbed her lower back. "Is it much farther to the main encampment?"

"This is the main encampment," he said. "We do not gather in groups larger than this, or we would invite a scourging."

It was the second time he had spoken of the possibility of a raid. "How often does *that* happen?" she scoffed, recalling how successfully he had avoided her knife thrust. Who would bother attacking an enemy who could not be hurt?

"Often enough," he replied. "Our memories are long."

Aerise supposed it would be annoying to lose structures and possessions. Everything she saw up ahead was either portable or easily replaced. It was comforting to think her people could inflict some sort of pain upon his.

By the time they were two-thirds of the way across the meadow, the majority of the inhabitants of the enclave had still barely glanced in their direction. Aerise thought it eerie that the children would take so little notice. Then she recalled the stories.

"How long *are* your memories?" she asked.

"We age no more than one year for every ten that pass."

These then were not children like any she had seen. They had lost the boundless inquisitiveness of the very young. Only the babies were her juniors. Of them, there were two. Both were nursing at the breasts of women sitting beneath the arbor. These women, and a third who sat with them, gave off a different aura than everyone else present.

Broodwhores.

The group regarded Aerise intently. Their gazes kept returning to her swollen belly. The scrutiny made the fine hair on the back of Aerise's neck stiffen. They thought she was like them! They assumed she had made the same choice they had.

Two other women—these movingly fluidly, at home in their environment—strode past the arbor and met Aerise and her escort at the edge of the enclave. One appeared to be only a little older than Aerise, and like her had hair that tended toward coiled. The other possessed subtle lines by her eyes and traces of grey speckled her hair, which was merely wavy, like that of the man.

"This is Cloud," the man said, and the older woman inclined her head. "And this is Fern. They will be the mothers of the child you bear."

Aerise blinked. Much as she did not want to think of herself as the child's mother, it took her aback to hear anyone else described as such. "Both of them?"

"It is our way. Go with them now. If you require me, you have only to ask."

"And whom do I ask for?"

"You may call me Morel."

Her brows rose. "You are named after a mushroom?"

"The morel is my favorite treat. We do not share our true names with one of the Uncursed."

He walked on toward the heart of the encampment. Two

elderly men and a woman met him there and ushered him into the large central tent. Aerise's eyes remained narrowed until the flap fell and he was lost to view.

When her attention returned to her escorts, she found both of them gazing at her coldly.

"You do not deserve the honor he bestows," Cloud said.

"I did not ask for it."

"Is it pity you seek? Pity us, who can only be mothers through the likes of you. Now come along. We have prepared a repast for you. Eat before you swoon from hunger. If we must needs shove food down your gullet while you sleep to keep our baby fed, we will not shrink to do so."

⋯⋯⋯

Modest as the Cursed Folk dwellings were compared to the sturdy buildings of Nine Vineyards, the tent Cloud and Fern thrust Aerise into was no hovel. It had four poles and enough headroom to easily stand straight. It even featured a lidded privy hole at the far end.

A roasted partridge, a kettle of porridge, and fresh greens waited on a stand made of interlaced forest twigs. Aerise set about devouring it at once, embarrassed at her directness but too ravenous to do otherwise.

While Aerise ate, Fern lit a large three-wicked candle to stave off the deepening twilight. Cloud unrolled and set up a trio of cots.

"That one." Aerise pointed. Her companions did not object. Within moments, food gone, Aerise was clambering onto the one she had chosen. She fell asleep moments after Fern covered her with a fur blanket.

At first her slumber was deep, but with a baby pressing upon her bladder, it was inevitable she stirred. She saw to her needs quickly and returned to her cocoon of warmth as fast as she could. Only afterward did she realize she was not alone as she had thought. Fern was lying on the farthest cot, so much in the other realm only her outline showed.

Fern seemed to be almost levitating upon the bed. She was unclothed—Aerise understood the woman had no choice but to be unclothed. She showed no reaction to the night's chill. Aerise checked for some further attribute of alienness. Hoofed feet. A tail. Perhaps the absence of a navel. But Fern did not look meaningfully different than any young woman of Nine Vineyards that Aerise had ever shared the sweat lodge with.

Some time later, Aerise was briefly awakened again by the noise of the tent flap lifting. Cloud entered. Aerise feigned unconsciousness, but watched from beneath the fur.

Cloud undressed by simply turning to her phantom form and letting her garments fall. As she leaned over the candle she solidified again for a moment to have the force of wind to blow out the flames. For a moment the nearness of the illumination accentuated the detail of her body. Cloud's bosom rode as high on her chest as a maiden's. Her lower belly, between the wide hips so well configured for the birthing of children, bore no stretch marks.

ಚಿ೦ಶ೮ಾಐ

In the morning, Fern and Cloud showed they meant their pledge to see that the baby was well fed. Before Aerise had been awake more than a few moments, Cloud was setting down milk and eggs and more porridge in front of her.

Aerise was perfectly willing to cooperate with that particular duty. It was different when Fern ducked under the flap carrying a bucket of steaming water.

"What's that for?" Aerise asked.

"We will bathe you," they said.

"I'm clean enough for now."

The two women moistened rags in the hot water and wrung them out. "Strip," Cloud said.

"No," Aerise said. She stood and folded her arms. At full height she loomed over her hosts.

Cloud cleared her throat. "We are smaller and weaker than you, it is true. But if you do not yield, we will call in some of our menfolk to hold you down, and we will bathe you anyway."

Aerise had known Cloud only a matter of hours, but she could already tell the woman did not make empty threats.

Sighing, she slipped out of her clothes.

Little did she imagine what the shadow women meant by "bathe." They scrubbed her until her skin was red.

"How many times are you going to do that?" Aerise objected when Fern lifted her arm to wipe an area she had already attacked more than once.

"If we are to share this tent, we don't want to smell your stench."

Aerise's jaw dropped. She pride herself on her grooming. "Well, that's easy enough to deal with. I don't want to share a tent with you. If my odor bothers you, put me with the broodwhores."

Cloud tipped Aerise's chin until they were gazing straight at one another. "Morel requires that we look after you. But while we are leashed to one another, Fern and I decide what we will and will not endure."

"Do I really smell that bad to you, or do you just enjoy tormenting me?"

"Every night we fade. Our lice, our fleas, and the dirt and sweat on our bodies stay behind when we cross to the dream realm. We start each day fresh. This is the standard you will observe."

But having said that, Cloud wrung out her cloth and nodded to Fern, who did the same.

"I take it I am fresh enough now?" Aerise quipped.

"We are weary. This will have to do."

Aerise threw her gown on, picked up the bucket, stepped outside, and heaved the water away. She turned to confront Cloud and Fern as they emerged.

She held up the bucket. "Where do you heat the water?"

The two women shared a glance. "We do not," Fern said. "We get it from the hot spring in the meadow."

"Tomorrow, I will rise early and fill the bucket, and I will bathe myself. I am sure I will meet your standard."

Cloud gave another of her infuriating shrugs. "May it be so."

A deep male voice sounded just behind her, making Aerise jump. "I see you have recovered some of your strength."

Aerise spun. It was Morel.

"And some of her spirit," Cloud added.

Aerise scowled at them both, wishing she had not yet emptied the bucket so that she had water to fling at each of them.

"Is there aught I can provide?" Morel asked.

"You can leave me alone," Aerise replied.

He pursed his lips. He gazed steadily at her. She glared back. Finally he gave her a short bow.

"As you wish," he said.

She blinked. "Truly?"

"Until the child comes, I will leave you be." He strode off. He did not look back.

Aerise found herself the subject of another round of Fern and Cloud's cold stares. "You are the poorer for your choice," Cloud said. Then she added, less harshly, "But it is better this way, I think. Clearer."

ೞೞೞೞ

Morel did as he had said. Over the next few days, Aerise only saw him from a distance. He usually remained in the encampment—Cloud assured her he would never be far away while she might go into labor. His tent stood near the center of the enclave, beside that of the elders. Young as Morel seemed to be—gradually Aerise came to understand that among his people, he was no further along than she was among her folk—he seemed to hold considerable status.

Her efforts at cleansing each morning were enough to save her from the humiliation of having Cloud and Fern handle her. The women dropped enough insults to imply they might have to take over, but she knew they were happy to be spared the task.

It was not long before Aerise began to appreciate the benefits of the ritual. The Cursed Folk really were astonishingly clean and well-groomed. Even the children began each day without grubby hands or feet. Their nostrils had no caked mucus. In the whole camp, only the broodwhores failed to maintain the same level of hygiene. Aerise saw the looks of contempt they received.

As the final stretch of her pregnancy wound down,

Aerise spent much of each day outside in the open air, trying to stay cool. She observed many small examples of alienness. Children slipped in and out of their corporeal state as they ran about. Small enchantments kept candles burning longer than they should, made mosquitoes stay away. Yet to her surprise, for the most part the Cursed Folk lived their lives as anyone would. They prepared meals. They gathered firewood. They talked. They laughed.

"You are more like my own people than I was led to believe," Aerise said as she sat in the open with Cloud and Fern, digesting a meal of brook fish and spiced acorn mash.

"Are we not all children of the First Man and First Woman?" Cloud asked.

"No. How could it be so?"

Cloud clucked her tongue. "We were one great tribe until a small group of fools sought out the god of dreams. All who descend from them bear the legacy of that misstep. If we were so different, could Morel have gotten a child upon you?"

"I have not heard this tale before."

"Your people have chosen not to tell it. When we remind you we are related, we are disbelieved. Nevertheless we are as you would be if you were continually swept in and out of the dreamgod's realm. You would never be a natural mother, because no child quickens in a womb that does not remain in the solid world for nine months."

"I see." Aerise slid her hand along the bulge of her belly. "Are you telling me then that I would condone rape?"

Cloud folded her arms over her chest. "Is it rape when it is a not a product of depravity, but one of necessity?"

"Yes," Aerise replied unequivocally. "But I suppose you and I will never agree."

"Indeed. We never shall."

"Morel had other means open to him. Why did he choose as he did, if not for lust?"

Cloud grunted. It almost sounded like laughter, but Aerise suspected it was astonishment. "Look at yourself. Look at them."

The "them" the shadow woman pointed to were the broodwhores, sitting beneath their arbor as they usually did.

Aerise had seen them every day, but she looked at them anew. The three women were unlike anyone else in the camp. They did not smile. Their sole activity, aside from suckling the babies, seemed to be endless rounds of runesticks, often punctuated by accusations of bungled castings. All three were marred in some way—awkward posture in one, a huge chin on another, pocked skin on the third. And of course, the sort of common dirtiness Cloud and Fern had demanded Aerise rid herself of.

Aerise, on the other hand, had smooth, well-complexioned skin. Her frame was solid and her flesh abundant, her hips wide, her eyesight keen. She had no birthmarks, no large moles, no warts. Duran had called her beautiful. He was biased, but even her rivals among the young women of Nine Vineyards had granted that she had no need to feel humbled by either her body or her countenance.

She was the sort of woman a man selects when he wants to choose a mate to bear his children. The broodwhores were...dregs.

Cloud had just tendered her a compliment. Aerise wished she did not deserve it. If she had been less appealing, she would not be where she was.

ଔଔଔ

The baby came right on time, a fortnight after her arrival. Feeling contractions in the middle of the night, Aerise awakened Fern and Cloud. Experience told her she had hours to go yet, but if she were going to be sleepless, she wanted them to share the misery.

As midwives, her companions were well schooled. They took her to a lean-to at the meadow's edge, where they had plenty of clean, hot water close at hand. They helped her walk back and forth to speed things along, get her water to break. They reminded her when to push, and when to breathe.

She sent her mind elsewhere when the agony reached a crescendo. She came back to full consciousness when the pressure between her legs abruptly eased, and a newborn's cry resounded through the forest. She opened her eyes. Cloud was cleaning the baby's face. She lowered the girl to Aerise's bosom.

Fern lay a light blanket atop them while the older woman turned her attention to the umbilical cord and the delivery of the afterbirth.

The baby continued to wail. "Shhhhhh," Aerise said, holding its head gently against her chest, snug enough to be near the reassuring thump of her heartbeat. The little one calmed down.

Aerise gazed at the tiny hand, the tiny mouth, the shiny eyes. She tried hard to find some fault, some aspect she could recognize as Cursed and therefore hate, but she failed.

ଓଓଷ୫ୌ

Even after the arrival of the baby, Morel remained clear of Aerise as much as possible, letting Cloud and Fern be his intermediaries, but he did not avoid his little daughter. He played with her, swayed her to sleep, let her nap in the crook of his neck. Aerise realized he was spending more time with the baby than she herself. The foster parents were loath to let her take possession of the child at all save for feedings.

One afternoon, three weeks after the birth, Cloud suddenly announced, "You may leave tomorrow, if you wish."

Aerise's head jerked up so abruptly it jostled the baby off the nipple. "What?" she asked, restoring things before the young one fussed.

"It is customary that a broodmother weans the baby before her service is done," Cloud said. "But Morel bids us set you free if you desire. The broodwhores can serve as wet nurses."

"Or you can stay until next summer begins," Fern said. "And in so doing, earn a greater reward."

Leave? Aerise hesitated. Part of her wanted to leap to her feet and scamper off toward whatever future awaited. But where could she go? The nights were growing crisp. The forest held no more welcome than it had the first time. She had not yet made a plan.

"If Morel had not insisted, would you have made me this offer?"

Cloud and Fern glanced at one another, then back to

Aerise. "No," Cloud admitted. "We pled the needs of the child. A mother's milk is best."

Aerise stroked the baby's cheek. The tug at her breast was strong and regular, a bittersweet reminder of the time not so long ago when her second-born had nursed in her arms just that way, before the bog fever swept the village, first stealing away the appetite of the child and then taking her life, along with the life of her toddler brother.

"I will stay," Aerise replied.

Fern actually smiled. Cloud let out the breath she had been holding.

"You truly thought I would leave?" Aerise asked, as if she had not been tempted.

"Your anger is deep," Cloud said.

Aerise nodded. "So it is. But none of what was done to me was *her* choice." She lifted the baby up and gave her a little kiss before cradling her in the crook of her neck to burp her.

Cloud lifted the tent flap. Morel was standing twenty paces away. Cloud gestured in the sign-talk the Cursed Folk used when they were insubstantial and incapable of producing sound from their throats. Morel's expression brightened. He gazed at Aerise long and appreciatively.

"Close the flap," she demanded. Cloud sighed, but obeyed.

⚜

The months passed. The baby thrived. When frost whitened the forest floor, the Cursed Folk moved their camp to an even more remote area, where the game was less wary of hunters and meat would be plentiful through the cold months. Snow fell thrice and it stuck to the ground longer than Aerise was used to from living nearer the coast. The Cursed Folk tents remained extraordinarily warm and snug, demonstrating the enchantments upon them.

Aerise never felt as though she were a member of the enclave. The denizens did not seek her out, invite her to join their games of chance or storytelling circles. Even the baby's presence could not meaningfully assuage her loneliness. But her turmoil remained at a simmer. She bickered less with Cloud and Fern. She deigned on rare occasions to mutter a few words to Morel or even accept the child directly from his arms when she cried to be suckled. She was made comfortable and kept well fed in all the ways that would keep her milk both good and abundant. The days blended together until an afternoon when birds were nest-building in the trees and mushrooms were sprouting thickly on rotted logs. It was the day the broodwhores left.

Aerise was watching from her favorite nursing spot, a long flat log near which Cloud and Fern had pitched the tent. The matriarch of the Cursed Folk met with the broodwhores in the center of the encampment. She handed the one with the pocked skin a phial containing a winedark liquid, which the woman quickly secreted away in a pouch, which she further hid away beneath her cloak.

The younger women received a purse made of deerskin. The woman immediately untied the drawstrings and upended it. A cascade of silver coins and copper bits dropped into the lap of her skirt. Counting, the woman restored the money to the purse.

"The Mother's Bounties," Aerise said.

"Yes," Cloud confirmed.

"Why do you give that one money? Why not a potion like the other? Did you find her service poor?"

"She served adequately. She wanted nothing magical. She chose thus the first time, and now wishes she had not."

Aerise hesitated. "The first time?"

"She bore a child for members of our enclave two years ago. The baby died of a pox when it was not yet weaned, but that was not the mother's fault, and so we honored the pact. At her request we gave her a snare otters would find irresistible. Her folk are fur trappers and she imagined she would rise high in their favor. Instead they recognized what she must have done to acquire such a treasure, and cast her into exile. They kept the charm, of course. I'm told they had good luck gathering pelts this past season."

"She spun you a tale," Aerise replied. "Her own kin would not treat her so."

"Did she cut off her own ears, then?"

Aerise jumped. Something about the broodwhore's features had always been disturbing. Cringing, Aerise finally perceived how the hair that the woman always kept down along the sides of her head hung too freely, without flaring around earlobes as it should. All at once she recalled the words shouted after her as she fled the village, telling her how lucky she was to be leaving with her skin intact.

"I never told you, did I, that the strain of yeast that makes the wine of your village so remarkable was once a Mother's Bounty."

"You lie," Aerise said, but her voice barely rose above a whisper.

"Your village was founded only three centuries ago. I was a girl when that sorcery was cast. I could introduce you to the man who wrought it, if you wish, though 'twould require us to journey to the next enclave to the south."

Aerise searched for a way to disbelieve what she was hearing, but all she could think was how many times she had heard, from her own people and from everyone at the fair at Traders Hollow, how the vintages of Nine Vineyards consistently surpassed those made anywhere else in the region.

"If she spun us a tale, it was one we had heard before. The Uncursed are glad enough to own and benefit from our creations, but the mothers themselves are condemned for consorting with us. This woman takes coin because she can conceal how she obtained it. Maybe she will be more fortunate this time. She knows to seek out a life where her face is not known, and spend the money a little at a time, never revealing how much she has in reserve."

The broodwhores shouldered their packs and set off upslope. Aerise guessed they would try to join a settlement of the Shepherd Folk on the other side of the range. The older woman, the one who had never served as a wet nurse during the whole time Aerise had lived in the enclave, trailed after the other two.

The latter had received no reward. Cloud anticipated Aerise's question and said, "She was paid long ago. Her childbearing years have passed, but we let her stay as long as the others were here. But when you leave us, we will move the camp again. We will accept no new broodwhores until we are reestablished."

It was the first time in many weeks she had made reference to Aerise's leavetaking. Aerise studied the fretful, tentative pace of the trio as they vanished among the trees. The one whose ears had been cut off looked back four times before she passed out of sight.

C8CR80RO

O ne evening, as twilight lingered far into the night and the warmth of the day clung like a garment, the baby suddenly felt light in Aerise's embrace, and the tug at her nipple vanished. All at once the child...faded. She slipped right out of Aerise's grip and out of her swaddling clothes and tumbled to the floor, landing silently. She lay there on her back, arms and legs waving, clearly wailing in surprise but producing no audible noise. Her form was misty—nearly transparent.

Fern transformed into her ghostly state, her clothes falling away. She picked the baby up, and held her close. Soon the baby stopped crying. A smile brightened her little face. Fern began playing their favorite game of pat-hands. She obviously— though silently—giggled when Fern swept her through a tent pole, and she passed right through.

"It is almost time for you to go," Cloud told Aerise.

"I know," Aerise murmured.

C8CR80RO

I n the next fortnight, the people of the enclave packed their belongings and moved away. On the final morning, friends took away Fern and Cloud's tent. Aerise was left sitting on her familiar log, nursing the child one last time while Fern, Cloud, and Morel waited by the central firepit, where the storytelling circle and elders' councils had been held for the past season.

Gradually the baby finished feeding. She burbled in contentment. She was eating solid food regularly now, and had only been nursing lightly once in the morning and once in the evening lately, sometimes indifferently. Aerise was glad to see her indulging in the experience this time.

Suddenly Fern was looming above them, naked and ghostly. The baby cooed and slipped into the dreamgod's realm. The swaddling clothes went limp and collapsed on Aerise's lap. Fern picked up her foster child and rejoined Cloud, who remained solid, carrying Fern's attire and the baby's necessities.

They did not say a word of farewell to Aerise. She said none to them. Within moments they were ambling off through the trees. They were soon lost to view. Morel alone remained.

Tears poured down Aerise's face. She stood up, as if to follow, but knowing it was not a choice open to her. "I don't even know her name," she murmured. She lifted a corner of her nursing vest to wipe her eyes. The aroma of her infant wafted into her nose.

Morel's voice was strangely husky. "There is only one thing left. The Mother's Bounty."

"So I am a broodwhore after all."

"A debt is owed. Simply that." He lifted the swaddling clothes that had fallen from her lap to the ground. Smelled them. "And more. I swore that if you grieved at this parting, I would grant to you whatever boon was within my power to create."

She opened her mouth. He raised a warning finger. "Anything save vengeance."

"Give me a life as fine as what you took," she snapped. "A life among my people. In my own village."

She meant it as a challenge—a demand he could not fulfill, which would put the lie to his sincerity. It was only when she looked up and saw the numb contemplation on his face that she even imagined her request might be possible to grant. Abruptly she sat back down on the log.

"What you ask..." He blanched. "To have any hope, you must take great risks. Are you willing to do what is necessary?"

Her breath had vanished so fully she could hardly get the words out. "Do you toy with my hopes? To have *that*? I will do whatever I must."

He rubbed his neck like a man facing the ordeal of his life. "If after I have told you the whole of it, your answer is the same, then our bargain is sealed."

 softCRISO

The first thing Aerise was aware of was the dustiness in her throat. She coughed.

Someone lifted her head up. The rim of an earthenware cup was pressed to her lips. She drank without opening her eyes, without truly coming awake. The second cup smelled of honey, anise, and something fiery. No sooner had she gulped it down than her bid for consciousness failed.

And so it went, how many occasions she could not say. Eventually she awoke fully. For the first time she managed to open her eyes and knew where she was. The stone vault of the cavern loomed over her. Light seeped in where the boulder sealing the entrance had been removed.

Morel leaned near, supported her head again, and served another draught of his potion. Gradually her eyes were able to focus. His countenance had changed. Fine lines had deepened where the skin had formerly been smooth.

"How...long?" she coughed.

"Sixty years. It will have to serve. I dared not leave you longer."

"Let me see," she said as she grasped the meaning of his statement.

He gently lifted her arm in front of her face. Where a plump hand and generous forearm had been, what she saw now was a crone's—no, a mummy's—desiccated appendage, looking as crusted and grey as she felt inside.

"The rest," she insisted.

He hesitated, seemed about to argue, but gradually he peeled back the blanket, unveiling her body. She tried to lift her head to view it, but could not until he assisted her.

She was speechless at the sight. When she had been lowered to the slab, her milk-laden breasts had perched heavily on her ribcage. Now they were empty, nippled flaps of skin. Her belly dipped lower than she could see from her angle, the hipbones rising like mountain peaks on the other side. Her legs seemed to be little more than bones overlaid with dried skin. She suspected the odd nest of coils by her feet were the remains of toenails Morel had recently trimmed away.

Aerise fought to contain her horror. He had told her it would be this way when he sealed her in this subterranean chamber. He had also said that, as long as she did not perish altogether, her body would ultimately have suffered no lasting harm.

"Drink," he said. "Drink and drink, then drink again. This will all change, and seem but a dream."

Surely he was a liar. But she did as he said.

ଔଓଃ

On the day Aerise and Morel journeyed to Nine Vineyards, her muscles were strong enough to help load the sacks of feed for the oxen. Her complexion had deepened from pallid to lightly tanned. She did not fill her new clothes as amply as she had her old ones, and she still craved twice as much water per day as normal, but as the shadow man had promised, her health was sound. She no longer doubted she would finish the recovery as he indicated—in a year or two, she would have her curves back, her cheeks would be rosy, and her hair would reclaim its bounce. In six decades of hibernation, she had in fact aged only three years.

She inhaled sharply as they rounded a bend and she caught her first glimpse of the village. Nine Vineyards had grown during her time away. The headman's house was now a stone manse three stories high, with a watchtower. A ferry sat at anchorage on the river bank where the smokehouse had been, and a newer, larger smokehouse stood a hundred paces upstream. A huge warehouse had been recently built beside the winery. The latter improvement provided the means to their goal. More wine and more storage space meant more barrels were needed, and someone had to construct those barrels.

"You are the new cooper?" asked the head vintner as Morel tugged back on the reins and brought his wagon and team to a halt.

Morel gestured at the piles of staves and strap in the rear of the wagon. "At your service."

"Let me show you your workshop," the vintner said.

Morel held up a hand. "If you please, my wife would like to see the quarters you've arranged. We took the long road getting here. She is very tired."

"Ah. Of course. Follow me."

Aerise's heart was beating fast as Morel helped her down from the wagon, but her spirits were high. Morel's command of modern vernacular, in which he had schooled himself these past decades, had not failed him. When he broadened a vowel or two to capture the accent of a denizen of Baymouth, the listener had believed him to be who he said he was.

The vintner led them to a cottage behind the winery. He opened the door for her. "I hope you will find this adequate."

When she reached the center of the main room, she turned in a slow circle, letting her eyes adjust. Fresh, tight thatch lay above the rafters. The floor showed no gouges and only a few stains. The dwelling was perhaps ten years old, not yet spoiled by the touches of those who had inhabited it thus far.

It smelled of home. Of wine vats stored near. Of the river. Of tilled soil. All the smells she had been deprived of in the Cursed Folk enclave.

She smiled. "Yes. Yes, it is adequate." She moved quickly to the larder, checked a crock to confirm it held cured olives, then began arranging space on the shelves for the goods from the wagon. She blew air to clear away dust and cobwebs—though in truth, the place showed every sign it had been well cleaned in anticipation of their arrival.

The vintner chuckled. "I will check back anon." He paused at the door. "Mind you don't exhaust yourself. Tomorrow night we will have festivities in the great lodge to welcome you. The whole village will be there."

She and Morel both caught their breaths.

"Is anything wrong?" the vintner asked.

Morel shrugged, appearing to make light of it. "My wife is somewhat shy. She was raised on a very small farm. But of course, we will be there."

"Good," the man said. He winked at Aerise. "I am sure you will enjoy yourself."

She smiled weakly. "I am sure I will."

After the man let himself out, Aerise went to the water

basin, moistened her scarf, and wiped her suddenly hot face.

"If it would put you at ease, we could concoct an excuse," Morel suggested. "I could go alone."

She steadied herself. "No. That would only raise suspicions. We must both be there."

ങርു

The great lodge was the same building in which Aerise's banishment had taken place. A nave had been added to increase its capacity, but the main chamber assaulted her with memories. It took all her will not to tremble as she moved about beneath familiar soot-stained beams, awash in scents known to her from babyhood.

Morel endeavored to be the center of attention, laughing, telling stories, cheerfully greeting one and all. Aerise gravitated to the periphery, avoiding the full light, speaking only enough to observe good manners. She and Morel had rehearsed her feigned background as a daughter of a recently-deceased dairyman near Baymouth, but she uttered only the dull outline of this tale when asked about her origin, for fear her listeners would take an interest and gather around her to listen. It was not in her nature to be reticent; she had to still her tongue more than once when she found herself about to carry on.

Whenever possible, she avoided the elders. Sixty years was a long time, but not as long as she and Morel had aimed for when they made their pact. So short a span meant not all of the people she had known were dead. In the first few minutes she recognized three individuals whom she had known. She had last seen them as children who had flung stems and spoiled grapes at her to drive her from the village. Much as she wished to avoid it, she knew she must put their memories to the test. She let herself be introduced to each, and exchanged a few sentences. They showed no sign that they made any connection between the cooper's bony, reserved wife and the plump, boisterous Aerise of Nine Vineyards they had known. Gradually the tension in her lower gut began to ease.

At one point, revelers parted in such a way that Aerise could glance right across the room. She spotted a white-haired, wrinkled matron on a bench against the wall.

The old woman lacked teeth. Her jowls hung low. Her eyes—one of them clouded over with white—could scarcely be made out amid the puffiness of her face. But by the time the crowd shifted again and hid her from view, Aerise had identified her as Zana.

"Excuse me," Aerise told her nearest companions, and rushed out to the privy. She barely managed to shut herself in before she began sobbing. She managed to suppress the noise, but not the shuddering and tears.

When she was able to control herself, she wiped her face dry and reentered the lodge. Spine stiff as a wagon yoke, she continued to mingle. She did not go to the side of the room where Zana sat until several of the oldest folk, worn out early, made their exit—Zana among them, a pair of adolescent girls assisting her.

Aerise longed to follow. The desire tightened her throat so much she spoke in rasps for the rest of the evening.

ⷠⷉⷨⷩ

That night Aerise tossed and turned. The bed, which had been so reassuring the night before, provided no comfort now.

"I cannot do it," she murmured aloud to herself. The pretense, the knowledge she would be dwelling near her favorite kinswoman and be forced to avoid her at every turn—it seemed too impossible, despite all she had gone through to get to this point. She had been a fool to ask for it. Had only done so because she wanted to punish Morel by asking for the impossible.

Enough. She would tell the shadow man, and make an end to it.

She rose and went into the main room of the cottage, where she had left him sleeping near the hearth. She had not been able to bring herself to let him share the bedroom, though to do otherwise carried the risk that some neighbor might notice clues and question whether they were truly husband and wife. Three steps within, she halted so quickly she nearly keeled over forward.

Morel was not simply lying there. He was writhing. His body twisted and bent, caught in paroxysms that distorted his shape in ways that would be impossible while he was in his solid form. Whether he was conscious or slumbering was unclear. While he thrashed, sometimes the glow of the embers fell on his face, and what she saw was a rictus, eyes squeezed shut, teeth showing. Muscles were bulging unnaturally all over his body.

"Morel!" she called. "Morel! Wake up!"

His eyes blinked open. All at once he shifted from misty to solid. As soon as he had completed the transition, he sucked in a desperate chestful of air. The breath seemed to quell the throes. The rictus subsided. Trembling, sweating, moaning, he tucked himself in a curl like a newborn.

"What happened to you?" she asked.

He coughed. She brought him a dipper of water. He tried to hold it, but his hand quivered too much. She took it back and tipped the serving into his mouth. He was calmer after he had swallowed.

"It happens most nights," he replied, voice sluggish and toneless. "All of my folk suffer unless they divide their existence between this realm and the other, never biding too long in either. Today, among so many witnesses, I tarried too many hours in only one."

"I had no inkling."

"It is not your concern. Do not trouble yourself. I endured much worse in Baymouth."

He referred to the period he had spent as an apprentice cooper, learning the craft, establishing a history that would stand up to scrutiny if investigated by anyone from Nine Vineyards. He had dwelled in Baymouth four years.

"Worse than what I saw just now?" she asked.

"Yes. I had no one such as you to stand guard. An apprentice works long hours, with little privacy."

Aerise said nothing. She fetched another dipper of water.

He drank. "Did you come in for a reason? My struggles surely produced no clamor."

"No," she said quickly. "No, I couldn't sleep. I was simply...pacing. Pay me no mind." She retreated quickly into the bedroom and shut the door.

She lay back on her bed. Everything seemed so different than when she had been lying there minutes earlier. She could not say she was sorry that Morel endured such agony. In some ways, he could never experience enough to satisfy her. But if he could keep to the plan despite all that, if he had somehow found the fortitude not to break his vow and leave her in the cavern for eternity, then she would have to find the means to cope with her own anguish. To do otherwise would be to let him shame her all over again.

ಬ೧೩౭౧৪৩

The next week was the worst of it. Aerise's heart would trip each time she glimpsed Zana or anyone similarly old. She limited the occasions she went out in public, using the excuse that she wanted to arrange the cottage to her liking. She accepted an invitation to a barrel tasting of the upcoming vintage, but only after determining that the attendees would only be workers and their spouses, all too young to have known her in the past.

Only on the seventh day did she dare to go to the one part of the village she had dreaded as much as craved to see. Checking regularly to be sure she was not observed, she approached the little house that she and Duran had shared. By now, having made a few careful, tangential queries, she had confirmed that Duran himself was dead, and she had learned what he had done with his life, once she had been erased from it.

The house had changed less than some in the village. Rather than expanding it as his family grew, Duran had built a second, larger structure that shared the same yard, and then expanded the latter, because he had fathered six children with his second wife, and in middle age served as stepfather to the three that came with the widow he married next.

The maple that had been a sapling cast thick shade over his grave. She did not go near it—someone might look out a window and see her—but she let her glance linger on the marker.

"Were you happy?" she asked the air. "Tell me my going did not steal your smile forever."

A beam of light glinted through a gap in the leaves and

touched the gravestone. Yes, he had been happy, the omen said. He had been happy, said the fineness of the workmanship of the second house, the orderly nature of the yard, the number of descendants residing in the community. Whatever anguish had lingered—Aerise could not find enough generousness of spirit to hope he had known no regrets at all—had healed in time. It gave her a model to follow, if she could manage.

⋘⋗⋗⋗⋘⋗

She could not have said, after the fact, just when she began to believe the scheme would succeed. Maybe it was as early as the first few weeks, when she ceased pretending to have a Baymouth accent—a part of the act that had never come easy—and spoke in her normal voice, and everyone accepted she simply had a good ear and had learned to mimic those around her. Maybe it occurred during the harvest, when she unconsciously joined in the singing of the classic village work chant, and no one thought it odd that a girl from a farm near Baymouth knew it, but just assumed she had heard it at some point in the months she had lived among them. Perhaps it happened in the winter, during the long sessions of storytelling in the great lodge, when one of her own nephews, now a wizened elder of seventy years, told the story of her banishment—never mentioning her by name, for that was forbidden, and never revealing that the harlot had been someone he personally knew—and not one person in the circle glanced her way.

Then came the evening at the sweatlodge. She felt a hand fall on her shoulder. Startled, she turned. A crone was leaning near to peer closely at her face.

It was Zana.

Aerise's throat went dry. She had encountered her sister many times since the evening of the welcoming feast. Widowed for a fourth time, Zana lived behind the weaver's house, cared for by a loving clan of children, grandchildren, and great-grandchildren, and Aerise had seen her taking daily walks to the river. They had both attended village funerals, weddings, and storytelling circles. However, in all instances Aerise had endeavored to stay outside the range of Zana's compromised vision. They had never before been in the sweat lodge at the same time. Like most of the elderly women of Nine Vineyards, Zana typically visited the place in the early evening, and Aerise always arrived late.

But at last, it had happened. Zana's good eye had settled upon her while she was unaware. In the past six months, Aerise's body had filled out again, becoming replete with the abundance and comeliness that Zana had often said she wished she had more of.

Zana stared. Blinked. Stared again. And finally a tear crept down her face.

Aerise began to cry as well.

Zana sat on the bench beside her. "Throw a little more water on the rocks," she said.

Aerise scooped the dipper into the barrel and splashed the hot cobblestones, sending a new dose of steam into the lodge's interior. Zana inhaled deeply.

"Do you miss your old home, cooper's wife?" Zana asked.

"This is my home," Aerise replied softly. "This is the place where my happiness lies."

Zana nodded. A short time later the other women in the lodge happened to leave. When they were alone, Zana reached out and grasped her sister's hand.

They sat together, the sweat of their palms mingling.

୪୦୪୫୭୧

Morel was waiting by the hearth when Aerise returned. She could tell he had assumed solid form a moment before, when he had heard her footsteps approaching. He wore only the blanket he had thrown over himself.

"I expected you ere now," he said.

"All is well," she said. "I believe the end of your service is nigh."

A brightness came into his eyes. It reminded Aerise of the emotion he displayed whenever he bounced his daughter in his arms. She had not seen that gleam in all the three seasons they had dwelt in Nine Vineyards.

To her surprise, she wished he had showed a trace of wistfulness.

"Tell me," he said.

She told him of her encounter with Zana. When she was done, he nodded. "As you say. Soon you will be free of me, and I of you. Here is how I propose to do it."

They talked deep into the night.

༄ଓଋ଼ଡ଼

A fortnight later, in the brightness of a springtime afternoon, a solemn knock resounded on the door of the cottage.

Aerise answered. Outside stood the vintner and the headman. Both hung their heads, avoiding eye contact, and shifted from foot to foot. The headman coughed. "Lady Cooper..."

"What has happened?" she asked with alarm.

"Your husband went fishing today at the rapids with a group..."

"Yes. I know."

The headman cleared his throat. "He slipped on a wet rock and fell in. He did not come back up. The men are still searching, but they have not found his body, but it has been too long now to hope. He...he has drowned."

Aerise let her face contort more and more with each word. When the headman said "drowned," she whirled, fell to her knees just inside the cottage, and pulled at her hair, wailing at the top of her lungs. The men hovered over her, trying to mutter condolences. She blocked them out, concentrating on her performance. Try as she might, she could not summon tears. She had not expected to. Not for him. But the rest of the act came surprisingly easy. She heaved and thrashed and wailed. They could not see her face to observe the lack of weeping, and they were only males. She knew they accepted her reaction as true grief.

And soon, so would the whole village.

ೞೞೞೞ

T he vintner told her she could stay in the cottage until the
replacement cooper was hired, and assured her that would
not be for many months. Out in the fields the grape canes had
barely started to show green growth and the crush was months
away. There were plenty of barrels on hand until then—the late
cooper, the vintner remarked with appreciation, had been an
industrious tradesman and had prepared plenty of stock.

Aerise had no fear that she would find new living
arrangements by then. Though not with Zana. The one thing that
might stir certain elders to recall one Aerise daughter of Makk
would be a sudden acceptance of a Baymouth cooper's wife into
the household of another daughter of Makk.

The only hardship remaining was that she was still
obliged to drag about, pretending to mourn. It was many weeks
before she allowed her step and posture to display the verve that
churned within. As soon as she did so, village bachelors began
"accidentally" crossing her path. They offered to do small favors
for her, from repairing her hen coop or splitting fresh cord wood
for her hearth, and bit by bit she said yes to some of these
overtures, preparing food for them in exchange.

She judged it best to wait a year before she wed. But it
was apparent that as far as the community was concerned, less
than that would not be taken amiss.

ೞೞೞೞ

S he saw Morel only one more time. On midsummer night, she
slipped away from the solstice celebration in the town center
and made her way down to the river.

The moonlight on the water became the white gleam of
his body, emerging. He did not come alone. Beside him rose a
girl child, looking to be about seven years old. She was robust
and round-cheeked like Aerise had been at that age—not lithe
like her father.

Aerise held out her hands. The girl clasped them.

How warm her hands were. Full of life's vigor. Aerise

gazed until the moon hid behind the leaves of a river alder, making her offspring's features too dim and ghostly—too much like what she was.

At the last, Aerise leaned in and gave her a kiss. She smiled.

Her daughter smiled back.

"My true name is Rahella," the girl said.

When they separated, Aerise was reminded of the moment the Cursed Folk foster mothers had cut the cord, that day she gave birth by the meadow. The severed parts would never be joined again. This was surely the last time she would ever see this child of her body.

Morel waited in the shallows. When the girl reached him, he cupped her chin. Seeing the tenderness of the gesture, aware of the pride in his eyes, Aerise could not hate him. Forgive him? No. But understand him? Yes. For him, it had not been enough to bring a child into the world. It needed to be a child as fine as Rahella.

The pair became intangible and walked off across the surface of the water. From time to time, until they slipped out of sight, Rahella turned to catch glimpses of her mother.

Finally Aerise climbed the bank and made her way along the river path to the village. It was not a short walk, but it seemed so.

No braids dangled from her head, tallying the number of her living offspring. She had no husband. For family she had only one aged sibling, not long for this world. But she had youth. She had time. And she had recovered her place.

She arrived back in the village murmuring a tune, and when the blacksmith's sons asked her to dance with them around the bonfire, jostling and nudging each other to be the first to twirl her around, she laughed and said yes.

BLACK GHOST, RED GHOST

by Jonathan Moeller

Jonathan Moeller writes mostly fantasy—his novel *Demonsouled* was published in 2005—in addition to some science fiction and freelance non-fiction. He says that if you wish to argue with him over the Internet, visit him at www.jonathanmoeller.com. Presumably you can also go there even if you don't want to argue with him.

I rejected the story he submitted early in our reading period. Striving for "exactly the opposite tone," he wrote this one. Sometimes that's what you have to do to make a sale.

The ballroom glittered with a fortune's worth of jewelry.

The guests stood in small circles, clad in bright silk and damask and fine linens. Caina watched them drink and laugh, listened to the edges of cloaks and skirts rustling against the gleaming marble floor. The Governor's guests were enjoying themselves, she reflected.

She wondered how many of them would die tonight.

A servant appeared, bearing a pewter tray, and Caina took a flute of expensive wine. She sipped, savoring the taste, and resumed her study of the room. The marble floor had been quarried from the Tauseni Mountains, the floor-to-ceiling glass windows imported from Jear, the wines and cheeses ordered from the heart of the Empire. The palatial mansion seemed out of place in the Governor's modest province.

Very strange, that the governor of a backwater province should have so much money.

Caina glided across the floor, taking careful steps to keep from tangling her feet in the expensive linen of her gown. She made polite noises with the other guests, exchanged empty compliments, laughed at insipid jokes. It took some time, but at last she made her way across the room to the Governor.

"Countess," Governor Druzen rumbled, planting a wet kiss on her fingers. "Truly, you do my humble house great honor." He was a paunchy man, with a broad bald head and a red face. He looked like a jovial priest, or a kindly grandfather.

He did not look like a traitor to the Empire. But, as Caina knew, appearances meant nothing.

"And you do me great kindness, my lord governor," said Caina. "When my father sent me on this tour of the provinces, I never thought to find hospitality so far from the Imperial capital."

Druzen smiled. "And I have heard fearful tales of the capital's decadence and hauteur. Who would have thought that such a charming young lady could come from there? Truly, you must come to dinner tomorrow...ah, excuse me. Duty imposes, I fear." Druzen hastened across the room to pair of Carthian merchants in white robes and jeweled turbans. Caina watched them from the corner of her eye. Were they his shadow partners, she wondered?

She turned, and saw the hawk-nosed man in the black robe staring at her.

Caina kept her face calm, but only just. The hawk-nosed man wore a black linen robe with a purple sash, and by law only the magi of the Imperial Magisterium could wear such garb. Caina turned, hoping the magus would lose interest.

He did not. The magus set aside his flute of wine and strode towards her. Caina braced herself, smiled, and turned to meet him.

"Forgive my intrusion," said the magus. He was a man in middle age, with glittering gray eyes and tangled black hair. "But I could not help but overhear your conversation with Governor Druzen. You came from the capital, no?"

"Yes, wise one," said Caina, bowing. "I am Countess Marianna, of House Nereide."

"I am Ryther, a brother of the Magisterium, as you no doubt have guessed." He bowed and placed a brief, dry kiss on her fingers. "A curious thought occurs to me, lady. I served for some years in the Imperial Court, and yet I never met anyone from House Nereide."

Did he know? "My father's House is ancient in dignity, yet has long been poor in coin. Recently his business met with some success, and we have come to prosperity equal to our honor."

Ryther's eyes glittered. "Indeed? Most remarkable. I never met a member of House Nereide, fair lady, because House Nereide was exterminated a century past during the War of the Fourth Empire." He smiled. "Your father is truly a cunning businessman, if he bargained his way back from the land of the dead."

Caina kept smiling, but her mind raced. Ryther had seen past her disguise. Would he expose her to Druzen? Could she kill the magus? No, it was too risky. There were too many witnesses. And if the magus worked a spell before she could kill him, then Caina would die, most likely quite painfully.

And, worse, her task would fail.

"Tell me," said Ryther, his voice a soft murmur, "why has a Ghost come all the way out to Varia Province? What draws the Emperor's spies here?"

"Ghost, wise one?" said Caina. "The Emperor's Ghosts? Those are just a story."

Ryther smiled, crooked a finger, and a flute of wine floated from the tray of a startled servant to his hand. "And some fools believe sorcery to be only a story, too."

Caina's teeth clicked behind her smile. No use lying to the man. It was against Imperial law for a magus to force his way into another's mind without proper warrant, but that never seemed to stop them. Besides, the magi were sworn to the Empire, just as the Ghosts were. Perhaps he could aid her.

"For six years now, a slaving gang has operated out of the province," she said, remembering the orders the circlemaster had given her. "They kidnap peasants from the countryside and children from the towns, and sell them to Carthian corsairs." It made her blood boil. "The coastline has become a nest of piracy, and sooner or later some bold brigand will try to conquer a city for himself. Therefore the Emperor has commanded the Ghosts to bring these slavers low."

"So I see," said Ryther. "Is that not a matter for the Governor? Why send a Ghost? Your particular...expertise...is hardly common."

"The Ghosts believe Druzen complicit with the slavers, perhaps even an active partner," said Caina. "The slavers' successes are too convenient. Druzen gives an order to move a garrison, and the next day a town is attacked. Or he orders a warship to sail south, and a corsair vessel slips past. At best, Druzen may be corrupt. Or, at worst, he plans to seize Varia Province for his own, set himself up as petty king. The Emperor will not suffer it."

"So you are here to kill Druzen?" said Ryther.

"Once I have proof," said Caina. "Then the Emperor can appoint a new governor, one both loyal and strong enough to destroy these slavers." She would murder, if her duty required it, but only if she had proof.

"So I see," said Ryther. "You have done well to confide in me. I, too, share your concern about these slavers' raids. Slavery violates the highest principals of sacred Imperial law." He spread his hands. "Yet that same law shackles my power, alas. I could not take effective action."

"The Ghosts answer to the Emperor alone," said Caina. "I have no such constraints."

Ryther's lips twitched. "Indeed not. When do you plan to kill Druzen? Best to have plans, lest the province fall into chaos."

"I said I might kill Druzen," said Caina, annoyed by his presumption. "But only if I have proof. It could well be another official, perhaps a legion commander, colluding with the slavers." Had she told him too much? The Magisterium and the Emperor's Ghosts were often at odds, and Ryther's goals might not match hers.

"Of course," murmured Ryther. "I'm certain you want proof before you act. Ghosts like to remain in the shadows, and murdering an innocent man might draw the attention of ghost hunters. But I am certain, Countess, that Druzen is guilty." His mouth twisted. "Yet I see the word of a brother of the Magisterium is not enough for you."

"Sadly, I am not skilled with magic spells," said Caina, "and so I must use more mundane methods to find the truth."

"Very well," said Ryther. "You can find the necessary proof in Druzen's study." He glanced sidelong at the high windows. "The north wing. Druzen has the bureaucrat's customary mania for useless paperwork. I doubt he could conspire to high treason without keeping detailed records."

"I thank you for the counsel," said Caina. "Perhaps I will use it to rid this province of slavers."

"Yes." Ryther looked both amused and unconvinced. "Perhaps you will. A pleasant evening to you, countess." He strode away through the crowd of nobles and merchants, his black robe grim against their finery.

Caina hid her scowl with a sip of wine. She never enjoyed dealing with the Magisterium. They had ruled the Empire in ancient times, and the magi seemed to think they still had the right to rule. More than once, Caina though the Empire would be well rid of the magi.

But that was a concern for another time. Caina set aside her wine flute and made her way through the mansion's deserted corridors. Paintings and statues adorned the walls, all of them expensive. At last she came to a mahogany door with polished brass hinges. Two men in servants' livery stood before the door. They seemed quite large and grim-faced for servants.

And servants didn't usually carry shortswords and daggers in their belts.

"You there," said Caina, putting the hauteur of nobility into her voice. "Is there a bedchamber through there? I'm feeling ill, and wish to lie down."

The man on the left looked her up and down. Not with lust, but with the cold-eyed assessment of a hunter contemplating his prey. "Begging your pardon, my lady, but those are the Governor's private rooms, and we've orders to let no one pass."

"Well, man, where can I lie down?" said Caina. The guards relaxed; they must have seen her as nothing more than another haughty noblewoman. That pleased her. "If I do not lie down at once, I'm certain I shall faint."

"If you feel unwell, my lady," said the man on the right, "the Governor keeps a chapel with an Amathavian priest." A scar had twisted his lip into a permanent sneer. "He can say his healing prayers over you, make you feel right as rain."

"Which way to the chapel?" said Caina.

"Head down the hallway," said the cold-eyed man, "and once you pass the library, turn right and go down a flight of stairs. The chapel's right there. One of us can escort you there, if it please you."

"No need," said Caina. "I can find my own way." She left them and made her way through the maze of Druzen's mansion. But once she passed the library, she went left, not right, and emerged into a small garden. She looked up, but the windows were dark and silent.

That was good.

Caina slipped out of her gown and crossed the garden, grateful that the cumbersome thing no longer entangled her legs. She had hidden her gear behind an overgrown hedge the night before. It still lay there, wrapped in her dark cloak, and Caina began to dress.

In the tales and songs, the Emperor's Ghosts were always women of perilous beauty, clad in skin-tight dark leather that left little to the imagination. That was ridiculous. Black leather reflected too much light, and was too noisy besides. Caina clothed herself in loose dark cloth, black leggings, a long-sleeved black tunic, soft-soled black boots, and black gloves over her hands. A belt with throwing knives and other useful tools went around her waist, and a black scarf hid the whiteness of her face.

The cloak came last.

It was a wondrous thing, truly. It weighed nothing at all, yet was dark as night, and flowed through her fingers like water. At night it rendered its wearer almost invisible. According to her circlemaster, the wizards of old had created it, using sorcery to fuse spider silk and shadow together in a cloak impenetrable to human sight. Caina wrapped it around her shoulders and pulled the cowl over her head.

She turned, and a red woman stood before her.

Caina's hand blurred, snatching a knife from her belt, but the other woman didn't move. At first Caina thought the woman wore a crimson gown, but that wasn't so. Blood soaked the woman's clothes, and glistened on her face and bare arms.

And as it happened, she was also translucent.

Caina tensed, but the specter made no move to attack her. Instead the woman raised her arms, as if in warning. Her mouth moved, shouting, but no sound came forth.

Then she vanished.

Caina let out a long breath, frowning. She knew better than to doubt her senses, and she knew ghosts existed, even if she had never seen one. According to her teachers, wraiths and other revenants had once been common, until the Empire had all but exterminated the practice of necromancy.

But where had this red ghost come from? Why did she haunt Druzen's mansion? Had she been a victim of the slavers? Caina's mouth tightened into a grim line.

If the slavers had murdered the red woman, she would be avenged soon enough.

෦෬෯෨෨෬

A short time later, Caina scaled the wall, opened a window, and found herself in an empty bedroom. She opened a door, glanced into the corridor, and saw nothing but expensive rugs and shadows. Across the hall stood Druzen's study, the door closed and locked. An expensive lock, but Caina's skill and tools made short work of it.

Druzen's study shared the mansion's opulence. A massive desk gleamed in the moonlight, and a marble bust of the Emperor gazed down from the wall. Caina's eyes swept over the desk, the shelves, the overstuffed chairs, the fireplace...and stopped on the huge iron box beside the wall. Strange, solemn designs covered its dark sides and bulging lid. Even in the darkness, Caina saw the dark slits on the box's sides, slits that might hide any number of unpleasant things.

A Strigosti trapbox.

Caina hissed through her clenched teeth. Strigosti-made chests commanded enormous prices due to their nearly tamper-proof locks. Even worse, the Strigosti always built fiendish mechanical traps into their chests. Try to pick the lock, and poisoned spikes might spray from the sides, or burning oil, or even deadly gas.

The perfect place for Druzen to hide his records.

Caina hesitated, considering. The simplest course was to find the keys. Most likely Druzen kept the keys with him at all times, and if she stole them, he might well know someone had looked into his affairs. And no hints of the Ghosts' involvement could become public. Besides, Caina had disarmed Strigosti trapboxes before, though they had almost cost her life.

Caina knelt, produced her tools, and set to work. Three keyholes stood just beneath the box's lid. Two for the traps, she knew, and one for the lock. She ran a finger below the locks, seeking for a hidden seam, and found it. A moment's work pried open the plate, revealing a bewildering maze of gears, cogs, and tight-wound springs. Caina allowed herself a tight smile. Countless thieves had tried to disarm Strigosti trapboxes by smashing the mechanical innards, and countless thieves had died soon after. Breaking the gears would release all the traps at once.

Instead, she set to work on the labyrinth of gears. Two traps, she guessed; to judge from the tiny iron bottles, one involved poison gas, and the other would launch spring-loaded blades from the slits on the box's flanks. A gear here, a spring there, a cog there, and Caina started to feel more confident.

Then she heard a click. The gears started to spin, faster and faster, and the cogs became a silvery blur. Caina flung herself backwards.

An instant later foot-long blades erupted from the box's sides. Greenish-yellow slime glistened on their razor edges. Caina recognized the poison. It caused paralysis, followed by a slow and agonizing death. She felt her face and hands anxiously, but found no cuts.

By all the gods, she hated Strigosti trapboxes.

After a moment, the gears began spinning again, pulling the blades back into their slots. Caina waited until her pounding heart slowed, and started to work once more. This time she knew what gears to avoid, and soon had both the traps immobilized. Or, at least, she hoped so.

Only one way to find out for certain.

The lock was the most complex she had ever seen, and it took a long time to crack. But at last it clicked, and Caina leapt back, prepared to flee if either poisoned blades or foul gas issued from the box. But nothing happened, and Caina threw open the lid. Some men kept jewels in their Strigosti trapboxes, some gold, and others rare magical treasures.

Druzen kept papers in his.

She leafed through the papers, her mood darkening. There were letters from the slavers, addressed to Druzen. There were orders to move ships and troops, signed in Druzen's own hand, sealed with his own seal. In one corner lay a thick leather-bound ledger. Caina flipped through the pages, scowling. The ledger recorded Druzen's inventory of slaves, listing them by sex, weight, height, and age, along with the expected sale price, all written in his own hand.

So the villain had condemned himself by his own words. Caina stood, her mind resolved. Druzen's life would end this very night, within the hour.

She turned, and the red woman was waiting.

The specter hovered between the door and Druzen's desk, her face twisted with fright and panic. The blood-soaked gown hung limp and sodden from her skinny frame. Her hands worked in frantic gestures, and her mouth moved in silent screams.

"Gods," whispered Caina. "What did they do to you? What are you trying to tell me?"

The red woman's face screwed up in concentration, and she seemed to speak slowly and clearly. And then, to Caina's astonishment, she heard faint words echoing inside her mind.

They're going to kill you!

All at once, Caina realized that the specter was gesturing for her to move.

And through the ghost's translucent form, she saw the glint of metal.

Caina ducked an instant before the crossbow bolt would have plunged through her throat. She sprang back to her feet, knives in either hand, as the cold-eyed man and the man with the scarred lip rushed into the study. The cold-eyed man tossed aside the crossbow and drew his shortsword and dagger.

"Well, well," he said, "it seems our clever little countess was a bit more curious than we thought."

"And here she is, going through the Governor's private papers," said the man with the scarred lip. "Scandalous, it is." He held two daggers, one of them by the blade in preparation for a throw.

Caina considered throwing a knife, but from the expert way the men held their weapons, she knew they could block it.

"Now we'll have to kill her," said the cold-eyed man, "and get blood all over this fine carpet. The Governor will be wroth."

"Better yet, have out her tongue and send her with the next shipment," said the man with the scarred lip, stepping to her right. Caina stepped back and swiveled, trying to keep both of them in sight. "A pretty little slip of a thing like her, why, there're Carthian emirs who'll pay a fortune for such a bed slave."

They were trying to distract her, she knew, lull her or scare her with their words. Dangerous men, then, and used to fighting as a team. She would have to startle them, do something to break their coordination.

"Girls with tongues fetch higher prices," said the cold-eyed man.

The man with the scarred lip barked laughter. "Bah! You've met my wife." He glanced to the side. "I'd pay a fortune in good gold for a woman who doesn't carp from dawn till dusk."

His hand whipped around, the dagger blurring for Caina's face. But she had seen through his feint, and snapped her left knife up, deflecting the blade. The scar-faced man lunged at her, stabbing with his remaining dagger, and Caina leapt aside, slashing at his face. The cold-eyed man came at her, and the scar-faced man circled to the side, trying to get past her guard.

Caina wrenched her cloak free and flung it at the cold-eyed man.

He slashed at it, no doubt believing it nothing more than normal cloth. But the mundane steel only passed through the shadow-woven fabric, and the dark folds fell over his face, blinding him. The man with the scarred lip snatched up his fallen dagger and attacked, his blades a dizzying whirl of steel. Caina let him drive her towards the Strigosti chest.

When they stood besides the trapbox, Caina smashed her foot into the trapbox's exposed workings. She threw herself to the side, and the scar-faced man's daggers ripped open her sleeve and slashed a cut along her jaw. She hit the ground hard, and the man turned for the kill.

Then the poisoned blades erupted from the trapbox.

Two of them plunged into his right thigh, a third catching in his left calf. His scarred lips dropped open in shock, and his eyes bulged in sudden pain. Caina sprang to her feet just in time to meet the cold-eyed man's furious attack. She caught his dagger on her left knife, slipped inside his guard, and drove her right knife hard into his throat. He gagged and toppled backwards, his blood pumping across the floor.

The Governor's fine carpet would be ruined after all.

Caina retrieved her cloak and turned to the man with the scarred lip. His eyes still bulged, every muscle rigid, and yellowish foam dribbled down his chin. He was already dead; apparently the poison killed quickly. A small mercy, that.

The red ghost had vanished.

Caina took the ledger from the trapbox, shut the study door, and went out the window.

CR3ROEN

The guests had departed, and Governor Druzen had gone to bed. No one had discovered the corpses in the study yet. That was good. Caina would leave the ledger besides Druzen's corpse. Between that, and the letters in the study, the truth about the slavers would come out, and the Emperor would send a new Governor to Varia Province. Druzen's death would remain a bit of a mystery, no doubt, but people would likely blame the slavers. No one would suspect the Emperor's Ghosts.

Caina opened the window and slipped into Druzen's bedroom.

The Governor lay sprawled in his bed. Caina glided across the room, knife in hand, the razor edge glittering in the moonlight. One quick slash across the throat, and the corrupt swine would bleed to death. She stopped, lowering her blade to his throat.

The Governor stared up at her.

Caina hesitated, stunned. Druzen had been asleep, she had been certain of it. She snapped back her arm, hoping to land a killing blow before Druzen called his guards.

Yet the Governor did not scream. He did not move.

He didn't even blink.

Caina frowned. Was Druzen dead? No; his chest still rose and fell. Caina waved a gloved hand in front of his face. The Governor blinked, once, but seemed unaware of her presence. She poked his chin a few times, but received no response. At last she scratched his jaw with the knife's point, drawing blood, but Druzen never flinched.

Had he been drugged? Or poisoned? Her fingers brushed his brow, but felt no fever, no sweat. She sniffed his breath, but smelled nothing but wine and garlic. As she leaned forward, the drape of her cloak fell across Druzen's legs.

The shadow-woven fabric billowed up, as if caught in a wind, and then fell limp. Caina stepped back in sudden alarm, her eyes sweeping the room. Only one thing could make that cloak dance so.

It had come into contact with a magical spell.

Caina looked back at Druzen, and the truth struck her like a blow. The stupor. The glassy eyes. Her circlemaster had described these symptoms to her, but Caina had never seen them before.

Druzen's mind had been enslaved by a magical spell.

That blasted magus Ryther had lied to her. His was a cunning plot, to be sure. Everything was done by Druzen's orders, the letters written in Druzen's hand, and when things fell apart, Druzen would take the fall. And when the Emperor sent a new governor to Varia Province, Ryther need only enslave a new mind to begin his operation anew. But why? The brothers of the

Magisterium were haughty, to be sure, but why would a magus turn to treason and slaving?

Caina looked up, and saw the red woman on the other side of Druzen's bed. The bloodstained gown hung sodden from her shoulders, the blood glistening on her arms and face. Through the tattered fabric, Caina glimpsed ugly gashes in the woman's chest and torso.

"Ryther killed you," said Caina. "You were one of his slaves, weren't you?"

The woman's mouth moved in soundless screams.

"Wait." Caina held out her hand. "Don't try to talk. Just nod. Can you understand that?"

The red ghost hesitated, then nodded.

"You were one of the slaves, and Ryther killed you," said Caina.

The red woman nodded again.

"Why? Why is Ryther trafficking in slaves? Do you know?"

The ghost shook her head.

"Do you know where Ryther is?"

The ghost nodded.

"Can you show me?"

The red woman drifted through the wall. Caina pushed open the door and stepped into the corridor. The red woman waited for her, and beckoned. Caina followed the red woman as she glided down the corridor. They went down a flight of stairs, into the gloomy cellars below the mansion's north wing. Casks of wine stood in dank alcoves, and furniture lay piled beneath dusty sheets. The red woman stopped before a stone wall and pointed.

Then she vanished.

Caina blinked, frowning. Why lead her to a blank wall? Had the ghost been mistaken? She laid a hand against the stonework, and felt the faint breeze blowing through the cracks.

A hidden door, then.

A short search revealed the trigger. Caina pushed it, and part of the wall swung open, revealing a narrow stairway spiraling down into darkness. Caina took the stairs, walking through the blackness, until she saw the glow of torchlight.

The stair twisted once more, and Caina stepped into a scene from a nightmare.

Torches lit the cavernous vault, and a score of metal tables stood on the stone floor. Corpses and parts of corpses occupied the metal tables, and the stench of rotting flesh choked the air. Wooden shelves held jars, and in those jars floated hands, eyes, hearts, and even entire heads, their mouths open in silent screams. Caina saw the corpse of the red woman lying on a nearby table, limbs caked with dried blood.

And across the vault, near a table piled with books and scrolls, stood Ryther.

"Well," said the magus, "for one of the Emperor's pet fools, it seems you're unusually clever." He took a step towards her. "Tell me. What betrayed me?"

"No secret can be hidden from the Emperor's Ghosts," said Caina. She dropped one hand to her belt. "Before you die for your crimes, you will tell me why."

Ryther laughed. "Then perhaps the Ghosts are not all-knowing after all. But crimes? What crimes? The Empire is a pale shadow of its former self. Once the Magisterium ruled the Empire, and it can be so again. Only the Magisterium can bring order to the Empire, not the foolish Emperor, not the corrupt lords, and certainly not skulking spies such as you."

"Oh, indeed," said Caina, fingers curling about a knife's handle. "A brilliant plan, I see that now. Kidnap innocent men and women and," her eyes glanced over a nearby table, and her voice hardened further, "and children, and butcher them like pigs. Surely that will bring down the Emperor's throne."

"This is not butchery, but science." Ryther gestured at the books behind him. "Necromancy is the only true magical science. With these corpses and my experiments, I will soon discover immortality itself. Think of it! A council of immortal magi, ruling the Empire for the good of all...think of the golden age we can create. What are the lives of a few peasants, weighed against that?"

"I had thought you a fool," said Caina, "but now I see that you're both a fool and a madman."

Ryther shrugged. "The same thing has always been said of great men. Fear not. You too will contribute to the new age.

Your blood will fuel my sorcery. Are you a virgin, I hope? A virgin's heart can be used in mighty necromancy..."

Caina's hand snapped up, and back, and sent a knife spinning at him. It struck Ryther square in the throat, but bounced away to the floor. Again her hand blurred down to her belt, and again she sent a knife flying for his face. The blade struck him square in the eye, and this time Caina saw the faint silver flash that deflected the knife.

A wardspell.

This was bad.

Ryther smiled, lifted his hand, and gestured.

Caina whirled to flee, but an unseen force seized her and threw her hard against the wall. She tried to squirm away, but the force of Ryther's magic kept her pinned against the cold stone. It felt as if an enormous hand pinned her against the wall, crushing her bit by bit.

"When the Ghosts trained you," said Ryther, "didn't they mention the fate of spies? No? Pity. Well, you're about to learn firsthand." He muttered under his breath, face drawn tight with concentration. "Spies, you see, always die at their own hand."

Then his will hammered into her mind. Caina felt his thoughts inside of her skull, like a wet groping hand, and shuddered. Her left hand moved jerkily of its own volition, pawing at the knives in her belt. She watched in horrified fascination as her hand drew a knife free, reversed the blade to point at her face.

"The left eye first, or the right?" said Ryther. Caina struggled to regain control of her arm, but her hand still inched towards her face. "Or perhaps the tongue? A Ghost can't report to her precious Emperor without a tongue, can she?"

Caina tried to fight, tried to move, but the grip of Ryther's magic held her fast, and his will filled her left arm. Dread choked her, and the knife moved faster.

Then the red woman appeared, screaming silent words.

Ryther's thin brows tugged into a frown. "What's this, then?" For a moment his attention wavered, and the knife stopped three inches from Caina's left eye.

Through her dread, Caina remembered. Her circlemaster had taught her how to fight off mind-controlling magic. Rage was the key. Only through fury could she throw off Ryther's will. She looked at the red woman's garish wounds, and fed her anger. She thought of all the people Ryther had murdered. And if she did not stop him, he would escape punishment for his hideous crimes, and that thought made her anger explode into molten fury.

With a scream of rage she wrenched her arm down, dropping the knife. Ryther's insidious will vanished from her mind.

Yet his magic still held her pinned against the wall.

Ryther staggered back a step, wincing in pain. "Ahh! You are both stronger and cleverer than I thought." He glanced at the red woman. "Did you raise her yourself? No...she was one of mine. An experiment gone awry." His gaze returned to Caina. "A pity you're not younger. You would have made a splendid apprentice." He gestured again, raising his hand. A block of stone rose from the floor. Ryther spun his fingers, and the block began to circle him, slowly at first, yet faster and faster, like a slinger whirling a stone, until the block flashed around him in a gray blur.

It would crush her skull like a melon.

Caina could not pull away from the wall, but her arms and legs were free, and one of the metal tables was just within reach. She drew back her legs and slammed her boots into the table. It toppled over, the body tumbling to the floor, and smashed into one of the wooden shelves. The shelf exploded, the glass jars shattering, their vile elixirs spraying over the floor. One jar sprayed a foul-smelling yellow ooze over one of the torches.

But instead of going out, the torch exploded in a snarling green fireball, spraying glass splinters in all directions. Ryther stepped back in alarm, throwing an arm over his face. Caina pressed her face against her shoulder, points of pain flaring in her cheek and neck and shoulder.

But for an instant, Ryther's will wavered, and she was free.

Caina hit the floor running. Ryther whirled, snarled a curse, and thrust out his open palm. The floating block of stone hurtled at her. Caina threw herself to the floor, rolling, and the stone block exploded against the wall. She came to one knee, drew a knife, and flung it. It flew true and struck Ryther's throat, or it would have, if not for his blasted wardspell. Ryther gestured again, and Caina dodged. The force of his will sent her spinning, and she bounced hard off the wall.

The red woman floated before her.

No! Not steel!

The cords on the specter's neck stood out from the effort of her scream. Caina jumped to her feet, fighting through the dizziness, and ducked behind one of the tables. An instant later the jagged remains of the wooden shelf flew overhead, driven by the lash of Ryther's spells.

No. Not that. Not that way.

Caina looked at the red woman. "What?" she managed, weakly.

Not steel. I tried. To save. My children. With steel. I couldn't. His magic. The wardspell. Not steel! Not steel! The ghost sagged, as if the effort of speaking from beyond the veil of death had exhausted her.

Not steel? What did that mean? Caina's knives were steel, and the wardspell blocked them with ease. But could the wardspell block living flesh? Or wood, or stone?

Caina didn't know, but it was time to find out.

She scooped up a chunk of shattered masonry and sprang to her feet. Ryther's eyes narrowed, and his hand came up. His magic hammered into Caina, tight as a vice, but not before she threw the broken stone. It slammed into Ryther's face, and the magus stumbled back with a shriek. Two of his teeth fell to the floor.

By the time he recovered his balance, Caina was on him. She slammed a palm into his face, snapping his head back, and drove a fist into his gut. The magus doubled over, and Caina put a hammer fist into the back of his neck. He dropped to his knees, and Caina gripped his temples.

"You can't," coughed Ryther, "you dare not, I am a brother of the Magisterium, I..."

She wrenched her arms and snapped his neck. Ryther fell dead to the floor. Caina managed two staggering steps and threw up. After a moment she looked up to see Ryther's glassy, dead eyes staring at her.

"And that," she croaked, "is why the Magisterium doesn't rule the Empire."

ᚳᚱᚨᚱᛋᛋᛞᛠ

Afterwards, it was easy enough to slip away. Someone had discovered the corpses in the study, and the mansion had gone into an uproar. Worse, the Governor seemed to have gone mad, babbling about voices in his head. With Ryther missing and Druzen incapacitated, by the time anyone thought to question Countess Marianna Nereide, Caina would be on the other side of the Empire. By then, Varia Province would have a new governor, and perhaps Druzen would have recovered enough to indict the Magisterium.

The ghosts were waiting for her.

Hundreds of them stood before the mansion, pale as mist in the moonlight. The red woman led them, but she was red no longer, her wounds healed, her gown white once more. Besides her stood two children, smiling.

Thank you, whispered the ghosts, their gratitude echoing inside Caina's skull.

"Go," said Caina. She managed to smile. "Do not linger here on my account. Go."

As one, the ghosts bowed, and then vanished like mist swept away by the wind.

Caina stood for a moment, thoughtful, her wounds throbbing. The unavenged ghosts, the murdered dead, could not avenge themselves.

But she was a different sort of Ghost.

Smiling, shadow-woven cloak wrapped tight about her, she vanished into the night.

THE DECISIVE PRINCESS

by Catherine Mintz

Catherine Mintz's work has appeared in a number of publications, including *Interzone, Asimov's, Weird Tales,* and the anthology *Whitley Strieber's Aliens.* Often it reflects her interest in languages, anthropology, and the history of genre literature.

One of the most enjoyable things about writing is playing "what if"—the intellectual game of changing an incident and playing with the possible consequences. The popularity of alternate history novels attests to the fact that readers enjoy this as much as writers do.

There was once a barbaric king, who, aspiring to be well-thought-of by his more civilized neighbors—the source of goods which the king resold at an extraordinary markup further north—instituted a novel method for dealing with those guilty of crimes against the state. He combined elements of southern law with his own thoughts in such a way that he could, with pride, show the resulting spectacle to envoys. In this manner he provided both an entertainment and a not-too-subtle assurance that he was under their sway, something that he had no intention of allowing to happen.

His method was to place the accused traitor into the arena that his southern neighbors had been happy to construct for him. It had cost not much more than three times what the same contractors would have charged had it been built on their own territory supplying their own laborers, instead of in his territory using his farm folk in their off-season. The contractors and their sponsors thought the king was not aware of this and he did not disabuse them of their notion.

The accused had to choose between two huge soundproof doors. Behind one was a fighting bull, pricked and goaded to the highest pitch of fury. Behind the other was a lady of the nobility, perhaps not the prettiest or the most accomplished—for those wed early—but nonetheless of good education, breeding, and with a substantial dowry, her gift from the king for accepting an arranged marriage instead of one of her own choosing. She was always a woman who would be a fit wife for an ambitious man, a woman whose family would see to their son-in-law's success—and his loyalty.

The barbarian king had but one child, a daughter, whom he had caused to be reared in every way as a prince. It was his intention that she, in due course, be the linchpin of a suitable alliance, yet defend her interests and those of her people against those of her husband and his folk. A fine match was in negotiation for a prince from the south, one second in line to a throne. In those days, when life was quite uncertain, such a one was a man of excellent prospects that might be improved by some judicious pruning of his family tree.

However, to bring the match to fruition, the king knew, his daughter must be delivered to her future husband a virgin, for such was the fashion of the southern lands where inheritance went from father to son. For a man to be certain a woman's child was of his own flesh, he must marry a virgin and keep her from all other men. The king, who was king because he was a sister's son to the former king, had his doubts about this, knowing women and their ways, but if politics dictated that his daughter remain chaste, chaste she would be.

With the southern monarch's envoys already sighted on the road, he found the princess deep in private conversation with a handsome, poor, and doubtless ambitious warlord who came from farther north than the king was certain his own power extended. The northern border was always a troublesome area, where it was often wisest to simply overlook various things as long as fealty was sworn. Nonetheless, the king declared this might-be lover an oath-breaking traitor and condemned him to the trial of the arena.

To the great wonder of the court and populace, his daughter, more prince than princess, made no complaint and the king, emboldened by her silence, selected as the young man's prospective bride one of her handmaidens, one whose favors the monarch had often sought and failed to win. It was his thought that, once married, the wife might be persuadable where the maid was not. Those the king found inconvenient often had bad fortune and it was whispered that his reach was not short of his grasp and his grasp was often deadly.

It was with pleasant anticipation that the king took his place of honor at the arena. The only blot on the day was that his daughter chose to appear veiled from head to toe. Being no fool, he had her drape back the black gauze for an instant that he, loving father that he was, might be sure of her. She had only one ring, a fine ruby much like the ones he wore, and that she toyed with restlessly. Her face, though calm, was pale as ivory, and her ebon eyes were lustrous, as if with unshed tears. In her saffron gown and gold-worked scarlet girdle, backed by the black cloud of her veil, she was stunning. The king heard the envoys—who had not seen the prize for which they bargained—murmur appreciation.

Presently, as the pomp and ceremony that might precede a funeral or a bridal went forward, the king became absorbed in delightful thoughts of the future. Serving girls came and went, bringing sweetmeats, wine, and sherbets. The southern envoys chatted among themselves, making complimentary remarks on the anticipated spectacle, comments that they intended to be overheard. The king, pleased, lolled against his cushions, waiting for the fanfare that would herald the moment of decision.

When it came, the might-be lover and therefore-possible traitor stood forth barefoot, in tunic and short cloak, weaponless. The king knew a moment of regret that events must play out as they would, for the man excited much favorable comment among the female companions of the envoys. Southern princes were reputedly soft with the comforts and lax ways of the south, not to mention that several were known to have handsome, painted pageboys in their households...

His daughter was not a woman to be happy with a man who was less than virile and there was, there always had been, that weakness on the northern border of his kingdom. However, the duties of a ruler often require that the joys of the marriage bed be, at best, tepid. Even as the king mused on his own marriage, which had produced only one child before his wife retired, permanently, to her own rooms under the protection of her own guards, the trumpets sounded again.

The king saw, in the corner of his eye, his daughter make a tiny decisive movement, and he smiled in his beard. She was indeed a prince. He had expected she would know how the lots had fallen. The monarch had not bothered to find out since either outcome was pleasing to him. The right door it was then. Had she chosen to see her lover trampled and impaled by the enraged bull? Or had she chosen a lifetime of seeing another woman, one who had been subject to her, have the man she might have desired?

Men pulled the ropes that opened the chosen door: it was the bull that came, snorting and stamping. The king felt a great satisfaction that his daughter was as tough-minded as he, a satisfaction that turned to bewilderment as the young man took off his cape and waved it at the beast, which charged the piece of red cloth. The man whipped his cloak up and out of the way as the bull thundered by. It wheeled in a cloud of dust, looking for a target for its pain and rage.

Again the man waved his cape, and the crowd roared as the bull passed the man by, futilely attempting to hook the fluttering thing with its horns. A third time the scene was repeated, and by then the entire crowd was upon its feet, beating upon the railings in excitement. Not least among them the southern envoys the king wished to impress. "The gods speak!" cried one and then cried all.

The king stared, uncertain how to retrieve the victim from the arena, for retrieved he must be, with the envoys as witnesses. "Father," said his daughter, and she knelt before him as if to plead for mercy. He sighed with relief: she would help him by letting him be the indulgent father rather than the strict monarch. "Yes," he said and bent close to listen.

She laid her hands, the hands he had so often held when she was a child, upon his. The king felt a sting. His arm went numb, to the elbow, to the shoulder, then to the heart. He who had had taught his daughter *all* the ways of princes, sagged back against his cushions, dying.

The crowd, enthralled by the spectacle in the arena, saw nothing. His daughter rose, raised her arms, flinging wide the black veil so it obscured any view of the king. She stood forth at the railing next to the royal standard, proud in saffron and scarlet, and gestured. The left-hand door, the door that supposedly hid the bride-to-be, opened, man-wide and no further, then closed behind the northern warlord.

The dusty, blood-streaked beast gored the unyielding planks. Finally, fury spent, it ambled down the passage to its stall. As the bull went on its way, the princess rested one long-fingered hand upon her scarlet girdle and smiled. It could stay, muzzle in manger, until it was sacrificed at the old King's funeral feast, a feast that would also be her wedding banquet, for behind the gold-worked silk of her girdle lay a future queen of her people or lord of his father's. She would have a secure northern border and the man she desired.

For all the new queen's tears as a serving girl discovered her father's fatal accident with his ring, some were thoughtful. The lady's composure when the northern warlord knelt and offered his condolences, his gratitude for his salvation, and accepted her offer of her hand in marriage was noticed by some. However, the wise majority paid no attention at all, for they remembered the ways of the dead king, her father, and knew that the princess *had* been reared as a prince.

As for the southern envoys, they went home to their court with nothing to show for their embassy, except for the whispered observation of the most senior of them in their king's ear, that it would be as well to be on good terms with those barbarians to the north, for they were nearly as clever as civilized men, far more ruthless, and reckless to a degree never seen in the south, for they dared to be ruled by a woman.

In appreciation of Frank R. Stockton's "The Lady, or the Tiger?" and with the observation that, being a man, he was wise to end his story before the princess made her choice.

CHILD OF THE FATHER

by Alanna Morland

After living in several US states and two European countries (courtesy of Uncle Sam), Alanna Morland now lives in Maryland with her husband, children, the world's most brilliant grandchildren, and the requisite two cats. She has published two novels, *Leopard Lord* and *Shackle And Sword*. Two cats and two novels—does this mean she has to get another cat in order to write another novel?

This is her first short story, and I knew I wanted to buy it when I not only remembered it the day after I read it, but kept thinking about it. Despite some stiff competition, this story has one of the strangest twists in this volume.

"Should we geld him first, or just skewer him?" the dark-haired woman asked.

I held very still. In my opinion, this is a wise thing to do when you're flat on your back and two women have swords on you, one at your throat and the other at your crotch.

To be fair, I suppose they thought they were doing a reasonable thing. After all, they had come back to their camp to find Anya pinned underneath me, fighting to throw me off (and succeeding, too, just as they grabbed me by the back of the neck). And I must have been enjoying it entirely too much, or they couldn't have come up on us like that without my noticing. But, dammit, Anya's a lively armful, and I'm no eunuch!

I glanced—*very* carefully!—over to my right. Anya was sitting up, rocking back and forth with her hands over her face and making strangled noises.

"Geld him, of course," the gray-haired one said. "Isn't that appropriate for a rapist?" She grinned and jabbed the sword harder into my crotch.

Stupid! If they'd bothered to look, they could see that both of us were still fully clothed. "Anya!" I yelled. (No matter what they tell you, I did *not* yelp. There is a difference.) "Tell them what was going on!"

Anya shook her head and continued making those weird noises. She did take her hands down from her face, and I thought I caught the glitter of tears.

"Nooo..." she choked out. "He—he—hehehahahooo."

She was laughing, laughing so hard she was crying. The other two let up the pressure just a fraction, looked at her, then back at each other. That was all I was waiting for. I twisted and rolled into the younger woman, knocking her off her feet as I scrambled to mine, snatching for my dagger as I went. The sword at my crotch dragged across my thigh, ripping my breeches and slicing my leg. One against two, dagger against swords, and me already wounded didn't make for great odds, but it was better than being gelded.

The prospect of out-and-out battle must have sobered Anya, for she gasped out through the giggles, "Iriana, Kalia, stop! I'm sorry, I—Lar, I am, really! But it was so funny, the look on your face!"

"My face isn't what I'm worried about!" I snapped. "Look, you two, I was teaching her a defensive throw. Would she be howling like that if I were trying to rape her?"

"He's right." Anya grinned. "I know I've told you about Larion."

"Uh," the younger one grunted as she picked herself up. "The one you shacked up with a couple of months ago?"

"Kalia, I did not 'shack up' with him. I spent the night with him—most pleasurably. Lar, these are Iriana Lyseksdaughter, and Kalia Bransdaughter. Kalia is my sister, and Iriana is our aunt."

"Larion Kirasson." I gave them a warrior's salute with my dagger but didn't sheath it until Iriana put away her sword.

"I apologize for ripping your clothes," she said stiffly. "I'll pay to have them mended."

That was as much apology as I was going to get, I reckoned, at least from her. She was highborn, by the look of her, and used to dealing with a scuzzy sell-sword like me only as a servant.

"Lar! You're bleeding!" Anya said with concern. "Get those breeches off and I'll Heal it for you."

"I knew it! It was all a plot to get me out of my clothes again!" I said loudly to the empty sky.

The other two just scowled when Anya giggled again. "Lar, you know perfectly well that I wouldn't have done it the last time if I hadn't had one too many mugs of that innkeeper's ale and you hadn't made that silly bet. Have I ever dragged you off to bed before?"

"We-ell—no. But not for lack of trying on my part." I sat gingerly down and pulled off my boots. The breeches followed, somewhat more carefully. The cut wasn't deep enough to be crippling but it was starting to sting like hell, besides leaking blood all over.

While I was stripping Anya rummaged through one of her saddlebags and brought out a small leather packet. She knelt down beside me and held out the packet in both hands, as if presenting it to me. She'd Healed me before, so I knew to put out my own hand and cover it. A flash of green light burst through our fingers, and Anya smiled and opened the packet. All the while she was crooning a soft wordless chant.

The humming became words as she sprinkled a pinch of bluish-green dust over the wound. Then she put her hands on my thigh. Warmth seeped from them and the wound itself grew uncomfortably hot. Anya nodded as if pleased and began to stroke the air over it, not quite touching it.

I still don't know how earthwitches do it. With every stroke the long gash closed just a little, first with a thick crusty red line like a scab, then a thinner pink one like a new scar.

Both of us sighed with relief when it was over.

"Just don't put too much strain on it for the next couple of days, or it could split open a little," Anya said briskly, all professional now.

"Can I get it wet?" I asked. "I want a bath, after all this."

"That shouldn't be any problem."

"Care to help?"

She aimed a mock blow at my head. "Get along with you. I'll watch your stew for you so it'll be ready by the time you're finished."

I heard a soft murmur of women's voices as I stood on the creekbank and finished stripping. They were quizzing Anya about me, I think. The only thing I could make out, "...cocky little bastard..." I ignored.

After all, it was all true. 'Cocky', yes. I have reason to be. I'm one of the best in the kingdom with a sword, and I'm *the* best when it comes to unarmed fighting. 'Little' I'm not so proud to admit to, but the gods decided that Lar was going to be just a hand taller than five feet, and that was that.

And 'bastard' is true enough too, as if you couldn't tell already from my name. I use 'Kirasson' out of choice, because I'm damned proud of the tough woman my mother is. I wouldn't use my father's name even if I knew it, but Mother didn't know herself whose seed sired me. Gang-rapists, even those disguised as priests, rarely introduce themselves.

For the rest—well, I've known Anya for years. If she wanted to tell them the rest of my story, how we met and all that, she was welcome to. Just as long as she left out the incriminating details.

The water was warmer than it looked. I didn't hurry bathing, and even took time to wash the grit out of my hair. The women may have gotten an eyeful, but so what? I very much doubted that any of them were completely unfamiliar with a man's body.

Maybe that was why the other two thawed out a little over supper. I shared my rabbit stew with them; they shared bread and cheese and new apples. And their news.

It wasn't good. The 'priests' of the demon-god Velichkor had crawled out from under their rocks, declared that it was the sacrificial year again, and proceeded to kidnap any young woman who caught their fancy.

Some were chosen at the slave-markets and their masters gladly 'donated' them to the god. Others were taken out of the marketplaces or off city streets and their families were helpless to protest.

Some had tried, I heard, a generation ago when those who conquered our lands had first installed Velichkor as the only 'True and Living God.' The 'god' had decreed that any girl his priests chose was immediately sanctified to him, and given his priests the power to kill any who 'blasphemed' by objecting. Entire families had died horribly, consumed alive by fire that no water could douse.

But the ones that made me want to vomit were those that freely offered their daughters to Velichkor, seeking to gain his favor. I will never understand why some people willingly follow those that they *know* are evil.

Anyhow, that was why Anya and her party were on the road, heading for Korovor. Anya explained while Iriana just sat staring grimly at the fire.

"Those—those—I don't know words bad enough to describe them, Lar! Those *priests* stole Iriana's daughter Elftheria. She was one of the first ones they grabbed. They just rode up to her in the marketplace, grabbed her, and threw her into a closed wagon."

"We're going to get her back," Kalia said, her face as grim as Iriana's.

"Get her back? Anya, are you *crazy?* Maybe when they've done with her, if she lives. Some of them do. What the bloody devil do you think you can do, just walk into the temple, spit in Velichkor's face, and walk out again with the girl?"

"Elfi's rescue is only part of it, Lar. We have a plan, worked out with all the senior earthwitches of the Sisterhood, to defeat Velichkor. Whatever he is, demon or sorcerer or whatever, he's not a god, not an immortal. After the last sacrificial year we sent a supplicant to the oracle at the Mother's shrine, clear down in Rakoma. And the message came back, 'The False One's downfall will come at the hands of one who is not what he seems.' We've been working for years on this."

"We have to try," Kalia growled. "Wouldn't you try, if it were your cousin? Wouldn't it be worth it, if we can eliminate this scum?"

"I never should have let her leave the house," Iriana muttered. "I didn't know, I just didn't know that the time was so close for choosing the sacrifices."

"It wasn't your fault," Anya said soothingly. "You know they keep it secret, so people won't hide their girls."

"But Elfi's not even thirteen..." Her breath caught in a harsh ragged sob, deep in her throat. Anya put her arms around her and began to hum softly. After a moment Kalia knelt down by them and clasped her aunt's hands.

I just kept my mouth shut after that. They didn't need to tell me what happened to those poor girls. I knew—my mother had been one of them.

ഗ❀ഔ

A nya came out of their tent and sat wearily down by the fire. "She's finally asleep," she said unnecessarily. "You can go on to bed. I'll take the first watch."

"In a little bit," I answered. "Got to finish this first."

She watched me as I yanked a comb through my hair. "Lar, you never told me your hair was curly. I know women who would kill for long honey-blond curls like those."

I swiped a line from the old granny-tale and added my best leer. "'The better to seduce you with, my dear.'"

Anya's one of the few people I let get away with teasing me, and she takes every advantage of it. She waved her eyelashes at me and cooed, "Oooo, yes, if it wasn't for the beard and mustache, you'd make a very pretty girl."

"Don't forget my big blue eyes, too," I said sourly. She was getting a little too close to the truth there, and I took enough hassles over my looks as a boy. If it weren't that short hair is the mark of a peasant, I'd chop this hair all off short in a heartbeat. As it is, I keep it back in a warrior's braid and try to ignore it.

Her face abruptly sobered. She took a deep breath and asked, "Lar? Will you help us?"

I should have seen that coming. "Why?" I finally countered. "I'm sorry for the girl, but she's no kin to me. Why should I risk my hide for her?"

"A lot of reasons. Friendship. Payment of old debts. Revenge, maybe. And...because of what you are."

The comb shattered as my fist tightened on it. "You told them?"

"No. I gave you my oath that I wouldn't, Larion Kirasson. I've never told anybody. I never will."

"I told you no sell-sword would do it, Anya," Kalia's bitter voice said from the darkness. "He'd make more money hiring out to *them!*"

That got me more angry than I've been in years. "Aye, sell-sword I am, Kalia Bransdaughter. But I'm no cringing, crawling slave to work for the scum that call themselves our *masters!*"

"Then do something to help free our land from their yoke!" Kalia hissed.

"And what payment does this sell-sword get out of it? Patriotism doesn't put food in my family's bellies!"

"Kalia! Lar! Nothing will be solved by the two of you bickering like children. Lar, will you sleep on it, at least, and give me your answer in the morning?"

I do owe Anya a debt. She deserved at least what she asked. "All right. I'll think about it."

CR3C880

I don't think any of us slept very well. It was just barely dawn and I was on watch when I heard someone stirring in their tent. Anya bolted out, half-dressed, and headed for the creekbank. She disappeared behind a screen of bushes and noises started to come from that direction that sounded like the morning after a three-day drinking party.

What else could I do? She was my friend, and she was sick. I went after her.

"Lar. Go. Away!" she gasped through the dry heaves.

"No. Here, drink this. Give your belly something to be sick with, stupid, and it will stop."

Anya clamped her jaw shut and glared at me, then grabbed my water flask and took two swallows. It all came back up immediately, of course, but I think it did help. She didn't puke any more after that.

"What did you do, eat something that might have been bad?" I asked. "Is anybody else sick?"

"No," she answered sourly. "Don't ask a Healer

diagnostic questions, Lar. I know what's wrong with me."

"Oh. You want to enlighten this poor iggernant sell-sword? Is it catching?"

"No. At least, you can't catch it from me, even if you gave it to me in the first place."

That was when I began to catch on. If it was something she had caught from me, it couldn't have been since just last night. And I wasn't sick, anyway. She had to have caught it two months ago....

"Anya? Are you...?"

"In a delicate condition? Carrying? With child? Pregnant? Take your choice, Lar. The answer is yes."

I did not ask the logical next question. She'd come to my bed virgin, though I hadn't known that until afterward, when I saw the blood on her thighs. That was *my* child in her belly.

And that put a whole different light on the help she had asked for last night. Would you let a woman who was carrying your child walk alone into danger?

"You asked me to sleep on a question last night, Anya. This morning the answer is 'yes'."

Gods above and below, I will *never* understand women! Her face clouded over and she started to cry. "I didn't want you to know!" she wailed. "You can't just because I'm..."

"Being very silly," Kalia's dry voice said behind me.

Iriana, only a step or two behind her, agreed. "I don't know why you insisted he was the person we needed, but if he's said yes, there's nothing to cry about."

"Yes, there is!" Anya said mutinously.

Kalia ignored her. "It's time to tell your loving kin why you want this man, Anya. And it had better be for something other than his looks, or how good he is in bed."

"His looks are a big part of it," she said sulkily. "Lar? May I tell them?"

"First you tell me what it is you want me to do."

"I think you are the one of the prophecy. I want to plant you as one of the sacrifices. After that...well, it will depend on your trust in me, your willingness to link magically with me. The baby is a bond between us, the best link we could possibly have."

"Plant *him* as a sacrifice? Anya, that's insane!" Kalia cried. "You can't beglamour him to look like a young girl, they'll see right through that. And an ordinary disguise—what will the priests say when they find out that one of their sacrifices needs to shave in the morning?"

"He won't need to. Lar, please, tell them!"

"They won't believe me. Who would? Let's see, the moon's five days from full—I can force Change if I have to, and show them."

It was almost worth it to see their outraged faces when I stood up, stripped off my shirt, and dropped my breeches. Before they could get up enough breath to protest, I Changed.

Change doesn't hurt, not really, not even when my bone structure alters. It just itches like hell when my scars smooth over, replaced by soft flawless skin. I only wish the rest of it wasn't so...unsettling. Bad enough that I lose beard and body-hair like a dog shedding its winter fur, but it gives me cold chills every time my male parts wither and pull themselves back up into my body. The breasts that sprout on my chest don't make up for it.

Even my center of gravity changes when my hips broaden and my shoulders get narrower. That's the worst part of it, I think. I move differently, and can't even swing my own sword properly. It's just too heavy for delicate female wrists, and of course I'm not female long enough (thank the gods!) to do anything about strengthening them.

"Well, Kalia," I asked sweetly. "Will I pass?"

"Blessed Holy Mother! I—you—but shape-changers are only in stories!"

"Don't I wish! Then I wouldn't have to hide the three days of the month that I can't control it."

"Every woman has to cope with 'that time of the month,' Lar," Anya smirked. "Yours is just a little different, that's all."

"Bite your tongue, wench. This curse is bad enough without that one too."

☙❧

After I Changed back, we broke camp and continued heading for Korovor. As we rode, Anya worked out a modification of the plans that they had already made to infiltrate the temple. Somehow Velichkor had heard of the prophecy, too, and no longer trusted men except his own sworn priests. For the last ten years all his personal guard had been women. What he didn't know was that many of them were members of the Sisterhood, spelled to forget it and the battleplan until someone released them with the right magic.

That someone was going to be Anya. 'Bounty-hunter' Kalia was going to bring her in as a prisoner, one of the outlawed earthwitches. As her reward, Kalia would ask to join Velichkor's Guard. She knew the release words, too, though she had no talent for magic.

And me? Iriana would present me as one of the voluntary 'offerings.' If Anya were imprisoned, unable to get near Velichkor, she could work through me. Or if I was lucky, I could kill him myself for what he had done to my mother. I didn't like it, not any of it, but I couldn't see any way to make it work better.

I didn't like it, either, that evening, when Anya refused to marry me beforehand. "You can 'give our child a name' afterwards," she said firmly. "She'll wait. This can't. If we don't bring down Velichkor now, we'll never have a second chance."

"She?" My child was a daughter?

Anya snuggled up close, kissed me, and put my hand on her belly. "Introduce yourself to your father, little one," she whispered.

At first there was nothing. It was too soon to feel the child kicking, and I wondered what Anya meant. Then something that was not words, not emotions, but something of both, washed over me. There was pleasure there, and a...a *bonding* that was blood calling to blood. She was mine and I was hers. I know, I know, it sounds stupid and sloppy and sentimental, but it was there all the same.

႙ႩჄႨჄ

We reached Korovor late the next afternoon. At the gates I had to watch indifferently and do nothing as Kalia shoved her bound and blindfolded 'prisoner' ahead of her and demanded to see the Head Priest for her reward. The gate-guards directed her to the Palace, and they disappeared among the crowds. Iriana and I were left alone to hunt for an inn and a market to buy me some girl's clothes.

I didn't have to force Change as hard the morning after that. By evening, when the almost-full moon rose, I would have no choice in the matter. After I dressed in the girl's clothes (how do women stand having skirts flap around their legs all the time?) we made our own way to the Holy Palace.

There we joined a line of families waiting to give their daughters to Velichkor. I kept my head down as befits a modest young maiden. All too soon we reached the head of the line and were admitted to the temple courtyard.

"Name please," a priest asked without taking his eyes from his tablets. He sounded bored. No doubt it was more exciting to go out kidnapping girls than to sit here waiting for them to be brought to him.

"Iriana Lyseksdaughter. I—please, this isn't a usual offering. You took my daughter Elftheria. Her cousin Lara here has volunteered to take her place."

"Indeed. We're very choosy, you know. You can't fob off just any homely unmarriageable cow of a girl onto *us.*" He raised his head then, and I saw more than a spark of interest in his eyes. In fact, his jaw dropped briefly. "But this one! If her body matches her face, yes, we'll take her!"

"Then you'll give me back my Elfi?" Iriana asked eagerly.

The priest ignored her. He was too busy stripping me naked. I expect he thought that I was trembling out of embarrassment, but I was trying to keep from strangling him right then and there. "Ooohhh, yessss," he whispered to himself. "Velichkor Himself will want you, my beauty." His hand strayed to places he probably wasn't authorized to fondle, as the sound of someone clearing her throat caused him to jerk back.

"Here, take this girl to Master Kopos," he said firmly as he beckoned to a guard. A hand closed on my upper arm to shove me away down the corridor. I heard Iriana's voice say, "But my daughter—" and the priest's laughter cut her off.

"The girl may volunteer if she chooses, but we make no bargains. You may leave now, woman."

If she made any further protests, I didn't hear them. A heavy door closed behind us; the guard behind me dropped my arm and began to curse softly in Kalia's voice. So, that part of the plan had worked as well.

"Well, I didn't think they'd swap," I whispered. "Where's Anya?"

"We'd hoped there was a small chance. Poor Iriana. Anya's in the north tower, they said. I haven't seen her since I brought her in. Messroom gossip says Velichkor will take her as part of the sacrifice."

It was my turn to curse. Kalia grinned and shook a finger at me. "Such language, young lady!"

She delivered me to another priest, presumably Master Kopos. Evil minions shouldn't look and sound like kindly old grandfathers, but this man did. He gave me a hellacious scare, for he just looked at me and said, "There is the smell of magic about you, girl. What is it?"

I said nothing and considered fainting or bursting into tears, as any properly frightened maiden would, but I couldn't quite manage it. Instead I just put my head down and trembled some more.

He stared at me intently. "Yes, definitely something magic. But not an illusion, not a bespellment. Not something you've done, or had done to you. Something you are."

Gods above, that scared me spitless! I could kill him, I knew, quickly and quietly and easily, but that wouldn't get me any further on with this damned-fool mission. Nothing to do but wait and see what he would do. He came toward me, still staring, took my shoulders, and turned me around. His fingers brushed my hair aside, exposing the back of my neck and the birthmark that I had been told about but had never seen. I heard the sudden hiss of his indrawn breath.

"Your mother was a sacrifice in her time, wasn't she?" he asked.

"Yes, my lord," I whispered meekly. "How did you

know?"

"You bear Velichkor's own mark, child. He will be *very* pleased to see you. He always is, when one of His own begetting comes back to Him."

�⋆

I've let Anya talk me into some of the damnedest things, but this one had to beat them all. Lustful Lar locked up in a harem with dozens of beautiful naked maidens—and not able to do a blasted thing about it.

But after I got a good look around, I didn't want to. Yeah, laugh if you want, but any decent man would feel the same. Only about half of those girls were of proper beddable age, maybe fourteen to sixteen. The others were barely nubile, with slim childish bodies and just-budding little breasts. Some weren't even that. One exquisite little beauty couldn't have been more than eight or nine, just the age of my littlest sister. I thought about my own daughter, still safe in her mother's womb, in this room a few years from now, and I vowed then and there to kill Velichkor or die trying.

One group, about a dozen or so, sat apart, chattering as gaily as if they were at a village festival. The others sat or lay numbly on soft bright pallets, just waiting helplessly for it to be over.

"Lar?" Anya's voice whispered in my head. *"I'm here."*

"Hey, it works!" I thought back at her.

"Told you it would. Maybe next time you'll believe I know my magic."

"Are you all right?"

"Yes. They knocked me around and I've got bruises, but that's all." Her laugh sounded hollow. *"They believed that old tale, that taking a witch's virginity makes her powerless. Kalia told them her partner raped me, but the bad luck I cursed him with killed him.*

"Look around for me, Lar. Ah, yes. Elfi's the little dark-haired girl over there, on the purple blanket."

"I see her."

She was one of the young ones. I wanted to take the man

who had chosen her and cut him into a few thousand screaming little pieces, starting with his privates. As I knelt beside her, I could see the tearstains on her little face. "Are you Elfi?"

She nodded without speaking.

"I'm Lara, and I'm here to help you. I have a message from your cousin Anya. She says to tell you it will be all right."

"Anya? You know Anya? And what she—" Elfi stopped and swallowed hard. "Don't let *them* hear you!"

"Who?"

"Them!" She indicated the happy group. "The ones that call themselves 'Velichkor's Brides'. They want this...what's going to happen...." Her lips started to tremble as she visibly fought her fear, then broke into fresh tears. So she knew, or thought she did, what Velichkor and his priests were going to do at their obscene ceremony. I *did* know. They would gang-rape these girls first, publicly, then use the power gained from their shame and fear and pain to feed their life force to Velichkor.

I couldn't stand it any longer. I sat down beside her and put my arm around her. She turned to me like the child she was, put her arms around my neck, and burrowed her face into my shoulder, her little body shaking with sobs. I just held her and stroked her hair while I talked to Anya. *"Anya? Can other magic-workers talk to each other like this? Or look through someone else's eyes, to be spying on these girls?"*

Her 'voice' hesitated. *"Without the same kind of blood-link that we have through the baby, it would be very difficult, but it can be done. And the spy would have to be like you, a willing participant."*

"So if there is a spy here, one of those Brides would be the most likely."

"Yes. What are you getting at, Lar?"

"I want to teach Elfi how to defend herself. Hell, I'll teach any of them that are willing to learn. Anything that will add to the chaos we've planned is worth trying."

"I knew I didn't pick you for your looks alone. Hm...relax your throat muscles and let me use your voice."

Everybody has had the experience of saying something without meaning to, almost as if somebody else has taken over your tongue, but hearing yourself singing without willing it is *really* weird. There weren't any real words, even, just the soft crooning sounds that a mother uses to soothe her child to sleep.

That must have been Anya's intent, for the Brides stopped chattering and drifted off to their beds. Soon they were all fast asleep.

Elfi stirred in my arms and raised her head. "That wasn't a very good lullaby," she said reproachfully.

"No? Anya seems to think so. Look."

She looked, and a faint smile came over her face. "Good. We can talk without those noseys sticking in where they aren't wanted."

"Right. Elfi, do you want to know how to fight back when the ceremony happens?"

"Yes," she said in a little voice. "I don't want to be a helpless little lamb going off to slaughter—but I don't know how."

"I'll teach you."

"You?"

I had to grin at the disbelief in her voice. "I'm older than I look. And I'm warrior trained, one of the best."

"Then teach me."

There was only time to teach the bare basics that day. You know, the kind of dirty tricks that don't take strength and work best when your opponent isn't expecting resistance. As they noticed what we were doing, most of the other girls came to ask for help too. I was proud of them. Young they might be, and scared spitless, but they were warriors at heart.

As I said, there wasn't a lot of time. I had my arms around Elfi, playing the part of her attacker as she practiced, when we were interrupted. The door opened, and a file of priests came in. "Playing girl-games?" one of them asked with a sneer. "That's not allowed, girls. You have to wait for men, tomorrow."

"The only games are in your filthy mind," I answered icily. "I'm trying to comfort these children who should be home in their own beds."

Little Elfi was no fool. When I released her she was already dripping with tears. "I w-w-wanna g-go *home*!" she wailed, and a chorus of girls burst into tears and joined her. The priests ignored them. Master Kopos made a sharp gesture and the noise cut off abruptly. "Now, no nonsense," he said sternly. "Line up, all of you."

I recognized the tingle of magic coercion, and did not fight it. No point to wasting strength you might need later, after all. They moved down the lines of girls, examining us closely and making their choice of victims for tomorrow.

About half of them, the most senior, had made their choice when another commanding voice spoke from the door. "A poor lot this year."

As one, every priest fell to his knees and bowed before the being they worshiped. Velichkor was beautiful, no denying that. White-blond hair, a sculpted face and body that belonged on a marble statue—and just as cold. The hair stood up on my neck and arms, and I shivered. Sheer, malevolent evil poured from him, and in that moment I believed every story that I had ever heard of his cruelty.

He looked bored as he surveyed the clusters of girls. My girls were still scared, and showed it. The Brides tried to flirt, fluttering their eyelashes and oozing adolescent charm. Blessed Lady, after a hundred years of frightened girls and simpering Brides, I'd be bored too!

And that gave me the hook to snare him with. When his eyes fell on me, I gave him back the look that has gotten me into trouble in taverns the kingdom over—the level challenging stare, the slow sweep of the eyes from head to foot and back again, and the amused insolent half-smile. Normally this causes my target to snarl, "Who're *you* lookin' at, little man?"

Velichkor, of course, did not. Instead, interest came into his eyes, and he reached out to finger a lock of my hair. "So. Even my own get don't usually have such foolhardy courage." He turned to the attending priest. "This one."

There were no lessons the next day, at least not in unarmed combat. Instead, body-slaves were admitted to groom the sacrifices for that night's ceremony. Manicures, hair styling, baths, stuff like that. Now, I enjoy a bath as much as anybody, but not in milk! Ewww!

The meals they served were only fit for invalids. More milk, this time served up in creamy custards, eggs, chicken simmered in almond milk, all of it white, all of it intended to tempt delicate appetites.

I ate it anyway. Years ago I learned that if I go into battle on an empty stomach, I get the shakes and want to puke. This stuff settled down as happy as a kitten by the hearth.

It was an endlessly boring day, and yet all too soon the golden light slanting through the windows high in the walls told us that sunset was near. The little slaves returned, and the priests directed them in their final preparations. The girls' hair was given a final smoothing, and husky male slaves brought in heavy chests filled with jewelry. The assorted priests took great delight in picking out just the right pieces to adorn their chosen victims.

And me? They arrayed me like a queen. Except, as I understand it, queens usually have clothes on. All I got was jewelry. A band of gold set with emeralds and tiny diamonds went around my forehead. A matching necklace circled my throat, and they pierced my ears for earrings that were thumb-sized drops of green fire. Wide gold bands set with diamonds and emeralds in swirling patterns clasped my wrists and ankles. (Any sell-sword worth his pay would have given his eyeteeth for any one of them, and for a moment I pondered the possibility of making off with them.)

⋘⋘⋙⋙

As they took us in torchlight procession to the city's amphitheater, we could hear the cries running before us. "Make way for the Chosen Ones, the Brides of Velichkor!" People lined the streets, open-mouthed with awe and fear. Although a few faces reflected the naked obscene lust of the priests that accompanied us, many more glittered with tears as they grieved for their daughters.

At the amphitheater, guards ringed the upper walls and the banks of seats were packed with unwilling spectators. They too had been seized off the streets, and forced into this place to witness the might and power of Velichkor. The pounding of drums and the wailing of flutes cast a pulsing spell as down on the stage dancers swayed in erotic postures, miming the ceremony that would follow.

As the dancers fell, the drums stopped dead without finishing the pattern of their beat. A soft groaning sigh swept over the crowd as we were dragged to the raised stage, each girl held firmly in the grasp of the priest who would torture and rape her. Good girls; they were following orders, pretending to be scared witless and helpless. Some of them probably were, poor things.

The 'god' was already standing there, waiting for me. He was arrayed like a king out of legend in scarlet and gold. A diadem crowned his head and jewels winked from his clothes. The ceremonial sword swinging at his side blazed in the torchlight with rubies as big as hen's eggs. An evil smile curled across his face as the two High Priests, those who would share Velichkor's Chosen, threw me to my knees before him. He beckoned, and slaves came forward to slowly and ceremoniously divest him of his clothes. The sword he handed to a guard, anonymous behind her armor and helm.

Velichkor took my hands, raised me to my feet, and put his hand under my chin, forcing it up so that my eyes met his. "So, little one. It will be more than pleasure to break you. You are very lovely, my daughter."

I smiled oh-so-shyly up at him and let my own hands stray coyly up his arms. "You may be my father, but I'm not your daughter."

"Riddles, child? Not now." He bent forward, intending to—what? I don't know. Kiss me, I guess, or bite me.

His mouth never touched mine. That was when I grinned and jabbed both thumbs into the nerve centers in his throat. "No. I'm your son."

If he wasn't dead then, he certainly was after I broke his neck.

All hell broke loose behind me. Light splashed like sunrise, strong enough to blind me if I'd been looking that way, as Anya's mental 'voice' cried words I didn't know. Kalia's voice was no quieter as she gave a shrill warcry. Several girls screamed; one of them might have been me.

No, dammit, not because I was scared! Change had hit me, faster and stronger than it ever had, and this time so agonizingly painful that it drove me back to my knees. When it was over, I was sweating and shaken and male again—and bare-assed naked on a stage full of fighting women where anything male had just been designated as 'target.'

At least, that was what I thought was my immediate problem. It turned out I was wrong. When I raised my head, *he* was still standing there above his broken body. He looked at me and grinned vaporously as his voice sounded in my head. *"How thoughtful of someone. My son, right here when I need a new body. And already a shape-shifter, too."*

"Oh no, you don't! There's only room in this body for *me!*" I backed up hastily and almost fell off the stage.

"That can be arranged."

Then—how do you describe something when everything happens at once? He raised his hands and I saw a tongue of mage-flame lick from them. Two voices, one inside my head and another outside, screamed, *"No!"* in chorus, and somebody tackled me from the side. As I went down, a sword swished over my head, and the mage-fire caught the priest wielding it instead of me.

"Lar!" Anya's mental voice screamed. *"Channel us, now!"*

Huh? Channel? I really, *really* wish Anya would explain magic stuff to me *before* things like this happen. Something that felt like tiny hands grabbed me from inside, at the base of my spine, and heat flared up my back and down my arms. Mage-flames started to stream from *my* hands. They fried another priest before I knew what was happening.

"Don't waste Power on them! Get Velichkor!"

Now, this was more like it! Give me a weapon, and I'll happily use it. I aimed blue-green lightnings at Velichkor; they flashed and crackled uselessly, as if he had an invisible shield around him. He grinned and reached for me again. I knew if his power touched me it would be worse than rape, worse than dying.

A body threw itself at Velichkor, swinging a sword madly. Light glinted off the rubies of the hilt and pommel—Kalia, wielding Velichkor's own sword. It caught him about where his waist would be, if he'd still had a body. His shields faltered, just for a heartbeat, and I threw everything that Anya and the Sisterhood could feed me. He stiffened and began to glow, blue-green building to blue, to blue-white, to a blinding white that made tears stream down my cheeks.

Something popped, almost noiselessly, and he vanished. There was nothing where he had been, not a puff of smoke, not a drift of ashes, just...*nothing.*

"Master! He's gone!" screamed one of the few priests still standing. He screamed even louder when the little girl who had been his intended victim kicked him in the crotch.

"You got him, Lara, you got him!" a little voice said in my ear, and the person who had tackled me, who was still sprawled half on top of me, hugged me from behind.

"Elfi-child, *we* got him!" I turned and started to hug back.

Her eyes widened and she blushed bright pink. "But—but—you're a *man!*"

"Damn right he is!" Kalia crowed joyfully. She hauled me to my feet just in time for Anya to nearly knock me over again. She'd been back in the wings offstage, held by guards to await her turn to die.

"Lar! Lar! We did it, we really did it!" She hugged and kissed me enthusiastically. Not that I minded, but I'd prefer to be either clothed or in private the next time, so that my...ah... response wasn't quite so noticeable.

ೞೞೞೞ

You know the rest of the story. The remaining Priesthood lost most of the magic powers they had when Velichkor died. Rioting spread from the amphitheater to the streets of the city, and from there into the countryside. Within three months we had taken back our land from the usurpers.

We're a trio sword-and-sorcery team now, Anya, Kalia and me. Elfi threatens to make it five just as soon as she turns fourteen.

Oh, the fourth? She's due to be born any day now.

I can hardly wait to meet her.

CHILD OF ICE, CHILD OF FLAME

by Marian Allen

Marian Allen has had three novels published in electronic form, and her stories have appeared in on-line and print publications, on coffee cans, and on the wall of an Indian restaurant in Louisville, Kentucky. She writes a food history column for the electronic recipe magazine *Worldwide Recipes* and teaches a non-credit Creative Writing course at Indiana University Southeast. She is a member of the Short Mystery Fiction Society and of the Southern Indiana Writers Group, and is a regular contributor to the SIW's annual anthology. For free stories, surrealist poetry, recipes, and links to novel excerpts, please visit her at MarianAllen.com.

This story demonstrates that a swordswoman may have a lot more to worry about than how well she fights.

Now Casilda squatted in the crisp air and weak sunlight, covered in another woman's blood, as the townspeople cheered and laughed. She had killed their champion, and they cheered her. They laughed at their champion's cooling body. She was certain this meant trouble.

She stood, lowering her sword so the blade pointed to the congealing blood pooled around the dead woman. An icy breeze zinged through every chink in her armor, succeeding where the swords of many another warrior had failed.

"Where is the tent of your chief?" she said, formally claiming the rights of a victor. "Where is my bath filled with scented oil and healing herbs, my victor's banquet, my bed above hot bricks? Where are your fair young men, so I may take my pick? Where is my prize—the treasure of your village?"

A whoop of joy went up from the crowd. As it died, she heard another cry in the distance: the cry she had expected from the villagers, a single voice of defeat and soul-felt sorrow.

"This way." A black-haired man in rich clothes spoke, a smile of peaceful satisfaction smoothing his face to agelessness.

She shifted her weight to take a step, then settled back.

Wrong, she thought. This place is wrong. Dangerous? No, not for me. For someone else? Perhaps. Certainly for her— the woman I killed. It wasn't only I who killed her. Well, then, let me take nothing for granted. Let me make sure the forms are observed.

"Where is the honor guard for your champion's body?"

No one came forward.

Casilda held herself motionless.

I will count to ten, she told herself. Then I'll tell them what I'll do after I've counted to ten again.

She had only reached the first *five* before four men and four women stepped out of the crowd, unwinding the woven scarves from their heads and shoulders. One woman bound the dead warrior's hands and one bound her feet, one swathed her head and one tucked the hilt of her sword beneath her hands and tied it there. The men lifted the body and passed their scarves beneath it. The men and women took the ends of the four scarves and lifted the body between them.

In the distance, the wail turned to wrenching sobs, inarticulate shouts of despair.

"Wait," Casilda said. She removed the dead fighter's helmet. Like all armor in Dairu, it was made of overlapping plates of lightweight forgewood—easy to cut and work and rivet together while it was green, hard as iron when it had cured. The woman who had challenged her when she had entered the village, looking for food and a night's lodging, had worn her blond hair short. The sightless eyes, which Casilda closed gently, were deeply blue.

Why? Casilda wondered. A test of strength, yes, that's common—a form of entertainment—a sort of hospitality, even. But a challenge to the death, to a stranger? And those heartrending cries, sunken to inaudibility—was someone mourning this death, or did a different tragedy wring them forth?

The crowd parted for them as they carried their dead champion to the pyre prepared for the challenge's loser.

Despite herself, Casilda let her reddened blade lift perceptibly toward the unarmed people as she said, "This was a valiant fighter. We will all pay tribute to her."

Grudgingly, the villagers encircled the pyre. With indifference that, toward a fallen warrior, equaled contempt, the richly dressed man lit a torch from the brazier at the foot of the pyre and thrust it into the kindling. He was still smiling.

As the flames engulfed her fallen opponent, Casilda chanted the Rite of Passage for the Valiant Dead:

I walk with you so far and no farther.

Now your steps proceed where mine will follow.

Soon, my steps will follow, but now they stop.

I stop and I stay on this side of the border,

The border of the land you tread without me.

Defend the land until I come.

I will come, after.

The forgewood armor was reluctant to catch fire but, when it did, it burned an incandescent white. Warriors called that a sign the Spirits of Heaven had accepted the departed soul—that flame the color of ice. Casilda thought of the pale skin of the village champion, nearly as fair as her own, and of the crowd's joy at her loss. When she turned from the pyre, the villagers were gone, all but the black-haired man in rich clothes.

"I am the chief," he said. "Come with me."

Perversely, she stood her ground.

"Did she have family?"

Frowning, the chief said, "Who?"

"Your champion. Did she have family? Did she have a name?"

"We guard our names from strangers."

"Hers is past guarding, don't you think?"

He smiled again. "Her name was Audris."

"Did she have a family? ...Family. Did she have one?"

"In this village, female warriors are chaste."

Ah, she thought. One of *those* places.

She neither moved nor spoke.

Reluctantly, he offered: "Her mother died at her birth. Her father died ten years ago. This is as far as we count kinship here."

Sensing there was more to be had, Casilda fixed him with her stare. She was still wearing her helmet, a casque of forgewood dyed forest green as it cured; all it showed of her face were her eyes, so pale a blue as to be almost silver.

As she had suspected, the chief was uneasy under her scrutiny. Irritably, he said, "Come. You'll see."

She shouldered her travel pack and followed him, passing from the arena at the edge of the village, threading through the irregularly placed wood huts. The huts were rectangular, the eave work of the shingled roofs carved with totems and floral elaboration. Children playing in the fenced gardens stopped and watched her pass, wide-eyed at the drying blood on her armor and her still-unsheathed sword.

He led her to a hut apparently no different from the others, though perhaps its carvings held meanings of authority for the villagers. The interior was familiar to her from more welcome stays in other places: Decoratively carved chests with hinged lids stood around the walls, each six feet long and three feet wide, each both storage and bed. In the center of the room, a mud-brick charcoal-burning oven, the same general size and shape of the chests, was the bed of honor at this chilly altitude.

At this time of day, just before lattermeal, the oven fires were stoked and the bricks shimmered with heat.

A girl—seven? eight?—with unkempt hair the color of dark honey struggled to carry two wooden buckets from the stove to a tin bath tub. Ropy muscles stood defined on arms devoid of baby fat. She dumped the water into the tub, and the scents of bay and rosemary floated to Casilda's nose—the smell of triumph, after a contest of arms. The smell of death, after this strange challenge. The smell of compulsion, manipulation, desperation.

The girl tugged at a folded screen, spreading it to conceal the tub from the rest of the room.

Eyes lowered, head bowed, she said, "The bath is ready."

"Congratulate her on her victory," said the chief, with his strangely peaceful smile.

"Did you fight with honor?" the girl asked, voice clear, eyes still on the floor.

Casilda's gloved hand deflected the chief's blow.

"Your servant is my servant until I leave. She is mine to punish, not yours."

Rubbing his arm, the chief nodded.

"I'll go bring the pick of our young men," he said. "Will you look at them before the meal or after?"

"I want none of your young men—nor your young women. I will bathe and eat, take my prize and go. Now, if I could have privacy?"

"Then I'll fetch my wife to cook our meal."

The thought of breaking bread in this village tempered her appetite.

"Have her fix something I can carry. I can stay no more than two hours."

Many warriors refused to linger in a place where they had killed. Let him believe she had taken a general vow to that effect, which she had not.

"I'll fetch her." His smile broadened as he turned. Then he was gone, leaving the atmosphere clearer.

"Did you fight with honor?" the girl asked again.

"I did. So did the Warrior Audris."

The filthy head bobbed a nod.

"May I attend you?"

A less subservient request to serve, Casilda had never heard.

"If you think me worthy."

The head bobbed again.

Casilda laid her sword on the floor, silver and garnet, steel and lost life.

The girl held up her hands for Casilda's casque. She dipped it into the bath, rubbing it with the scented water inside and out, then set it on the floor.

Meanwhile, Casilda slipped off her forgewood-plated gloves and tunic, her armguards and shinguards. One by one, they went into the bathwater and were set out to dry. She untied the broad pepperbark leaves that protected her precious leather boots and dropped them into the bath, where they added their spicy aroma—and their burden of dried blood. The water was distinctly pink, now. Off came her gray silk tunic and trousers, so much tougher than their delicacy suggested. Normally, she would let them be cleaned and aired, but now she would roll them up and take them away to do herself.

Finally, she raised her sword and held it on both hands, pommel on her right and blade on her left. She knelt and lowered it into the water.

"By the sacred tree," she said, "I have done no wrong."

She felt the vibration as the sword—or her hands beneath it, she could never decide which—discarded all residue of the fight.

She withdrew the weapon and slid it, spotlessly shining, into its scabbard. The water it left behind was clear and pure—cleaner than it had been to start with.

Unbinding her waist-length hair, the startling color of scraped carrots, she lowered herself into the bath.

"Three times, I attended her," the girl said, pouring thick soap into Casilda's upturned palm. "Three times before this, since I've been old enough to remember, her challenge was accepted. She always won, before. I thought she would always win."

The regret was almost too faint to be heard beneath the simple statement of fact.

The girl scooped up water in a wooden cup and poured it over the warrior's back-tilted head, then worked soap into the bright hair.

"She told me if she ever lost, it wouldn't be for lack of will. She said I should attend the winner as I attended her, if the fight was won with honor."

Casilda ducked into the water to rinse. When she came up, the girl had raised her head and Casilda looked into her eyes—proud eyes—blue eyes—deeply blue, the living eyes of the dead champion.

In our village, female warriors are chaste.

And if one fails in her vow.... If she carries her "shame" to term and gives birth to a living reminder... the child is taken and used as a servant? The warrior becomes a village champion, forced to challenge all comers to mortal combat? She looked into those eyes and understood she had just been bathed by the daughter of the woman she had killed. And the child knew it.

Before she could speak, the chief's voice sounded outside the hut, ordering someone to be silent.

"My wife is here. May she enter and prepare your food?"

"She may enter. You may not."

"The warrior speaks and I obey."

The chief's wife shuffled across the floor as if her sight were poor. A muffled sob, a smothered groan escaped her.

It was this woman, Casilda realized, who had cried out at the news of Audris' defeat.

"Help her," she said to the child.

She regretted the order a moment later, when the woman hissed, "You!" The child yelped as if hurt.

Casilda hurriedly dried herself and dressed in fresh silk from her pack. She twisted her baby-fine hair into a knot at her nape and pushed back the screen.

The wife of the chief was a young matron, her eyes swollen with tears.

The warrior took pity on the woman's grief, until she saw the bruise on the child's upper arm. An expert in reading wounds, she recognized a savage pinch.

Still, she kept her voice gentle as she asked, "What was your champion to you, woman?"

The chief's wife spat into the fire, her face twisted with loathing. That was the only answer she gave.

Quickly, the woman mixed flatbread and rolled two translucent rounds onto the top of the oven. She chopped a mara root next to them and left it there to soften in the heat, flipped the bread, and swung a stew pot from its place above the coals.

Casilda had made many a quick meal for herself; she could see she would be on her way within five minutes. She put on her armor and sheathed sword, lashing her casque to the travel pack. By the time she was dressed, the woman had two bundles wrapped in pepperbark leaves and tied with mara vines.

The warrior folded her arms when the woman tried to hand them to her.

"I was promised a prize."

The woman bit her lips.

So that's her trouble, Casilda told herself. It isn't the champion she hates to lose—it's the prize.

The chief stuck his head in at the door. "I have it with me. May I bring it in?"

With her hand on her sword, she said, "You may."

A boy strode into the hut, a travel pack over his shoulder. Casilda guessed him to be around six, but he had a dignity of bearing many kings would envy. His hair was thick and black; his face was a miniature of the chief's wife's, even to the swollen, red-rimmed eyes. Those eyes, the color of wet ashes, stared blankly, in odd contrast to his assured manner.

"Here is your prize," said the black-haired man. "My son. The son of a chief."

The chief's wife groaned and wrung her hands.

"I will not take your child," Casilda said.

"Look!" said the chief. He raised the short sleeve of the boy's tunic, showing a red and blue tattoo of interwoven vines. "This is my mark. All the traders know it. Whoever owns my son can claim special trading status with us. Our pottery and woven cloth are much in demand. My son is a prize of value. Or keep him for yourself. He's been trained to serve a warrior. He'll make a good squire for you."

Trained to serve a warrior. To serve Audris? Audris' daughter here, their child there....

"Take him," Audris' daughter said. "Please. If you leave him, they'll kill him."

The chief's wife crossed her arms, holding her own shoulders as if to restrain herself from rushing to her child.

Casilda read the truth in the woman's body, in the chief's eyes.

"Why?" She asked them all, but knew it would be the girl who answered.

"Because he's blind. They would have killed him when he lost his sight, just as they would have killed me at birth. My mother bought my life by agreeing to challenge every passing warrior who would accept a fight to the death. As long as she lived, I would live. When the chief's son lost his sight—"

"A curse from the gods!" the chief shouted.

His wife, to whom the shout had been directed, shouted back. "Because you spared the warrior and her spawn! You cursed our son!"

As if they hadn't spoken, the girl went on, in her clear calm voice. "My mother and I bought his life by trading me for him. While she lived, he would live and I would serve. Now that she's gone—" The girl's eyes flickered, the only sign of emotion she had displayed.

"I'll take him, then. Give him the food to carry. We leave immediately. Say your goodbyes, boy."

His head turned toward the girl. His proud young face was pale. "Goodbye," he said. "You and I and my mistress your mother will meet again, under the roots of the sacred tree. Until then, I envy you."

The chief's wife said, "Here. Take the food." She pressed the bundles into his outstretched hands. Her fingers strayed to caress his, but he pulled away.

"Corrupted!" the woman growled. She glared at the chief. "More of your doing."

The chief stood away from the door, the relaxed, contented smile back on his face.

Casilda could read him now: The gods' curse was leaving the village. She had rid them of the impure warrior and was taking his imperfect child. She was quite the benefactress.

She placed a gloved hand on the boy's shoulder and they left the hut.

As they entered the forest beyond the settlement, she felt freed of a strain, as if the air of the village had become difficult to breathe. "I am Casilda. Where I come from, we guard our honor, but give away our names."

"My mistress told me the real world worked like that." His voice was vague, as if his mind were on something else. "My name is Cecilio."

"And the warrior's daughter? What is she called?"

Bleakly, he said, "She was Izella. She was my only friend. She would talk to me. She would give me sweets and toys she made out of scraps. My mistress loved her. I loved her."

Casilda shook his shoulder gently. "Don't put her in the past. You may meet again. She isn't—"

She stopped, her hold on Cecilio's shoulder stopping him, too.

"You traded places," she said. "She *told* me you traded places. I heard, but I didn't understand. With her mother gone and you gone, they'll kill Izella. Won't they?"

He nodded, tears reflecting the green of the leaves, the green of her armor.

She dropped her travel pack.

"Wait here."

Though she ran, the path to the arena seemed endless.

They were back—all the adults, and the older children—lining the arena's rim. One figure stood in the center. Izella. As Casilda shouldered her way through the ring of villagers, three stones struck the child, one of them drawing blood from her cheek.

The warrior stood behind the girl, her gloved hands protecting the delicate face, the deep blue eyes.

"Stop!" she commanded.

"Outlander!" the chief shouted. "Our ways will not be mocked! We have been more than lenient with our law-breaker. We have been more than compassionate toward our living curse. What we're doing now, we have to do. How dare you interfere?"

"A *warrior* broke your law. It's your *own* child you call a curse. And yet it isn't a *warrior* you stone. It isn't *your* child in this circle. How dare *you* use me to give yourselves an easy mark for your hatred?"

The chief's gaze swept his people. When he had gauged their mood, he said, "Very well. Let the gods take you both."

He nodded. Casilda heard the thuds of stones hitting her armor, was buffeted by blows from all sides.

Then she was on her hands and knees, her head spinning and blood running into her eyes. She reached forward and pulled the fallen child under what shelter her armored body could afford.

She drew her sword.

"You can't," Izella said, turning to look up at her. The girl's face was a mask of red and dusty brown. "You can't raise your sword to them. They aren't warriors."

"They aren't unarmed, either."

"They aren't warriors."

Thud! Thump! They were using larger stones, now.

"Your life is worth more than my honor," Casilda said.

"Not to me."

"Well, *mine* is!"

Young people! Casilda thought.

She placed her sword on the ground and concentrated. The blade dulled with frost. A web of crystals seemed to explode along the ground. Before the villagers could cry out or step backwards, the web had caught them, running up legs and along fingers, slowing their hearts and locking their muscles. The rime on the sword hissed away, and the blade shimmered. The sandy dust around it melted to pebbled glass. Sand fused in a line from the point of the blade, moving slowly, then faster and faster, in a wandering path between the huts, straight to one hut, no different from the others, unless the carvings of the eave work held some meanings of authority to the villagers. She grinned as she heard the *whump!* of sudden conflagration.

Casilda stood with some effort and sheathed her sword. She held out a hand to Izella, who frowned.

The warrior flapped her fingers in an irritable demand that her hand be taken. "I didn't *raise* my sword to them," she said. "Did you see me *raise* my sword?"

The girl, with a slow smile, shook her head and took the offered hand.

The warrior pulled her up. "They'll recover, as soon as we're out of sight. Your friend is waiting. So, unless you have anything to keep you here...."

In the forest, the girl and the younger boy embraced, and the girl shed the first tears Casilda had seen from her. They moved quickly, Casilda carrying Cecilio, until they were beyond the village territory and a little way past that.

A high vantage point with a stream bubbling through it seemed a good spot to stop and eat the food Izella had helped prepare.

While the warrior and the warrior's daughter washed away the blood and dirt, Izella told the boy what had happened.

"And now," the girl said, "we're going home."

Casilda stopped, her face half-done. "Home?"

Izella pulled a handful of leaves from a nearby bush and rubbed a patch of mud from Casilda's discarded armor. "Your home. Every warrior has a village or an estate. Which do you have?"

"I have an estate. A small one. Not far from the foot of this range, as it happens. No more than a week's walk. But why would I take you there?"

The girl looked smug, as if she had been asked a trick question she could see through. "You won't want to drag us with you, young as we are. I know that. We'll need training."

"Training for what? What 'we'?"

"We." Izella tossed away the leaves and put an arm around the boy's shoulders. "Izella and Cecilio, apprentice and squire of the Warrior Casilda. That's who we are, isn't it?"

Absently, Casilda finished cleaning her face.

"Yes," she said, after a moment. "Yes, I suppose that's who you are."

SKIN AND BONES

by *Heather Rose Jones*

When Heather Rose Jones wrote a bio for *Sword & Sorceress XXI*, she had just turned in her PhD thesis and was temping for Bayer as a technical editor. She now works there permanently as a discrepancy investigator. (She says she's essentially an industrial detective. Something happens that shouldn't have and she has to find out what, why, how, who, and all the rest, then figure out how to prevent it in the future and determine whether it affected product quality. And as dessert, she gets to write thick, juicy reports.) She's had her first book published, *Baby Names For Dummies* (under the pen name Margaret Rose) and has joined the 21st century with her own web site at heatherrosejones.com.

This story evolved out of a plot-brainstorming session with her friend Sharon, where a question about the "rules" of the skin magic led to a cascade of "what ifs." Given that she's been writing Skins stories since *Sword & Sorceress XII*, it's probably time to work out the rules for the magic involved.

When the Marchalt of Wilentelu summoned me, I came— not for fear, but because I had bound myself to his service for a time. And when the Marchalt asked a question, he was used to being answered quickly. But I hesitated when he asked if I knew anything of a village of skin-changers five days' ride east through the hills.

"You know I mean no harm to your people," he said sharply when the pause had grown too long.

I answered as carefully as I ever did. "Harm or not, if they don't care to be found by outsiders, it isn't my secret to share. But truth to tell, I don't know. There have been a few Kaltaoven from time to time in the marketplace, but it isn't polite to ask of their homes if they don't offer. Even we can only find each other by rumor sometimes."

He gave a bark of laughter. "Come. Walk with me away from all...these." He waved his hand to take in the guards and servants, clerks and waiting officers who always buzzed around him in the Shalen—his hall of office—like bees in a hive. Then he led me out into a private garden where the only buzzing bees were in the flowers.

It was a hot day so I slipped the cloak of wildcat fur off my shoulders and draped it across my arm.

"Are you never without that?" the Marchalt asked—but teasingly. It had become a joke between us.

"But I never know when you may need my services," I joked back. And then more seriously, "It reminds them—" I nodded back toward the hall, "—who I am, that I am your skin-singer, your Kaltaoven witch."

He grunted in acknowledgement then went straight to his business. "When I was new to the king's service—twenty years back or more, long before I was made Marchalt—I was given the task to survey the extent of the king's lands in Anwella. My quarter was the uplands from where the hills overlook the river back as far into the unknown lands as the king's hand might reach. And on that survey I came across a village of skin-changers, of Keltowin." He never had learned to say it correctly.

"They laughed at the thought that the king in Mergenel might have a say over their lives; and I may have been a green puppy, but I had the sense to laugh with them. But that was when I first had the idea...." He gestured at me—or more accurately, at my skin-cloak. "There was an old man, Emeen his name was—the one who put the magic in their skin-cloaks. He asked for stories of the wider world and gathered the children around to hear them. Now, it wasn't as if I'd traveled the world myself, but I could tell stories. And I thought, if I could have two of these people in every company of soldiers, I could.... Well, best not to speak too loudly. But I asked if any wanted to follow me into the king's service and see more than their little sweep of hills. There were one or two interested I think, but nothing came of it at the time. We had stayed too long already. But when we left, the old man whispered to me that if he were thirty years younger and free to choose...but he was their only skin-singer, and his duty bound him."

The Marchalt stared at nothing for a moment then shook his head. "I always hoped I'd planted a seed there, but who was I? Not even a captain of my own troop yet and no one to be listened to. When the king put the keeping of Wilentelu into my hands, I tried to find them again, but the village was deserted, and we didn't have the luck of stumbling across them again. But you, perhaps, will make better luck."

"What message would you have me take?" I asked hesitantly.

"Ashóli, this is nothing against your services. I have no complaints. But I've grown too used to having skin-changers around. Some day the road will call you back—you and your companion—and it will be easier for me to let you go if there are others to take your place."

I couldn't help but be reminded of the bargain I'd had to strike to convince him to let my predecessors leave. And it hadn't escaped my notice that somehow it was never convenient for my Eysla and me to leave the city at the same time.

"You know my needs well enough," he continued. "You know what I expect and what I offer. Find them. Tell them, and see if any are interested." He didn't need to add that if I were persuasive enough my own interests would be served as well.

⋘⋘⋙⋙

"How long will you be gone this time?" Eysla asked me sleepily after the candles had been blown out that night.

"Not long. Two, three weeks. I suppose it depends on whether they are hidden or have just drifted elsewhere. And on how they listen to the Marchalt's offer. I don't think he expects anyone to return with us at once, just to listen and consider."

"Us?"

I sighed. "*That* is what will slow me down. He's sending two of his men with me—not guards, I think, just other eyes and ears. But that means we'll travel at a horse's pace."

Eysla snorted in mock insult and I had to laugh. "Your brother may breed fast horses, but wings are faster across hilly land. So until he breeds horses with wings, I'll call them slow."

She was silent for a moment, but I knew better than to think she was angry. "Ashóli," she asked. "How many are there? How many Kaltaoven?"

I propped myself up on one elbow to look at her in the faint moonlight. "Why?"

"I know your clan. And Laaki, your teacher, and her adopted sons. But their families are dead or lost. And the family whose place we took here. And this village of the Marchalt's. But that isn't very many. So many places we've been where they'd never heard of skin-changers. What if...?"

A shiver ran through me as I counted along with her list, but it passed. "You forget my mother's kin—she was a stranger to my clan. I've never met them, but they're out there somewhere. And here in Wilentelu there have been a few Kaltaoven travelers. More than the Marchalt's men know about. With our skin-cloaks packed away we look enough like everyone else. And what's more—" I stroked her nose in the way I always did when teasing. "—if there weren't enough interesting strangers showing up from time to time, why, we'd all have to fall in love with *sálen*, with ordinary humans, as I did."

But Eysla's words rode with me in the days that followed as we made our way over hillside tracks and stony fords, following the Marchalt's careful map. Back at home, secrecy had been an unquestioned habit, but since I'd left on my wanderings I'd grown less cautious and had taken little hurt from it. And yet it was different for Eysla and me. We could slip away and run if we needed. Laaki told darker stories of jealousy, greed, and fear, and what could happen when you'd put your heart into a house of stone and your children were hostages to the turning of fate. Today I had the Marchalt's protection, and if there were people in Wilentelu who feared me enough to harm me, they feared him more. But what of tomorrow? I'd seen enough of the king's court in Mergenel to know that not every *talodesh* had a Marchalt of similar quality.

When we found the overgrown foundations of the village's clan-hall and traced the ghosts of old fields in the pattern of the meadows I put away my favorite cat-skin cloak and took out a cloak of falcon's feathers. Halkun and Kers had hobbled the horses to graze and begun to make camp, but they stopped to watch me change. A skilled skin-singer can put on any skin without needing to know its song, but I chanted one anyway. It made for a better show.

"*Kael-keol i'éle i'óe,*
"*Yetaovog v'tev.*"

⋯⋯⋯⋯

In the end, it took four days to find the new village: one for each point of the compass, with no luck until the last. But I saw no signs that they had tried to hide it. Indeed, the northern edge of their planted lands lay along a travelers' track continuing further up into the hills and beyond. Clearly they had no objection to surprise visitors, so I returned to collect Halkun and Kers before making myself known to them.

It was a larger village than the one I had grown up in. I counted maybe forty buildings besides the large clan-hall. And an even more welcome difference from my childhood home was the crowd of children who swarmed out to meet us. Each one of a proper age wore a well-crafted skin-cloak. New. None of the fading and roughness that spoke of hoarded family heirlooms. I remembered too well the meanness that was bred by the lack of a *byal-dónen*'s skills.

The children were followed at a dignified distance by a group of five men and women, and it was to them that I made my courtesy. "My name is Ashóli of a clan near Ganasset, but I come as the messenger of the Marchalt of Wilentelu, as do these men." I introduced my companions who were bearing patiently with not understanding a single word.

One of the older men stepped forward—he wore a cloak of cinnamon-colored bear skin and he introduced himself as Laeno. "I wondered if we would see you here some day."

When he spoke, I recognized him. He was one of those who had entered the city gates with his cloak hidden in his baggage. For that reason, I hadn't claimed an acquaintance at the time, although our eyes had met and recognized our kinship. "An invitation would have brought me sooner," I said, trying to convey respect for their privacy rather than reproach. "The Marchalt remembers this clan with friendship from when he was a young man. And he honors the memory of the *byal-dónen* you had at that time—he gave the name as Emeen, but I fear his tongue isn't skilled with our language and he may have meant Amyen." I hesitated in confusion as sharp glances darted between them. One man turned so pale I thought he might be sick. Clearly I had trodden on a sore toe, but how I couldn't guess. I pressed on with what seemed a safe compliment, nodding towards the children. "My compliments to your current skin-singer, I can see the signs of great skill. I hope that I will be allowed to pay my respects while I am here."

"That may not be possible," Laeno said in a closed voice. "But we can offer you food and warm beds, and we will listen to the words of your Marchalt."

೫೦೩೫೦೪

That first evening, as their custom dictated, we were fed and entertained but business was set aside. The next day word went out to those working further afield, and there was more of a true feast in the clan-hall for all who gathered. The words the Marchalt had sent were fairly few—I was the message he wanted them to hear. So I told stories of the errands and tasks I was sent on, of the types of work that made a Kaltaoven valuable to a man with power.

"And what is he like, this Marchalt?" they asked. "Does he deal fairly?"

I'd been expecting the question, but was still groping for an answer. I couldn't say that I trusted him, other than to be what he was. We had come to be on easy terms, but I knew their limits. But there was one thing my people understood. "He will drive the hardest bargain that he can," I said at last. "But he will not break it once it is made." I could hear sounds of approval and see a few nods.

It seemed, in the end, that the Marchalt's errand might come to bear fruit. But on one point I was still waiting. The *byaldónen* had not come to this gathering with the others. I'd looked closely around the hall and seen no one that they gave that deference to. In telling my tales they had learned that I shared the skill to sing power into skins. If I held to the oldest customs, it would be an insult for me to be refused a meeting. Yet it was curiosity, not pride, that made me ask again, only to be met by the same prickly pushing aside of the matter.

The next day we settled down to more ordinary business. The Marchalt's men had brought gifts, politely disguised as goods to trade, and I left them playing bargaining games with a few of the Kaltaoven who shared enough of their speech to play. For my part, I put on feathers and was shown more of the lands they had made their own in this wilderness. Then there was time to speak more closely with a few of the younger men and women who thought it might be worth some years of exile to see more of the world before settling down. And more than one questioned me about other clans, other wanderers—and there was more than one soft glance thrown in my direction. It was not only adventure that might lure them into strange lands.

I asked again that evening if I might pay my respects to their skin-singer. We would be leaving in the morning and my curiosity was now an itch. Again I received an answer that was not an answer and I lay awake that night chewing on my mystery. At length I gave up on sleeping and put on my cat-skin against the cold and padded out along the moonlit path, enjoying the scents and sounds my human senses could not catch.

The sounds of an argument caught my ear, and I would have gone another way, but someone was speaking of their *byaldónen* and I paused, cupping my ears forward to catch more of it.

"She must meet him." And then something indistinct. A younger voice saying, "You promised me it was the last time." Something about no one else being ready. The younger voice was louder, but it sounded more like fear than anger. "One last time. And in return you let me go with them in the morning—to this place called Wilentelu." There was a long silence then and I nearly turned away to my bed, but then the voice came again, slowly as if nearly asleep. Brief and with an old, formal feel to it, but unmistakably a song of power.

"*Ada-gaom ebe-gyam; ebe-kael-gyam adye.* I am thy bones; be thou my skin."

Another voice then, saying, "Go fetch her."

I scampered back to the place they expected me to be, drew off the cat-skin, and did my best to pretend to be drowsing. Shortly, a voice called from the doorway, "Ashóli. Ashóli, wake up. The *byal-dónen* would speak with you."

I rose and followed, with my guide explaining, "He is old and has been ill. Do not spend his strength in mere pleasantries."

It was like a strange dream. They brought me into a small house, lit only by a pile of coals on the hearth. The old man sat wrapped in a heavy cloak patched together of all manner of skins, nodding as if in sleep. My guide touched his shoulder saying, "Ashóli is here to see you."

He stared at me without focusing; his hands clutched and stroked at the cloak he wore, as if he were working his craft. "Ashóli," he repeated and the word was slurred as if by drink. I was suddenly embarrassed, knowing they had wanted to hide this from me.

"*Byal-dónen,*" I said, not having been given his name, "I wished to do my courtesy to you. I have seen your cloaks throughout the village and have rarely seen such fine work."

"Ashóli," he repeated again. "I thank you." And then, as if a curtain were drawn aside, his eyes focused and he truly *saw* me. Something flashed across that gaze briefly—hope? Purpose? And then his eyes closed again and he shuddered.

My guide pulled me away. "Enough, let him rest."

I wanted to ask what his illness was. I wanted to know why he had no students to take the burden from him. I wanted.... But I was a stranger as of yet, and I had already bullied them into revealing this weakness to me. I let it go.

ଔଓଽଓଌଠ

In the morning when we had packed and saddled the horses, I pretended to be surprised when a young man was presented to me as a companion for our journey. A woman who I took for his mother presented him to me. "Daolesh has decided to bargain his services to your Marchalt. May he travel with you?"

I nodded, taking in the fox-fur cloak he wore. "Daolesh, can you ride?" I had seen a few horses around the village, but that was no guarantee among people more used to being, than using, animals.

He ducked his head and said, "A little."

"Then we can share," I said, "and take turns in skin-form. Give Halkun your bag to carry and see if you can keep your balance back here." I patted the pad behind my saddle, hoping that the horse would behave.

He handed over a small sack of his things to be strapped on, made his goodbyes, put on his skin, and leapt to the horse's rump. There was a brief argument between the two of them as to his presence, but in the long run his lighter weight in skin-form would be carried easier than as a man.

ⰌⰍⰎⰁⰄⰃⰑ

With one or the other of us in skin-form while moving, I had few chances to ask the questions that puzzled me. Kers took it upon himself to begin teaching Daolesh more of the speech of Wilentelu when I was the one wearing fur behind the saddle—or taking briefly to the skies. That first evening I tried to draw him out, but on any question touching on the affairs of his clan he was silent and for the time I let it be.

Our return was swifter than our road out. How could it not be, given that we knew the way this time? I remembered my thoughts the first time Eysla and I had topped the rise of one of the hills bordering the great river's valley and seen the green fields rolling endlessly into the distance and the startling solidity of Wilentelu sitting where the river bent—as if the river itself had changed course around it. When the same vision appeared, Daolesh exclaimed aloud and we stopped a few minutes to rest the horses and let him look. From there on, he and I rode double in the human way and I told him an endless stream of things it would be useful for him to know in the city. More, perhaps, than I should have poured into him at one time. By the time we rode in through the gates he was stretched as tight as a cornered hare.

"Don't worry," I assured him. "Remember that you're an invited guest. That means as much here as it does at home."

That reassurance was off the mark, as things came to pass. We went first to the Shalen. It was expected, though I would rather have returned straight to Eysla's arms. And we were expected—the word would have been passed as soon as we were seen riding down from the hills—but the welcome seemed a bit cold.

When we came before the Marchalt, he gave only the briefest of glances at Daolesh and asked, "Where is Eysla?"

The question made no sense and I stared at him.

"Two days ago she disappeared. From your house...from the city, for all I can tell. I wonder that—"

Fear loosened my tongue. "How can you have lost her? You have her watched when I'm away—we both know you do. Were your men asleep? What is the use of all your walls and gates if she can be taken from under your noses?"

He stayed me with a wave of his hand. "That answers my first question. But for the second, who might have taken her, and why?"

All I could think was that our home might hold some clue, and with nothing that passed for asking permission I strode from the hall, trailing the remainder of our party in my wake.

The house seemed untouched, with no more disorder than if she had stepped out for a moment. I went first to the chest in the bedroom where she stored her skin-cloak. Eysla wasn't yet enough of a Kaltaoven that she wore it everywhere, but if she had left with a purpose—word from her brother perhaps?—surely she would have taken it. No, the horse-skin lay folded neatly as it always did. And then I saw the carved token laid on the covers of the bed and snatched it up. It would have meant little to the Marchalt's men.

"What is it?" one asked.

I turned instead to Daolesh, demanding fiercely, "Do you know this?"

"It's a *gelkov*," he said uncertainly.

"No, do you *know* it? Do you know who made it? Why it was left here?"

He shook his head mutely.

I turned to the others and explained, "It's a trading token. The message can be read as 'You have something I want; I have something you want.' Whoever left it...they took Eysla."

"And what of this boy?" the Marchalt asked. "Is this about him?"

I shook my head. "I don't know how it could be. We saw him take leave of his kin. There was no secret about it and no complaints." Only that strange night-time argument. "Search our bags," I demanded quickly. "I swear we came away with nothing that wasn't honest trade."

The baggage had been left back in the Shalen, so it was back there again in a crowd and then everything was dumped in a heap on the floor. There were the usual bits of clothing, remnants of travel food, tools and trinkets, and from the bottom of Daolesh's sack, a small tied-up bundle of leather.

He cried out when he saw it. "No! No, I swear I didn't... I wouldn't...."

I heard terror in his voice, but the Marchalt's men heard guilt and seized him fast.

"This is what they think I took?" I asked him.

Daolesh nodded. "It must be. But I swear...."

"Don't swear me any oaths," I snapped. "Just tell me how it comes to be among your things if you didn't put it there. Was this a trap for you? For me? Was it meant to poison the Marchalt's bargaining?" I paused for a moment to explain for the others when Daolesh had no answers for me.

"What is it?" the Marchalt asked curiously. "One of your magic cloaks, I assume."

I bent and picked it up—and nearly dropped it again. The leather was smooth and buttery-soft, but like nothing I had handled before. And as I touched it the power trapped within it reached out to meet me, like a whispering or muttering in my head. I untied the knots and shook it free. A short cape, just enough to drape around the shoulders. A thing of power, definitely, but strange... and wrong somehow. Daolesh had recognized it, but when I brought it close, he struggled against the hands holding him and clearly feared to touch it.

"What type of skin is this?" I demanded. "Who wears it? Why is it important to you?"

"*Nalyev*," he whispered. "It is *nalyev*." And that was as much as I could get.

Once again I translated for the others. "It is...I don't know a good word for it...a secret? A mystery? Something it isn't appropriate to speak of, not to strangers. He is—" I tried to think of a way to explain that would make sense in this place. "—under a vow not to speak of it." I looked the Marchalt in the eye. "You could force him, but it would mean the end of your plans among his people." He scowled, but nodded.

I was far less satisfied and turned back to Daolesh. "This is no longer a private matter for your clan. Someone has made it our business as well. They have taken my *kólvyashen* and I will do what I must to get her back." I wadded up the cloak and stuffed it roughly back into the empty sack and took some pleasure to see him flinch at the handling.

"Ashóli." The Marchalt was back in a mood to command. I knew it sat ill on him to deal in matters he had little power over. "Ashóli, this isn't king's business. I will do what I can, but it won't go as far as sending armed soldiers after these people."

"No need," I said. "They *want* to bargain."

"Is that why they came here and took her? Why they didn't simply go after you in the wilds?"

That brought me back enough to smile. "You're learning more about us than I thought. Yes, better an elaborately-staged bargain than a simple demand. It's our custom." I thought hard for a moment. "They won't be far away—unless they have a skin-singer with them, they can't carry her inside someone else's skin against her will. And to get here so soon before us, the ones who came must all be wearing feathers."

The Marchalt picked up the trail of my thoughts. "So they can't have carried her off any further than humans can carry an unwilling captive. No horses have gone missing, of that I'm certain."

I frowned, trying to imagine myself in their place. "Not within the walls, I think. Too confined, and too unfamiliar—although at least one will have been a regular visitor here. They knew where to go and what Eysla meant to me."

"Will they have been watching for you to return?"

I thought of soaring high over the river valley on falcon's wings and nodded. "If we ride out of the gates, they will find us."

I was not as confident as I sounded, but it all made sense. They wanted a trade, not a feud. And I wanted Eysla back, not revenge. But I also wanted to understand what had happened. And that skin...it bothered me. Laaki's stories had told of people who worked evil magic—not Kaltaoven, different kinds of power-working. If this skin-cloak were not of Kaltaoven make, I would have thought it might belong in those stories. And that made me tempted to cheat on the bargaining. Or at least to try. So before we went out of the city, I took a small thing—a very small thing—from the skins I had worked, and borrowed the use of one of the Marchalt's scribes.

⊗⊙⊗⊙⊗⊙

There were seven of us who went out for the bargaining. The Marchalt changed his mind at the last moment and stayed behind. I think he felt his rank was not well served if he could only stand by and watch. But he sent not only the two men who had traveled with me, but another pair to keep watch over Daolesh and one whose duty was only to carry the skin-cloak and not let anyone take it by force or trickery. They were armed, but only with swords and knives, not with anything that might threaten a Kaltaoven in bird-skin at a distance.

The guess that they would be close by was only partly true. We rode out the gates and down the road towards the river landing at a slow pace, looking carefully in all directions. But the sign came from above, in the form of a raven that circled three times over our heads and then soared south following the river bank two hours ride to where the land grew marshy and grown over with willows. To come this far they must have stolen a boat, but that would have been easier than stealing horses. There were only three that came out to meet us, all in feathers as I'd guessed, but none wore a raven cloak and Eysla wasn't there, so I knew there must be more in hiding.

"I don't see that you have anything to trade," I began, breaking several of the rules of the game. "Until I see Eysla and take her hand, we have nothing to discuss." And for our side, I nodded to the man carrying the sack who pulled out the skin-cloak for them to see then put it away again.

They couldn't have expected to begin so one-sided, which gave the advantage to me. I suspected that I had another advantage—I was certain both Daolesh and I were innocent of the theft. There was more waiting and Eysla was brought forth from the screen of willows. The man who wore the raven cloak was Laeno, who had a bear's skin when I had seen him last—the man I had seen once in Wilentelu. This was important enough that someone had lent him both skin and song to speed ahead of us.

Eysla hadn't been taken easily. I could see bruises, and they had her hands tied before her and kept one hand on the rope. And her appearance was heralded by a stream of curses that were wasted on her captors as the only ones she knew that were strong enough were in her cradle-tongue. But she was sound and whole and she shouted when she saw me.

I pushed past them to greet her, giving no one a chance to forbid it. I took her bound hands and kissed her cheek. And as I slipped that small furred something into her curled fingers I said, "It's not quite as bad as that time your brother locked us in the store room, is it?"

She was completely bewildered for a moment, then closed her fingers tightly around the tiny pelt and smiled. "No, not quite that bad. But I'm not sure I remember how you got us out of that place."

"Try your best," I said, completing the confusion for anyone who was listening.

CONTENTS

Custom demanded that we sit, and so we spread our cloaks and sat with the damp from the river rising around us. Custom demanded that those who had offered to bargain begin, and so I waited, which was a hard thing. Laeno took the lead. He wasn't the eldest of those present, but I thought all this may have been his plan—certainly his knowledge must have been behind it.

"*Byal-dónen*," he began, giving me the title that courtesy demanded. "Ashóli, since you have no patience for the old ways, perhaps we can finish this quickly. You have something of ours; we have something of yours. The trade is even. What do you say?"

"This was never an even bargain," I countered. "You know what Eysla is to me—the one to whom I've bound my heart. I know nothing of what this skin is to you."

"You don't need to know, except that we value it."

I interrupted, as if I found what he had to say of little importance, "And you have taken pains—and caused pain, I see—to steal away something of mine, but I never took your property. I have it now, but I did not take it. Look to those around you and ask who put it in Daolesh's baggage. He never took it, and neither did I."

"Liar!" one of the others cried.

From where he sat behind me I heard Daolesh answer, "No!" before he was hushed.

"This is no ordinary skin-cloak," I continued. "When I know what it is, then we can begin bargaining for it." I stood and began walking away, leaving the rest in my party to scramble after. I half expected to be called back but the call didn't come.

⊛⊛⊛⊛⊛

It was well after dusk when we came again to the walls of Wilentelu, with one gate left open waiting for our return. My body and heart were both exhausted. I had succeeded in giving Eysla a possible key to her prison, if she could learn a skin-song from writing rather than speech. But I was no closer to solving the riddle of the skin. Was it foolish—to believe something was wrong and that it was my task to fix it? Had I gotten too much in the habit of fixing other people's difficulties? The Marchalt asked me much the same thing when we reported our failure to him.

"Maybe I'm wrong," I admitted, "but maybe this skin came into my hands for a reason. I can't think of any profit that would come to anyone from all this trouble. Maybe I'm supposed to solve the riddle."

"If what you want is to know what sort of skin it is, why not just put it on?" the Marchalt asked. "You say you can wear any skin you choose."

It was a simple enough answer. I can't say I hadn't thought of it, but that wrongness worried me. I took the cloak out of the bag and shook it loose. Daolesh made a strangled noise—no one had thought to do anything else with him, so he was still dragged willy-nilly into all our councils. "One last chance," I told him. "Is there something I should know?" He shook his head—not in answer but in refusal. With a sudden motion I threw the cloak around my shoulders and reached out to take on the spirit within it.

෴

Through a fog, I could feel myself falling to hands and knees. But they were still knees, and still hands. My mouth moved, and another's voice came from it saying, "Be as quick as you can. The knife is sharp, and I am a dead man already." Then pain, like a fire wrapped all around me, and a voice chanting words of power. I flung the skin from me and heard screaming in my own voice.

෴

The pain remained crawling all under my skin, but faded slowly. When I opened my eyes, I saw the high ceiling beams of the great hall of the Shalen. And the Marchalt kneeling beside me with a stricken look.

"Emeen," he said. "You put the cloak on and you turned into Emeen. He looked just as he did twenty years past, but that can't be. He was an old man—by now he must be..."

"Dead," I finished, struggling to sit up. "Dead. But not before *that* was cut from him." I pointed where I had thrown the crumpled wad of leather.

I heard oaths and curses from many of those standing nearby, and the one of the Marchalt's men who had carried the sack and handled the cloak started scrubbing his hands against the fabric of his clothing. I leaned on the Marchalt's arm to rise and staggered over to Daolesh. "What have you done? Do you know what they did to him?"

The haunted look in his eyes was answer enough but he said simply, "I've worn that skin. I and others before me. They have to drug us first, so we can bear the pain. But not so much that he can't work."

Things started falling into place, but still I asked, "Why?"

He almost shrugged. "He is our *byal-dónen*." Telling some part seemed to have freed him to tell all. "I was a child back then but we all know the story. Our luck turned bad and then worse. Four students he had trained over the years to make skin-songs and all had died: a fever, one attacked by a beast, one in childbirth. Then he fell ill with a growth gnawing on his insides. This—" He gestured at the skin-cloak. "—was his answer. A way to preserve his skills for us to use. But only he could make the skin-song, and he could only make it while he still lived. I don't think he knew...." Daolesh's voice had dropped to a cracked whisper. "They say...they say that he put the knife in his own brother's hand. And they say that the day after, his brother put on feathers and rose out of sight and then fell back to earth as a man."

After that, no one spoke for a long time.

ഗരുൽ൞

W e rode out again in the morning, down along the river to where the willows grew thickly. I and Daolesh and the Marchalt, and two of his men for guards as was his custom. They came out to meet us looking angry and bitter and I knew Eysla had succeeded in working the song. I reached out with my power to call her and stood waiting until I saw a small movement in the grass at my feet then bent over to cup my hands under a small brown mouse. I whispered a song to reach under the skin and then it was Eysla who filled my hands and arms. I kissed her proudly before pushing her back towards the Marchalt's waiting men and turning to bargain.

"I did not steal your skin-cloak, it stole itself." I waited until the denials and accusations had faded before I continued. "And it is with the cloak that you must make your bargain." With a shuddering breath I unwrapped the cloak and put it again around my shoulders. It was much harder this time, knowing what would come, but I knew why I had been chosen. I sang the song I had overheard that night in the village, "*I am thy bones; be thou my skin.*"

The fire wrapped around me again and I heard a voice crying out, "Forgive me! Forgive me, but let me die!" And when I could bear it no more I shed the skin and stood gasping as if I had run seven miles.

When the roaring in my ears faded I could hear birds singing in the willows, so quiet had everyone become. "Let him go," I echoed.

"We have no choice," Laeno said quietly.

"You have plenty of choices!" I shouted. "You are not the only Kaltaoven in the world. He was not the only *byal-dónen*. Is this what we come to when we hide in our villages and fear to speak to each other in the marketplace? You could have a dozen children with the skill to craft skin-songs and you would never know it because you cling to this... this sad abomination. My own clan wasted a generation doling out second-hand skins. Why do we never *talk* to each other!"

I had heard Eysla behind me translating my words for the Marchalt and the others, and as if summoned he now came forward with one of the Kaltaoven phrases he had mastered, "*Geol-dón pen-deah.* I would make a bargain."

I walked away to cool my anger and heard him distantly speaking of making Wilentelu a meeting place for all Kaltaoven. Of sending word out and bringing people together. Teachers, traders, skin-singers, suitors. And there would be work for those who chose to take it on. I remembered what he had said to me that day in his garden, *If I could have two of these people in every company of soldiers....* And I wondered what might be set in motion today.

After a time, Laeno came to me where I stood apart. "Is it something that can be done?" He seemed unsure what to ask. "To... to release him from the skin?"

"I can try, if that's what you choose." I was growing ashamed of my earlier words.

"We didn't choose this," he protested. "Amyen chose his own path."

I wanted to ask whether Daolesh and the others had made their own choices to wear the old *byal-dónen*'s skin. But perhaps they had, given the choices they knew. "I can try," I repeated.

They brought me Amyen's skin-cloak and I sat holding it in my lap. There was a part of the death-song that we sang when skinning a beast for a cloak that bade farewell to its spirit. And there were songs for funerals, for sending human spirits on their journey. I took the part of a skin-song that bound the power into the skin and turned it inside out, then braided the three together. As I sang it I could feel unseen things loosening inside the cloak. It only needed one last push. I whispered, "*Lyev-gaal adye*, it's time to go," and the cloak crumbled to dust between my fingers. A breeze lifted the dust of Amyen and scattered it across the grove and up until it disappeared against the sky.

CROSSWORT PUZZLE

by Michael Spence & Elisabeth Waters

Michael Spence and I have been collaborating on and off since we were in high school. Our first joint published story was "Salt and Sorcery" in *Sword & Sorceress XVI* in 1999. Eight years later, we're still trying to get Stephen to pass his Senior Ordeal, but Michael has finished not only his comprehensive exams but also his dissertation ("Secular Theology in the Fiction of Harlan Ellison") and graduated with a PhD in Systematic Theology—all with the indispensable support of his wife, Ramona, who can outdo Melisande at kick-hubby-into-motion wizardry any day, and to whom this story is appreciatively dedicated. So at least we've made some progress, even if only in the Real World. Since graduation Michael has ventured into Internet-based radio, storytelling, and criticism; see his website "Brother Osric's Scriptorium" (http://www.brotherosric.com).

The Internet may bring the world together, but, as this story reminds us, the world has been coming together for a long time. Be careful what you allow in; there are things a lot worse than computer viruses.

If looks could bring on a dark and stormy night, Laurel's glower would have plunged the College into a monsoon.

She slammed the door to the resident advisors' house behind her. *Stupid sister-in-law,* she thought. *Bad enough that the rest of my family thinks I'm some kind of whiz-kid mage; now she thinks she has to balance them out by calling me an idiot. Idiot. Idiot!*

She made it as far as the statue of Tertullian in the northwest courtyard before she slumped to the ground.

Moonlight cast the statue's shadow on the stone pavement, and in that shadow she sat, face in her hands, wrestling to hold back tears.

I'm such an idiot.

ᘓᘓᘔᘖᘓᘔ

"Laurel, how could you do such a thing?" Melisande was normally the most serene young woman whom Laurel had ever met. She never, ever lost that calm. No wonder Stephen loved her. But now she was shaken, and her eyes, catching the late Monday afternoon sun, looked as though they were trying to find their way along the narrow line that divided scorn from horror.

"Thing? What 'thing'? I saved time. I got the job done faster. That's what they're always talking about in business classes, isn't it? 'Work smarter, not harder'?" Laurel sat on the sofa, feet up on an ottoman. The living room was small, like their previous apartment, but whereas that had been cramped, this was cozy. Chairs and the sofa formed a half-ring opening onto the fireplace; lamps adorned the wall in strategic locations; flowers decorated the long, narrow table behind the sofa and the low, wide table in front of it; and—*mirabile dictu!*—the only books in the room were Melisande's. Stephen's had been banished to his new, adjoining office. "We could have been poring over those applications until tomorrow afternoon, there were so many!"

"Yes, I understand," her sister-in-law replied. "But there's a reason why you're supposed to check each item. Yes, it takes longer. And yes, sometimes you want to pick them all up and throw them out the window—"

Laurel broke in, just as Melisande was pantomiming that throw. "Which would be interesting, given that I work in the Customs Building, right on the harbor, and my office window is over the water."

Melisande's arms halted mid-mime and returned to her lap. "Um...all right. So then it's not only out of your hair, it's either on the bottom or waterlogged and ink-run. Neither of which does a thing for your performance record. So—" She paused, and an eyebrow went up. "Tell me again why you chose the Customs Ministry for your internship?"

"It was either that or the Signal Corps—and tending signal fires and testing scrying relays is *such* fun. And since—thanks to Edward—Stephen can't use his magic, he can't pass his Ordeal, and Grandmother's *geas* still keeps me here until he does pass it. If she hadn't modified it to allow Stephen and me to go into the city during the day, I wouldn't be able to do an internship at all, and there's no way I can go overseas. So I thought I'd let overseas come to me." She grimaced. "They said there'd be clerical work, but I just thought that would be good experience. I hadn't done that much of it before, and now I know I never want to do it again!"

"Do what again?" came a tenor voice from the opening front door. They turned to look as Laurel's manipulative, snake-in-the-grass, thoroughly-ex-boyfriend Edward entered with a double armload of packages, followed by her brother, Stephen.

Laurel scowled. "Oh, you do *not* want to hear the answer to that."

Melisande quickly spoke up. "Laurel was having a difficult day at the Customs office."

"Desk work?" said Stephen. "I suppose so. You never really liked that sort of thing."

"Well, it's been okay, if boring. But your wife thinks I caused some kind of disaster today."

"Oh?" said Stephen, as Edward headed toward the kitchen with the packages. "Which kind?"

His wife threw a small cushion at him. "You're not helping. She's screening applicants for commercial agents, and I'm afraid she may have let in something that we don't want."

"And that would be—"

"Crosswort."

From the kitchen came Edward's voice. "Crosswort?" He returned to the sitting room to join them. "I hope you're not saying you don't want that," he said. "We just brought you several ounces of it for Easter dinner."

"Well, no, I don't mean that. Of course we need it. I mean maybe some bad crosswort. One of the applications Laurel approved today sounds suspect."

"But why?" asked Laurel. "It didn't *look* suspect."

"That's the problem. You didn't give it a long enough look." She turned back to her husband. "Last Thursday they assigned her to process application forms from people who take dock-side delivery of imported goods on behalf of the people who actually ordered them."

"And...?"

"She was supposed to do a reference check on each of them, using the customs library."

"Good grief," said Stephen. "Each one?"

"That's why the job requires a mage and why I'm interning there," said Laurel. "I do a Summon-and-Bind spell that links the form to the appropriate books, and use the spell to check each entry on that form. Normally it works fine, although it takes time because I have to do a spell for each item on each form. It's quicker than pulling down the different volumes and flipping through them—but it still adds up to a lot of time, since all agents have to submit fresh applications for each shipment."

"So she tried to reduce that time, and—"

"Well, today I had to! We got a huge pile of applications, and there just wasn't any way I could get them all done by the end of the day. I'd still be there, working on them, and probably wouldn't get finished until tomorrow afternoon, by which time there would be still more of them."

"Hmm. So you shortened the checking routine," said Edward. "How?"

And you have the right to interrogate me? she thought. *Boy, what a relationship this turned out to be. Boy meets girl, girl likes boy, boy uses his Talent to damage girl's brother's brain during brother's Senior Ordeal, girl realizes boy is basically pond scum. Your classic romance story. And since his atonement for his crime is to help heal the almost-permanent damage he did to Stephen, I'm still* stuck with him.

Shooting him a glare, she said, "I figured that the primary entries we were concerned with were—" She ticked them off on her fingers. "—*who* was applying, *what* they were importing, and *where* it came from. So I worked up a batch spell that would go through all the applications, focusing on those three items and looking for—" She manually counted again.

"—whether the agents had criminal records or complaints against them, whether the proposed import was on the Ministry's list of goods we don't want brought in, and whether the country it came from was on our we're-at-war-with-or-soon-will-be list."

Edward nodded. "Seems like an efficient method to me. I like it."

She scowled. *Trying to make nice, are you? Forget it. You took away Stephen's magic, and now you have to help him get it back. But even with magic, you'll never have me for a friend again.*

Stephen looked thoughtful. "So far, so good. What's the trouble?"

"That's just it. It *isn't* so good," said his wife. "Tell us about the crosswort application."

Stephen's eyebrow went up. "Imported crosswort? Someone doesn't like the domestic kind?"

Edward joined in with, "How did you notice it, if you were using a batch spell?"

"I did look at them, you know," Laurel retorted. "I didn't just cast the spell over them sight unseen." To her brother she said, "From what I understand, we don't have a large surplus. If everyone in the realm makes Easter lamb with the traditional recipes, we might wind up with a shortage afterward. It seemed to make sense to me. But that's why I remembered it."

"So what was the problem?" asked Stephen. "The agent?"

Laurel shook her head. "Hawick & Scarborough— reputable, well-established. 'Official Supplier to His Majesty,' et cetera, et cetera."

"And they'd be acting for..."

"The Royal Guard. That's another reason I remembered this one. It isn't every day something royal crosses your desk. I assume it's for Easter dinner."

"So what's the problem?"

"The problem," said Melisande, "is that the shipment is coming from the province of Dreismark in Grestig. *That's* what the problem is."

The men wore blank looks. Edward said, "So Grestig exports crosswort. Doesn't sound unusual. What's the problem with that?"

Melisande harrumphed. "With Grestig, none. But the soil in Dreismark province has something in it that does strange things. Flowers are okay, but some of the other plants.... You know that normally crosswort has a slight euphoric effect?"

"That's right," said Edward, "in larger amounts it's used to treat melancholia. I suspect that's also one reason it was ordained for the traditional Easter dinner—besides adding flavor, it would also lift everyone's spirits. So?"

"So," Melisande shot back, "for a few people this herb has the opposite effect—they wind up deeply melancholic, even suicidal. And when it's grown in Dreismark province, that would be *all* people, not just a few. This stuff is dangerous—possibly deadly."

Stephen let out his breath slowly. "Wow. And the Royal Guard ordered this? Wouldn't they know what they were doing?"

"I have no idea; I don't think it's common knowledge. Maybe there's someone in the Guard who does know; and then the question becomes, who and why? Or maybe Hawick & Scarborough placed the actual order, and *they* need to be checked out. But whatever the case, someone's about to be seriously drugged—and today's events helped to make it happen." She looked at Laurel. "Your 'batch spell' looked for political problems, but not for *health* problems. I'm sure the Customs library has documents on them—and the regular check would have caught this."

The room was silent for a long moment, and then Edward said, "So what can we do about it?"

He looked at Stephen, who shrugged. "I don't know. Ordinarily I'd go to Lord Logas; he's the advisor to the King. But he and Lady Sarras are away for the next two weeks with an investigation of their own. I suppose we could talk to Grandmother—"

Melisande broke in. "Not unless we have to. I don't think Laurel would want her here—her comments would probably start at 'idiot' and get stronger from there—"

"*Idiot?!* Is *that* what you think of me? Well, you can—" Laurel couldn't finish the sentence. She jumped up and ran out the front door.

Stephen turned to his wife. "What was that?"

Melisande's face was ashen. "Oh, no. Oh, no. And I'm supposed to be the Sensitive here. I didn't pay attention—"

"She'll be back." Stephen held her as tears started down her face and Edward beat a hasty retreat, closing the door quietly behind him. "Um...if that thing about Dreismark isn't common knowledge—and this is the first I've heard of it—how do you know about it?"

She searched her pockets for a handkerchief, found it, and wiped her eyes. "My mother the gardener." She buried her face in his chest. "What do we do now?"

"First we wait for Laurel to come back."

"Do you think she will?"

He smiled, lowering his face to kiss the top of her head. "You forget the *geas*. She has to."

Melisande laughed softly amid her tears. "Thank the Lord for domineering relatives."

଼ଃଠଃ଼

The next morning, Tuesday, Laurel—who had indeed returned, but had gone straight to bed without a word to anyone—got up, dressed, and immediately went to work so she wouldn't have to face anyone over breakfast. Her day was quiet, without incident—and also without any shortcut techniques. It was early evening before she made it back to the College and home, where Melisande was waiting for her with tea and cookies.

She was on her second cup before she was able to speak. "I'm sorry."

"No," her sister-in-law replied. "*I'm* sorry."

"But I *was* an idiot. Grandmother would have been right."

"That's why. I should have realized that you'd feel that way and react badly to the word." She smiled. "I'm sorry. Really in-Sensitive of me."

Laurel heard the capitalization and chuckled. "But typical of me, I guess." She stood, went over to Melisande, and gave her a hug. "Thank you."

Sitting down again, she asked, "So what do we do? I checked, and the shipment comes in tomorrow. If we can't do anything about that, we have only three days to figure out an answer before Easter Sunday."

"Can the authorization simply be cancelled?"

"No, it's in the system now. We can't handle this through paperwork."

"Is there some kind of transformation spell that could change the crosswort into something else?"

Laurel snorted. "I'm a Strong talent, but not *that* strong. You're talking world-class wizardry. Besides, I've no idea how to make it selective; I'd wipe out all the crosswort in the realm."

Melisande put down her cup. "Council time. Stephen!"

He came in from his office-library and, seeing his sister, went over to give her a hug. "How are you feeling?"

Laurel smiled sheepishly. "Idiotic. So what do you think we can do about this?"

"Well," he said, "probably the first thing we need to do is get word to the palace and the King's guard detail." At that, Melisande's eyes widened and she started to say something, but he went on. "If this is really a plan to make him and his household vulnerable, then somehow we need to shore up his defenses."

Again his wife tried to interrupt, but he continued. "And that means contacting the chief of the Palace Guard and filling him in. If we can get him to believe us—"

Melisande waved her hand in front of his face. At last he stopped, and his eyes followed her hand as she pulled it back. "Why," she asked, "are you talking about the Palace Guard?"

"Well, if the King's in danger, doesn't it follow?"

"It might, if the attacker were already there. But that's unlikely. He'd have to get past the Harbor Guards first, then the City Guards, and then the Guards at the palace gates. All that *before* he could even get inside the palace grounds. Laurel, how much crosswort is in that shipment?" Laurel told her, and she said, "There. We're talking about several companies at least. Whoever's planning something, they aren't in place yet."

Laurel nodded. "And they're feeding their weapon to

Guardsmen throughout the city. 'An army marches on its stomach,' after all. It is what it eats."

Stephen looked thoughtful. "Well, yes...but I'm guessing the saying means that the food had to get *to* the army, not that it had to be high-quality."

"We've all heard about how good army food isn't," said Melisande. "*Q.E.D.* But Laurel's right; it's the supply lines. That's how we've got to tackle this."

"Hold it," her husband said. "Suppose we do get to the right people. How do we get them to believe us?"

"Oh, you just realized that?" she said with a smile. "I have an idea."

⳥ⳛⳏⳡ

Wednesday Laurel reported to work as usual and, after an hour of general office work, went to her supervisor's office. She found him at his desk, which was neat as the proverbial pin, as tidy as he himself. *My brother could learn so much from him...* "Would there be a problem with my leaving early today?" she asked. "My brother and sister-in-law want me to go to the Tenebrae service with them."

He set his mug of tea onto a coaster and regarded her over small wire-rimmed spectacles. "Is your work finished for today?"

"Um...I estimate that I have about three hours' work remaining. If I haven't finished it all, I'll stay late tomorrow. Would that do?"

"Hmm. Normally I would prefer not to stretch things that way. Still," he sighed, "it is Holy Week. Do what you need to do."

She nodded and smiled. "Thank you."

⳥ⳛⳏⳡ

That afternoon, Stephen stood on a hill between the harbor and the Royal Guard headquarters, peering through a small telescope.

Not far from the headquarters entrance, Melisande watched her husband put down the telescope, pick up his cloak, and wave it over his head. "That's it," she said. "The ship just finished off-loading. We have about forty-five minutes before the delivery gets here."

She regarded the headquarters gate some fifty feet away. "I read the sentry as very, very cautious, even suspicious. This could be tricky."

"You're 'reading' him?" asked Edward. "How's that?"

"Did you forget that I'm a Sensitive? It's like body language and facial expression, only with something added." She chuckled. "I noticed it first with Stephen, but I thought it was just a husband-wife thing. Now I think Stephen believes that I always know what he's thinking. It makes him nervous."

Edward looked steadfastly forward. "No comment whatsoever."

"It's odd," she said, as they walked up the short rise toward the gate, "but I think Stephen actually likes not having his magic for a while. I didn't expect that."

"We talked about that," Edward said. "He sees it as an opportunity to look at things from the perspective of the magic-blind; he says it's educational. I also suspect he relishes the chance to let Laurel have all the magical responsibilities—but please don't tell her I said that. She barely speaks to me as it is. If we can't restore Stephen's Talent, I expect she'll never forgive me."

"Mm. I'd like to think she's better than that. But," Melisande spoke the time-honored words, "we shall see."

They continued walking. "I really would rather not do this," he said for the second time in as many days. "You know what it did to your husband. Do we want to risk anyone else?"

"If I knew any alternative, we'd try it," she replied. "Besides, if we don't act, Sunday will come and we'll have every Guardsman in the city unable to perform his duties. Which risk would you rather take? We can't avoid both."

They reached the gate, and the sentry moved to block their way. "Sorry. The compound is off-limits."

"We need to speak with the quartermaster," Melisande said earnestly.

"I'm sorry. Not without entry clearance."

There was an awkward silence. Edward was evidently still building up his courage. Melisande frowned inwardly. It was now or never....

"There you are," said a voice behind them. "I thought I told you to wait for me."

They turned, and saw Stephen approaching them in Guard uniform. "Good day, Yeoman...Kilroy," he said as he scanned the name stitched on the sentry's tunic. From a pocket he took a paper and handed it to the man. "I think you'll find this in order."

The soldier examined the paper and handed it back. "Yes sir. Uh, sir, we've been told that all visitors must be escorted while they're on the grounds. Will you be doing that?"

"Indeed I will," said Stephen. "Carry on."

"Yes sir." The sentry stood aside. "Enjoy your visit, Captain Rafton."

The three passed quickly through the gate and into the compound. Reaching a nearby administrative building, they turned and walked behind it, out of sight of the gate.

Edward stared at Stephen incredulously. "How did you conjure up a uniform and papers? You haven't shown the slightest hint of magical response for three months!"

"Who said it was magic? Don't you think I might have found a real captain and just taken them?"

"You could have..." said Edward, "...but you wouldn't. I've known people who would do that, but you're not that sort. Besides, you wouldn't want to risk showing them a familiar name with an unfamiliar face."

The face and uniform abruptly changed into an entirely different appearance. "I guess he wouldn't have, at that," said Laurel with a grin. "Glamours. I love them. I'm glad I knew the proper markings of rank, though."

"Amen to that. Um... 'Rafton'?"

"I don't know," Laurel said, shrugging. "It just sounded right."

"It would be better not to show that particular face for much longer," Melisande said. "Stephen might need to come here on legitimate business some day, and we don't want people asking the wrong kind of questions. Can you change the face a little?"

Edward broke in. "I have a better idea. A little something Stephen and I put together. He did the theory; I worked out the application." He pronounced several syllables, at the same time weaving a pattern of gestures. "There. It isn't exactly invisibility; we call it a 'move along, nothing to see here' spell. Hopefully, that's what they'll do. They won't notice us."

From there to the main kitchen, things mostly went well. No one did seem to notice them, not even Yeoman Kilroy, whom they were surprised to encounter not once but twice during their walk through the compound. "Must've just come off watch," Edward remarked.

There was one awkward moment, when they passed someone standing outside an office door, preparing to knock. Rather than knocking, however, the man suddenly charged forward, smacking full force into the door and falling backwards on his rump.

They watched him rub his nose, looking thoroughly puzzled. "Oops," said Edward. "I think the 'move along' part needs a bit more work."

oଓେଅଃ୫ର୦ଃଠ

In the massive kitchen, they identified the voice of the chief cook with no problem. A minute later they could see him, berating another cook for sloppy handling of a meat grinder. "Gentlemen," said Melisande as they approached, "would you come with us, please?"

Silence fell. The two men looked at each other quizzically, as if asking, *Who is this and how did she get in here?* But they came.

By the time the group reached the corridor outside the chief quartermaster's office, the delivery cart was pulling into the outer drive. Melisande had everyone wait until the driver entered the anteroom, then motioned them outside and toward the cart.

It didn't take long to find what she was looking for. "Sir," she said to the chief cook, "If I understand correctly, this crosswort is for the troops' Easter dinner. But I have it on good authority that it comes from the Dreismark province in Grestig. Would you please examine it?"

With a bemused expression, he pulled one of the burlap packages open, reached in, and took a small handful of the root. He broke a piece apart and sniffed at the break. "Hmm," he said noncommittally. He scraped some of the root from the newly-exposed area with a thumbnail, ground it between his fingers, and put it to his tongue.

"You're right!" he said after half a minute's consideration. "This is—" Laurel's ears burned with the description he gave it. He turned and strode off, back to the quartermaster's office.

Melisande and the others followed him and the second cook as far as the anteroom, where the assistant quartermaster sat at his desk, head bent over his work. From the office within they heard the chief cook proclaiming, "I don't know who ordered this, but it's not going to the men!"

"And what," another voice came back with equal force, "do you propose to do about Easter dinner? You're the one who told me it has to have crosswort in it!"

A third voice said, "Sir, we might be able to find another source. I don't know. But I agree, this shipment is trouble."

Silence. Then a weaker voice: "Don' look a' me! I just drive th' cart. I don' know *where* th' stuff comes from."

The three mages listened, intrigued. The assistant quartermaster put the documents he had been working on in the desk drawer and casually stood, taking his cloak from a hook. Melisande frowned at his back, and nudged Laurel.

The chief cook's voice could be heard again. "We'll have to get it somewhere else, then. But that poison gets burned, now! Unless you really *want* to see the men standing around doing nothing at best—killing themselves at worst!"

The front door closed a bit too loudly as the assistant quartermaster made his exit. Edward, suddenly picking up on what Melisande had noticed, said, "Hey, wait a minute!" and took off after him.

They found the two of them outside, sprawled on the drive, Edward's arms around the assistant quartermaster's waist in a flying tackle. The man hollered, "Will someone get this moron off me?"

"All right now," said the quartermaster. "What's going on here?"

The assistant quartermaster, looking up from the tangle, shouted, "This numbskull started chasing me!"

The quartermaster looked at Laurel. If he had any modicum of patience left, it was fast evaporating. "Well?"

Laurel looked at Edward, who was clearly hoping she would explain. "I have Hawick & Scarborough's agent application," she said, holding the document that had masqueraded as their entry clearance. "His signature is on it."

"But it would be there normally, wouldn't it?" said the assistant cook. "He does the clerical work, after all."

But he did choose that exact moment to leave, Laurel thought. She saw the question in Edward's eyes, and nodded.

He inclined his head slightly in acknowledgement. Turning to the assistant quartermaster he said, "If you know anything about this, I suggest that you TELL THEM." Although his voice sounded casual, Laurel knew that it was reverberating through his captive's mind.

The man told them.

⊗⊗⊗⊗⊗⊗⊗

Stephen met the three some distance from the headquarters gate. "Well?"

"Mission accomplished," said his wife. "And I don't think anyone will give us much thought." To Laurel she said, "We'll see if any inquiries get back to Customs later, but it's possible that the matter may be ignored, since nothing came of it. You do get a lot of applications, after all."

Laurel sighed. "And if not—well, I'll have to deal with it, that's all." She looked at Edward, and in her head she heard words she had said at mass that morning, words she said every day when she said the Lord's prayer.

Stephen chose that moment to hand a small package to his sister. "I found this in town and thought it looked nice. I hope you like it."

What? A gift, and you're not giving it to your wife? You're slipping, brother dear. But then she opened the package and found a silver pendant that bore the very words she had been thinking about. *Dimitte nobis debita nostra sicut et nos dimittimus debitoribus nostris.*

Forgive us our debts, as we too forgive those who owe us.

And you say you have no magic. Well, maybe I can't forgive him yet for what he did to you, but I'll try to forgive what he did to me.

She turned to Edward. "Thank you." If the words were a bit forced, at least she said them. "You did something really good today. I know you didn't have to do this."

He smiled at her. "Yes, I did." To Melisande he said, "But really, there wasn't that much to do. Laurel took care of the sentry at the gate; otherwise I'd have had to give him a hard nudge—but I didn't. The 'nothing to see' spell was non-invasive. The cook's decision about the crosswort was his own; I had nothing to do with it. The only one I had to use force on was the assistant quartermaster."

"I'm glad to know that," said Melisande. Then she looked him squarely in the eye. "You don't have to feel guilty about *him*, Edward. It was needed. You probably saved quite a few lives. And what you did brought out the truth."

He frowned. "I tell myself that...but I keep running into the end-justifying-the-means problem again. Is what I did today any different from what I did to Stephen?"

Stephen clapped him on the shoulder. "Be glad we have the opportunity to ask that question. For what it's worth, I don't know what else we could have done—for this we needed you. At least the end *was* right and good. It's like the difference between poisoning someone and giving them medicine to heal them. Literally. And I," he said, stretching, "am hungry. It must be teatime."

Laurel laughed. "Sounds good to me. Come on, I'm sure there's a teahouse around here. You saved my internship; I'm buying."

ଔଔଈଔ

As they left the teahouse, they heard a familiar voice. "Good evening, Captain Rafton! I hope you enjoyed your visit." They turned to see Yeoman Kilroy coming toward them, his eyes on Stephen.

Stephen raised an eyebrow. "I beg your pardon? I have no idea what you're talking about."

Kilroy surveyed the group, noticing for the first time that a new young woman was present. "Right, sir. Not a word." He put his finger to his lips, gave Stephen a broad wink, and turned to disappear into the crowd.

"I declare," said Melisande. "That man is *everywhere.*"

Stephen just stood, staring at the yeoman's retreating back. "Will someone please tell me what in the world that was all about?"

Melisande took his arm and steered him toward the road back to the College. "I'll explain it later, dear. Let's go home."

FAIRY DEBT

by T. Borregaard

T. Borregaard has a Masters of Science in Archaeological Materials (which she says only *sounds* interesting), and is listlessly engaged in PhD studies that seem to revolve, in equal measure, around ancient pottery and torturing undergraduates. She is freckled in person, organized by nature, and obsessed with motorcycles, medieval kilns, corsets, blue hair, and tea—one of which (or probably all in combination) will eventually be the death of her. Her work appeared previously in *Sword & Sorceress XVII*, and she has a story coming out in the anthology *Sails & Sorcery*. She's written the obligatory unpublishable fantasy series (there are plans for a rejection-slip database), so is optimistically writing a paranormal stand-alone novel instead. While she is godmother to several cats, she would like it known that she does not actually keep one of her own. Take that, stereotypes! Certainly the creatures in this story are anything but stereotypical.

"I won't do it, I tell you!" I was mad, and I had a right to be.

Aunt Twill sighed dramatically and swished about where she sat in the lake shallows. Aunt Twill did most things dramatically. She was the naiad of the Woodle River, and it was a bit of a dramatic river, full of small but excited waterfalls.

"Unfortunately, it's your debt to pay."

I crossed my arms and glared at her.

She explained as though to a child, "Your mother was rescued from certain death by a human King. That's a great debt of honor for a fairy to endure."

"Yes, but these things are easily taken care of," I insisted. "All mamma had to do was show up at the christening of the King's firstborn and grant it something humans care about." I tried to come up with examples. "You know: bravery, beauty, boxing, beekeeping. That sort of thing."

My aunt fluttered her webbed fingers about her face in exasperation. "Yes, but your mother missed the christening and, most inconveniently, died."

I sighed. I was only a nestling when she died, so I didn't remember much. They say it had to do with a golden barbell and a frog, but it was all kept very hush-hush.

My aunt reached down and gathered a few water lilies about her. "So the princess has no fairy godmother, and you can't grow wings." She began braiding the lilies together into a chain with her magic. "An honor debt warps wings, you know, especially in the young."

I fluttered my four stubby wings angrily. They weren't of any use to me, but I liked to flap them for effect.

"Debts carry forward to the next generation," my Aunt continued, draping the water lilies about her neck. "You owe the princess."

"But I've no working magic without working wings. Nothing to pay her back with."

"You have your Child Wishes."

I snorted. A fairy's Child Wishes had power over only one thing, usually to do with human domestic life. Evolutionarily speaking, this ensured that mankind would always find value in sheltering fairy offspring. My cousin, Effernshimerlon, could manufacture safety pins as needed. My Wishes improved baked goods. For a fairy potluck I once made banana puff cupcakes so delicious they caused a visiting earth dragon to cry. Earth dragons are fond of cupcakes. They have notorious (and very large pointy) sweet-tooths.

"What could I do with my Wishes?" I asked Aunt Twill. "Make sure the castle's bread rises perfectly for the next one hundred years? Is that sufficient payback?"

I was being facetious, but my aunt took me seriously. She bobbed about slightly in the lake water and the lily chain fell from her neck.

"No, I don't think that's enough. Not unless the castle's bread is cursed."

I raised my eyebrows at her. "What do you suggest, then? I can't be fairy godmother to the princess; she's my age, that'd just be ridiculous." I felt as though everywhere I looked there was a troll with a club pointed at me, and no troll pacifying-porridge in sight. Was there no way to pay off my mother's debt? "What do I do?"

Aunt Twill shut her damp old eyes. I could practically hear her thoughts sliding about in her head, like water over pebbles. Very slow water over very large pebbles. She opened her eyes after a long time.

"You'll have to pay it back the hard way."

"Oh yeah. What's that?"

"Old-fashioned servitude."

CSCRSORU

I packed up and trekked west, away from the Woodle River, toward the Small Principality of Smickled-on-Twee. There lived a king who'd once rescued my mother from certain death. What else was I to do? I wanted wings. What good is a fairy without wings?

I'm tall for a fairy (all that naiad blood) but really very short for a human. I come up to about the knees of the average adult male. With my stunted wings tucked under a tunic I looked like a hunchback. There's only one role at a royal court for a short hunchback—court jester.

I knew it would all end in tears the moment I saw the hat.

"Do I have to wear it?" I asked the High Jester in shock, staring at the ghastly thing.

He jiggled his own at me. A three-pronged confection of red, blue, and green plaid tipped with silver bells. "Required uniform, I'm afraid," he replied. Clearly he'd gone into the profession out of physical necessity as well. He was extremely tall and decidedly skinny, with a great beaked nose and a very, very low voice.

His hat was elegant compared to the one presented to me. Mine had four prongs and was worn so that one prong always fell directly in front of the eyes. Two of the prongs were yellow with pink spots and the other two were purple with white stripes. Mankind may have made uglier hats, but I seriously doubt it. And don't even get me started on the subject of the bells. The darn thing was covered in them.

I put it on, and the accompanying checked green pumpkin pants and doublet (which, next to the hat, seemed quite somber), and slouched after the High Jester toward the Throne Room.

"Your Majesty." The High Jester bowed low to the king. Too low, however, for he toppled forward, stumbled, and sprawled flat on the floor. The assembled courtiers laughed appreciatively. "May I introduce our new Least Jester?" He waved a spade-like hand in my direction from his prone position.

I had fairy grace at my disposal even if I didn't have working wings. So I did a flip and two somersaults to end in a bow at the king's feet.

The king nodded at me happily, and the princess clapped. Not every court was lucky enough to have a tumbling jester.

"Why," said the princess, looking at me closely, "you can't be much older than me."

I looked up at this human who held my fate in her hands. She didn't seem all that bad—a little chubby for a princess, and rather graceless. Hadn't she been given *any* fairy gifts? I know my mother fell down on the job, as it were, but this poor thing was practically ordinary! She seemed to know it, too. She slid off her throne in the most humble manner, and bent down in order to properly introduce herself to me.

"Princess Anastasia Clementina Lanagoob. How do you do?"

I came out of my bow. When I stood upright my head ended just below her waist. I reached up and shook her pudgy hand with my tiny one. "Bella Fugglecups," I replied. I couldn't give her my fairy name, of course, too recognizable. Aunt Twill had invented this one as an alternative. It was silly. But so was my hat.

"I shall call you Cups," announced the princess.

"Only if I can call you Goob," I shot back.

The king seemed appalled by this impertinence, but the princess was clearly delighted. The statement made her laugh. Which is, after all, a jester's job.

"Done," she said, letting go of my hand. "Will you teach me how to tumble?"

I looked dubiously at her full white skirts covered in gold beads and silver embroidery.

"Now? All right, but I hope your under-things are as attractive as your outer ones."

The princess laughed again. The rest of the court gasped in shock. The High Jester made a frantic sawing motion across his neck. I had no idea what he was on about.

"Anastasia Clementina, I forbid such an undertaking!" The king rose from his throne and glowered down at the two of us. He was a large sort of human, full of hair, and prone to some kind of disease that made his face go all red and splotchy when he was upset. It was doing so now.

"Please Daddy." The Princess turned big muddy brown eyes on her father. Cow eyes. "I'll change my clothes."

The king sighed.

What I didn't know then was that the princess rarely took an interest in, or asked for, anything. When she did, her requests carried more power. It's a good approach to life, generally getting one what one wants. (So long as one doesn't "want" too often.) I would come to appreciate this character trait greatly over the course of my association with Princess Goob, for all too often we fairies are on the receiving end of demanding humans. Take Cinderella, for example, with her gown, and her coach, and her glass slippers, and on and on. I mean, really! But I digress.

"Very well." The king ceded defeat. He looked at me. "You don't mind?"

I tilted my head way back. "It is my honor to serve Your Majesty." What else could I have said?

I did a back bend, kicked my heels up, and walked away from the two royals on my hands until I'd rejoined the High Jester. Then I flipped to standing.

The princess clapped delightedly.

I bowed to them both.

"Tomorrow at noon, Cups," she ordered.

"Noon, Princess Goob. Noon," I agreed, and followed the High Jester out of the audience chamber.

ೞಞಜೕ

"Do you think it's enough of a service?" I asked Aunt Twill that evening through a small cup of tea.

Her image wiggled slightly in the brown liquid. Normally tea talking is a delicate spell requiring both parties to use bone china, Earl Grey, and silver stirring spoons. But Aunt Twill had a contract with the tea daemons that allowed her conversational access (between the afternoon hours of half-past three and five o'clock, of course) to any cup in the kingdom. (It's a naiad gossip thing.)

Aunt Twill extracted a small gudgeon fish from her hair and ruminated. "I doubt that teaching a princess acrobatics constitutes proper repayment of an honor debt. Though it is a nice thing to do. Why would she want to learn, though? It certainly isn't normal princess-y behavior."

I shrugged. "She isn't a normal princess. More like a normal dairymaid. Poor thing."

Aunt Twill nodded. "Plain ones happen sometimes. I'll do a little research and get back to you on the tumbling. Until then, I'd proceed as though this were not the answer."

I sighed. "Very well, Aunt Twill."

"Oh, and niece," I looked up, "that's a hideous hat."

I stuck my tongue out at her and lifted up the bone china cup. Her face wavered in the brown liquid as I drank down the tea. Fairies invented tea, did you know that? It was one of our best collective spells, until the daemons stole it from us, and humans got in on the idea. Still, it explains my Child Wishes: baked goods go very well with tea.

ೞಞಜೕ

There wasn't much for the jester contingent to do during the daytime at court. Most of our entertaining work was done at night, or at feasts, or at festivals. The rest of the time we were left pretty much to our own devices.

I spent the first few weeks poking about looking for spells or curses I could break: princes disguised as dung beetles or the odd evil loom wight. Nothing. Not a single enchanted sausage. Smickled-on-Twee had to be the most boring principality in the entire province of fairy-kind. The princess was painfully average. The queen had died a perfectly respectable death (by plague). The only thing out of the ordinary the king had done, in his long and uninteresting career as ruler, was rescue my mother. And he didn't seem to remember doing that.

Princess Goob and I became fast friends. She was hopeless at tumbling: far, far too clumsy. But I soon realized the lessons were only an excuse. What she really wanted was the company of someone her own age, and to get out of the castle once in a while. In keeping with these two desires I announced that we really must practice on a mossy lawn every afternoon, so took her through the castle gates and over the drawbridge to a sheep pasture near the moat. There I pretended to show her handstands, cartwheels, and flips. She pretended to try and learn them. Mostly we just lounged about and chatted.

"I always wanted to be a shepherdess," she confided in me one afternoon. "I think I'd be better suited to that kind of life."

I looked at her from my supine pose on the grass. She wore a very plain dress, borrowed from one of her maids, and long brown bloomers underneath, which were supposed to be for riding. She'd tucked the skirt of the dress up on each side and tied a kerchief about her hair. She looked very like a shepherdess.

"I think the role would suit you," I replied.

"That's what I like about you, Cups. No silly pandering or hedging. Everyone else secretly agrees when I say such things, but they all pretend to be shocked. Or worse, tell me what a perfect princess I am."

She flipped onto her stomach and began picking away at the grass. "I never had a fairy godmother, you heard by now I suppose? Shocking thing. Dad spent a good deal of time trying to find and rescue fairies in his youth, hoping to gather honor debt, but it didn't work. So I got nothing."

"You're probably better off that way. I always felt that princesses with all those boosts in looks and manners probably have no idea how real people feel. How can anyone be a good ruler if they have no understanding of those they rule?"

The princess looked at me and nodded. "You're absolutely right, and I want you to arrange it for me."

I sat up, wondering what I'd suddenly gotten myself into: small fairy, big mouth.

"What?" I asked, nervous.

"This 'understanding.' Since I can't learn acrobatics during our afternoons together, I should learn something useful. What better thing is there to learn than the lives of my people?"

I squinted at her. She may have looked nothing like a princess, but she certainly spoke like one. If she kept her mouth shut, we should do all right. It was a bit like the enchanted leading the enchanted, though. The only person less likely to know about the common lives of humans than a princess was a fairy. But an order was an order.

So our afternoon tumbling sessions turned into afternoon field trips. First we visited the shepherdesses (because she really *was* interested), and then the dairymaids. Then we visited the stable hands and the goose-girls, the portrait painters and the gatekeepers. I learned a lot on these journeys. I found the lower-class humans far more interesting than the nobility.

Eventually we ended up in the castle kitchens.

My Child Wishes made us quite the popular visitors there. The princess liked it too. Even without my help she seemed to have a natural talent for cooking. She invented a roasted peacock dish stuffed with dates and sage, slathered in a thick gravy with wild mushrooms and cubed ham, that caused the king to give the entire kitchen staff a raise.

Of course, the staff all knew she was the princess, but they pretended not to, and that seemed to work well for everyone.

Me, on the other hand, they called their Lucky Least, as whenever I was around pastries and breads seemed to turn out moister, chewier, fluffier, and more delicious than when I was away.

"Why is that, Cups?" the princess asked me, dusting flour-covered hands on pure silk petticoats.

"I like baking, so I'm good at it."

"But you don't actually touch anything. You're too short to reach."

I shrugged, a movement made very odd by my hump of hidden wings. "I keep an eye on things. Make sure they don't mess up."

Princess Goob looked at me skeptically, but she let it at that. She'd learned that if she questioned me closely I got all philosophical, so it was better to stop before things got epistemologically out of hand.

CRWEDY

I'd been there nearly a year, and was no closer to repaying my debt, when the peace of Smickled-on-Twee was finally disturbed by something terrible.

It was a festival day and everyone was sitting down for high tea. We jesters were gallivanting about jestering, when an earth dragon waddled into the main banquet hall.

He was a smallish, fat sort of dragon, only about two horses long and probably that many wide, with muddy bronze scales, six sad little horns, lots of sharp teeth, and a sour expression.

Still he was an *earth dragon*, and as such, terrifying to humans. Earth dragons take food seriously, you see. They collect interesting recipes and bags of fizzy lemon candies to stash deep in the recesses of their muddy caves. They also consider humans crunchy little treats of meaty goodness. Other dragons don't care a jot for such things. Air dragons eat birds and collect kites as a general rule, while water dragons eat algae and collect fishing tackle. Fire dragons are the ones who hoard gold. No one is quite sure what *they* eat, though they have a nasty reputation. Difficult to get close enough to find out.

As a fairy, I don't find earth dragons all that bad, but then I'm a fairy. Magic in the blood makes us far too spicy for consumption.

This particular dragon headed straight for the high table. Where he squatted across from the royals and gave Princess Goob a very toothy grin. Princesses tend to be succulent: well fed and soft skinned. It was earth dragons that started the whole "kidnapping of princesses" policy. They like to steal them away and keep them around for late night attacks of the munchies.

The king knew this and panicked. His face went redder than I'd ever seen it, and he began to sputter like an over-filled teakettle.

I snuck under the table to sit at the princess's feet. I could touch the dragon's baby toe from there. It was about the size of my head.

I touched the princess's toe instead. She twitched slightly. I touched it again. She lifted the edge of the tablecloth up and looked down at me.

"Tell your father," I said, "that the only way to get out of being eaten by an earth dragon is to serve it a high tea far better than the one *you* would be."

The princess nodded and her head vanished.

A moment later I heard the king bang hard on the table and call for service.

This dragon was unlikely to be particularly impressed with the king's tea. Smickled-on-Twee was a very small principality and not precisely prosperous. The honey-glazed whole pig with thyme and raisins was not as big as it would have been in the principality of Bugdoon-near-Schmoo. Nor were the great mounds of tiny new potatoes drizzled in melted butter and sprinkled with mint quite as small or as minty as they would have been in Schmoo itself. But the bread was certainly up to par; I'd been lounging about wasting Child Wishes on it all morning. There were huge crispy brown loaves shaped like tortoises and filled with sweetmeats; small round honey-soaked buns rolled in cinnamon; and long skinny cheese-encrusted baguettes. The dragon ate sixteen loaves in all, and I had to sneak away to the kitchen to make sure the second batch came out as good as the first.

The dragon consumed three of the princess's famous peacock dishes, eight racks of lamb smeared with roasted garlic and rosemary, two platters of pork sausage with hot mustard, and several spit-roasted pheasants. Between each course the dragon picked up his teacup and gazed deeply into the murky depths. The fifth time that he did this the princess stopped me when I came in for a bread check and asked me about it.

"He's doing what?" I said.

"Talking dragonish into his teacup."

I looked at the dragon. At that moment he was stuffing his face with a trencher of bacon-and-tomato-stuffed quail. I was suspicious. So far as I knew, only naiads and daemons used the teacup network. What was this dragon doing?

I examined the huge beast carefully. There was something oddly familiar about his markings. Had we met before? I crinkled my forehead in thought. Then I remembered. Once, long ago, an earth dragon had turned up at a fairy potluck. Could this possibly be the same one? I squinted at him: six horns, sour expression...yes, it must be. And if this dragon was talking into his teacup, I bet I knew whom he was talking to.

I snuck a cup of tea off of the high table and retreated into a corner of the room.

"Aunt Twill," I hissed into the cup.

The surface of the tea shivered slightly and Aunt Twill's wrinkled face appeared in the dark brown liquid, looking harried.

"Aunt Twill, what are you up too?"

"Add a little milk will you, dearie? You know the spell is easier in milky tea."

I ignored her and said firmly, "Aunt Twill!"

Aunt Twill had the good grace to look slightly guilty. "He's been asking about your banana puff cupcakes for ages. So I thought, why not just send him along?"

I was shocked. "Aunt Twill!"

Aunt Twill straightened her spine. "Now don't go taking that tone with me, nestling. This is quite the opportunity. The princess is at risk, the castle in danger, and you and your Child Wishes can save the day."

Just then, behind me, the dragon sent up a great roar and tipped over the high table. There was a cacophony of sound as plates, platters, knives, and teacups slid to the floor.

"Gotta go," I said, drinking the tea unceremoniously.

I turned and rushed towards the chaos.

The dragon was yelling in dragonish—a sort of rolling fuzzy kind of language. I don't speak it well myself, but I gathered he wasn't entirely pleased with the meal.

I ran up to Princess Goob. "Stay out of his reach as much as possible and keep feeding him bread. It's very filling." She looked at me with wide eyes and I could tell she really wanted to ask how I knew so much about earth dragons. But instead she just nodded.

I turned to run back to the kitchens.

"Where are you going?" asked the princess in a panic.

"I have to make banana puff cupcakes! Your life may depend on it," I replied.

Strange as that statement was, Princess Goob merely nodded again. That's what I liked about that girl, no silly interfering when there's work to be done.

Once in the kitchen I marched straight up to the High Cook.

"I need to make banana puff cupcakes," I said.

The cook looked at me in a harried kind of way. He had about a hundred desserts all going at once. "At the moment," he said, "the needs of the Least Jester don't particularly concern me."

I stared up at him earnestly. "The princess's life depends upon it."

The thing I've learned about humans is, if you make a bizarre enough statement, they simply don't know what to do. In this case, it was easier for the High Cook not to argue with me. He pointed at a small oven and a bit of counter space in one corner and I went off to find myself a stepping stool so I could use both.

With the help of Ernest, one of the Least Cooks, who was very tall and liked helping me, I managed to gather all the ingredients and get to work. There were only six small bananas, almost completely black and very sad, so I used every last Child

Wish I had on that one batch of cupcakes. I decided to let the earth dragon eat up as much of the other desserts as possible first so that he had very little room left for my cupcakes. That way they would come as a kind of crowning glory to the whole high tea experience.

Eventually evening rolled around, which signified the end of high tea. All the cooks were looking exhausted, there was very little food left in the storage cellars, and servants began to slink down to hide in the kitchen away from the dragon.

I removed my banana puff cupcakes from the oven, popped them out of the pan, sprinkled them with cinnamon and sugar and arranged them on a platter using up the very last of my Wishes to make sure they were as perfect as they could possibly be.

Then I whisked them up onto one shoulder and carried them into the banquet hall. A hush had descended upon the room in my absence. Everyone was looking at the dragon, who was polishing off the last of the raspberry parfait and muttering into his teacup between bites.

"Where are they?" I heard him grumble into his tea.

I inched up beside him and slid the cupcake platter onto the table in front of him.

The dragon sniffed and looked up.

He poked a claw into one of the puffy yellow cakes and delicately popped the confection into his mouth. He chewed for a moment, and swallowed thoughtfully. Then he closed his eyes and sighed contentedly.

"Just as I remember," he muttered to the teacup in dragonish. The teacup chirruped back at him in the dulcet tones of my Aunt Twill. I couldn't hear exactly what she said but the dragon nodded vigorously and replied, "You have a deal."

He poked a cupcake onto each of his front claws, leaving one behind on the platter (for Mr. Manners). Then he turned away from the table and slithered awkwardly out the front entrance, on his elbows to keep the cupcakes from dragging on the floor.

He turned at the door to look back.

"I await my Wishes, little fairy," he said looking directly at me.

I realized what Aunt Twill had done. When a fairy reaches adulthood and trades in child's magic for the real deal, she has a choice as to who gets to keep her Wishes. (How else do you think human wizards got magic in the first place?) Obviously, Aunt Twill had promised my Wishes to this earth dragon.

He left, moving awkwardly across the cobbled stone bailey, out the barbican and over the moat. Soon he was out of sight.

The courtiers heaved a collective sigh, and then everyone, including the king and the princess, stared at me.

I wasn't paying attention because something very strange was happening to my wings. I took off the jester's hat in order to concentrate better. Then I found I had to take off my whole uniform as my wings were starting to push against it. It was a good thing I always wore fairy garb underneath.

Sure enough, in a very short space of time, there I stood in front of the whole court—with fully grown wings!

I looked at the king. He was staring at me in wonder.

"You saved my mother once," I said, "but she died without repayment. So I've been serving your daughter in secret in her stead." I flapped my wings experimentally, and they lifted me easily into the air. I was a little wobbly, but I could stay up and that was the important part. It was nice to look down on people for a change. "My cupcakes have saved your daughter from certain death, so my debt to you is fulfilled."

I looked down at the princess fondly. "Goodbye, Princess Goob."

She grinned up at me. "Goodbye, Cups."

"But wait," said the king, "Don't you have to stay? Be her fairy godmother, make her beautiful and graceful and stuff like that?"

I shook my head. "I could choose to stay if I thought she needed my help. But I think she'll do perfectly fine without me." I thought about all the gatekeeper's daughters Goob and I had met, and the miller's sons we'd laughed with, and the servants who'd helped us in the kitchen, and the goose-girls who'd gossiped with us. "I think there are others who need fairy godmothers far more than princesses," I said. And with one more wave to Princess Goob, I flew out of the castle and away into the forest.

I sent the earth dragon my Child's Wishes by butterfly post the very next day. I also sent him the recipe for banana puff cupcakes. I understand he grew even fatter.

I kept in touch with Princess Goob. Right up through the time when she became Queen Goob. She'd married by then. A rather nice young writer-fellow I found for her, named Adolfus Grimm. They had two children, both boys. I became a kind of adopted aunt, since I had far too many fairy godmother gigs by then to take them on as well. I did tell them about my exploits though, usually over Sunday tea. Fairy-tales, the boys called them. I had no idea they would write them all down. But that's another story.

TONTINE

by Robert E. Vardeman

Robert E. Vardeman is the author of more than 50 fantasy and science fiction novels, as well as numerous westerns under various pen names. *Alien Death Fleet*, written under the pseudonym Edward S. Hudson and reprinted under his own name for the first time, should be coming out the same month as this anthology. For more of his work, see his website www.cenotaphroad.com. He is a lifelong fantasy/science fiction reader and a long-time resident of Albuquerque, New Mexico; he graduated from the University of New Mexico with a BS in physics and an MS in materials engineering, and he worked for Sandia Labs in the Solid State Physics Research Department before becoming a full-time writer.

In this story, he takes the concept of the tontine—which started out as something that vaguely resembled life insurance—and gives it a very unusual twist.

"Let's get it over with," Captain Jonna el-Marran said. She forced her voice to remain level as she spoke to the wizened old tavern keeper, though she quaked inside. The Boar's Spit tavern had gone quiet when she walked in. Ignoring the soldiers in her training cadre had been easy enough. She held her head high, looked straight ahead, spotted the empty chair at the rear where she could have the wall to her back and strode to it as unerringly as one of her arrows. The silence passed quickly once she was seated. The soldiers were celebrating their victory over the Loee and protracted mourning held no place in their world. Better to laugh, joke, get drunk and deny that any of them could have died in battle. As a quarter of their company had before the armistice they now celebrated.

Like Asenthena.

"It is only right," the tavern keeper said, bowing his head to her until it hung under his hunched shoulders. He backed away as if in the presence of royalty and then shuffled to the locked cabinet behind the bar. Jonna had seen fights break out and bulky men slam into that cabinet over the years. It never so much as creaked. She thought that this might be the safest place in the entire country. Nothing could break the ironwood or breach the intricate brass lock. There might have been more to protecting the contents of the cabinet. A spell? Perhaps, considering the contents.

Although she did not want to, she strained to look past the tavern keeper as he opened the cabinet door. On a single shelf within stood three bottles. The tavern keeper's arthritic hand curled around the middle one. Carefully drawing it out, he held it close to his frail body so as not to drop it. Jonna sucked in her breath as he shuffled back and placed the dusty bottle on the table in front of her along with an ordinary drinking cup. She had expected more. A goblet? A chalice?

"You don't have to," the tavern keeper said when he saw her hesitation.

"You want me to."

"I only store the bottles. Nothing more. You are the one who took the vow."

"Has any survivor refused to drink?"

He nodded slowly, his rheumy eyes becoming sharper as memories poured back like a freshet.

"Not many. It is an honor."

"There's no honor in it," Jonna said sharply. She reached out and started to fling the bottle against the wall but stopped when she saw the faded label with four signatures alongside hers. The woman sagged a little, feeling the weight of the years on her. It had been in this inn more than thirty years ago that they had been young soldiers, full of arrogance, ambition and strength, sure they would live forever. It was more difficult for her aged eyes to focus now but the names were as vivid as if they were freshly written. Jonna had been the first to sign the

label, then small, dark, powerful, cocksure Bellarine. Torian and
Freda had jostled each other to be next and had settled their
never-ending argument by signing side by side. The last name
caused tears to come to Jonna's eyes. Asenthena. She had been
the last to affix her name and almost the last to survive.

"You want anything more?" the tavern keeper asked,
starting to back away to leave her to her decision.

"Wait. How is it you were selected to keep the bottle of
wine?"

The tavern keeper shrugged and smiled faintly, the move
almost vanishing in the wrinkles on his leathery face. "It is my
duty to those of you who give your lives protecting us."

"Against the Loee? They were only a problem crawling
from their pits in the last year."

"The Loee. All the others. The corridors of time are long
and dangerous." The tavern keeper turned and shuffled off,
leaving Jonna in a curious bubble of silence. She saw the other
soldiers celebrating their victory, yet she heard none of it. Her
strong fingers closed around the dusty bottle and then she drew
her knife. A quick slash took off the red wax seal around the
cork. She bit down on the protruding end of the cork, tossed her
head and yanked out the stopper.

Jonna had no idea what she expected to happen. Ghosts
rising from the bottle? A sudden rush of cold shouldering away
the heat building inside the crowded tavern? Never had she
spoken with or even heard tales of those in other tontines. They
had to exist. Hers did. And there were two other bottles in the
tavern owner's cabinet.

Jonna realized she was procrastinating. She spat the cork
onto the table. It bounced once and jumped to the floor. She did
not bother retrieving it. There was no need for a stopper since
she would finish the contents tonight. Hand shaking just a little,
she poured a full glass of wine. The heady aroma made her
nostrils flare and brought back memories of the day they had
sealed the bottle.

For a moment she stared into the ruddy depths of the
wine, then took a deep drink. After all the years, the wine
retained its body and color. It slipped easily over her tongue and

down her throat. As she leaned back and closed her eyes, the world began to fade about her and she became...

...Bellarine.

Jonna tensed when she realized she no longer looked through her own eyes but those of her dear friend and sworn blood-sister. Bellarine turned slowly, missing nothing—not even the faint outline Jonna made in her hiding place.

Jonna wanted to cry out, but she dared not. The scene was as acid-etched now as it had been just twenty years ago when she and Bellarine had gone on patrol. Only now she saw it through her friend's eyes. Bellarine had been promoted to sergeant and was in command of the scout unit hunting for the invaders infiltrating from the northland. No one knew who they were but they were deadly, fierce fighters. None had been taken alive for questioning to learn their home country, much less their intentions. Did they come to conquer and occupy or were they simply freebooters?

As Bellarine, Jonna moved forward like a ghost. In spite of her muscular body she disturbed not a single leaf. No twigs snapped under her broad booted feet. Even the birds and other wildlife in the forest accepted her as one of theirs as they continued mating calls and loud barks and yowls proclaiming their territory.

Jonna was startled to realize that she—Bellarine!—was uneasy with her promotion. It had been well deserved and obvious to all in the company. But Bellarine felt Asenthena was a better choice. Jonna wanted to tell her it was not so, that Asenthena was hot-tempered and prone to make poor decisions in combat. Only her skill with a sword kept her alive. But Bellarine was exactly what made a good leader. Calculating, cool under pressure, skilled.

None of that came through to Jonna now. Bellarine saw soldiers moving through the woods and panicked. Bellarine dug her toes into the soft forest detritus to flee. Bellarine crashed full into a northlander and instinctively grappled with him.

Jonna did cry out now. The northlander had been crawling up to kill *her*. Bellarine flushed him and fell on him, rolling over and over as they fought. Jonna tried to look away but could not because she saw through Bellarine's eyes. She felt hot blood on her belly and reached down to wipe it away. It was not hers but Bellarine's. She smelled fetid breath in her face and felt the knife slicing painfully up into her until she abruptly died.

Shaking in reaction, Jonna thrust the empty glass from her and stared at the wine bottle. Four portions remained.

Jonna had always thought Bellarine had given her life that day to save her. Jonna remembered how she had scrambled to her feet and driven her short spear into the back of the northlander who had killed Bellarine. She had evaded the rest of the northlander patrol, returned and told how Bellarine had not only saved her but had prevented a massacre. Even the company commander had not known the northlanders were so close. They had barely strengthened their defensive line when the enemy attacked. Bellarine had been credited with so much. And she had fled out in the forest to save her own life.

Or so Bellarine thought. Jonna was not sure after peering into Bellarine's thoughts and memories of that death day where lay the truth. She poured another glass and drank it down so fast her head spun. Jonna poured another glass and swallowed it, going more slowly this time only because her throat constricted against the onslaught of alcohol.

The world had spun before. Now she felt completely transported, body and spirit, to a day not ten years prior.

"You're not going to make it back to camp," Torian said, kneeling down to stare into Freda's eyes.

"Go on. Fetch help."

"No! I won't leave you. The rebels will find you for certain sure."

"I can't walk," Freda said, "not with an arrow through my thigh."

"It missed the big artery. You can hobble."

"Oh, so you'll support me?"

"Don't I always?" Torian said.

The bickering went on until Jonna's head felt as if it would explode. She saw and heard everything her friends did from within their heads. The rapid changes as they swung about made her giddy, but deep down she knew that under their perpetual argument seethed fear that knew no bounds. Torian was afraid she would fail her friend and Freda feared being less than heroic, in spite of the pain. Jonna almost gagged when a new wave of giddiness struck her—struck Freda.

"I won't lose you to scum like that," Torian said. "They're not worthy of killing you. Only I can do that."

Jonna/Freda looked into her friend's eyes and saw the anguish. The pain from her thigh spread downward so that her entire left leg was little more than a lump of dough baking in an oven. Worse, her loins burned with a fire that refused to die down. The arrow had been poisoned, as so many of the rebel weapons were.

"Then do it," Freda said, her voice low but firm.

Jonna cried out as the words slipped from her lips—from Freda's. With a gasp, she swung from Freda to Torian. Torian looked up and saw the ring of rebels closing in, faces grim with murder and weapons already dripping with blood.

"I can't escape. You can." The words rang in Torian's ears. "Kill me. Don't leave me for them. You know what they do to prisoners. Then escape and slaughter them all!"

Torian looked into the forest and saw movement as the rebels worked to close a circle around her and Freda. She looked down into Freda's anguished face.

"Forgive me, Freda, forgive me! I can't kill you. They'll only take you prisoner. They won't kill you. I swear, I'll rescue you before anything harms you."

Torian saw that she gave no false hope to Freda.

"For once," Freda said softly, "stop arguing. Please."

"By all that's holy, forgive me," Torian said. She slid her dagger free and drove it expertly into the armhole of Freda's armor. The woman died with a gasp. Pink blood foamed her lips, then nothing. Jonna felt the resolve steel Torian and she tried to cry out, to tell her friend not to fight, to run, to find the rebels another day when they were not so strong.

A shriek of hurt and pure rage ripped free from Torian's lips as she drew her sword and rushed at the nearest rebel. With sword and dagger she slew four rebels before an archer cut her down.

Jonna stayed with her—*as* her—until Torian died. The berserk rage faded, leaving only suffering that she had killed her friend and had hardly begun to avenge that death.

"Are you all right, Captain?"

Jonna swiped the sweat from her forehead and looked up. For a moment her eyes refused to focus. Then she saw one of the new cadre she trained. Leah of Obregsdon. One of the finest, though still filled with the impetuosity of youth. Couldn't she see that Jonna wanted to mourn alone?

"I...I have had too much to drink," Jonna said weakly. The visions of Torian dying were less vivid and lingering than the bloody dagger in her hand that had stolen away Freda's life. How necessary it had been! And how utterly awful. The rebels had fought like rabid dogs for more than three years until the last of them had been brought down. Not once in those years had Jonna heard of a rebel taking a prisoner. Their captives were all tortured to death.

She held up her empty hand—and saw a ghostly dagger dripping Freda's pale blood. There must have been some other way. Torian had not seen it. Neither could Jonna.

"You look the worse for wear, if you don't mind my saying so," Leah said. "You need some company, eh?"

Jonna rubbed at her eyes and stared at the empty cup in front of her. Only two measures left. Her hand shook as she poured, leaving one in the bottle.

"I want to drink alone. For the moment," she said in a voice that almost cracked with strain. She looked up sharply at her trainee. Leah and her four friends had proven themselves against the Loee and were the best of the recruits. Just as Jonna had declared herself and her four friends so many years ago as the best of the best.

"I understand, Captain," Leah said. "Losing a friend and boon companion must be soul-tearing."

Jonna nodded, thinking more on how Leah had never lost anyone close to her. So many fallen over the years, but those in the tontine were the closest. They had been more than sisters. They had been comrades-in-arms. They had shared everything— or so Jonna had thought. How little she had known of Bellarine's and nothing of Freda and Torian's last moments alive. She dared not linger on the courage—or was it fear?—that had guided Torian's hand when she killed Freda. Torian had never been known for blood rage, either, and yet she had refused to slip away when she might have and had attacked, knowing she could never survive. In its way, she had killed both Freda and herself that day. Jonna had never suspected. Always she had thought they died in a rebel ambush. Their bodies had never been found to give testimony to what had happened.

Jonna closed her eyes and lifted the cup to her lips.

"Asenthena," she said softly before downing the wine in a single gulp.

It felt as if she had been hit with a war hammer.

Doubt flooded her senses and more. Ever so much more. But not fear. That was alien to her—to Asenthena. But the pain gnawing at her breast inspired something akin to it. Jonna struggled to decide what she really felt. What *Asenthena* felt. Not fear. Anger. Hatred at her own weakness, but not fear at the cancer slowly stealing away her life.

Tears ran unabashedly down Jonna's cheeks now. She had not known and Asenthena had never told her. Side by side they had fought and Asenthena had never told her. Why?

Jonna saw the answer inside Asenthena and wept even more. Asenthena had not believed she would react well.

"No coddling," Asenthena said. "That's what Jonna would do. Coddle me, treat me differently. That would be worse than the slow death."

"I wouldn't have pitied you," Jonna gasped out. But what she saw was not fear of that. It was stark panic at the notion of being thought of as less. Asenthena was a warrior, the finest, always at the forefront, always braver and stronger than the rest. She was driven by what Jonna thought of her, now that the others were lost.

"I loved you," Jonna sobbed out. "I could never think of you with pity."

Even as she spoke, she saw how true Asenthena's vision was. If she had known of the cancer she would have behaved differently. Asenthena would not have been an equal but something less, not because of failing strength—never that. Asenthena was always so strong! Jonna felt it deep within, a different power from that of the cancer. The tumor might consume her body but could never taint her soul. It was something else.

"Never give Jonna reason to show her own weakness. Only give courage."

"Can I be so fragile?" Jonna wondered aloud, almost expecting a response. "Did Asenthena not see more in me than a delicate flower? I've fought long and well. Would I have crumpled knowing of my—your—my illness?"

Jonna sat straighter on the bench and told herself she would have never changed how she thought of her friend, and knew she lied. She would have. She had seen comrades distance themselves from the critically wounded to lessen the blow of death. She would never have done that with Asenthena, the last of the cadre, the last of her truest friends. But Asenthena had the clearer vision deep into her soul.

"Jonna will falter at the slow death, even as she squarely faces the quick death of battle. I must never give her that choice. It is my only legacy to her."

"Only?" cried Jonna. "No, no, your friendship! Your—" She broke down sobbing, only to feel a strong arm around her shoulders, steadying her. She drew back, confused with the thoughts and visions of Asenthena leading the assault that broke the Loee spirit and forced them to sue for peace. In the face of such ferocity as shown by Asenthena, the Loee realized they could never prevail.

"You've had too much to drink, Captain. Need some air?" Leah looked at her curiously. Not as a friend. Hardly as a subordinate. There was no pity for weakness, but there was no charity, either. It was as if she was a relic of the past that had tipped and fallen off the shelf to the floor. Not a tragedy since the relic had outlived its usefulness, but still something to be dealt with expeditiously because of what it had meant once.

"I need drinking companions now," Jonna said. She lifted the bottle and sloshed the single measure remaining. So long ago there had been five. Now only she remained.

"Easily done. I'll even buy," Leah said, laughing. She waved the others of her cadre over. They came reluctantly. To drink with their training officer was not right.

"No, I'll buy," Jonna said. "What good is coin if it's not spent wisely on wine?" She moved her bottle to the side of the table, trying not to look at the few ounces left sloshing over the bottom.

The others gathered around the table and accepted the wine brought by the tavern keeper.

Tales were told and bawdy songs were sung but Jonna sensed that Leah, if not the others, wanted an explanation for their captain's hesitation in finishing the wine in the bottle.

"Do you know what a tontine is?"

"A teenaged ton?" guessed one.

Jonna smiled wanly. A joker, like Freda.

"A pact among only the best of friends," Jonna said. She lifted the bottle. "I and four others signed this bottle of wine long ago. The survivor of the group is required to drink it." She sloshed the wine about inside. One draft left. She had sampled magically the dying thoughts of her friends. Only one drink remained—hers.

"So you get to drink to their memory," Leah said. "That's a fine idea."

"I don't drink to their memory but *of* their memories," Jonna corrected. "I thought I knew them all so well." She shook her head. "Even sharing their last memories, I don't know them as well as I thought." She took a deep breath and let it out slowly. "Perhaps I know myself a little better." *Or not at all,* came the considered thought.

"Or mayhap it's the wine," Leah said.

"It might be the wine," Jonna said. Her head swam with the memories of her four friends, all so different and yet as one in death now.

"This is a good idea," spoke one of Leah's cadre. "Why can't we do a tontine? The last of us gets to drink free wine!"

They all agreed too hurriedly, Jonna thought. They did not realize what they did. But then, neither had she and her friends.

Jonna looked up and saw the tavern keeper shuffling toward them, clutching an empty bottle with a blank label on it. He said nothing as he placed it on the edge of the table, then pushed it to the center.

"What do we do?" Leah asked.

"Each of you pours an equal amount into the bottle," Jonna said. She watched as they did so. "Then you sign the label."

"In blood?"

"Ink's fine," the tavern keeper croaked out. He dropped a quill onto the table and then produced an ink bottle from an apron pouch. Each in turn signed with a flourish, laughing and jostling. How like it was, Jonna reflected, when she and the others had signed. Closing her eyes for a moment took her back, without need of the wine. She opened her eyes to the five soldiers toasting one another with what remained in their cups. A cork had been thrust into the tontine bottle and within minutes the tavern keeper had sealed it with red candle wax. He left them to place it safely within the sturdy cabinet behind the bar.

"How many bottles has he kept?" Jonna wondered aloud.

"Who cares? This is fun," Leah said. She downed the rest of her wine, clicked the cup on the table and ordered more.

But after the wine was served, Leah edged closer to Jonna and whispered, "Captain, what of the wine remaining in your tontine bottle?"

Jonna emptied the last drops into her cup. She stared into the shimmering surface rippling as the table was jostled by the others. Vague reflections of other times fleetingly appeared and then subsided.

"What of it?"

"You said you drank the memories of those who had died. Asenthena was the last—save for you. You're still among the living."

"The last time I checked I was," Jonna said. Entranced by the blood-red wine in her cup, she could hardly pull her gaze from it. Patterns formed and died as she watched intently.

"What is it you'll see when you drink? Your own death? Or nothing since you haven't died yet?"

Jonna upended her cup, drained the heady liquid in a single gulp, licked her lips and then smiled as she gently lowered the cup to the tabletop.

"Well, Captain, what is it?"

"You'll see for yourself," Jonna told her. "If you are the last, you'll see."

On unsteady feet, Jonna left the tavern and plunged into the freezing night, invigorated by what lay ahead of her.

THE MENAGERIE

by Sarah Dozier

Traditionally we end the anthology with something short and funny. As we got further into the reading period and I was getting stories that made me go back and check the guidelines to make sure that I had not said that 9000 words was my *preferred* length, I began to fear that we wouldn't get anything suitable for the last story. (I even wrote one myself, just in case.) Then, the day before the deadline, this arrived—not only short and funny, but from a brand new writer. Her writing professor suggested that, considering she had been reading Ms. Bradley's work for almost eight years, she should write something for *Sword & Sorceress*.

Sarah Dozier is a junior at Texas Christian University, working towards a BA in English and a minor in Theatre. She has been reading and writing, mainly science fiction and fantasy, almost as long as she can remember. When this book comes out in November she will just be turning 21. (Her birthday is on the 15th, so if that turns out to be the release date there will be a huge party in Texas and every one is invited). *[Publisher's addendum—guess what? Happy birthday, Sarah!]*

I like her approach to ending a war; I can think of a few world "leaders" I'd love to see it used on.

I didn't start the war, but I finished it, so I might as well tell the story. At least this way it might be told correctly.

అ౦ఎ౩౨౦ఙ

The war started out as most tend to. One king was offended by another at some banquet honoring someone else entirely.

The offended one then wanted the other's land as an apology. Scuffles broke out but nothing official, yet. Slowly the kings turned to the use of assassins and magicians. Then the documents were signed and war officially started. That was ten years ago. By now the original argument must have been forgotten.

One of the two kings sent out the call for me. No messenger will ever admit to knowing how to get in contact with me, but all know my inn. My inn and the menagerie next door are well known; most just don't realize who runs it.

King Jereth's messenger reached me in November of the eleventh year and commanded my assistance. Of course my talent is not that easily bought; my reply was "no." A month later the same messenger showed up in my inn seeking refuge. The Black Death Inn and Creature Menagerie has always been a safe haven for all who ask. This time he came with the death count, from both sides. Thousands were dying and more would die. The messenger told me that King Jereth again commanded me to save his people and assassinate the other king. Again, I said no.

About six months after that, the other king, Aramond, sent his messengers asking for the same thing. Kill the other king. Their offers were truly impressive: my weight in silver, then jewels, and finally gold; half the kingdoms; a Prince for a husband or slave; finally, whatever I wanted. People were fleeing both countries and going to neighboring neutral countries, including the one where my inn was located. It was always filled with people from both countries, people who used to live just across the borders from each other. Friends and family.

After seven months of messengers, a child came up to me. He was fleeing from Aramond's country with his mother. His father had been slaughtered for not fighting.

"Daddy said the Black Panther could stop the fighting. Would you ask her for me?"

That was all that was needed. I told the small family that they would have free room and board for the evening. I showed them to my bedroom. I instructed a messenger from each side to return to his king and say I would end the fighting before noon tomorrow.

Aramond's daughter had sent me a message the same day the boy and his mother arrived. The day before Jereth's son also sent me a message. They had somehow managed to meet and fall in love and just wanted the war to end so they could marry. I knew the two kingdoms would be in good hands.

I went to my work room and changed into my tight dark leather pants, old worn thigh-high leather boots, and a soft black cotton shirt which fell to my thighs. A belt on my hip held several pouches of various potions and other items which might come in handy. A harness went over the shirt so that my sword would sit comfortably between my shoulder blades and the hilt would poke out over my right shoulder. The mask was actually a black kerchief to tame my mane of brown curls; it rested low on my forehead giving the illusion of disguise. Two silver webbed bracers fit comfortably on my forearms. Two black opals hid in the webbing; they worked the magic, not I. My black gloves hugged my hands as I walked into the common room of the inn. A hush fell over the whole room as I strode out in my regalia. For the first time in years I was dressed as the Black Panther.

I sent messengers to request that the kings meet me at the edges of their lands in a wood not far from my own inn.

At this point I should tell you about my menagerie. I have some of the exotic creatures that are found all over the world, but most are unique to my little menagerie. I have bears with wings, black unicorns, purple dragons that are the size of cats, cats the size of horses, and many more creatures. Every time I go out on a mission I return with another creature for my menagerie.

In the woods I hid behind a tree and watched the two kings approach each other. They were alone as I requested. I stood, feeling their energies bouncing around the small clearing. I was trying to determine what would become of them. Would the children like them? Would they behave?

"Gentlemen, are you prepared to provide me my payment?"

At that they both began to protest that I had neither completed the task nor specified my payment. They looked at each other. Eyes wide, each realized for the first time that the other wanted him dead.

"No, please. Panther, do something."

"I can't die; I'm not ready."

"My kingdom will fall."

"My child is too young to take over."

They protested, trying to drown each other out.

"My lords, neither of you is going to die just yet. Your children have both spoken to me. They plan to marry and merge your two kingdoms and rule together in peace. Your kingdoms will prosper and grow. People will flock to be part of the growth. New cities will emerge. Your legacy will go on. I am about to make you immortal. You should be thanking me."

They stood looking at me in wide-eyed fear, not sure what was about to happen. Then they tried to run. They always try to run. I flicked my hands and froze them.

The next day I was showing some of the children staying at my inn around the menagerie. I showed them the black unicorn and I let them play with the purple dragons. The dragons coiled around the children like cats.

I glanced over at my two newest additions, still in their cages. A winged kitten and a young chimera glared out at me.

"See, my lords? If you learn to behave, you can come out and play with the children."

LaVergne, TN USA
28 July 2010
191219LV00006B/178/A